Also by Edwin Oliver
Praise for

A Fiend Unveiled

Barnes & Noble Events
August, 2000

Edwin Oliver… has now established his creative versatility and talent as an author of a book that takes you through twists and turns of terror and suspense. In his first novel, "A Fiend Unveiled" he tells a story of greed, murder, buried secrets and frightening surprises.

Deerfield Times
March 2000

Haunted by dreams slowly uncovering the mysterious murders plaguing unsuspecting victims… as you cautiously turn every page, afraid of uncovering the truth, but anticipating every word of it. As you continue reading, you become drawn to the characters, drawn into the story, so engrossed with every detail, so involved in the plot, that you find yourself screaming out to the characters to "watch out", and to "run". A Fiend Unveiled" is full of just enough suspense to keep you guessing right down to the last page. The details are so realistic and the wording so thorough that Oliver's book is a definite mystery thriller you won't want to miss. Your skin crawls and every strand of your hair stands on end as your strive to solve the mystery and mayhem concealed within every twisted situation of Edwin Oliver's new creation.

Tamarac Times
June 2000

"A Fiend Unveiled", Edwin Oliver's chilling mystery complete with vampires, murder, greed, and long buried secrets, has an impressive amount of twists and turns for a debut novel from someone who, until recently, never dreamed of becoming an author. His characters developed lives of their own and wills to match. His book's protagonist, Daniel Hull… is a computer programmer with a keen sense of observation and a passion for solving mysteries… very observant when it comes to human behavior and small details.

The Forum
April 15, 2000

Author, author… Meet a Tamarac resident who's new mystery novel is available for sale on the Internet. "A Fiend Unveiled" by Edwin Oliver will keep you up all night guessing its surprising ending.

The
Terrestrial

The Terrestrial

EDWIN OLIVER

THE TERRESTRIAL

Scripture quotations marked RSV are taken from the Revised Standard Version of the Bible, copyright © 1946, 1952, 1971 by the Division of Christian Education of the National Council of the Churches of Christ in the USA. Used by permission.

iUniverse books may be ordered through booksellers or by contacting:

iUniverse
1663 Liberty Drive
Bloomington, IN 47403
www.iuniverse.com
1-800-Authors (1-800-288-4677)

Because of the dynamic nature of the Internet, any web addresses or links contained in this book may have changed since publication and may no longer be valid. The views expressed in this work are solely those of the author and do not necessarily reflect the views of the publisher, and the publisher hereby disclaims any responsibility for them.

Any people depicted in stock imagery provided by Getty Images are models, and such images are being used for illustrative purposes only.
Certain stock imagery © Getty Images.

ISBN: 978-1-6632-0283-3 (sc)
ISBN: 978-1-6632-0284-0 (e)

Print information available on the last page.

iUniverse rev. date: 06/19/2020

PROLOGUE

The Garden of Edin
Date: ?

She looked towards the door from her cage. It was feeding time. Her custodian was about to enter the room with his pail of slop. The smell of the inedible swill he must have mistaken for food assailed her nostrils even before he walked into the room. Watching him closely, she crawled closer to her pen door.

The other caged creatures rattled their cages, screaming, demanding to be fed. Not her. Restraining her intense hatred for the man, she quietly, extended an open hand towards him; a simple, but effective gesture.

Every day, when he stopped to feed her, he spoke to her. It was all beyond her understanding, except for one word. A word he often repeated and emphasized as he spooned food onto her plate. Every day, after he would leave, she practiced, whispering the word to herself, repeatedly. Now, she was ready.

She waited for him to pour the slop into her plate, and then looked into his eyes.

"Food," she whispered.

His face showed his surprise, stopping cold and staring at her with a blank look. None of the beasts had spoken before or shown any semblance of intelligence.

She repeated the word softly, slowly. "Food," she said, her eyes moving back and forth from his eyes to his bucket then back again.

Full of excitement, he scooped more slop out of the bucket. "More?" he asked, showing her the full ladle.

She hesitated, but decided to try the new sound he just made. "Moorre?" She slurred it. Again, she extended her arm towards him with her open hand facing upwards.

The custodian dropped the bucket and ran out the door.

It didn't work, she thought, moving towards the back of her pen to curl in the corner. Her leathery wings hurt. The small cage forced her to keep them tucked in. Had it not been for the weekly fifteen-minute walk they allowed her in the enclosed backyard, her muscles would be atrophied.

She lay down, resting her head over her arm. The beast in the next pen, too weak to move or feed itself, looked across the bars. She returned her gaze and knew it had given up hope. She had seen the look before.

She tried to pass it some of her own food but the beast only smiled weakly. If it survived before the next feeding, the custodians would pull it out of its cage and slaughter it in front of the others. Their jailers must have thought there was a lesson to be learned by doing this.

This was her world, a lonely cage where she knew not the tenderness of a mother, with no memories of kindness.

Her custodian's routine included a weekly hosing to clean the tray under the bottom bars and remove excess excrement from their bodies. Whenever that time came, she would face the back wall to curl herself into a ball. Her wings never healed properly because of this, but it was better than meeting the water pressure head on.

Now that her plan to gain her custodian's attention failed to work, she gave serious thought to lie down and die. She closed her eyes and cried.

The lab door suddenly swung open. The custodian rushed into the room with two men dressed in white lab coats following close behind. He pointed at her excitedly as they stopped in front of her cage. Their agitation startled her.

Words made no sense, but she slid towards them, her head tilted sideways in a desperate attempt to understand what they said.

The men in the white-coats talked to each other while the custodian waved his hands in her face. Other than to tilt her head from side to side, she made no further movement. Soon, their voices lost intensity, and the men in the white-coats walked out of the room, leaving the custodian standing there, dejected.

His hands fell to his side; she met his eyes. He said something, but she just blinked, tilting her head again, as if doing that would make his words sound clearer. Picking up his pail with a deep sigh, he started for the door.

Frustrated, with a sudden loud grunt, she shook her cage. "Food!" she groaned, forcefully this time, extending her arm towards him in a desperate attempt to make him understand.

The custodian yelped and ran out of the room again. He was back almost immediately, with the two men from before. They stopped in front of her cage. The custodian raised his pail in front of her, pointing at it with his finger. The meaning suddenly exploded in her head.

"Food, food, food," she repeated.

The men in the white lab coats, not knowing how to respond, looked at each other puzzled. To the custodian, this was his very own accomplishment. He turned to the men to stop them from talking, and then faced her again.

"More?" he said, showing her the empty ladle.

They giggled as she repeated the word in an elongated slur. It was a good sign. The rest of the caged creatures joined in by jumping and screaming. Soon, the whole place turned into a chaotic cacophony of animal noises.

The custodian sprinted out of the room, only to return with a leash and muzzle. The time for her walk was a few days away, but as soon as she saw the leash, she knew something new was happening. She squatted next to her cage door, moving her head back, exposing her neck for the leash. It pleased him when she did that. As soon as he tied the leash over her neck, she lowered her head to allow the muzzle to fit over her face.

The custodian made a clicking sound with his tongue as a signal for her to step out of the cage. She did it slowly, unhurriedly. A necessary precaution to ensure they would not feel threatened - otherwise, one of them would touch her with the zap-stick. A dangerous thing, the zap-stick. Getting touched with it, meant death or several days of unconsciousness. Her measured moves ensured her safety.

In hand to hand combat she could have taken all three of them, and the thought crossed her mind a few times before. Had it not been for the zap-stick, she would have already torn their hearts out. Nevertheless, obedience was preferable. With these men, death was just a short step away.

She started to shuffle towards the backyard, as she did on her weekly walks, but the custodian pulled hard on her leash. This time, they were going elsewhere.

One of the lab men opened the other door, the dreaded door that led to some unknown destination. Her heart pumped fast as she cautiously crossed the threshold, expecting to see more cages, more animals trapped and locked, such as herself. Instead, the room had many tables arranged parallel to each other with all sorts of bottles full of multicolored liquids. Some bottles connected to others with transparent tubes and bubbling liquids passing from one container to the next.

They continued towards another door, finally stepping outside. The spectacle of the mountains in the vastness, beyond the wall that surrounded the compound, almost made her faint. Tears swelled in her eyes.

The custodian pulled her towards another building, ordering her to keep up. On top of the wall, several men walked back and forth, scrutinizing her as they passed by.

They entered a new building, into a long corridor, where she saw another wondrous thing; something she had never seen. A large mirror hung from one of the walls.

'Impossible', she thought while looking into the mirror.

The custodian, or someone looking remarkably like him, seemed to be inside the shiny thing. His reflection pulled an ugly looking creature on a leash; a large, hairy beast with a squashed nose and long fangs. Forgetting herself, she approached the mirror, dragging the custodian along, almost making him lose his grip on the leash. She touched her reflection, but he barked at her, pulling her away.

They continued towards a large door at the end of the corridor, but she kept looking back, trying to make sense of the mirror.

A guard opened the door, and ushered them inside.

A long, rectangular table stood across an large room. Several men sat from one end of the table to the other. The custodian stopped in front of them and forced Lilitu to kneel. Every pair of eyes in the room was upon her.

A long silence followed.

There was no mystery now. She was expected to perform, and perform, she did.

They all gasped when the single word came from her mouth.

"Food!"

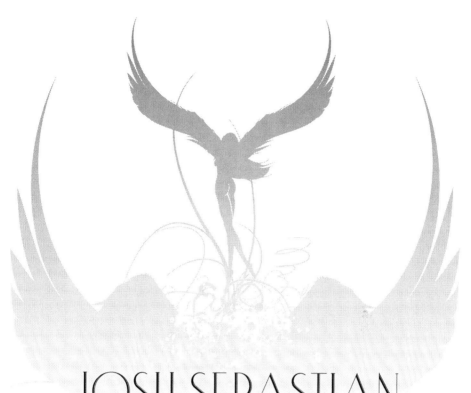

JOSH SEBASTIAN

MAY 3, THE PRESENT

ONE

The school bus turned the corner as Josh stood by the sidewalk with a faint heart, hoping Norton wouldn't be in the bus today. The bus stopped to pick him up, hissing loudly at him with its open mouth. As always, Josh got ready to be digested. He greeted the bus driver, but she just snorted, waiting until he climbed aboard to close the door. From the back of the bus, one of the boys, mocking a high-pitched female voice said, "good morning, Pinhead." Everyone giggled. Josh felt like crawling right back out of the bus. It was too late for that. He sighed deeply and walked towards the back; his eyes avoiding contact with anything but the floor - a precaution he learned to take a long time ago, to prevent getting tripped by some wise-ass.

"Where ya' goin, Pin?" someone jumped directly in front of Josh, blocking his way. Josh looked up; Norton, of course.

"Please, let me pass," said Josh, trying to sidestep him.

"But I saved a seat for ya', man," said Norton, his olive-green eyes narrowed down to a slit. His thin-lipped mouth twisted cynically. "Ya' don't wanna turn down your old buddy, do ya'?" He slipped a strong arm over Josh's shoulder and gently nudged him towards the empty window seat.

Josh looked for a sympathetic face. They were smiling. They were all smiling.

"Here," said Norton. "I'll hold your books while you get in."

"No, that's okay," replied Josh.

"Oh, but I insist." Norton pulled the stack of books from Josh's arm. "Go on, sit."

Josh complied. Contradicting Norton would have been the shortest route to getting hurt. There was a reason why they called him 'The Destroyer'; he was the meanest defensive tackle the school ever had.

"Ya know, Pin," said Norton, dropping his weight on the seat next to Josh, "I've been thinking..."

I'll bet you have, thought Josh as he looked out the window. Josh racked his brains out trying to understand what motivated this asshole to come after him, day after day, after friggin' day. He could almost pinpoint it to the day when Miss Frankel, the history teacher, asked Norton a simple question: "Who's the President of the United States?" Norton just stared at her with a blank look, then finally said, "Lincoln?" Josh was stupid enough to volunteer the correct answer.

"Business ain't been goin' well for me lately. Maybe cause I been too greedy . . . know what I mean . . .?" Norton slipped an arm over Josh's back seat and winked an eye at the kid sitting behind him. "How'd ya' like to be my partner?"

Josh kept an impassive face, but didn't answer.

"Now," continued Norton as he pulled a joint out of his shirt pocket, "we can start ya' off with the small stuff. You know, sort o' have ya' work your way up to the top. And I'll give ya' a good price too..." Norton pushed the joint in front of Josh's face. "Here, wanna try it?"

Josh looked at the joint, and then turned his eyes towards the window. "No," he said.

"What was that?" said Norton, changing his tone of voice.

"No, thank you." Josh stressed the 'thank you'.

"That's okay," said Norton, back on his friendly tone. "No need to thank me now. I'll just put it in here, inside one o' your books . . . after all, what's a salesman without goods to sell, right?" Norton shuffled Josh's books about, finally placing the joint inside 'Grammar and Composition'. "Just bring me ten bucks by tomorrow, and we'll call it even."

"Ten bucks!" said Josh unable to control himself.

Norton turned and grabbed him by the collar. "Any objections?"

In the violence of Norton's move, Josh dropped his books. "Okay, okay. I'll get you the money."

Norton let him go and began to fix Josh's collar – mockingly behaving as if he was a valet. "Good," he said, patting him in the face.

Josh reached down to pick up his books and began to stack them one over the other on his seat. Norton watched with amusement. The last thing Josh picked up was his sandwich.

"Hey," said Norton loudly. "Is that my sandwich or is that my sandwich?"

"No, Please," pleaded Josh. "That's my lunch. Please…"

"Did ya' put more peanut butter on it, like I told ya'?" said Norton grabbing the sandwich away from Josh.

Josh looked sadly at Norton, and then sat. He turned to the window as Norton gulped down the sandwich.

"Thanks, Pin," said Norton. "But, this is no better than yesterday's. No wonder you're so skinny. Ya' gotta put s'more jelly in it too... needs more body, know what I mean...?"

Body? thought Josh. *Wait till you get through with this one.*

"I guess you'll be joining the rest of us at the cafeteria today now that ya' lost your lunch. Don't worry. I'll save a seat for ya'." Norton brought his hands to his own lap; he had a wide grin on his face.

Josh didn't reply. He just turned back to the window. Usually, he avoided the cafeteria and did not intend to go today. Josh felt something tickle his shoulder, but it wasn't Norton; he could see Norton's hands resting on his lap. *Just ignore the asshole*, thought Josh. He hoped they wouldn't get physical with him. Whenever they got into those moods, he would hurt for the next couple of days. The tickling at his shoulder persisted. Shrugging his shoulders forward, he then turned his head around, towards the kid sitting behind him. The large Tarantula that rested on Josh's shoulders raised its two front legs. Josh screamed and jumped forward, landing on the seat in front of him, trying desperately to brush the spider off his shoulder. All the kids in the bus broke into uproarious laughter; Josh screamed uncontrollably.

When the bell rang for the third period class, Josh looked around for Norton, but Norton wasn't there. He smiled. He knew exactly where to find him and wouldn't miss this for the world. Walking happily down the hallway, he went directly to the infirmary. When he got there, the door was open.

"Hey. Norton," said Josh standing by the infirmary door. "What are you doing here?" His face showed concern, but not surprise.

"Get outta' my face, Pin," replied Norton with his hands held tight to his stomach. "Leave me alone."

"You ought to get a doctor to see you," said Josh.

"I said 'get outta' here'!"

"Hope you feel better." Josh turned around and headed back to his next class. Although Josh never got the chance to eat his sandwiches, he enjoyed preparing this one immensely; he had been specially creative; peanut butter and jelly, and enough Ex-Lax to knock down a horse. Tomorrow, he would change the recipe.

Josh hated sitting in the first row of the classroom every day, but it was the best way to deter most of the guys from pulling anything funny with him; not that they didn't try, but at least, he thought, the teacher was close by.

School was no picnic. Janet Phillis usually sat in the front row also. She was Josh's female counterpart, except that she was much more unpredictable than Josh; normally, she bore insults without answering back, but with her, you could never tell. Once, right after school, the students were waiting for the school bus, and there was Janet, minding her own business when Bobby - one of Norton's friends - teased her about her looks. Before anyone knew what was happening, she grabbed a baseball bat from a nearby kid, and broke it on Bobby's head. It took nine stitches to put his scalp back together. The day she got off the wrong side of bed was the day to avoid her.

The kids had a name for her too; they called her 'Blockjaw' because of her long, protruding jaw. Nevertheless, they used it sparingly, and would never say it to her face. When Josh met Janet, he knew the meaning of 'ugly'. Her legs, in contrast with the rest of her body, were much too skinny; she looked like a fat Canary with a flat ass. The only redeemable physical quality about her, were her well-rounded, large-but-firm breasts.

At first, Josh thought nothing of Janet. But when the kids started picking on her, he began to feel empathy towards her; he began to think about her more each passing day, until, without realizing it, he became infatuated. Then, her ugly face didn't seem so ugly anymore; her skinny legs didn't matter anymore. He thought of a thousand ways to get her to talk to him, but she too was a loner.

'I wonder if she ever goes to the cafeteria', thought Josh. With Norton out of the picture, he figured he could get by unnoticed; most kids ignored him if Norton wasn't around to tease him. That afternoon, arming himself with a thick layer of protective indifference, Josh walked towards the cafeteria.

Janet sat alone in one of the tables near the corner. Josh purposefully came in late, to avoid having to make a line; he didn't feel like getting pushed around today - not in front of Janet. Mrs. Ballin stood behind the food counter with her arms crossed in front of her, her rotund figure almost spanning the width of a full section of the dessert counter. When she saw Josh, her face lit up.

"Why, Josh," she said with a thick Creole accent, "what brings you around these here parts? Ah' thought you'd given up on food." She winked at him.

"Hi, Mrs. Ballin," replied Josh with guarded enthusiasm.

"Here," she said as she filled the large spoon with yellow rice, "let me put something on your plate before you decides to change your mind." She leaned forward a bit, and in a conspiratorial hush said, "Ah'll put in a double portion o' dessert for you. It's Chocolate cake."

Janet sat on the table with her hands on her lap and her eyes cast downward; she had not touched her food. "Hi, Janet," said Josh shyly. "May I sit with you?"

"No," she said without looking up. "Go away. Leave me alone."

"Look, I brought you something." He put his tray on the table and placed the cake in front of her.

"Goddammit," she said. When she raised her head, he saw how swollen her eyes were. She threw the cake - plate and all - at him. The dark frosting hit square on his face, and the edge of the plate cracked heavily against his skull. "I said 'leave me alone'!"

The room disappeared as Josh's ears rang with a loud high-pitched hum.

"Way to go, Janet," yelled one of the guys at the table next to them.

"Hey, people," said another voice from behind Josh, "Blockjaw is letting Pinhead have it!"

In a matter of seconds, the whole cafeteria began to mill around Janet's table, laughing and teasing Josh. Janet stared at his cake-covered face and, for a moment, it seemed to Josh that she too was laughing.

Josh threw his tray against the wall. "Go to Hell!" he hissed at her.

⬥⬥•⬥•⬥•⬥•⬥

Later that day, after coming home from school, Josh went upstairs and locked his bedroom door behind him.

By dinnertime, his mother called from the kitchen. He didn't answer

"Josh," called Mary Ann from the foot of the stairs. "Did you hear me?" She waited for him to answer, but he remained silent. "Josh, are you going to make me come up?"

"I'll be down later," he said through the door. He had a knot in his stomach. "I'm gonna' lie down for a while."

"All right. I'll call you when dinner's ready." Her voice sounded tired.

Hoping she would go to bed early and leave him alone, he lay in a daze, staring at the ceiling. Then he remembered...

He walked towards his bedroom door, listening for his mother. She was still in the kitchen. He opened the door and tiptoed towards her bedroom.

When his father died, Mary Ann was prescribed Seconal to calm her nerves but she never used it. Josh found they worked fine for him. He opened her closet and found the bottle, hidden way back on one of the shelves. Normally, he thought, one did the trick, but today, well . . .

He shook three pills in his hand and placed the bottle back in the closet.

TWO

Josh reluctantly rode in his mother's car. She drove.

"Please, mom," pleaded Josh. "I'm okay . . . It won't happen again, I promise."

"I'm sorry," said Mary Ann without taking her eyes off the road. "The way you've been behaving isn't normal. You need help . . . God knows, I do too." For a woman old enough to have an eighteen year old son, she looked remarkably young and trim. Her waist was not an inch wider than the day she got married twenty years ago.

"It was an accident," he said emphatically.

"Swallowing a whole bottle of Seconal? An accident?" she said, raising her tone of voice.

"It wasn't a whole bottle," he said irritably. "It was just three lousy pills." He paused for a moment and looked at her. "Okay, so I got a little carried away, but I don't need a psychiatrist. Honest, I don't. I just felt a little depressed. That's all."

"It's not good for a kid your age to live like a hermit. You should go out more; meet some people, get a girlfriend."

"Oh, gimme a break!" Josh gave Mary Ann a steady look. "You wanna' know why I act the way I do? Come with me to school someday. See if you can find out why they call me Pinhead; see if you can find out why every asshole in school feels it's okay to take a poke at me whenever I walk by." Josh's voice broke. "Then, maybe you can tell me why no one understands I have feelings too; maybe you can tell me why those stupid bullies make me the butt of their jokes and why everyone thinks it's funny. And when you do find out, please tell me, cause I can't figure it out!"

"But why don't you fight back?" Her tone betrayed her irritation; her hands tightened on the steering wheel.

"Fight back with what?" he yelled. "Mom, look at me and tell me what you see."

"I see someone I could feel very proud of," she said.

"You couldn't even bring yourself to say it, could you?"

"Say what?"

"You didn't say you were proud of me, because you're not. And you didn't answer my question."

"Well," she said, making an effort to smile, "you could use a few more pounds."

"A few more pounds!" he interrupted. "Oh, come off it, mom. I can read the reflection on the mirror." Josh slumped in his seat and looked out the window.

Mary Ann didn't reply.

"Look, mom," said Josh. "If you forget about the head shrink business, I won't do it again . . . Okay?" He tried to make her look into his eyes. "Is it a deal?" he continued; she still wouldn't answer. "Answer me, will you?"

"I can't. I'm too busy driving," she said with glassy eyes.

"You can't afford a doctor. You know that," he pleaded, trying to manipulate her. But he was no match for her.

"I can't afford a funeral either." She pulled the car to the edge of the road and turned towards Josh. Her face softened as she spoke to him. "Josh, you're all I've got to live for." She smiled at him and gently touched his cheek. "Besides, you've got a whole life ahead of you; don't throw it away." Their eyes met sadly. "If you don't want to live for yourself," she continued, "then do it for me. I need you."

"How many times do I have to say this? I wasn't trying to kill myself," said Josh looking straight at her.

"I believe you," she said unconvincingly. "But why don't you humor me for a change . . . Please, tell me you'll see the doctor. That's all I ask." Her hand reached under his chin and moved his face towards hers. "Please?" she said.

Josh didn't answer.

"Well, I'm taking you, whether you like it or not!" She turned back to the wheel with a frown on her face and drove on.

Doctor Montague's waiting room had a plush, wall-to-wall, dark green carpet; several, comfortable, evenly placed, light green chairs, complemented the decor. The center of the room had a table, full of old medical journals and magazines that, clearly, no one bothered to read.

Josh and Mary Ann waited for nearly two hours before the nurse called them in.

Josh saw the psychiatrist a few more times, until Mary Ann, curious about his progress, insisted upon talking to Doctor Montague.

That was Josh's last visit. He waited outside the office while his mother went inside. After ten minutes with Doctor Montague, Mary Ann rushed out of the office in a storm. "Oedipus Complex, my ass!" she said, as she slammed the door on the doctor's nose. "Come on, Josh. Let's get out of here!"

Two days later, Josh watched Mary Ann drive away as he stood on the steps of St. Patrick's church. He would have walked away in the opposite direction had Father Roberts not been standing next to him.

"Come on," said Father Roberts gently placing an arm over Josh's shoulder, "let's go into my office, and have some coffee before we begin." Father Roberts was in his mid-thirties, and had an athletic quality about him that gave Josh the impression that he was more a semi-retired boxer than a priest; his face, however, projected kindness and understanding.

Josh put his hands in his pockets and followed the priest inside.

Later, that evening, Josh lay on his bed with the door locked when he heard Mary Ann pulling up the driveway. She'd be knocking at his door any moment now. He mentally followed her movements as she closed the car's door, and walked from the driveway to the front door, looking for the house keys in her handbag. He knew exactly what she would do when she closed the front door. He could almost mouth her words when she loudly said, "Josh, I'm home." He heard her climb up the stairs.

"Josh?" she said as she knocked on the door. "Are you in there?"

"No, he's not," replied Josh with restrained anger. "He's still talking to that jerk priest."

"Come on, open up the door." She fumbled with the doorknob.

Josh walked slowly to the door and released the lock. He went back to his bed and lay down again. Mary Ann walked in.

"All right," she said as she sat next to him. "What happened between you and Father Roberts?" She gently placed a hand over his knee.

"Nothing happened. I just think it's a waste of time. We've never been religious, never been to church, so why all of a sudden do you want me to see a priest?"

Mary Ann leaned her elbow on the bed, a look of uncertainty registered on her face. "I don't know. I honestly don't know..." She looked at him for a long moment, her eyes searching into his, trying to find an answer. "Maybe because I'm worried about you," she said softly.

He leaned away from her. "Then don't. I'm okay."

"Josh," she said, as she moved closer to him, "stop seeing me as the enemy. I'm on your side, can't you see that?" Her voice almost broke to the verge of crying, but she held on. Josh noticed, but reacted by simply moving away.

A barrier was building between them that could soon prove insurmountable. She straightened up and allowed her fingers to softly brush through his hair. "All right, no more priests. I promise." She sighed deeply, then, with a strong feeling of inadequacy, walked out of the room.

THREE

Josh stepped out of the school bus with a nasty lump on the back of his head; today's hard dose of knuckles for protesting Norton's sick jokes - but he'd rather have a thousand lumps than allow anyone to grab at his ass. He wondered about Norton as he saw the infernal school bus turn the corner.

Well, Norton, he thought, *tomorrow's another day.*

It was nearly three o' clock, and he had to hurry if he wanted to catch Laura - his next-door neighbor - before she took Trinket out for her walk. He stood by the front porch of his house, fumbling for his keys, when Laura closed her garage door - she had Trinket's leash in her hands.

I'd better hurry, he thought as he finally opened the door, dropping his books by the doorstep. This was going to be fun; good, dirty fun.

Laura Mackle was closing the door to her front porch, when Josh, who had come running from his house, stopped behind her. She was in her mid-fifties, but her wrinkled, weather-beaten skin made her look much older. In her younger years, however, she had been a very attractive model; all she had now was her memories, a pot-bellied know it all husband, and Trinket.

"Hi, Mrs. Mackle," said Josh with his breath caught in his lungs. "Time to walk Trinket, huh?"

Trinket wagged her tail at Josh, pulling at her leash as she tried to reach Josh. The dog's coat was silky and white, and, as Maltese went, smaller than average - a spoiled, but likable dog. Josh often came to Laura's house to play with Trinket – today he had something else in mind.

"Where have you been these past few days," she said turning away from the door. "We've missed you." When she said '*we*', Josh knew she didn't mean her husband.

"I'm sure my little friend here can't live without me." He allowed Trinket to lick his face. "Isn't that right, Trinket?" Trinket jumped up and down around Josh, barking playfully, inviting him to romp around with her. He stood up and faced Laura. "I've been around. You know, lots of homework and stuff."

Laura's telephone rang.

"Oh, dear," said Laura, unsure whether she should go back inside to answer the telephone. Trinket kept pulling at the leash; nature was also calling.

"I'll walk her for you, Mrs. Mackle. You go answer the phone."

Laura hesitated for a moment, then handed Josh the leash. She took out her house keys, opened the door, and ran towards the telephone in the living room. Josh waited by the door.

"Hello." She signaled at Josh with her hand, indicating that he should wait. "Oh, Malcolm, yes. Hold the line a minute, will you?" She placed her hand over the speaker then said to Josh, "Don't keep her out long. As soon as she makes 'wee-wee' and 'poo-poo', you bring her right back, hear?"

"Sure thing," said Josh. *'Wee-wee' and 'poo-poo'?* He grinned to himself as Trinket pulled at the leash. "Come on, Trinket. Let's see how well you can take a shit."

Thirty minutes later, he brought the dog back to Laura.

Josh was busy in the kitchen preparing tomorrow's sandwich when Mary Ann pulled in the driveway. He quickly threw the disposable rubber gloves in the trashcan, and placed Norton's sandwich inside a small plastic 'zip-lock' bag. He hoped Mary Ann wouldn't notice the smell.

"Josh," called Mary Ann as she opened the front door, "I'm home!"

"I'm over by the kitchen, mom." Josh hid the sandwich in one of the kitchen cabinets and walked out to greet her. He kissed Mary Ann.

"Did you eat?" she asked.

"No, why?"

"You smell like Onions... and Mayonnaise." She knitted her eyebrows as she sniffed the air. Leaning against the dinner table, she raised her right foot and looked at her sole. "Goddammit! I think I stepped on some dog poop." She raised her other foot and checked it too.

He shifted nervously as he glanced towards the cupboard. "It was probably me. I took Trinket out for her walk today and stepped on it by accident. But don't worry, I took care of it."

"Well I hope you didn't mess up our rug. We just had it cleaned last month."

"Sure, Mom," replied Josh. "Oh, before I forget," he continued as an afterthought, "Laura wants you to call her."

"What about?" asked Mary Ann.

He shrugged. "She didn't tell me."

A while later, Josh sat in front of the television set trying to concentrate on 'Star Trek'; but Mary Ann's phone voice cut loudly through Captain Pickard's orders on the bridge.

"Okay," she said. "Only if you promise... I'll see you later then. Bye'" Mary Ann placed the phone back on its cradle and came back into the family room.

Josh looked up. "What's going on, mom?"

"What? Oh, that. Laura is bringing a hypnotist to her house tonight and wants me to come over." Mary Ann studied him for a moment. "Want to come with me?"

"I don't know," he said, almost by reflex.

"Well, don't think about it too long. I'm leaving in a half-hour." She turned around and walked upstairs to her bedroom.

Josh stopped watching Star Trek. He'd heard a lot about hypnosis, but never had the chance to see anyone being hypnotized before. He wondered if it might be useful with Norton.

Josh watched Malcolm Jaffe carefully as the man moved back and forth in the middle of Laura's living room. He spoke to his small audience with authority. The furniture had been rearranged in a semi-circle, and the man's imposing personality impressed everyone who sat there.

Malcolm was not a blue-eyed, six-foot tall, hunk. He was a rather short and chubby middle-aged man, with a receding hairline, and thick eyebrows. There was nothing physically attractive about him, but his eyes flowed with power; his best asset, however, was his deep, mesmerizing voice.

"There's nothing mysterious about hypnosis," said Malcolm, "and certainly, nothing to be afraid of." Malcolm paced the room slowly, deliberately; his eyes made contact with whoever sat in front of him as he walked by. "The greatest misconception most people have about the procedure is that you lose consciousness, that you lose control. That is not true."

Malcolm stopped in front of Josh, and smiled. Josh gave him his undivided attention.

"I cannot hypnotize you by just looking at you, not unless you are already predisposed. If you believe I can do it, then, it is possible; but only because you allowed me to.

"Tonight," said Malcolm, "I'll show you some of the things you can do through the power of suggestion. But I want to make one thing clear to all of you - and I'm sure this will set your mind at ease - I will never misuse hypnosis to make anyone behave like an imbecile. You won't see any of my subjects clucking like a hen, or crawling on all fours, barking like a dog."

"Now," continued Malcolm, "in order to demonstrate the power of suggestion, I'm going to ask for a volunteer. I need one of you to allow me to place him, or her under hypnosis."

Everyone looked at each other, but none dared come forth. That is, none, but Josh; he jumped at the chance.

Malcolm stared at Josh for a long moment, then, as he smiled, approached him. "Very well, young man." He placed a chair in the center of the room, and asked Josh to sit. Josh sat in the chair and nervously stared at Malcolm.

"I want you to look deeply into my eyes..."

Five minutes later, Josh just seemed to sit there with his head slumped forward. But he was wide-awake, as aware of his surroundings as he had ever been.

"Tell me," said Malcolm as he addressed Dave, "you consider yourself to be pretty strong, don't you, Mister Harris?"

"I'm not exactly a weakling," said Dave with pride. "That's why I lift weights regularly."

"Good," replied Malcolm. "Would you like to try some arm wrestling with Josh?"

"Come on," said Dave. "That's no contest. Why, he's not even a hundred pounds... wet!"

"Then you have nothing to worry about, right?"

"All right, but I still don't see what this is going to prove." Dave stood up and walked to the small coffee table that had been set in the living room for just this purpose. He reluctantly sat on the folding chair, and placed his right elbow over the table; his forearm stood upright and his hand open. "I'm ready. Bring on your champ."

Josh sat quietly in his chair with his eyes closed; both his hands rested over his legs. He listened to everything that went on, but felt completely detached; all he wanted to hear was Malcolm's voice. Being under hypnosis, thought Josh, was a wonderful experience.

"Josh," ordered Malcolm, "I want you to open your eyes, and walk over here. I want you to sit on this chair." Malcolm stood right behind the chair that was meant for Josh. Josh opened his eyes and meekly complied.

"Now, Josh, listen to me carefully. There is a man sitting in front of you, and he's going to arm-wrestle with you. He's a very weak man. Very weak. There's also something important that you should know. You are strong. Extremely strong. There is no one in the world that can beat you. You are the strongest person in the world." Malcolm paused for a moment, allowing his suggestions - to both, Josh and Dave - to sink in. "Now," he continued, "I want you to take his hand and show me how strong you are."

Josh placed his elbow on the table in front of Dave's, and grabbed his hand firmly. Dave smirked.

"Is he still under hypnosis?" asked Laura.

"Yes, he is," replied Malcolm.

"But his eyes are open."

Malcolm gave Laura an understanding look. "That doesn't matter."

"When do we start?" asked Dave impatiently.

"Whenever you please," said Malcolm.

Dave looked at Josh as he raised his left eyebrow. "Okay, kid. I hope this doesn't hurt."

Josh remained silent.

Dave made a move to push Josh's arm against the table, but found a solid-rock resistance; Josh didn't even flinch. Sweat began to trickle down Dave's forehead when his efforts to down Josh failed. Then, with a surprisingly strong and swift movement, Josh brought Dave's hand against the table with a resounding crash.

Fifteen minutes later, Josh was comfortably back on his chair. He was now out of his trance. Malcolm had more than a few tricks up his sleeve for his 'demo' nights. Some impressive memory feats were always effective, but the real decisive factor was his closing number.

"Through hypnosis," said Malcolm, "you can learn to develop your extra-sensory powers. Even though this requires specialized training, I'll give you a small demonstration of the unlimited resources we have at our beck and call." Malcolm opened his briefcase and pulled out a black bandanna-like mask.

"I want you to inspect this mask," said Malcolm as he gave it to Jamie, "until you are sure there's no way I can see through it. Please pass it around."

Jamie inspected the bandanna and placed it over his eyes, but could not find any pinhole or semi-transparent spot on it. After he was satisfied with it, he passed it over to the person next to him.

Josh watched with fascination as Malcolm cut a few strips of adhesive tape to cover his own eyes with them.

"Josh," said Malcolm, "I want you to place this bandanna over my eyes and tie it behind the back of my head."

Josh walked towards Malcolm - it made him feel important to have been chosen by Malcolm for his demonstrations. He took both ends of the bandanna, placed it over Malcolm's eyes, and then made a tight knot behind his head.

"Thank you, Josh," said Malcolm. "Please, stay here. I'm going to need you."

"Sure," replied Josh as he stood behind Malcolm.

"I'm sure you all realize," continued Malcolm, "that I can't see a thing. What I want you to do is to select an item, any item, and hide it somewhere in this room. I'm going to find it."

"How do you propose to do that?" asked Laura.

"Ever heard of telepathy, Mrs. Mackle?"

"Of course."

"Well, I'm going to pick Josh's brain, in a manner of speaking. Josh is going to transmit to me the location of the object."

"You mean you're going to put him under hypnosis again?" asked Jamie.

"No, not this time; however, since Josh does not have the experience to transmit effectively, I will ask him to allow me to hold on to his arm while I conduct the search."

"Why?" countered Jamie suspiciously.

"Because I need to be in touch with his aura."

"Aura?" said Dave.

"To put it simply," explained Malcolm, "the aura is something like the spiritual extension of every human being. It fully surrounds our body, and emanates, approximately, from three to six inches beyond the skin."

"Come on," snarled Dave. "Gimme a break!"

"I'm not asking you to believe this," said Malcolm firmly. "We have digressed from our little demonstration. Shall we continue?"

Jamie volunteered to lead the blindfolded Malcolm out of the room, while the group decided where to hide the set of keys they had chosen. When Jamie brought him back into the room, Malcolm asked Josh to stand to his left, as he lightly held on to his arm. Slowly, he began to walk forward. He stopped for a moment.

"Josh," whispered Malcolm, "you can't just stand there. You must move with me. I need you to concentrate. Think. Try to transmit, through your arm, the location of the keys. You have the power. Now do it!" He started to walk forward again as Josh, with a concentrated look on his face, walked beside him.

It took Malcolm less than three minutes to find the keys. Everyone was impressed by Malcolm's extraordinary powers. It was a con game as old as the world.

⬥•◦⬥◦•⬥

Sometime after the demonstration was over, Josh waited for Malcolm to leave and followed him to his car. He felt an unexplainable rapport with this man.

"I guess I'll see you next Monday, Josh. Your mother asked me to train you some on the power of hypnosis. I know you'll enjoy it." Malcolm opened his car's door and threw his briefcase in the front seat.

Looking at Malcolm, Josh smiled. His demeanor betrayed his doubts. "How did you do it?" he asked.

"How did I do what?"

Mary Ann and Laura walked slowly down the driveway talking to each other. The party was over and everyone else had gone home by now.

"Come on, you know what I'm talking about," Josh continued in a hush. "The keys, man; how did you find the keys? What's the trick?"

Malcolm, avoiding Josh's searching eyes, laughed gently. "That was no trick, Josh."

⬥•◦⬥◦•⬥

Josh now felt a vibrant lust for life as he discovered a New World within his meaningless existence.

He learned the art of profound concentration and self-hypnosis as well as anyone Malcolm had taught before. He also found a new friend in Malcolm. As for Mary Ann, as long as her son was happy, it was all that mattered.

Malcolm's home was a four-bedroom, two-story ranch house, in the suburbs of Linden town; its white washed walls, with clay-red shingles on the roof, made it look as plain as any of his neighboring suburban houses - on the inside, however, his home exuded warmth. Antiques filled every corner, giving the impression of being transported back a hundred years.

Josh and Malcolm sat in the relaxed, shaded atmosphere of the back porch, deeply immersed in esoteric conversation.

"...And according to the 'Hatha Yoga'," said Malcolm, "we have a total of seven chakras along the length of our spinal cord, running from the base of the spine to the top of the skull."

"Chakras?" asked Josh.

"They are psychic centers of power which, if stimulated properly, allow us to develop an almost superhuman control over our mind and body." Malcolm paused for a moment. "I know what you're going to ask me," continued Malcolm as he slid his right hand over his balding head, almost as if checking to make sure his hair was still there. "Now, we both know that what I'm about to say is not true and it will sound fantastic to you, but for this to work as it should, you've got to use your imagination - make yourself believe it."

Josh imagined himself performing psychic feats; showing off to his schoolmates. He leaned forward on the rocking chair, resting his elbows against his knees as Malcolm continued.

"At the base of your spine, in your coccyx to be exact, lies a dormant divine potency, called 'kundalini', the serpent power. There is also a vein, known as 'sushumna' that runs through the backbone, linking 'kundalini' by way of the psychic centers, or chakras, to the supreme center of psychic power, at the top of the skull - the pineal gland. This supreme center is known as 'sahasrara'." Malcolm laid back on his rocking chair with a sigh; he was bored and tired. "The purpose of the 'Hatha Yoga', is to raise 'kundalini', through this vein, from one chakra to another until it unites with 'sahasrara'. When that happens, you will have achieved 'nirvana'. Or perhaps I should say, salvation."

"Sure," said Josh.

Malcolm smiled at him as he took a writing pad from the coffee table and drew a circle with a small, coiled serpent inside the circle. "This is your coccyx," he said. Then he drew another, much smaller, circle, about three inches away from the first one. "This is the pineal gland, somewhere inside your skull." He drew a line that joined both circles. "This is 'sushumna'; your spinal cord. Now," continued Malcolm as he drew six tiny circles - equidistant from each other – alongside, and on each side of the line, "these are the chakras. When kundalini is awakened, it sends up your spinal cord a small electrical charge which stimulates each chakra individually."

Malcolm placed the pad back on the coffee table, and then lay back on the chair; Josh did the same.

Looking at Malcolm, Josh moved to the edge of his chair. "But how do you awake kundalini?"

"Think of your spine as being two separate hollow tubes connecting from your nostrils all the way down to the base of your coccyx." Malcolm took the paper pad in his hands once more, and drew two hollow tubes along each side of the spinal cord; he connected them through the coccyx. "You must first assume the 'lotus' position, then go into a light hypnotic state. Once you are completely relaxed, you will cover one side of your nose and breathe in as you - very slowly - count to seven; hold your breath for a count of fourteen, then let the air out the other side of your nose for an additional count of seven. You must do this seven times in a row, then reverse the process by breathing in from the other side of your nose."

"Seven times?" asked Josh with knitted brows.

"Seven is a mystical number which will help you attune your body to the spiritual world." Malcolm appeared to be glad that today's discourse was almost over. "When you do this, you must make believe that you're breathing cosmic air; this 'cosmic air' enters, not your lungs, but your coccyx. It travels through one side of your 'imaginary' hollow spine, enters kundalini's chamber, finally exiting through the other side of your hollow spine."

"What does that do?"

"Cosmic air bothers kundalini; it makes him want to shake it off. As he reacts, he'll send an electrical charge up your spine, stimulating the chakras it finds along the way. The more you stimulate a chakra, the more you will develop specific extra-sensory powers, depending on the chakra that you reach." Malcolm allowed a sigh to escape. "Of course, as your lungs get used to the strain, you may augment the time you take for breathing, but it must be done by multiples of seven."

Josh made a face that clearly indicated he was lost.

"If at first you start by a count of seven for each breathing step - that is, breathing in; holding it; and breathing out - when you augment it, it must be to a count of fourteen, then twenty one, and so forth. It should take you at least two months of daily practice before you try more than a count of seven." Malcolm looked at Josh, who seemed to be miles away.

"Are you listening?" asked Malcolm.

"Yes, I am." Josh straightened up, trying to look alert.

"There's one thing I must warn you about. Keep in mind that you'll be stimulating the lower part of your body, where your sexual organs lie. If you're not careful, you'll find you may develop a strong sexual appetite. Self control is of the utmost importance."

FOUR

For the next month, Josh maintained contact with Malcolm occasionally. As intense as he often was, a stronger force grew within him. Obsession. His nights were his anchor to sanity, his bedroom, his "sanctum sanctorum."

The solitude of his bedroom afforded him the best of retreats. Now that summer vacations were almost at hand, he could lock himself in his room all day, if need be. Voracious reading and Yoga exercises filled his hours. Relieved that Josh had finally come back to life, Mary Ann didn't mind his newly acquired eccentricities.

One thorn remained under his skin. Norton. Lately, the more he tried to stay out of his way, the more Norton tried to hurt him. He needed help, someone to turn to. But he was on his own in this. Not even his father, had he been alive, could do anything about it. Besides, Norton wouldn't care who got hurt.

School would be over in less than a week, and Josh had a bad feeling. He wanted to forget the guy even existed, if only Norton could do the same for him.

This unusually uneventful day worried him. If Norton was quiet, thought Josh, something was about to happen.

Josh walked out to the schoolyard to meet the bus, when Janet stepped in his way.

"I need to talk to you," she said. Her deadpan expression spelled trouble.

Josh sidestepped her. "We have nothing to talk about." He continued towards the bus, avoiding her eyes.

"God!" she said walking behind him, waving her arms in frustration, "can't you accept an apology?"

"Okay, I forgive you." He lightened his step. "Now leave me alone."

She grabbed his sleeve, pulling hard, forcing him to stop and face her. "I won't leave you alone." She let go of his sleeve, nervously placing the offending hand behind her back. "I'm sorry. I didn't mean to do that."

"Sure you didn't," he said angrily. "Just like you didn't mean it the day you threw that cake in my face, right?"

She lowered her eyes and swallowed hard. He turned around and began to walk briskly towards the school bus.

"Wait," she said, running after him, pulling at his sleeve again.

"Will you please stop it?" He said, raising his voice as he turned to face her.

"I have something to say, and you're going to listen, even if I have to kick your ass!" She growled, making a fist in front of his face.

Josh faced her impatiently, but with caution. His eyes watched her hands for any sudden movements in his direction.

"The day I threw the cake in your face," she continued, "was an honest mistake. Some jerk - and don't ask me how he did it - managed to switch my apple juice with a glassful of piss. I drank a mouthful while everybody watched."

"Oh, Jesus!" said Josh making a face.

She looked at him steadily; seemingly ready to punch him in the nose if given half a reason. "Now, if you don't want to accept my apologies, then you can go screw yourself!"

Josh thought of the many times she - like him - must have needed someone to reach out to. "How do I do that?" he said after a nervous pause.

"Do what?" she replied.

"Screw myself?" This time, there was a wide grin on his face. He remained on guard, but not obviously so.

They stood silent for a moment. She looked into his eyes, searching for a meaning. A nervous laugh broke from his lips, and she caught on. Soon, they were laughing together -guardedly, but the tension was gone.

All the kids were in the bus by now, and Josh heard the driver release the brakes.

"Look," said Josh finally, "I'm going to lose my bus. I'll catch you later, okay?"

"No," she said, losing her smile. "That's what I wanted to talk to you about. You can't go home. Not now, anyway."

"Why not?" he asked intrigued.

"Norton put something in your locker." She grabbed his sleeve once more, and tried to pull him towards the school building.

"What are you talking about? I have a combination padlock in my locker. There's no way he could..."

"I saw him steal the passkey from the janitor," she interrupted. She opened the main entrance door, pulling Josh back inside the school.

◆◇◆◇◆◇◆◇◆

Josh and Janet stood in front of his open locker, staring at a small plastic bag full of Marijuana. Norton was up to no good all over again.

"What do we do now?" He glanced nervously towards the end of the empty hallway hoping none of the teachers - especially the principal - were coming this way.

"We get rid of it," she said, taking the bag from the locker, hiding it in her skirt. "Come on, let's go." She started to walk away, nervous and eager to get the hell out of the place..

Josh closed the locker door, placing the padlock over the swivel eye, and then gradually, pushing it home. He stood in place for a moment with the closed padlock in his hand, looking at it intensively.

"Come on, what are we waiting for?" she said, looking down the hallway.

"No, wait," he replied, turning towards Norton's locker. "I've got a better idea." He walked to Norton's locker and stood in front of it. He raised his arm and took the padlock in his hand. "I'm gonna' turn the tables on him." Josh closed his eyes, gently massaging the lock between the palms of his hands. A tingle cruised through his body.

"Come on, Josh. Somebody's gonna' catch us if we stay too long." She pleaded with him, but he seemed strangely distant.

He didn't listen. Silently, his right hand moved over the Norton's padlock, then, with his eyes still closed, began to move the dial.

"What are you doing?" she said. She moved closer, not able to make sense of whatever he was trying to do.

He didn't answer. Instead, he continued to move the dial back, and forth, and then back again.

"Josh? Are you all right?" she whispered, bringing her face near his.

"There!" he said triumphantly, as he let go of Norton's lock, stepping back from the locker. The lock was still closed.

She looked at the lock, and then looked at Josh with a sneer. "There what?"

"Pull it," he told her.

She raised her eyebrows and rolled her eyes impatiently. "We don't have time."

He fixed his eyes on her, and slowly hissed, "pull the lock."

"Okay, okay." Startled by Josh's sudden change, she pulled on the padlock and felt it slide open in her hands. "You knew the combination?"

"No, I didn't," he said.

"But how did you...?"

"I'll tell you later. Let's get outta' here," he said as he quickly took the Marijuana bag from her hands and placed it in Norton's locker.

By the time they came out of the school building, the school grounds were practically deserted. "I guess we'll have to walk," he said.

"Josh, what happened back there? You acted kind of funny," she said, narrowing her eyes. "How did you know the combination of that padlock?"

"I don't know," he replied with confusion. "It just came to me."

"But you acted like you were somebody else, like it wasn't you standing there."

"I said, 'I don't know'."

She stopped walking and just looked at him, studying him.

"I'll walk you home," he said uncomfortably. After a long silent walk, Josh broke the ice. "How much further do we have to go?"

"We're almost there," she replied. "About one more block." Her shoulders moved with an involuntary shrug. "How about you? Where do you live?"

"Not far, really. Just four blocks away." He wanted to walk closer to her, but an exasperating awkwardness held him back. "I guess I owe you one, huh?"

"Owe me one?"

"Yeah, for telling me about Norton."

Her cheeks suddenly felt warm. "It was nothing, forget it."

"Thanks, anyway," he said, noticing her blushing face. "I guess that makes you my friend, doesn't it?"

"I guess it does," she said as they turned the corner near her home.

❖◆❖◆❖◆❖◆❖

Josh didn't have to wait long before Norton's plan was placed in motion. The next day, just before the second period began, Josh was called into Mr. Jefferson's office. Two tall, unfriendly looking police officers stood by the office door; they looked at him steadily as he opened the Principal's door.

"Did you want to see me?" said Josh, closing the door behind him.

Raising his eyes from his desk, with a grim expression on his face, he said, "Yes." Then he stood up and walked towards the door. "Come with me." He opened the door, and addressed the police officers. "Gentlemen," he said. Without pausing, he continued towards the hallway; Josh walked next to him. They passed the gym, and climbed the stairs leading to the student lockers.

"Please, open it," said Mr. Jefferson as he stopped in front of Josh's locker.

Josh looked at Mr. Jefferson, then at the police officers standing next to him. "I don't understand. What's going on?" His face flushed.

"Do as I asked, Mr. Sebastian," insisted Mr. Jefferson.

Josh hesitated, and then turned towards his locker to open it.

Mr. Jefferson crossed his arms, his eyes traveling back and forth from Josh to the police officers. He seemed to be holding his emotions in check. When Josh finally opened the locker, Mr. Jefferson pulled him gently, but firmly by the arm.

"Let's allow these gentlemen to look inside." He waved his hand towards the locker, inviting the officers to search it. Releasing Josh, he crossed his arms again.

Josh's locker was almost empty, except for two yellow notepads.

"There's nothing inside," said one of the officers, stepping back from the locker.

"What?" blurted out Mr. Jefferson, pushing the officer aside. He fished inside the locker, and took the notepads in his hands; he flipped through the pages, then, in frustration, threw them back into the locker. He was about to say something, when Mrs. Green came running briskly down the hall.

"Mr. Jefferson!" she called. "I'm afraid there's been a terrible mistake."

"What are you talking about?"

"This note was just slipped under my door," she continued short of breath. It was clear she ran part of the way.

"Well, what does it say?"

"Here," she said handing him the note. "You read it."

Mr. Jefferson snatched it away and read it. "Who owns locker number 235?" he asked Mrs. Green.

"Norton," she said in between deep breaths. "Norton Parish."

Mr. Jefferson brought his right hand to his chin, and then looked at Josh. Finally, placing a gentle hand over Josh's shoulder, he said, "I'm sorry about this."

Josh shrugged, placing both hands in his pockets. "That's okay, sir. We all make mistakes." He avoided Mr. Jefferson's eyes.

"You may go back to your classroom now," said Mr. Jefferson.

As Josh walked away, he heard the Principal say to Mrs. Green, "please ask Mr. Parish to report to me, immediately."

When Josh entered the classroom, he looked straight at Norton with a wide grin. Norton's jaw dropped in disbelief. Savoring the moment, Josh turned towards Janet and winked at her. He sat next to her.

"What took you so long to deliver the note?" he whispered.

"Mr. Petersen took his time to let me go out to the bathroom," replied Janet, also whispering. "I almost didn't make it."

"Anyone see you?"

"Are you kidding?"

At this moment, Mrs. Green walked halfway into the classroom, motioning at Mr. Petersen to come to the door. She spoke with him briefly.

"Norton," said Mr. Petersen from where he stood, "come here, please. And bring your books."

Norton left his chair and walked towards the door. When he saw the police officer standing behind Mrs. Green, he looked at Josh. His eyes burned into Josh with hate.

Josh decided to walk home again. Not because Norton might be in the bus - he knew he wouldn't be - but because he was worried about the consequences of what happened today. He had a lot to think about.

Carelessly, he forgot to avoid Linden Mall, but this time, Ratface and his gang were not around. He entered the mall and decided to check the bookstore. It was a small bookstore by most standards, but its owner was very selective; many items in his inventory could not be found in the large chains. Browsing through bookstores was something Josh enjoyed. It helped him take his mind off his problems.

"May I help you?" said the middle-aged woman from behind the cash register, looking at Josh over her glasses

"No, not really. Thanks," he said politely as he walked towards the 'new-age section'.

After browsing for a while, looking at books on hypnosis, E.S.P., ghost houses, and even philosophy, he saw the title: "Experiments in the Occult", by Beryl Malone. He opened it in the middle and read a paragraph, then turned to another chapter, and read some more. He stopped, almost as if he was afraid the book would slip through his fingers and disappear from his life forever. Holding it tightly, he quickly brought it to the cash register.

He walked home with his nose buried within the book's pages - almost managing to get run over by a car when, distractedly, he stepped out of the protective territory of the sidewalk. His bedroom provided a safer reading place for the rest of that afternoon. Norton was, by now, the furthest thing from his mind.

Later that evening, Josh tried to rush his way through dinner. Mary Ann, as always, would have none of that. She insisted in having her little "after dinner" chats; her way, Josh supposed, to prove she was a good mother. It drove him up the wall but it paid off to humor her – she usually left him alone afterwards. After that, they watched a movie.

The evening wore on slowly for Josh, but by eleven o'clock, the movie was finally over. His mother kissed him goodnight. "I'm going to bed. Don't stay up too late."

"I won't," he said watching Mary Ann put on her slippers, and shuffled her way upstairs. As soon as she closed the door behind her, he went straight to his bedroom, locking the door behind him.

Midnight was still some time away, and he had his daily exercise on telekinesis to work on; that would give him a good forty-five minutes before getting ready for today's new experiment. He set his timer for five minutes before midnight.

All sorts of paraphernalia covered his desk, from erasers to broken pencils, and a Ping-Pong ball.

Clearing up the desk, he placed the ball at the center. Both his elbows rested at each side of the ball while his hands lightly touched his forehead, providing a resting-place for his head. His eyes attacked the small spherical shape with the assurance that today, it would move.

For the next forty-five minutes, Josh focused unswerving attention on the ball, never budging a muscle, barely batting an eye. At times, it seemed to him as if the little plastic object mocked him, refusing to move. At five minutes to twelve, the timer went off. End of exercise.

Placing the ball back inside the desk drawer, he replaced it with two three-inch candles - one to his right, the other to his left. From his closet, he pulled out an old medium sized mirror - big enough to reflect his torso. The mirror was adequate for his purpose; its chipped upper right hand corner wouldn't bother him. Everything was ready. He reached for his new book and began to read.

"Chapter Twelve
'A Window to the Netherworld'

...and mostly, due to its inherent dangers, has the practice been abandoned. Soundness of mind and strength of soul, are no guarantee to anyone willing to subject himself to the visions. In the best of cases, the sighting of supernatural beings or scenes, which are unavailable through normal sensory channels, seem to be accompanied by an emotional response, producing a permanent change in a practitioner's personality.

This particular ritual, allegedly used by the Rosicrucians - a mystical brotherhood, still in existence today - has been largely abandoned. Although we have described the ritual in some detail, it has been included in this work only for the sake of completeness, not for any other reason. We cannot stress strongly enough its inherent dangers."

With the mirror carefully set on top of the desk, and the two candles standing upright in front of him, he sat and waited.

At the stroke of midnight, Josh lit the candles and turned off the lights.

The first remarkable sensation came from the spectral gloom of candlelight; tonight promised to be stimulating. Crossing his legs Indian style - it was the closest he could get to the yoga's lotus position - he gently placed his hands over each of his knees; his eyes clamped onto his own reflection's eyes like a steel vise, not to move away until the ritual was over.

The candle flames flickered slowly, producing a leisurely swaying motion of shadows against the walls. The room grew dark, full of menacing life; his perception distorted slightly with shifting images looming above and behind him. The eerie silence of night amplified the murky atmosphere transporting Josh's imagination into a phantasmal, old dark house.

Don't lose concentration now, he whispered to himself. *Don't let your thoughts wander. Focus on your eyes; don't even blink!*

Slowly, the room got darker. The candles shone steadily, but their flames no longer seemed bright. An unsettling uneasiness settled over Josh; the reflection on the mirror began to form a smile; a smile he knew was not on his face. The shadows etched on his features turned sinister; the gloom lurking behind him grew larger. He concentrated on the muscles of his face, but the harder he tried to relax them, the more his reflection insisted upon the fiendish smile.

It's not possible, he thought. *I'm hallucinating.*

He wanted to bring his hands to his cheeks, just to make sure it was not true, but he could not do it; his body was paralyzed, out of control. The disgusting smile on the mirror, somehow, felt obscene. The large bags under the reflection's eyes made him look like a wicked old man.

His stomach took a fluttering dive towards emptiness as the sensation of unadulterated fright held him captive to the chair; a tear trickled down his left cheek.

Josh felt desperate. He knew he had to stop. Closing his eyes for a moment, he hoped to regain a sense of reality, but his heart would not let him; it was beating itself out of his chest. His eardrums stretched to their limits with the wild panicked message of fear. Every blood corpuscle strained to burst out of his veins.

He opened his eyes again, but the sardonic sneer was still there; and there was something else. He was not alone. Someone, or something, stood behind him.

Although he felt tempted to knock out the candles, he realized how naked he would be in total darkness. The form behind him stood vaporous and wavering, like an amorphous cloudy image.

Yet, not for long. Suddenly, the shadow was a shadow no longer. A faintly discernible sneer fixed itself upon the spectral, but humanoid silhouette. Everything in the room now had a menacing appearance; even silence took solid shape.

Josh closed his eyes again. In a desperate attempt to disengage from the nightmare, he turned his head towards the floor. The vast emptiness in his stomach spread out to the lower parts of his spine as every hair on his body stood on end.

Josh was ready to scream when a cold, damp hand touched his shoulder; then his body went limp; and he lost consciousness.

An hour later, Josh came to. His head spun as he pushed himself up to a sitting position. The room was still dark and ominous. The candles had burned beyond their mid-point, and the mirror looked like an oppressive window to a forbidding, alien world - he shuddered at the sight of it.

The unpleasant sensation of hysteria, again, froze him with fear. With surprising speed and decision, he jumped on his bed, scrambling up towards his bedside lamp - almost knocking it sideways when he flicked the switch. The yellow softness of his night lamp bathed the room with light, but he could not fail noticing the candles flickering lightly from the sudden rush.

He curled himself into a ball, his back resting against the headboard, and his knees, pulled up to his chest. Although he wanted to put out the candles, he failed to gather the courage to do so. He didn't even dare look at the mirror. It still reflected the flickering candles and the darkness of the world behind it.

He sat in his bed, afraid of his own shadow, with no one to turn to. The loneliness of adolescence sliced into his soul deeper than ever.

After a half-hour of hesitant deliberation, Josh placed his feet on the floor, almost sure that some evil creature, lurking under his bed, would soon grab him by the ankles. Nervously, he walked towards the candles, and after blowing them out with a long puff, threw them into the wastebasket. He then covered the mirror with a pillowcase.

For the rest of the night, Josh remained in bed with his night lamp on. He didn't watch television, he didn't read. He just sat with his eyes open, until dawn.

FIVE

Josh Zombied his way through his final exams. He knew the material well enough to breeze through them, but not without being nudged awake by Janet on several occasions. The final bell rang and Janet walked outside with Josh. A strange mood of sadness ran among the seniors, creating a sharp contrast against the feeling of elation of the rest of the students. Summer vacations had officially begun.

"What's going on with you?" said Janet. "Didn't you get any sleep last night?"

"No, not really," replied Josh, not wanting to talk about it.

"Are you all right?" she insisted. She looked worried.

"Yeah, I'm okay."

"Hey, you know Norton got kicked out of school?" she said with obvious pleasure.

"I figured he would," he said, approaching the water cooler and splashing water on his face. "Where is he now?"

Janet giggled at Josh's wet face. "I haven't the faintest idea. He's probably in jail or something."

"That's unlikely."

"No, it's not," replied Janet. "He's flunked several times. And he's caused too much trouble to keep letting him off the hook." Josh raised his eyebrows with surprise. They walked out to the schoolyard, but instead of going towards the bus, he turned in the opposite direction.

"Hey," said Janet, "where are you going?"

Josh turned to face Janet, but continued walking backwards.

"I brought my bike today. I'm going to see Malcolm."

"I thought we were going to spend the afternoon together?" she asked knitting her eyebrows.

"I know, and I'm sorry, but something very important came up. I really need to talk to him."

"Come on, Josh. You promised."

"Look, I don't have time now," he said as he bent down to unchain his bike from the post. "I'll call you soon."

"Will I see you again, after graduation?" she asked anxiously.

"Of course you will," he said as he winked at her and got on his bike. "You're my best friend."

Josh put his bike in gear, then pedaled away from her. "See you later."

When he turned the corner a block away, he managed to glance back. Janet still stood there, looking at him.

Malcolm was clearly upset as he sat on his favorite wicker chair speaking to josh in the back-porch. "What possessed you to do such a stupid thing?" asked Malcolm.

"I had to find out, I..."

"You had to find out? Didn't you just say that the article warned you of the dangers in such an experiment?" Malcolm's voice was harsh.

"I know how you feel," said Josh, as he dropped his head. "You got every right to be mad at me."

"I'm very upset with you." Malcolm leaned forward, trying to make Josh understand. "I thought you were smarter. Some things are not to be taken lightly."

"Don't tell me you believe in demons and warlocks?" said Josh with unintended sarcasm.

"That's not what I meant," replied Malcolm raising his arms in frustration as he dropped back against his chair. His eyes seemed to search the floor, looking for something to say. "No, Josh," he finally said, "I don't believe in any of that nonsense, but it's obvious you do."

"Come on, give me a break!"

"Then tell me, what were you so afraid of last night?"

"I must have had an hallucination or something. I just thought I saw someone standing behind me, that's all."

"That's precisely my point." Malcolm got on his feet and began to pace slowly around Josh's chair. "That's what I've been trying to get across to you," he continued, almost giving the impression he was thinking aloud. "Yes," he emphasized, "you saw a demon last night, but not a demon in any real sense. What you saw last night came straight out of the deepest recesses of your subconscious." Malcolm circled around Josh and stopped directly in front of him. "It's very easy," continued Malcolm, placing his hands in his pockets. "For a man to convince himself outwardly that there are no such things as ghosts and goblins, but if he has the slightest doubt, and the right circumstances occur, any man - even the bravest - can scare himself to death, like you almost did last night."

"You're saying that what I saw standing behind me came from within me?"

"Yes!" Malcolm dropped his full weight back upon the wicker chair; the chair creaked in protest.

"I caught a glimpse of the evil that lurks in my soul?"

"What happened to you last night, was not the result of evil within you, but the direct consequence of placing yourself in a vulnerable situation. What you saw was the result of your own fears, not from your soul, but from your mind."

Josh remained pensive for a moment, while Malcolm carefully studied him.

"What if a man is able to turn his fears around?" said Josh.

"I'm afraid I don't understand."

"What if a man, who is able to control his subconscious and emotions, were to try the experiment? What would he see?"

"I haven't the faintest idea. You're talking hypothetical here. Every man is a world unto himself, and each has his own personal inner fears. These are not things easily put aside."

"Okay. Let's take for example, a saint."

"This hypothetical saint of yours would be specially afraid of falling into temptation... All the demons his religion has taught him to fear might take form in his imagination. The subconscious is a powerful force. Heaven knows what he might see, but I wouldn't like to be in his shoes." Malcolm paused for a second, and looked straight into Josh's eyes. "You're going to try this again, aren't you?"

"Why do you say that?"

"I don't have to be a mind reader. I know what's going through your mind, and I warn you that anyone can easily manage to scare himself to death, like you almost did. The next time could be worse."

They sat there for a long, embarrassing moment of silence. Malcolm was concerned about Josh. He finally broke silence. "Josh, I wish there was some way I could reach you."

"But you have," countered Josh. "My whole life has changed. I have learned so much, You've taught me so much."

"I know. That's what worries me." Malcolm interlaced his hands as he leaned forward, placing his elbows over his knees. "From now on, I want you to call me before you try something like this; and when I give you advise, I want you to listen."

A heavy silence came between them, as Josh lowered his eyes and said nothing. Malcolm decided to pursue the subject no further.

"Come on. Let's go to the kitchen and get a coke."

Josh looked up at a smiling Malcolm; he smiled back.

Malcolm's eat-in kitchen looked as beautiful as it looked old, from the 1925 General Electric refrigerator, to the antique, oak-wood kitchen cabinets. Malcolm had a passion for the past; modern technology had little place in his heart, except for his computer, which he usually used for research on the Internet.

"So tell me," said Malcolm as he poured himself another Coke, "have you been doing your Yoga exercises?"

"I have, but so far, Kundalini doesn't even know I exist."

"I see. Well, don't give up, he'll come around."

"Maybe he has, and I haven't noticed."

"Don't worry. When it happens, believe me, you'll know."

"That's what I mean. Maybe that explains what I told you about that padlock I opened at school."

Malcolm sighed. "There's only two explanations for that. Either the padlock was already open, or you hit upon the combination by accident."

"You're trying very hard to discount a still a third possibility," said Josh calmly.

"What is that?"

"That I made all this up to impress you."

Malcolm knitted his eyebrows, looking at Josh with interest. "So now you're a mind reader too." He placed his glass in the table and walked towards the cupboard. "I'll tell you what," he continued, opening one of the drawers. "I have, somewhere in this house, an old combination padlock."

"Forget it," said Josh.

"No, no. Wait. I know it's in here someplace," said Malcolm. He opened another drawer, and searched through it.

"Can't you just forget it?"

Malcolm stopped searching, then turned to Josh with a smug smile on his face. His expression said it all. He had called Josh's bluff and it worked.

"Oh, damn!" exclaimed Josh, leaving his chair and walking to the kitchen sink. He opened the cabinet under the sink, then pulled out and old shoebox. "Is this what you're looking for?" he said, handing the shoebox to Malcolm. He went back to his chair.

Malcolm stood there with the shoebox in his hand. "Wha...?"

"Open it," said Josh, resting his elbow on the kitchen table.

Raising his left eyebrow, Malcolm took the lid off the box. His startled face stiffened when he saw the padlock. "But, how did you...?"

"I just knew." He met Malcolm's eyes with mild suspicion. "I have no other explanation." Josh looked into Malcolm's eyes and saw the doubt. "Why are you surprised? Isn't this what you do on your demo nights?"

Malcolm's eyes shifted from Josh to the padlock, then to Josh again. "Yes," he hesitated. "Yes, of course." He placed the padlock back in the box, and then put it away under the kitchen cabinet. He looked confused as he came back to the table.

"Kundalini, right?" said Josh.

"I don't know. Maybe." Malcolm seemed to be lost in his own thoughts. He slumped into his chair, scratching his head. Suddenly, his face lit up with a sympathetic smile. "Yes, maybe you're right."

Josh took a long swig from his cool glass of soda. There was no confusing Malcolm's obviously puzzled face. Either the man was a fraud who didn't believe what he taught, or was taken aback by his student's sudden progress. Josh preferred to believe the latter.

◆◆◆◆◆◆◆◆

Josh rode his bicycle from Malcolm's suburban house, all the way home - a good three-mile stretch of thick trees and fields, then four more miles of the city's cement jungle. It was already early evening, and he worried that part of his route would take him through the seediest part of town; besides, his mother expected him to be in time for dinner.

As he pedaled along the way, his thoughts wandered. He didn't recognize where he was until he came to a stop light on a two way street; a group of five teenagers eyed him carefully from the opposite side of the road - to Josh's left. He recognized 'Ratface' and his gang of bullies.

Josh avoided looking straight at the group, but he knew what they had on their minds. From the corner of his eyes he saw them whispering at each other while they studied him, devising a plan of attack.

Before the light changed back to green, three of them crossed over to the other side of the street. If he continued straight, he would run right into them. He looked around, praying for a patrol car, but none was in sight. As always, he would have to fend for himself.

'Ratface' and another kid remained on Josh's side of the street; they waited for the other three to get into position before starting towards him. As soon as they stepped off the sidewalk, Josh bolted his bike to the right, almost managing to get run over by a passing car; not even bothering to glance back, he heard 'Ratface' yell to the others, "come on, he's getting away!"

The running footsteps loomed closer behind him, as he pushed his legs to pump harder than he had ever done. He would have to change this route after today, that is, if he could get out of this alive. The streets were not deserted, but as far as Josh was concerned, he was out there all alone, waging his own private war.

Josh came close to another stoplight hoping it wouldn't turn 'red' on him before he could pass it. Otherwise, he would have to risk running it.

I wonder which is worse, he thought, *getting run over by a car, or getting beat up by the local gang of assholes.* He looked back for half a second, and saw a 'miniature Ratface' coming after him. It was 'Ratface's' little brother

"Come on, Michael," shouted 'Ratface'. "You almost have him!"

Michael's long right hand stretched out in a concentrated effort to grab Josh by the neck - Josh couldn't afford a slack of speed now. He was almost seventy feet away from the stoplight, when it suddenly changed to yellow. There wasn't time to think about what he must do. He had to risk it. The 'stop light' continued its downward change to red, while he still had twenty-five more feet to go. From the left hand corner of his eyes, Josh saw the large truck advancing towards the middle of the street; if he wanted to avoid crashing into it, he would have to swerve to his right. He gave his bike a desperate burst of speed, barely avoiding the rushing juggernaut as he passed in front of it. The kid running behind Josh wasn't so lucky.

The terror-stricken faces watching the scene was not what made Josh pull on the brakes of his bike, but rather, the horribly screaming tires of the monstrous vehicle, and the sickening crunch of grinding flesh and bone. Josh stood aghast as the blood-saturated pavement hungrily drank the precious liquid.

The four remaining teenagers stopped dead on their tracks at the sight of their companion's mutilated body.

The heart-rending cry of despair that came out of 'Ratface's' throat when his brother was caught under the wheels of the truck made Josh realize the enormity of what happened. If he didn't get out of there soon, surely, he would end up dead as well.

He shifted his bike into low gear, and glanced back towards the truck before pedaling away. Only one face from the crowd looked back at him. A steady gaze darted from the tearful eyes of 'Ratface's' unmoving expression. Josh's blood froze in his veins.

THE SUCCUBUS

SIX

By the time Josh got home, he was shaking. This was not going to be the last he'd see of Ratface either. The last thing he needed was to make Mary Ann upset, as he was, again, late for dinner. He put his bike away while mentally working out some excuse for his lateness. Instead, he found her crying over the kitchen sink. He rushed towards her with concern; she was not a habitual crier.

"What is it, mom? What's wrong?" Josh gently placed his left arm over her shoulders.

Mary Ann dropped the dish she was drying and turned towards Josh. She embraced him.

"Are you okay?" said Josh, returning her embrace. "Look I didn't mean to be late. I..."

"It's not you," she interrupted with a controlled sniffle as she patted his cheek.

"Then what is it?" Josh waited for a reply. "Come on... Tell me."

Mary Ann hesitated, turning away from Josh. "I just..." she took a deep breath and, with a new lump in her throat said, "lost my job." Her eyes swelled up with tears as she bit a trembling lower lip.

"You what?" exclaimed Josh with surprise. He was silent for a moment as the news sank in. "Mom, I... I'm really sorry." He embraced her again and repeated, "I'm sorry." He closed his watery eyes. This time he needed to be strong for her. He took her hand and pulled her towards the dinner table. "Let's sit down." She followed and sat across the table from him. "Here," said Josh, handing her a napkin. "You got make-up all over your face..."

"Thanks." She reached for the napkin, but held it in her hand for a moment, before wiping her face.

"Tell me what happened," asked Josh

Mary Ann had, by now, calmed down enough to talk. "Well, Mr. Davies - the General Manager - came into my office this morning and began to flirt with me. I tried to ignore his attentions, as I usually do, but... just then, my supervisor walked in as Mr. Davies sat on my desk. He was sweet-talking me into calling him by his first name."

"You mean Ms. O'keefe walked in?" Josh didn't get it. "So what's it to her?"

She looked at Josh, forcing a smile. "You wouldn't understand." Mary Ann stood up and paced the kitchen floor. "Or maybe it's me who doesn't understand," she said. "I've always been able to handle him; he always seemed harmless enough to me, but Ms. O'keefe..."

Josh listened intently, without interrupting her.

"Ms. O'keefe and Mr. Davies are..." Mary Ann came back to the table and sat down again. "She created a scene." She placed her elbows on the table. "Not in front of him, mind you. She turned red as a beet, but didn't say a word till he went back to his office... and, boy, did he go to his office! As soon as he realized she stood behind him, he disappeared."

Mary Ann raised her hand to her face and, with a dejected expression, scratched her forehead. "Miss O'keefe, waited for us to be alone, then she gave me a dirty look and told me to clean up my desk." Mary Ann repeated Ms. O'keefe's words mocking her with a shrill voice *"you're not coming back tomorrow!"*

"She can't do that!" protested Josh.

"I thought she was just talking, but by the end of the day, she gave me a written notice."

"Does Mr. Davies know?"

"As far as I know, no one in the office knows, but I plan to be there tomorrow. I'm going to have a talk with Mr. Davies."

That evening, after a quiet dinner, Mary Ann went early to bed.

Josh went to his room, trying to calm down, yet unwanted images kept creeping back. He approached his desk and opened the top drawer. He stared at the Ping-Pong ball. It would be no use to try any mental exercises today. The power of concentration eluded him. "Damned bitch!" he growled, as he thought about Ms. O'keefe.

His adrenaline level brought his body and mind to a point beyond alertness. He visualized Mary Ann turning in her bed in the next room, doing her best to catch some sleep, while hopelessly thinking of how to make ends meet without a job. An almost uncontrollable anger ate him up inside. He moved away from his desk and sat on the edge of his bed.

I need to relax. He turned off the night lamp, rested his back on the headboard, and assumed a semi-lotus position.

He took a deep breath, closed his eyes and began... a slow count of seven breathing in... a double count of seven holding in the air... a count of seven breathing out. Seven full breathing cycles... and starting tonight, seven additional cycles; concentrating on the tiny serpent, Kundalini; watching it in his mind's eye as it stirred uncomfortably. His breathing was serene, uniform; his body felt light, non-existent. Then, as he completed the tenth cycle, he began to feel his lungs cry out for a large gulp of air, but he held on.

I must keep my rhythm, he thought. I must! The strain of maintaining an even flow of air in and out of his lungs gave him an uncomfortable emptiness in his stomach; his muscles tightened. *Breathe in. Hold it. Breathe out.* Cycle twelve. For the first time, since he started his exercises, he experienced strange sensations. His testicles contracted in his scrotum with life of their own, unwilling prisoners of their fleshy cage. *Breathe in. Hold it. Breathe out.* Cycle fourteen. Then he felt it. A sudden explosion of electrical discharges snapped from his coccyx, spreading upwards through the spinal cord and into his brain. A bright sparkle of blood corpuscles rushed in his eyelids breaking into fireworks of red and yellow.

His body slumped suddenly forward, landing headfirst on the mattress. His eyes opened and his mouth dribbled.

Josh suddenly came out of his trance and pushed himself straight. "What the hell was that?" His heart beat wildly; had he finally awakened 'Kundalini'? It had to be. There was no other explanation. Jumping out of his bed, he went straight to the kitchen and grabbed the telephone. Malcolm had to know. As he took the receiver off the hook, the kitchen lights suddenly came on.

"Josh," said Mary Ann half-asleep, "what are you doing?"

"Damn, mom. You startled me!"

"Who are you calling at this time of night?" she said as she approached him.

"Malcolm..."

"Come on. Let it wait till tomorrow!" She pointed at the clock on the kitchen wall. "It's two o'clock in the morning."

Josh looked at the clock as he gently placed the receiver back on its cradle. "Sorry. I... didn't notice I the time."

"Go to bed." She turned around and went back to her bedroom. "And don't forget to turn off the lights," she said before closing the door.

He turned the lights off, and walked back to his bedroom.

●◆●●◆●●◆●

Josh lay wide-awake in the dark, his head softly rested on his pillow, his eyes staring at the ceiling. Now that he had stirred 'Kundalini', if that was indeed what happened, the possibilities of developing psychic powers were real. His mind drifted to visions of showing off at school; reading people's minds; visiting far away places with astral projection.

Astral projection. Why not? he thought. *It's worth a try!* He made himself comfortable and began the process of self-hypnosis, concentrating on his astral body.

Before long, Josh was in deep trance, and fully aware. What happened next, he wasn't sure, was an illusion, or reality. His astral body drifted slowly upwards, towards the ceiling. It floated about six feet away before moving downwards once more, until it came to rest, in a standing position, by the foot of the bed.

As Josh looked at his body, he noticed a thin, transparent, liquid-like filament running from his astral chest to his physical chest... like an umbilical cord.

'This MUST be some kind of dream.'

Then, a sweet, musical voice spoke. "This is no dream, Josh."

He looked to his left, and was startled by the vision of an incredibly beautiful woman standing by his bedroom door. Her alien eyes looked straight into his as she smiled while moving her body with the grace of a goddess. A slight glow surrounded her body.

Josh heard a loud 'whoosh' as he felt himself sucked inside of a vacuum. His astral body returned in a flash to the sanctuary of its physical dwelling. He woke up. Nothing he read had prepared him for such an experience. Quickly, he stretched his hand towards the night lamp, turned on the light, and sat on the bed. He looked towards the door, but there was no one there.

"What the hell...?" he exclaimed. It was such a vivid dream and her body was so solid. Who was she? What was she? More importantly, could he do it again? His mind suddenly clouded with lust. He'd read about such a thing before.

The Catholic Church spoke of a being that would come at night to tempt their priests. A Succubus, he believed was the name. He went to his desk and pulled out his dictionary.

Suc·cu·bus: noun
Etymology: From Medieval Latin, alteration of succubare to lie under, from sub- + cubare: to lie, recline
A lascivious spirit supposed to have sexual intercourse with men by night.

Even if it was only in dreams, his body screamed for release, and by God, he was going to get it. He turned off the lights once more and stretched his body on the bed. The process of self-hypnosis was second nature by now. Before long, his astral body began its slow journey towards the foot of the bed.

This is incredible, he thought. I'm floating in the air!

Finally, he came to rest on the floor, standing upright. His astral body, although a little less solid looking, was otherwise a carbon copy of his physical self.

"Hello again," said the mellow voice.

Josh quickly turned towards the bedroom door. Sure enough, there she was. Her back reclined lightly against the wall as she sensuously raised her left foot, allowing it to rest on her right knee. She smelled of sweet incense. Both her hands moved back and forth along her thighs. Her well-proportioned breasts curved upwards, challenging the law of gravity, begging to be touched. Only her eyes made her appearance look alien... she had no pupils.

"I thought you weren't coming back," she purred.

Josh stood there, nailed to the floor. He had seen naked women in pictures only, but this creature was a poem in movement. "Am I dreaming you?" asked Josh.

"I already told you. This is no dream."

"Who are you, then?"

She moved her hands up her body, caressing herself. Her movements were slow, deliberate.

"Are you a spirit?"

"No more than you are."

"What are you then?"

"Don't ask who I am, ask what I want."

Josh simply stood there, afraid to ask, afraid to move, afraid to wake up.

"I want to help you," she said sweetly.

"Help me? Help me with what?"

"That." she said, pointing to the bed where Josh's body lay. His arousal was obvious through his underwear.

"You know you want me!" Her hips swayed rhythmically while slowly implying the intimacy he so desired.

Josh, no longer able to control himself, moved closer to the apparition.

"NO! DON'T TOUCH ME!" Her tone of voice changed as her body stiffened for a moment, and then relaxed again, regaining her composure.

Josh was somewhere between fear and fascination. He kept still as she resumed her seductive movements. "What do you want me to do?" he asked nervously.

"Stay where you are," she said, moving - floating - across the room. She reached the edge of the bed, near Josh's inert body, and stretched her right hand, softly stroking him. "Aaaah, yes. I can see now," she continued caressing him. "Can you feel?"

Her hand felt strangely warm. This was ecstasy. Although she touched his physical body, his astral self felt her every caress. "Yes," he said, turning his head up and closing his eyes.

"I want you." Her hands maintained a slow, but steady caress on him.

"Yes, yes. Take me."

She paused for a moment, and then moved away from the bed. Her hands went back to caressing herself.

"Wait. What are you doing?" he said, his body shaking in desperation. "Why did you stop?"

Looking at him hungrily, she walked towards his opened closet door. Suddenly, a bright luminosity spewed forth, seemingly, from inside the closet. It bathed the room with a blinding, unnatural light.

Josh's jaw dropped in disbelief. "What the hell is that? How'd you do that?"

She moved halfway into the light, looking back at Josh with the look of a woman in heat. "Come." she said, beckoning with her hands. "Come with me!"

"I don't get it," he said. "Where are you going?"

"We can't do anything here. Not in the physical world. It won't work. Come with me and I assure you, from this day on, you may have me forever."

He trembled with anticipation, needing her more than he needed life itself. Josh entered the light, and a sudden surge of power fed into him. The feeling was exhilarating. It was like crossing a huge tunnel with myriads of beautiful stars of different colors flashing on and off. The creature flew slightly ahead of him, but she checked back several times, as if to make sure they wouldn't lose each other.

At the end of the tunnel floated a large sun-like gate that opened and closed with the steady cadence of a heartbeat. The creature floated right up to the edge and stopped to wait for him. Josh suddenly realized he wasn't flying of his own volition. He was being pulled towards her. The trip lasted but a few seconds, and yet, it seemed an eternity.

When he reached the creature, she swiftly dove into the gate, drawing him in with her. A soft 'POP' indicated the end of the journey and the brightness was now gone. They were now in a gloomy looking room, about the same size as his bedroom, but there the similarities ended. There were no windows and no doors; only four moss-covered walls with two small bunk beds - each on opposite sides of the room. One of the beds was empty; the other had a piece of cloth-like material covering a large bulk underneath.

"What is this place?" he asked as he turned to face her. Somehow, she looked different now, not quite as alluring. She stared at him, but stood there motionless, not saying a word. "Wait a minute," said Josh apprehensively. "I don't like this." He moved towards the light on the wall. "I want to go back."

"No!" she said sweetly. "Do not be afraid." Her left hand made a pass over the wall and the light disappeared.

"I'm not sure I want to be here," said Josh.

"Nothing has changed. I promise you will never forget this night." Her hands came up to his face as if to caress him, but stopped short of touching him. "I want you to lie there," she continued, indicating the empty bunk bed.

Josh sat, still excited, but somewhat nervous.

Standing directly in front of him, exposing her body, she brought both hands to each side of her hips. "Do you not want me?" she asked raising her eyebrows.

He didn't answer, but his eyes remained fixed on her feminine beauty.

"Concentrate on your physical body back in your room. Look at it through your mind's eye. Can you see it?"

Josh closed his eyes for a moment, then said, "yes, I can see it."

"Can you feel it? Feel its slow breathing?"

"Yes," said Josh, somewhat surprised with the vividness of the experience.

"Good," she continued in a breathy, sexual tone. "When I go back to your plane of existence, you will feel me; you will see me. I will make you enjoy the glories of the flesh."

"Wait!" said Josh. "You're leaving me here?"

"It's the only way. Our spirits cannot touch."

Josh sat on the empty bunk bed nervously thinking that tomorrow he would wake up and this would have been nothing more than a dream.

She looked at him and allowed her tongue to travel around her lips. "Lie down and concentrate on what I'm about to do. You're going to feel sensations you never even knew existed."

Josh meekly complied.

The creature turned back to the wall and opened the gate once more. The light disappeared behind her as she crossed the tunnel.

And he remained alone.

Closing his astral eyes, he followed her in his imagination. He saw her crossing the tunnel of light, saw her enter his bedroom and stand naked in front of his bed. He was there - with her - yet he was a million miles away. There was such a look in her face, as he had never seen or imagined. Her breathing turned deeper, studying his inert body from head to foot. Her mouth twisted with desire. She climbed on the bed and straddled him, allowing a deep, full penetration. The entry was deliberate and slow, attacking each inch of him leisurely, very much aware that Josh watched, felt.

His climax was near. The timing was crucial. As his body thrust with instinctive force, she bent forward, until her mouth touched his mouth, forcing his lips open. Her body began to vibrate like a tuning fork. She didn't move, she didn't undulate. She just vibrated.

Her vibrations grew stronger, and soon his body began to vibrate with hers. Her kiss quickly moved within his mouth, like a serpent seeking refuge in a deep cave, caressing his teeth and palate, expertly exploring, savoring his virginity. Then her tongue slid deeper, impossibly deeper - past his esophagus. Her mouth opened wider, and her tongue thickened, continuing an unstoppable trek into his stomach; her face distorted horribly when her jaw became unhinged. She slithered like a snake inside of him while he suffocated.

Something from within her squeezed his virginity firmly. Her hands moved under his buttocks, digging her nails deep into him as she pulled his hips towards hers. Whatever held on to him, held with determination. A sharp pain shot through his spine when a finger-like appendage penetrated his urethra, inching its way into him, stretching his flesh almost beyond its limit.

His body thrust wildly as he tried to shake off the alien invasion. She held on like a steel vise. Josh was in pain. Their vibrations grew in intensity to the point where Josh felt his body about to shatter. Then, the pain went away, as quickly as it had started. Her form melted into his skin, and the transition was complete.

◆◆◆◆◆◆◆

The next day, Mary Ann knocked on Josh's door but got no answer. "Josh," she said through the door. "Josh." She knocked again, and then tried the doorknob. It was locked. *Funny,* she thought*, he doesn't usually lock the door.* "Josh," she called again.

"Hmm?" Josh was not a morning person. Getting up at any time before ten o'clock was a prodigious ordeal.

She heard the lazy response. "Listen, I left some breakfast on the table for you. Don't wait till it gets cold, okay?" She waited for him to reply, but he didn't answer. "Josh, did you hear me?"

"Yeah, mom," he said morosely. "Just let me sleep for awhile." With his eyes still closed, he smacked his lips, feeling a bad taste in his mouth. He made an effort to look towards the door, but his eyelids kept closing on him.

Mary Ann could hardly make out what he said, but it sounded like his usual morning struggles with getting up. She was going back to her office today. It was very important to straighten things out with both Ms. O'keefe and Mr. Davies. She wasn't about to lose her job because of some jerk coming on to her. "I'm going to the office. If things turn out okay, I'll call you."

"Sure, sure," he said in his sleep.

Mary Ann walked out to the car. A bird chirped happily away from some distant tree.

It was a beautiful morning.

SEVEN

The telephone rang for a full half-hour before Josh found the strength to get out of bed. Dragging his feet, he opened his bedroom door. He was still half-asleep when he finally picked up the receiver. Last night's events had not yet surfaced to his awakened, conscious state.

"Hello," he said with his eyes closed.

"Hello, Pin?" said a familiar voice.

"Yeah, what?" He spoke on automatic.

"You'll never guess who this is," said the voice playfully, but aggressively.

"I can't stand the suspense," said Josh with a yawn. His brain wasn't clicking yet.

It's your pal, Norton."

Josh froze. The sound of the name was enough to bring him to instant attention, but he didn't reply.

"Hey, Pinhead, I'm talkin' to ya'." Norton was ready to kill. There was still no reply from Josh. "Ye'r dead, pal," continued Norton. "Dead! Ya' hear what I'm saying?"

It was eleven o'clock in the morning, yet, Josh felt hardly rested. To him it was as if a ten-ton truck had just run over him. His skin felt sticky and his breath tasted like rusty iron.

"I'm gonna' kill ya', ya' little shit!"

Josh stood there with the telephone to his ear, wanting to hang up, but unable to do it.

"...And y'all never know when it's gonna' happen. Today, tomorrow, next week..." Norton continued talking, but Josh had stopped listening. He looked at his hands. They were smeared with blood.

"I'm gonna' have a barbecue soon, and ye'r gonna' be the main course."

The receiver fell to the floor with a loud 'crack' as Josh ran to the bathroom. He looked in the mirror. There was blood on his face; his teeth reflected a dull deep red. He shivered, afraid of thinking about what was going on. Instinctively, he smelled his hands. There was no question about it. This was blood. Without a moment's hesitation, he jumped into the shower, clothes and all. He remained there for an hour, not knowing what to do, not knowing what to think.

After a lengthy gargling with soap and water, and almost scrubbing himself raw, he finally stepped out from the shower. He grabbed a tube of toothpaste in his left hand, managing to squeeze most of its contents straight into his mouth. He brushed his teeth, his palate, his tongue, and his cheeks. Then he did it again.

"What the hell's this shit?" he said, throwing the toothbrush aside. He wandered around the house taking his time cleaning every spot he had touched. Then he took his shirt, his jeans, and his bedspread and threw then into the washing machine. After that, he put them in the dryer and continued the cleanup.

An hour later, he took the clothes out of the dryer, carelessly folding them over his arm. Dropping the bundle over the dining room table, he continued towards the kitchen. He couldn't understand how he woke up with his clothes on, when he clearly remembered going to sleep in his underwear.

Suddenly, the fleeting image of a frightened woman's face assaulted him. It stopped him cold. The image went away; almost as fast as it came, but there was no doubt he had seen it. He paused for a moment - unsure of what had just happened - then turned his head. His eyebrows knitted together. His eyes scanned the kitchen, as if trying to find the woman somewhere within the house; there was no one there. A cold chill went through his bones.

Then, the image flashed back; it was the same chubby faced woman crouched in the corner of some unknown house with one hand extended in the air while her other hand covered her face. She cried. Begged. Then again, the image disappeared.

That woman, thought Josh with a shudder, I know her from somewhere.

Then it flashed back again. This time, her face was much closer. She pleaded for her life. It was to him she cried. It was to him she begged.

It can't be, he thought. This is another nightmare. He quickly ran up the stairs to his bedroom and closed the door behind him. He couldn't lock the image out. It persisted stronger every second. He saw his arms reach in front of him, grabbing the woman by her shoulders, effortlessly lifting her in the air. Then his mouth, once more, tasted the coppery flavor of blood.

In panic now, Josh opened the bedroom door and ran towards the bathroom. He jumped under the shower with his clothes on. The shocking spray of cold water washed straight onto his face. The image eventually went away.

❖━❖━❖━❖━❖

An hour later, Josh sat on his bed, looking straight ahead, not seeing anything, and not hearing anything. His hair was still as wet as when he came out of the shower. A persistent, irregular noise came from his bedroom window. At first, he was too far out to hear, but then, it got louder and louder, until he could no longer ignore it.

"Hey, Josh," called a voice from the front yard. Another click came from his window; someone was throwing pebbles against the glass. He moved towards the window and looked down.

"Oh, no," he said when he saw Janet waving her arms at him from the front door.

"Hey, open the door, sleepy-head."

Reluctantly, he turned around and went downstairs to get the door.

She stood half-smiling, shyly shifting her weight from side to side. "Hi!" she said.

"Hi," he replied without returning her smile.

She hesitated for a moment. "Can I come in?"

"I... huh... sure." He opened the door wider and moved aside, allowing her to pass.

"Look, if you're busy right now, I can..."

"No, that's okay. Come on in."

She placed her hands behind her back, and walked in. "Wow!" she said. "Your house is nice. I thought you said your mother had a lousy job."

"She does. My... my father..."

"Life insurance, huh?" she completed the sentence as she continued towards the living room.

"Yeah. I guess." He closed the door behind him. He wasn't in much of a mood to talk.

"Listen," she said turning towards him. "I can't stay too long, and I wasn't planning to butt in on you like this." Her body language told him there was something important on her mind.

"Can I get you something? A coke or a beer?" A feeling of awkwardness swept over him. Here he was, alone with her in his house.

"Sure. Coke's okay."

"Good," he said, turning towards the kitchen.

"I guess you must be wondering why I came by," she said walking behind him.

He glanced at her, and now that she was here, he was glad. Things didn't seem as bleak.

"I've been kinda' worried about you. Norton's been spreading the word around that he's coming to get you." She leaned against the wall as she fidgeted with her fingernails.

"Yeah, I know. He called me a while ago."

"Well, I don't want to scare you or anything, but I also heard about what happened between you and Ratface."

"News travel fast in this town," he said as he opened the dishwasher and pulled out a blue plastic glass. "Who told you this?" He dumped three pieces of ice in the glass.

"Ratface did. He's my cousin." She lowered her eyes to the floor, as if ashamed to admit it.

"What?" said Josh, dropping the glass on the floor.

She bent down to help Josh pick up the ice cubes. "We're not close or anything, really. I hate his guts. But dad made me go with him to the funeral parlor this morning - we didn't stay long; my father can't stand his own family - that's when I heard Ratface talking. He blames you for what happened to Mickey." She plunked the ice cubes back in the glass, and then looked at him. "I'm afraid for you, Josh."

"You're afraid?" said Josh yanking the glass away from her. "How do you think I feel?" He threw the glass in the sink. "What about your family? What do they think?"

She was surprised at his reaction. "They know what happened. The problem is, they're all afraid of him. Nobody in my family even speak to him."

"Shit," he said angrily. "You've made my day, haven't you?" He tried to catch himself before he said it, but it was too late.

Janet's eyes turned red as a tear trickled down her cheek. "I don't think I deserve this." She turned and ran towards the front door.

"Wait!" shouted Josh, running after her. He stopped her just as she grabbed the doorknob. "I'm sorry. I didn't mean that. It's just that..." He paused. "Things haven't been going well for me." He too had tears in his eyes.

"Oh, Josh," she said as she turned around and hugged him.

Josh and Janet spent most of the afternoon sitting in the back porch, not saying much, just keeping each other company. By four o' clock, she had gone home. He didn't tell her about the nightmare; he didn't tell her about the blood.

※◆※◆※◆※◆※

As soon as Janet went out the door, Josh rushed to the telephone to call Malcolm.

"Come on, kid," said Malcolm over the telephone. "You're pulling my leg."

"But the dream was so real."

"Most dreams feel real, Josh. You and I know that." Malcolm paused for a moment, then continued. "Look I'm not saying I don't believe you experienced something, but…"

"What about the vision I had this afternoon? I was wide-awake then. And what about the blood?" Josh desperately wanted a rational explanation. *What's wrong with Malcolm?* he thought.

"You worry me. Maybe you've been taking all this too seriously. I want you to stop doing your exercises for a while. It'll give your mind a rest."

"Dammit, Malcolm. You taught me all this stuff and now you're telling me I'm imagining things?"

"Come over to my place. I seriously want to talk."

"No, forget it. I'll call you back some other time." Josh felt furious, disappointed. "Maybe when I stop acting like a lunatic." He hung up on Malcolm. '*What a damn jerk,*' he thought. No sooner had he released the receiver than the telephone rang again.

"YEAH, WHADDA YA' WANT?" said Josh with anger.

"Josh?"

"Yeah!"

"Are you all right?" It was a sweet voice.

"Oh, Mom?" he said, suddenly changing his tone of voice.

"What's the matter? You sound like you're having a fight or something."

"No, no. I'm okay."

"Good. Listen, I might be a little late tonight. Can you make yourself a sandwich?"

"Sure, no problem." Then Josh remembered. "Hey, how'd it go at the office today?"

"That's why I called you," said Mary Ann. "I have to stay overtime."

"Great! That means they took you back?"

"Well, yes and no," she replied with hesitation.

"What do you mean, yes and no?"

"No one knows I was fired yesterday."

"Oh, I see. Ms. O'keefe got soft on you, huh?"

"No, not really." There was a short moment of silence over the line. "Ms. O'keefe is dead," she said.

◆━◆◆━◆◆━◆◆━◆

That evening, Josh sat in the family room, watching the evening news with Mary Ann.

"*The woman's body,*" said the television announcer, "*has not yet been fully identified. The police, however, have reason to believe that the human remains found in the house belong to its present occupant. Ms. Judith O'keefe. There is speculation by police officials that what killed the victim was some kind of animal. The species remain undisclosed at this moment.*"

Mary Ann briskly walked to the television set, and turned it off. Josh sat there in a daze. When they showed an early photograph of Ms. O'keefe during the news, he immediately recognized the face - he had seen her earlier this afternoon, begging for her life, and yet she was murdered last night.

"It solved our problem, didn't it?" he whispered. His eyes were glued to the floor, his face showing no expression.

"I don't want to hear you talking that way," she said raising her voice, taking two steps towards him. "Ever again. Do you understand?"

He did not reply, but his cheeks flushed with confusion.

"Oh, I'm sorry," said Mary Ann as she came close to him and knelt by his feet. "I didn't mean to shout at you." She tenderly touched his face. "Forgive me?"

Josh looked at his mother and smiled. "Sure." He playfully mussed up her hair. His mind was somewhere in outer space, but Mary Ann seemed to follow close behind.

She stood, pulling Josh by the hand as she did so. "Come on," she said. "I want to have a drink before I turn in." He followed her to the kitchen. She poured him a soda, and then got herself a stiff glass of whiskey. Not much conversation happened between them. They were two zombies sitting alone in the kitchen. Half an hour later, she kissed him goodnight and went to bed.

◆◆◆◆◆◆◆◆◆

Josh stood alone outside his bedroom, anxiously looking at the door. What else was going to happen today? Why was there blood on his body when he woke up? How had he been able to see Ms. O'keefe's last dying moments? How much of last night was a figment of his imagination? And what about Norton and Ratface? Those two jerks were real enough.

He felt tempted to go into his mother's room and hide under her bed sheets, just as he did when he was a little boy. Thunderstorms still made him shudder, and this was a whopper. Of course, that was out of the question; he was no longer a child. Besides, his mother had enough worries of her own.

He opened his bedroom door. He would not be afraid. As he closed the door behind him, he scrutinized every inch of the bedroom. These were not just four ordinary walls with a ceiling to him. This was his castle, his world.

In this room, he sat endless nights, conjuring up all those wonderful scenarios for his 'Role Playing' adventures. Here he lived, countless times, the life of a hero, surmounting impossible odds, fighting the forces of evil with his alter ego's strength and cunning.

By the wall to his left were four shelves full of his hand-painted figurines. He walked towards them and grabbed one of the miniatures from the lower shelf. It was a barbarian-type fighter holding an oversized sword in its right hand. "We haven't gone adventuring in a long time," he said to the figurine. He looked at it with pride, and then carefully placed it back on the shelf.

His eyes wandered over the figurines in his collection, but stopped cold at the sight of one of them. He recognized the face. The face of the woman from last night! He grabbed the figurine from the shelf and brought it close to the night lamp. He remembered when he painted its eyes bright red, as well as the tip of its fangs. He looked only at the face, not at the bat wings that loomed upwards from its shoulders, nor the menacingly sharp claws at both its hands and feet.

Malcolm is right, he thought as he held the figurine in his hand. *I should take a break from all this mystic stuff.* Placing the figurine back on the shelf, he decided. Tonight there would be no hypnosis, no yoga. He took his pants off, went to bed, and turned off the night lamp. Tomorrow, he'd think about how to deal with Norton and Ratface.

◆━◆━◆◆━◆◆━◆◆━◆

"Hello, Josh," said the mellow female voice. Although this time there was no attempt at seduction.

"Huh? What?" replied Josh as he stood near the foot of the bed. She smiled at him from the threshold. "It can't be! I'm awake now."

"Are you?" She pointed to the bed where Josh's inert body lay. He had fallen asleep.

"But I didn't call you," he protested. "I don't want you here."

"Don't be a fool. You have no control over me." Her voice wasn't menacing, but there was no longer a seductive tone in her singsong; her beauty, however, were still as appealing.

"Well, you're not going to trick me like you did last night," he said.

She laughed. "I needed you to invite me in only the first time. Now I have the key. You cannot stop me. Besides, I don't believe you want to stop me. Don't you want to have me again?"

"You didn't make love to me, you raped me, and it was painful too!" Josh turned his back to the creature, bringing his hands up to cover his eyes. "No! Go away. You're just in my imagination. You're not real."

"There is no need for you to fear me. I wish you no harm. Besides, you will not feel pain this time."

"Yeah, right!" He turned to face her. "What do you want? What's in it for you?"

"I promise you our relationship will be strictly give and take. I give you pleasure, then you lend me your body for the night."

"What?"

"Of course. I used it last night. Do you not remember?"

Josh remained silent.

"That's a pity," said the creature. "You would have enjoyed my outing as much as I did." She began to move towards Josh's sleeping body. "It's a shame you're such a weakling," she continued with a sigh as she looked at his frailness with disappointment. "I found myself having to draw from my own resources." Then she smiled. "But you'll get stronger; you'll see."

She turned towards the closet, making a slight movement with her hands. The closet revealed a bright light inside. Josh recoiled away from it. Their eyes met for a fleeting moment and he understood.

"I'll be a prisoner again in that shithouse, is that it?" he said with anger. The creature's eyes narrowed to a slit as a dull reddish glow began to emanate from them. Josh stepped back cautiously.

"Wait," pleaded Josh. "I need to know more. Don't send me there."

She turned back towards him and smiled. "Not as eager tonight?" She flaunted her body at him. "Do you not want what I offer?" She said as she brought her face close to his.

"What is it you offer? Death?"

"I bring you the gift of power; to make anyone grovel at your feet, to crush your enemies with the flick of your little finger. Surely you can't still think I offer nothing?"

"You... you killed Ms. O'keefe, didn't you?"

She tilted her head to her left as she grinned. "Well, we did," she said slowly. "I used your body; remember?"

"I had nothing to do with it!" protested Josh trying to back away from her; he was already against the wall.

"As you wish." She said as she turned towards Josh's collection of figurines. "But the feeding did us both a lot of good." She approached one of the figurines and studied it for a moment. "I'm sorry I was a trifle careless last night. All that blood. It won't happen again." She gave him a mischievous look. "We can't afford to have anyone discover our secret, now can we?"

Josh felt nauseous. He felt like a cannibal. "How did you find out about her?" he managed to ask between gags.

"You mean that woman I saw last night? You forget I'm using your body. I have access to your thoughts. I know everything about you."

"You speak of her as if she was nothing."

"She was nothing to me, except a good meal. But to you," she turned from the figurine on the shelf to face the bed. "Well, let's say it made a difference to you." With a soft smile, she tilted her face a bit to the side. "I'm glad we had this little talk. In time, you'll learn to accept me. It's inevitable."

"Oh God," whispered Josh.

"Come, come, my sweet. You can't be any different than any of the other humans I have had the misfortune of possessing, are you? However, if you're curious about what we'll be doing tonight, you can find out tomorrow." As she straddled his physical body, Josh felt himself being irresistibly pulled away into the light. "All you have to do," she continued, "is to think about it. After all, your eyes will be there with me."

◦◆◦◦◆◦◦◆◦

The light closed up behind Josh. Again, he faced a long night, trapped within the prison his own folly. He was back in the room with the blind walls. He looked at the wall from which he entered, but it looked solid. His hands touched cold rock as he tried in vain to push them through.

"Let me out!" he shouted. "Let me out!"

Desperation gave way to frustration; he dropped to his knees and cried. After a bit, he sat on the floor and leaned against the wall, hugging his knees close to his body. His eyes scrutinized the room. Although there was light enough to see with, there seemed to be no direct source. *Is it possible the astral body sees no darkness?*

The walls were not just solid rock; they were made up of large blocks, one on top of the other. Quickly, he turned around and brought his face up close to the wall. I'll be damned, he thought. This is no astral limbo. This place is real. He stood and systematically probed the walls. There had to be a way out.

The west-end was impregnable. He touched every block, studied every seam; no results. Each block was perfectly fitted to the next so perfectly, not even a microbe would fit between them.

He tried the north wall; it was the same. Then he tried the east wall, first trying to push aside the empty bunk bed, but his astral hands had a weak grasp. There was one wall left, and he was almost afraid to check it. He sat on the bunk bed for a moment, casting his eyes downward, almost defeated.

"God," he said, "let there be a way out."

He sat for a long time. Then, with sudden determination, raised his chin, straightened his shoulders, and boldly jolted to his feet. He grabbed the other bunk bed by the end and tried to pull it away from the wall. It was too heavy.

The tarpaulin-like material covering the bunk bed hid something underneath. It seemed light enough to move. His left hand trembled as it reached towards the cover. He grabbed the cloth as firmly as his astral form permitted, and, with a quick motion, pulled it. It moved enough to let him see what was underneath. It wasn't a bunk bed at all. It was a glass chamber, or a coffin.

He gasped in sheer terror when he saw the demoniacal figure that lied inside. Scurrying quickly away, he ended up in the opposite corner of the room, almost managing to blend into the wall. His eyes fixed upon the creature, expecting it to get up at any moment.

It didn't.

Josh remained glued to the wall for a long time before he gathered enough courage to move towards the sleeping creature. *It seems to be dead*, he thought as he reached the side of the glass chamber. The sight of its hairy complexion and its pointed, protruding fangs made him shudder. The top end of two large bat-like wings showed from behind its shoulders; they were neatly tucked away under the body. The thing looked dangerous and strong.

With his weak astral grasp, he managed to cover the creature again. He couldn't bear the sight of it. Turning on his heel, he strode back to the opposite wall and sat on the floor. Things were different now. He was not alone.

EIGHT

The creature sat on the bed exhilarated by the new found freedom. She was growing stronger within Josh's body. Tonight was her second night out and she expected a good catch. *Josh would eventually see things her way,* she thought. *In the end, he would accept and enjoy it; they always did. Humans were so power hungry it made them predictable.* She stretched a skinny hand towards the night lamp and turned on the light switch. Bringing the right hand up to eye level, she studied it with interest. She didn't like what she saw; it made her feel weak.What an ugly species these humans are, she thought. Specially this one.

There wasn't much she could do for now but accept using this puny shaped body; later, things would be different. She sat on the bed for a while, moving the hand in front of her, and looking at it with disgust. Then, with sudden determination, took a deep breath, and closed her eyes as she turned her head upwards.

She trembled slightly for a brief moment, and then the shaking got more intense. Beads of sweat covered her face, her pupils dilating from a crimson pinpoint to a large fiery circle. The arm swelled and palpitated, growing stronger with layer after layer of new steel-like muscles; her fingernails slowly extended outward, shaping themselves into large, sharp claws.

Her facial expression changed back and forth from one of intense pleasure to one of unendurable pain. Waves of electrical discharges visibly turned her aura into a nightmarish vision from hell. A strong smell of ozone filled the room. Her shaking was uncontrollable now. She had to stop. A loud gasp escaped her lips as she broke away from her trance-like state.

"I'm not ready yet," she whispered. "It's too soon."

Mary Ann's voice came through her bedroom door; she sounded half-asleep. "Josh. Josh, is that you?"

The creature looked towards the bedroom door; her eyes narrowed to a slit. "Yeah, mom. It's me."

"What are you doing up so late? Go to bed."

"I will, mom; I will." She turned off the lights and waited.

The creature slipped out of the house, quickly disappearing into the night. It was difficult, during the first few days, to adapt to these clumsy bodies. All she needed were a few more feedings, just a few more feedings. She walked through the streets in awe of the progress these humans had achieved in so little time. She didn't like it.

She missed the days of gas lit street lamps, or even before that, when only the moon and stars served to guide her through the darkness. She missed the superstitious peasants living their vulnerable, isolated lives, afraid of their own shadows. She missed the grandiose castles, and the powerful lords that had served her so well in the past.

Yes, she thought, *that was a good life then.* She remembered the few years she spent with the countess. The luxuries of royalty were a dream. It's a shame that Elizabeth had no self-control; a murdering sadist that no one dared oppose. It was inevitable she would finally be discovered. The countess was a stupid and careless woman. Finding another body to possess was a difficult project, and time consuming – but her choices were, unfortunately, limited. Experience taught her to protect her alter ego's identity as best she could.

She also remembered her time with the prince. Another cruel beast she had to put up with. She could not forget the impalings on the wooden stakes; the endless counts of bodies the prince left every night - like meat on toothpicks. She would rather have fed on him instead, but that was impossible. He was her host. All the humans left to rot out on the roads, for all of Vlad's enemies to see. She helped write humankind's greatest and worst moments in history. Yet, no one knew she had been there. No one knew she existed. She did what she did to survive. Whatever else her hosts did with her powers was beyond her control.

Suddenly, she realized she was being followed. The stillness of the night betrayed her stalkers. This was better than she expected. No need to find food. Food was coming her way. She couldn't afford to attack out in the open in Josh's shape. She had to find some dark alleyway and wait.

A large building loomed right in front of her, a block away. She headed towards it, hoping to be followed. The footsteps behind her broke into a brisker step as she reached the building and turned left, into its isolated parking area. She looked for the darkest spot and waited.

Three figures stopped by the entrance, blocking any possible means of escape. Escape, however, was furthest from her mind. The tallest of the three walked forward.

"Hello, shithead. I've been looking for you," said Ratface. He held a knife in his right hand. The creature did not stir. "Thanks for saving me the trouble of breaking into your house," continued Ratface as he moved towards her. "Now I can have you all to myself."

The other two remained close behind Ratface. They too had knives. She had to act fast; strong as she was, this body was not indestructible. A swift fist slammed into her face before she reacted. Her body flew in the air, hitting hard against the front fender of the car behind her. The almost forgotten feeling of pain swept through her. Before she picked herself up from the floor, a strong kick buried deep in her stomach, turning her on her back.

"How's that for starters, jerk," said Ratface with a smirk. He knelt down and brought his face close to hers. "Oh, I almost forgot to tell you, after we're finished with you, we're gonna' have some fun with your dear little mommy. Gonna' have myself some sweet lovin' tonight." The three of them laughed aloud.

Ratface didn't expect the expression he saw on Josh's face. Josh smiled! He never expected the skinny hand that flew up to his neck either. She clamped on to him with the strength and determination of a bulldog. Within the creature's eyes burned an inhuman fiery glow, creating a weird light that scorched into her attacker's face. As she stood up, she pulled Ratface's body up in the air, lifting him with ease. His efforts to escape her grip were useless.

Without letting go of Ratface, her free hand swiftly grabbed the kid that stood motionless next to her and, with hardly an effort, threw him clear across the air. His body smashed - head first - against the front windshield of a parked car, ten feet away.

The third kid finally reacted. "You sonofabitch," he said as he moved forward with his switchblade. He never saw the hand that went through his chest like a sharp chainsaw. He only felt his heart stop and the indescribable pain as it was torn away from his body. Tonight was feast time.

❖❖❖❖❖❖❖

Next morning, Josh vaguely heard his mother say goodbye through the door as she left for work. He remained in bed a while longer, morosely trying to sleep away his tired feeling. Then, with a start, he sat on the bed; the overwhelming taste of blood brought him back to the sudden realization of his predicament.

The closed window shutters kept out the cheerful brightness of the sun. Josh flung them open; he had to look at his hands. This time, they looked clean.

He sighed with relief when he went back to bed and sat. The awful taste in his mouth persisted. His face wrinkled like a prune when he ran his tongue over his teeth, convincing himself this was the normal morning taste of an unclean mouth.

His bedroom looked normal enough, he thought as he glanced around; there were no signs of bloodstains. But there was this awful taste in his mouth. With some hesitation, he left the sanctuary of his bedroom and walked straight to the bathroom. He faced the mirror. There were some bruises over his left cheek, but otherwise, no blood. Not until he opened his mouth to check his teeth.

A feeling of revulsion overpowered him, barely giving him enough time to bring his face to the toilet bowl to throw up. Gobs of half-digested, half-clotted blood and pieces of flesh spewed violently forth in endless sprays of vomit. Irritated by his vomit, he coughed in rapid succession. He was choking. His lungs needed air, but his body refused to stop convulsing.

After a short while, he fell to the floor, unconscious.

Josh got up from the bathroom floor deeply shaken. What, in heaven's name, was happening to him? He saw the mess of bloody vomit and thought of Mary Ann. She would probably wring his neck if he didn't clean up. Or maybe he was being unfair to her; maybe she'd be more concerned about him than the mess in the bathroom.

He pulled the towel off the rack and began to clean up. An hour later, after a thorough bath and a good amount of scrubbing, he put on his jeans and sneakers. He ran out the front door with no specific destination, just a mindless determination to shake off the feeling of insanity. City buildings and houses passed like a blur in his eyes. His subconscious failed to register when he passed the city limits and the tall suburban trees came into view.

How far he ran was of no concern to him now. His body aches took his mind from the thoughts that invaded him; the powerful rays of the sun made his skin sting and his eyes burn. I mustn't stop now, he thought in desperation as his body forced him to ease the pace.

Before long, he stood in front of Malcolm's home. As if guided by some invisible beacon, his instincts led him there. With his breath caught in his lungs and his legs aching like they had nails driven through them, he walked towards the front door and knocked. After a short wait, Malcolm came out.

"Josh," said Malcolm, "what a pleasant surprise." He stepped aside to allow Josh to enter. Josh stood unmoving. Malcolm came closer to Josh, searching his eyes. "What's the matter?" he asked with concern. "Are you all right?"

Josh hid his hands in his pockets and shyly shrugged his shoulders. He shifted nervously, but said nothing.

Malcolm reached out towards him, grabbing him by the arm. "Come on in, kid," he said, closing the door behind them. "Sit there while I get you some coffee."

Josh meekly obeyed. He dropped his body on the sofa and rested his head on the back cushion, staring at the ceiling in silence. Three minutes later, Malcolm returned.

"Here," said Malcolm, offering Josh a cup, "this will perk you up."

Josh sat straight, welcoming the warm coffee.

Malcolm sat on the lounger across from Josh, waiting. "Well?" said Malcolm after a short silence. "I suppose you have it in your agenda to speak to me."

"I need a ride back home."

"You came here walking?"

"Running. I came running."

Malcolm eyed him carefully. "Are you still blaming yourself for what happened to that woman the other night?"

"Yes," said Josh, suddenly raising his voice. "Just as I blame myself for last night!"

"Last night?" asked Malcolm. "What about last night?"

"It happened again."

"Josh," said Malcolm, his whole body suddenly tensing, "you need help. You need to see a doctor."

Josh jumped from the sofa and almost in a scream said, "I need no doctor! I'm perfectly sane." He paced the room nervously; his hands flew into his pockets. "I don't want your sympathy... I want your help. Can't you see I'm desperate?"

"Yes," replied Malcolm, "I can see that." Malcolm sighed and allowed his tired body to fall on the lounger's backrest. "I'm listening. Please, sit."

For the next hour, Josh poured it out; Malcolm listened patiently. After Josh finished, a long silence passed between them. Malcolm stared at the floor.

"You don't believe a word I've said, do you?" said Josh.

"Hmm?" Malcolm didn't seem to be all there. His mind wandered.

"Damn it, you haven't even been listening!" Josh stood again to pace the floor once more.

"Pipe down," said Malcolm. "I have listened to every word you said."

"Then, tell me I'm not going crazy. Please tell me that much!" Josh's voice broke.

Malcolm raised his eyes to meet Josh's, and calmly said, "I want you to spend the night here. Can you arrange that with your mother?"

"You're going to help me?" He suddenly felt a glimmer of hope.

"I'll see what I can do," said Malcolm with uneasiness. "I'm no psychiatrist."

"This is something no psychiatrist would know about," replied Josh with conviction. "What do you have in mind?"

"First, I want to hypnotize you. Then, we'll see."

"But nothing happens to me when I'm hypnotized. This thing only takes over my body at night, after I'm asleep."

"Then, we'll have to keep a close vigil while you sleep, won't we?"

"You know you're placing yourself in grave danger."

Malcolm gave Josh a weak smile. "Perhaps." He stood. "Let's go into the parlor; we can work better in there. Maybe we can find out what's really on your mind." When they entered the parlor, Malcolm pointed at the telephone. "Call your mother now."

The parlor was furnished with a heavyset antique wing chair, a comfortable lounger, and a small sofa. The dark mahogany wood gave the room a dark, but warm feeling. Malcolm moved the wing chair close to the lounger, where Josh sat deeply hypnotized.

"This creature, where does she come from?" asked Malcolm as he leaned forward on the chair, his elbows resting on his knees.

"I don't know," replied Josh in a soft, subdued voice.

"You say she knows your every thought?"

"Yes."

"How does she do that?"

"When she's inside me, she probes my mind."

"Is she inside you now?"

"No."

"Can we call her?"

"No."

"If she has been able to enter your mind - and use it, if you will - would you agree that it's also logical to assume that, deep in your subconscious, there might be a part of her; her own thoughts, her memories?"

Josh nodded slowly.

Malcolm reclined back on the chair, resting both hands on the armrests. "I want you to look deep into your mind. You will now see what your subconscious has been holding back. Look deeper... deeper. I want you to think like her, tell me about her."

Josh moved his head as if his neck was in pain, then his mouth opened with a loud gasp. He thrust his body forward for a second, and finally dropped back against the recliner chair.

Malcolm crossed his left arm under his right arm, bringing his right hand up to his face. "What happened to you just now?" asked Malcolm.

"I don't know. It felt as is a blast of fire went through my brain."

"Is she here?"

"No."

"What are you feeling?"

"Strange. Like something inside of me. Thoughts, memories that are not mine."

"Can you tell me about them?"

"I can't. It feels like I'm watching a movie going by at ten times the normal speed." Josh's voice broke into a nervous high pitch.

"Okay, calm down. Relax. You are in command of yourself. Relax. Don't look at the images. Take a deep long breath."

Josh obeyed.

"That's it," continued Malcolm. "Now, let's go one step at a time." He leaned forward and spoke in a hushed tone. "Can you tell me anything that you didn't know before?"

"Her name. I know her name." Josh hesitated for a moment. "It's Lilitu."

"Who is she? What does she want with you?"

"She wants my body."

"She wants to kill you?"

"No. She wants to use it."

"But it doesn't make sense. If she's had full possession of your body, why would she want to leave it? Why should she release you?"

"She's afraid."

"Of what?"

"Sunlight… but only when she's inside me."

"I see." Malcolm stood up and walked towards the window, leaning his body against the frame as he glanced outside. The sun had already set. "This creature, where does she come from?"

"I don't know. She was born here."

"What do you mean 'she was born here'?"

"I mean on this planet, on Earth. She's a prisoner of some kind, or an exile." Josh began to sweat profusely, his breathing irregular.

"What's wrong, Josh?" Malcolm looked at him.

"She's here," he replied nervously.

"She's inside you?"

"No. She's here in this room. I can sense her."

Malcolm scanned the room with disinterest. "I see no one."

"You can't see her, but she's here." Josh's breathing got heavier.

"Then, why doesn't she enter your body?"

"She can't. Not while I'm in it." Josh moved his head in a circle. His hands shook. "She's trying to speak to me. Please, keep her away." His voice rose to a nervous pitch, as his breathing became irregular. "Keep her away!"

Malcolm walked briskly towards Josh. "Josh, listen to me. I want you to slowly come out of your trance. I want you to relax. Take deep long breaths."

Josh didn't seem to be listening. His breath was short and spasmodic.

"I am going to touch your arm, and when I do, you are going to relax. You will hear nothing but my voice."

Josh was now shaking, almost uncontrollably.

Malcolm spoke with authority as he raised his commanding voice. "When I get to the count of three, I will touch your arm, and you will wake up remembering nothing. One. Take it easy. Two. That's it. Now breathe slowly. Three!" His hand lightly touched Josh's arm.

An abrupt change came over Josh's face. He slowly opened his eyes and looked around the room as if nothing had happened. He stretched his body and yawned.

"Are you okay?" said Malcolm softly.

Josh looked at him and smiled. "Sure."

Later, that evening, they had a quiet dinner. Malcolm had, not for a moment, talked about what just happened. He circumscribed himself to the essentials, like: "Dinner is ready. Please, pass the salt. Do you want a Coke? Etc." Josh ran out of patience.

"I know you don't want to talk about it," said Josh, interrupting the silence, "but if you were in my place, you'd be more insistent on discussing this."

Malcolm was busy attacking a delicious chicken drumstick. He stopped chewing for a moment, took a large gulp from the glass of soda, and then smiled at Josh. "If I were in your place, I'd go see a doctor, but I'm not in your place, so that takes care of that, doesn't it?"

"You hypnotized me an hour ago, but you refuse to tell me what you found."

"I discovered nothing different from what you told me this afternoon."

"That corroborates what I said was true, doesn't it?"

Malcolm looked at Josh calmly, as if carefully weighting his words. "It only confirmed you are totally convinced that what you said to me is true. That doesn't mean it is."

"Look," said Josh standing up and moving away from the dinner table, "If you can't take me home now, I'm going to bed. I suggest you lock yourself in your room and don't come out till morning. It'll be safer."

Malcolm left his chair and approached Josh. "Look, I'm sorry if I seem so uncaring. I do care. I care a lot what happens to you, but put yourself in my place. Would you believe?"

"Why don't you put yourself in mine. Can't you see what I'm going through?"

Malcolm placed an arm over Josh's shoulder with a fatherly gesture. "I know, and I apologize." He turned Josh around, placing both hands on each shoulder, then looked straight into his eyes. "I want to believe you. Do you understand that?"

Josh lowered his eyes and sadly nodded.

Malcolm then walked towards the kitchen switch and turned the lights off. "Come on," he continued, "you must be tired, after all that exercise you got this afternoon. It's getting past your bedtime."

"I dread bedtime."

"I'll be there with you. I'll be standing guard." He meant it.

Josh lay on the large brass bed looking at Malcolm, who was reading on an easy chair by his bedside.

"Malcolm," said Josh, his head resting sideways on a pillow.

"Hmm?" replied Malcolm without raising his eyes.

"I'm not going crazy, am I?"

Malcolm closed the book while carefully placing his index finger between its pages. He looked at Josh. "Who knows what crazy means?" He placed the book on the night table and approached him. "Are you cold?"

"A little," said Josh.

Malcolm leaned down and reached under the bed. He pulled out a wool blanket. "Here," he said, "this will keep you warm. Try to get some sleep."

Josh nodded as Malcolm went back to his chair.

"Would you rather I turn off the night lamp?" asked Malcolm.

"No, don't," said Josh nervously. "I'll just turn and face the wall. It won't bother me." He shifted towards the wall and promised himself to remain awake.

An hour later, Josh was fast asleep.

"Hello, Josh," said the creature.

Josh reacted nervously. He looked to his bedside and saw Malcolm sitting there, calmly reading his book. The man was completely oblivious to the creature's presence.

"He can't see us. He doesn't have the power."

Josh turned back to face the creature. "What are you going to do to him?"

"What makes you believe I plan to do anything to him?"

"Because all you've done since I met you is kill people. Please don't harm him."

"I have been around long enough by now to make sure none of what I do is traced back to you." Her eyes reflected a pink glow. "Do you know how many years I have spent without a host? It took me too long to find you. I don't intend to jeopardize our relationship by killing everyone that comes near me. Besides, as much as you may think it, I don't just kill indiscriminately."

"Why don't you find someone else? I don't want this."

"Then you're the first. I like that. You might prove to be a pleasanter experience than most humans have provided me so far."

"So far?"

"One day I, after I get my strength back, we'll have time to talk."

"Answer me, what did you mean by 'so far'?" asked Josh.

"You might never believe the things I have to say," she said brushing him off.

"And you think what's happening to me now is believable? I can't even convince myself this is not a dream."

"I have been here since..." She paused for a moment, changing her mind about what she was going to say. "Just to talk to me might be worth your sacrifice, if sacrifice is the way you prefer to see it. Right now, you're not ready."

Josh didn't know what to make of what she said. "I want this to end. I want you to leave me alone." He knew it was useless to beg. He looked at her pleadingly. "I'm stuck with you for the rest of my life, aren't I?"

She said nothing. Instead, she moved closer to Malcolm and brought her nose near his face. She sniffed him and made a face as if she enjoyed his smell.

"How can I make you go away?" What she just did to Malcolm made him apprehensive.

"You can't," she said turning her face towards Josh. Her hand caressed Malcolm's head. "But there's no reason why we can't make our relationship enjoyable."

"How, by letting you screw me in exchange for killing people?"

"You're looking at the obvious, but I need to survive just like anything in this universe. It's nature's law."

Josh recoiled at the thought of what she meant by survive. "We are nothing but food to you."

"Perhaps, but what you will come to realize soon is that I will be much more to you than you suspect." She moved away from Malcolm and approached Josh. Her movements were sinuous, but natural. "Just relax and let it happen. You'll soon see what I mean."

"I'll never give in to you," said Josh as he stepped away from her.

"That's your prerogative. But if you continue to resist me, you might not like the consequences." Her face betrayed no loss of temper. She simply stated a matter of fact. "But you will change your mind. I know." She made a slight gesture with her hands, and suddenly Josh felt himself being pulled away. His astral body flew out the window, through no will of its own. The evening air rushed around him as he traveled to his inevitable destination. The city down below passed quickly by. Before he knew it, he was back inside the dungeon, trapped once more.

Josh crawled as far away as he could from the tarpaulin-covered glass coffin, allowing his back to rest against the wall. Having gone to Malcolm for help was the worst thing he could have done. Malcolm will probably get killed, he thought. Not knowing what was going to happen tonight was more than he could bear. Suddenly, he remembered. There was a way. Moving carefully, so as not to awaken the sleeping beast that lied under the tarpaulin, he stretched himself over the empty bunk bed and began to concentrate on his physical body. The strain was enormous, but he had to try. He had to see.

The creature sat on the bed facing Malcolm. "I want to go home," she said.

Malcolm raised his eyes from the book. "What's the matter, Josh? Bed too soft?"

"I said I want to go home!" she said with authority.

"Hey!" said Malcolm standing up to face the creature. "I can't let you go home at this time of night, your mother will kill me."

"Surely you don't mean that," she said as she got out of the bed, moving swiftly towards the bedroom door.

"Wait!" shouted Malcolm, "don't leave yet. I want to talk to you."

The creature hesitated by the threshold. "What do you want?" she asked.

"Your name. Tell me your name."

"What?" replied the creature knitting her eyebrows, her back towards Malcolm. "You know my name. What is this?"

"I need you to tell me your name." Malcolm came nearer to her.

The creature turned around slowly. "I see you decided to humor me."

"Perhaps, but you still haven't answered my question." Malcolm was within arm's length now.

"What do your eyes tell you?" she asked.

"What do you want me to say?"

"I'll tell you what's on your mind," said the creature with smugness, "you believe I'm crazy. That I need psychiatric help. A case of split personality, am I wrong?"

"I don't know," said Malcolm coming closer.

"Stay away from me." She said forcefully.

Malcolm stopped. "Surely, you can talk to me. Can't you?" He looked deep into the creature's eyes. "I can help you."

"Help me?" The creature laughed. "During my lifetime, I have met many fools and charlatans, wiser than you. What possible help do you believe I need?"

A momentary change of tone in her voice, quite unlike Josh's high-pitched tone, took Malcolm by surprise. His face registered the change.

The creature studied Malcolm for a moment. "You do not seem afraid."

"Why should I fear you?" replied Malcolm calmly. "There's nothing about you to frighten anyone. Besides, you're my friend, aren't you?"

The creature took a step towards Malcolm. "Quite so, quite so." He could now feel her breath on his face. "Perhaps you'd like to see something frightening?"

Malcolm took a casual step to his right and replied, "I'm not interested in your power plays." He stopped moving as he neared his chair and faced the creature. "What is important, however, is what is happening to you."

"You flatter me," she said. "You feel you can manipulate me. How refreshing, how stimulating." She shrugged, and while turning her face towards the ceiling, took a deep breath.

Malcolm sat comfortably on his chair. "Do I amuse you?"

"Yes, as a matter of fact, you do," she said, moving closer. There was a minute of silence between them; the creature did nothing but stare at Malcolm.

"Tell me," said Malcolm, "Why?"

"Because," she replied turning her face sideways.

"Ah, the Philosopher's answer," said Malcolm. "I didn't know you had it in you."

"What do you want to know? Josh has told you all you need to know." The creature sat back on the bed. After many years of loneliness, conversation was, oftentimes, a welcome thing. "Actually, you know more than you should. Perhaps I should kill you."

"And risk being discovered?" said Malcolm lightly; his hands interlaced while he crossed one leg over the other. "No, you can do better than that."

"Of course I can! That's my power. I can afford to be generous. I grant you life if I choose." She laughed.

Malcolm brought a hand up to his chin, studying Josh with interest. She waited for him to speak again.

"Why?" asked Malcolm once again.

"You begin to bore me."

"Why him? Why Josh?" His tone was impatient.

"Ah! That's better," she said. She slid closer to the edge of the bed. "He is - how shall I put it - special. He has talents seldom found in your pathetic little species. His kind comes along once every hundred years or so - more, if I'm lucky."

"Our pathetic little species? That implies you're not human. What are you, then?"

"I'm unique. There's no other like me, so it's hard to explain what I am, but I could tell you what I've been." She leaned her elbow against the pillow.

"I'm curious."

"You will find me in the legends of every corner of this revolting world. I have written the worst parts of your history, and some of the best also. Find death, and you'll find me near. You want to know about Vampires? I am here. What do you want to know? You are talking to the only vampire that ever was and ever will be. Have you heard of werewolves? You are looking at one." She paused. "Let me rephrase that. I am *the* werewolf. How about things that go bump in the night? Do I need to tell you?"

"Are you that old?" said Malcolm with amusement.

"I was here when the first of your species was born. I helped nurture him, helped him develop; I was the guiding light in his insignificant little life. Then your creator threw me aside for him. I never liked him very much, anyway."

"My creator? You mean God?"

"You are such a simpleton. Is the father of a child a god?"

"I'm sorry," said Malcolm, playing along with Josh. "If not God, then who?"

"One day I may tell you. If you live through the night, that is. Although I find you quite interesting for a human, I've said enough for one night."

"Then," continued Malcolm, "let's get back to Josh. Why did you choose him?"

"Let's just say, his body is tuned to mine."

Malcolm leaned his heavy-set body forwards, then with a sudden change of tone, he said, "Josh, listen to me." His eyes showed a mixture of emotions played inside of him. "I'm no doctor, but I have friends who can help you. I…"

"You must be what Josh refers to as an asshole!" said the creature dispassionately. "Why have you been wasting my time? Must I show you?" The creature moved swiftly towards Malcolm, grabbed him by the neck, and raised him one foot above the floor. Malcolm's struggles were futile. "Look at me now!" she said. Her eyes lost any semblance of humanity as her pupils dilated wide; a deep red spread outward from the middle of her eyeballs until both eyes were nothing but two fiery burning coals.

Malcolm looked on with horror. The creature's face no longer looked like Josh; it changed into a goyaesque caricature of him. A strong, protruding jaw, gradually replaced Josh's weak chin. The last things Malcolm saw before he lost consciousness were the fangs that grinned wickedly at him. She threw his limp body clear across the room, against the wall. He landed on the bed.

"I know you're watching, Josh," she said out loud. "I will destroy you if you don't stop resisting me. She looked at Malcolm for a moment. "Do not worry, he will live..." she said before turning around towards the bedroom door and down the stairs.

Josh, unable to continue holding the vision for much longer, cut off communication just before she flew away into the night.

NINE

"Josh! Come on, wake up!" Malcolm's strong hand shook Josh from side to side. He held an ice pack to his neck; his face was badly bruised. It was early morning.

"Malcolm!" shouted Josh sitting up with a start. "Are you all right?"

"My God, Josh," said Malcolm with disgust. "Go rinse that blood from your mouth." He turned away from Josh, half in shame, half in fear. "And be quick about it. I'm taking you home."

"But now you know. You believe me," said Josh, trying to understand Malcolm's reaction.

Malcolm walked to the window and leaned on its frame; he could not bring himself to face Josh. "I don't want to know, Josh. I want you to leave." He lowered his eyes. "Don't call me again." Malcolm stood unmoving as he looked out the window.

"I don't understand..." Josh's eyes glazed with tears.

"Please, go wash your face," said Malcolm sternly.

"Burying your head in the sand won't make her go away. You saw her, you know she exists." Josh took a step closer to him. "There's only one reason why she didn't kill you last night, and that's because your death could be easily traced back to me."

"I know that," he replied.

"Then you must do something before she comes back for you!"

Malcolm looked out the window as if paralyzed while Josh waited for an answer. "Go get ready," Malcolm finally said.

◆◆◆◆◆◆◆◆◆

The ride back home was torture for Josh. When Malcolm dropped him off, he didn't say goodbye. As soon as Josh closed the car's door, Malcolm sped away.

Inside the house, the telephone rang, but Josh didn't rush in to answer. He sat on the front doorstep, and stayed there the rest of the day.

"Josh," said Mary Ann stepping out of her car. "What are you doing out here?"

"I forgot my keys," he lied with a forced a smile.

"Oh," she said casually. She fished into her purse and took out her set of keys. "Do you know who called you last night?" she continued with a broad, self-congratulatory smile.

"No." He didn't care.

"Janet," she said after opening the door. She went to the kitchen, and then hung her set of keys on a nail next to the sink. He dragged his feet behind her. "You never told me you had a girlfriend," she continued.

"She's not my girlfriend. She's just a friend."

"Anyway," she continued, "she wants you to call her."

"Sure," said Josh with disinterest.

"There was also some jerk asking for a guy called Pin." She opened the cupboard and looked inside. "Let's see. I had black bean soup somewhere in here." She shuffled some of the cans around as she spoke. "I told him he had the wrong number, but he kept calling back every half hour or so. Kept me up all night." Her eyes then widened. "Ah, here it is." She held the can in her hand and showed it to Josh. "This okay with you?" she said indicating the can of soup.

"I'm not hungry now. Make whatever you want."

"What's the matter? Are you all right?" she said, placing the can of soup on the counter. Her tired eyes suddenly looked worried.

"I'm okay," he said upset. "Why is it that everything I say turns into a major production number?" He walked towards the stairs. "I'll be in my room. Call me when dinner's ready." As he climbed the stairs, he glanced back. She stood there, in the middle of the kitchen, looking at him sadly.

Five minutes later, the telephone rang.

"Will you get it, Josh?" shouted Mary Ann from the kitchen. "It's probably for you."

He cursed. Why can't they leave him alone? He went to the upstairs hallway and picked up the telephone. "Hello?"

"Hi, Pin," said Norton. "Where've ya' been hidin'?"

"Listen, you jerk, you'd better leave me alone if you know what's good for you."

There was a brief moment of silence.

"Who the hell is this?" asked Norton. "Pin? Is that you?"

"Go pin your mother!" Josh raised his voice.

"What'cha been eatin', Pin? Nails?" he said laughing.

"Why don't you come get me tonight?" challenged Josh. "I'll be glad to accommodate you."

"Ooh," Norton mocked him. "I'm sooo scared."

"Josh!" shouted Mary Ann from the foot of the stairs. "What' going on here?"

"Don't wait up fer me, Pin," continued Norton. "I may not show up. But maybe tomorrow, or when ya' least expect me."

Josh slammed the telephone against its cradle. He went to his bedroom, ignoring Mary Ann. He slammed the door behind him, but he knew she'd be coming up the stairs any moment now. Sure enough, just before he reached his bedside, she opened his bedroom door.

"I want to know what's going on," she demanded.

He plopped himself on the bed. "Nothing's wrong, all right! Nothing."

"Who was that on the phone?" She took a step forward. "Is that the guy that's been asking for Pin?" Her voice betrayed her irritation.

"So what if it is?" He refused to face her.

She walked over to the bed and sat by his side, wanting to touch him, but refraining from doing so. "What is it, Josh?" she said softly, in an effort to sound understanding. "What's bothering you?"

"Right now, you are."

She lowered her eyes, half-angry, half-sad. Then she stood up and walked towards the door. "I'll call you when dinner's ready," she said walking back downstairs.

◆━◆━◆━◆━◆

An hour later, they awkwardly sat at the dinner table. Neither of them touched their plate, both of them avoiding each other's eyes. Josh knew she expected an apology.

"Mom?" he finally said. She met his eyes with a steady stare. "I'm sorry I spoke to you that way."

"That's all I wanted to hear," she said sternly.

"I know. I…"

"When you're finished eating," she interrupted as she got up from the table, "make sure you do the dishes. I'm going to bed early." He got no second look, and got no goodnight. She went upstairs in a huff.

If only she knew, he thought, maybe she'd understand. But then again, probably not. Parents never understood; they don't react the way you want them to. For a moment, he wished his father were alive. As he looked towards his dinner plate he realized he hadn't eaten all day, yet, he didn't feel hungry. The sight of food repulsed him. He pushed the plate away.

There was a long night ahead. He had no way to stop Lilitu, except by avoiding sleep altogether, or sleep during the day and stay up all night. But that would solve nothing. When the next school semester came along, he'd be in trouble again.

Suddenly, his eyes shifted towards the telephone. It didn't ring yet, but he knew Janet would call him within the next five seconds. As soon as it rang, he picked it up.

"Hi," said Janet. Josh replied with indifference. "Where've you been hiding?" she continued. "I called you last night."

"Yeah. I was out."

"Are you okay?"

"Why do you ask?"

"You don't sound right. I mean, has Ratface been bothering you?"

Josh remained silent for a moment, and then said, "I need to talk to you."

"Go ahead. I'm listening."

"No, not over the phone. Can I come over?"

"Sure," she said brightly. "I'll wait for you by the porch, but you'll have to leave by ten. My father is…"

"I'll see you in a while," he said, before hanging up the telephone. He walked to the front door, hesitating by the foot of the stairs. Looking up towards his mother's locked bedroom door, he sadly realized he could never confide in her. Not this. She must never know. His hand went into his pocket to check the house-keys; they jingled softly. As he opened the front door, a rush of warm air hit his face. It was a hot summer night.

❖⸺❖⸺❖⸺❖

Josh and Janet sat by her doorstep. A look of disbelief swept over her face. "You don't believe me either," he said staring into her eyes.

"I'm trying very hard," she said sincerely.

"Have you heard from Ratface these last two days?" he said in more of a statement than a question.

"I told you how I feel about him. I don't give a damn what he's up to."

"I tell you he's up to nothing. He's dead." He turned away from her in frustration.

Janet raised her eyebrows as she pressed her lips together. She moved closer to him. "You say this woman came to you and forced you to go through a light in your closet?"

"Yes," replied Josh.

"How about when you were in Malcolm's house? Was there a light in his closet too?"

He faced her with anger. "Are you making fun of me?"

"No," she said sliding a little away from him. "I just wonder what's in your closet that's so special."

"Just some clothes and my collection of books," he said bringing his voice down to normal.

"You're wrong," she said as if she was having a brainstorm. "Unless you threw the mirror away."

He looked at her with wide-open eyes as his jaw fell open. "You're right!" He stood up suddenly and paced the front porch. "That's it. It's the mirror. It has to be the mirror!"

Janet's face lit up with joy as she also stood up and watched him pace back and forth.

"I gotta go," he finally said stepping down from the porch.

"Where are you going?" she said disappointed.

"Home. I've gotta figure out what to do."

"Will I see you tomorrow?"

He walked backwards, away from the house, facing Janet. "I hope so... bye," he said quickly turning around and running down the dark street. He left his bike behind.

❖❖❖❖❖❖❖

When Josh got home and opened the front door, Mary Ann sat by the kitchen table with a heavy expression on her face.

"Where have you been?" she asked as she stood up and approached him.

"I... I went out," he said knitting his eyebrows together.

"What am I to you? A painting on the wall?"

"I wasn't doing anything wrong," he replied defensively raising his voice.

"That's not the point!" She raised hers even higher.

Josh turned his back on her and started to walk up the stairs.

"Stop right there, Goddammit!" she shouted. Josh stopped, but kept his back to her. "Don't you ever ignore me while I'm talking to you!" She took a couple of steps up towards him. "I'm not going to take anymore of your teenage bullshit. I have done my best to get through to you, but you don't seem to care about me. I'm tired of it, you hear me? Tired!"

"So what else is new?" he replied defiantly as he turned to face her.

Before Josh could react, she raised her hand and slapped him hard on the face. The sting of the blow threw his head sideways when a sudden rush of anger brought him to a state of alertness. He clenched his teeth, holding on check an impulse to hit her back, but the look he gave her hit her harder than any physical retaliation. Her eyes turned red with pain as she looked away in utter defeat.

"Are you finished?" asked Josh calmly.

She did not reply. Instead, she went upstairs, towards her bedroom. She locked the door behind her.

A tear trickled down Josh's cheek. She had never hit him before. His right hand clenched into a fist as a painful torrent of unfamiliar emotions overcame him. Mary Ann, he knew, cried in her bedroom. For a brief moment, her thoughts were his thoughts, and her feelings, his feelings.

It wasn't easy to deal with him, and he knew it. Maybe nature was saying something here; maybe it was time for him to go away. But he wasn't ready for that. What would he do out on the streets? Could he work behind the counter of a fast food restaurant for the rest of his life? No way. Yes, he knew she was hurt and confused.

He looked sadly towards her bedroom door. Tomorrow he'd apologize. Tonight he had things to do. He turned towards his own bedroom and, with his hands in his pockets, walked slowly upstairs.

Later, Josh sat on his bed with the mirror in his lap, looking at his reflection. This was no ordinary mirror anymore. It was a gate; a window to hell, and he had no idea how to close it. His first impulse had been to break it, but he knew that was not the answer. One mirror was enough to handle, let alone a hundred little pieces of it. He racked his brain searching for an answer, but none came. Putting the mirror aside, he laid back on his pillow with his hands interlaced behind his head.

His eyes wandered over his display of lead figurines. *Amazing,* he thought, *how much Lilitu's face resembles the winged vampire-like figure on the shelf.* It was one of his favorite characters from his "Role Playing" adventures; the best paint job he had ever done.

Suddenly, he sat up - almost jumped. *Paint! That's the answer. Cover the mirror with paint - the blacker the better - it might just be enough to shut her out.* He went to his closet and pulled out several boxes. The paint kit was neatly stored on a corner, just behind his stack of books. He hoped there was enough paint left. There were still six small, unopened vials in the kit; three black, one gray, one white, and one red. The rest of the vials were empty. He rushed back to the closet to get his set of brushes, and a plastic cup to mix the colors.

A half-hour later, the mirror was nothing but a black piece of glass, an ordinary black piece of glass. That's what he wanted to believe, what he had to believe.

Carefully, he wrapped a pillowcase over the mirror, and then placed it back in his closet. "Goodbye, Lilitu," he whispered. "Hope I never see you again." He went back to his bed. "Here goes nothing," he said as he closed his eyes, beginning a slow count to ten. Before long, Josh was fast asleep.

The next morning, the sound of Mary Ann's car pulling out of the driveway awakened him. She hadn't called to him through the door to say goodbye, and for sure, no breakfast waited for him on the kitchen table either. She always did that when she was pissed at him.

When he sat on the bed, he moved his tongue around his mouth. There was no funny taste. Then, he looked at his hands; his fingernails were clean. With his breath caught in his throat, he jumped towards the bedroom door. He had to look in the bathroom mirror. The reflection that stared back was clean. His teeth were clean.

"Clean," he yelled. "Goddammit, I'm clean!" He ran back to his bedroom and jumped on the bed, bouncing on it several times until he almost hit the roof. The bed frame gave way, collapsing to the sides; the mattress hit the floor. Josh couldn't stop laughing, not even when his head bumped hard against the backboard. After a while, he lay on the bed, lightly rubbing the growing bump on the back of his head. Looking towards the ceiling, he smiled.

An hour later, after the feeling of elation passed, he got up to fix the bed. As he pulled the mattress aside to put the frame back together, he lifted it single-handed without breaking a sweat. He remembered the day Mary Ann redecorated his bedroom and how she almost gave up on the idea because they found the bed - particularly the mattress - too heavy to move.

Knitting his eyebrows, he leaned it against the door. His hands and arms didn't look any stronger. So far, all of this seemed like a nightmare. Could it be this was the end of the fairy tale, where the wicked witch dies, and the hero finds the pot of gold at the end of the rainbow? Was he now wiser, and stronger?

His brain registered the incoming call five seconds before the telephone rang. Pushing the mattress aside, he went to the hall and picked up the telephone. The caller hung up as soon as Josh said hello. Josh knew who it was from the moment he grabbed the receiver. He held it in front of him as if half expecting it to explain why Norton would bother to dial his number only to hang up again. Somehow, the thought of Norton no longer made him shudder - well, maybe a little bit. Hell, nobody's perfect.

Walking back to his bedroom, he inspected the frame. *Thank God, it wasn't broken*, he thought. By ten thirty in the morning, Josh finished fixing the bed. He stepped back a few feet, with his arms crossed, looking towards the bed as if he was studying a serious work of art. Then, with the flair of a fastidious artist, he stretched out toward the bedspread and straightened out a small wrinkle.

"Now," he said aloud, "let's call Janet." He went to the telephone, and dialed. The line was busy. Five minutes later, he tried again. Busy.

He went back to his room to put on an old pair of jeans and his dirty sneakers; *might as well walk over to give her the good news.* He opened the top drawer of his dresser, grabbed a T-shirt, and then ran down the stairs while pulling the shirt over his head. Mary Ann hated it when he did that.

'One of these days,' he often heard her say, *'you're going to break your neck! Nobody in his right mind runs down a staircase while getting dressed.'* Skipping the last three steps, he turned towards the foyer almost at the same time his feet landed.

When he opened the door, he found an unpleasant surprise. Norton stood at the doorstep with a big grin on his face.

"Hi, Pin," said Norton, shoving Josh back into the house. "Missed me last night?"

Josh lost his balance, falling flat on his back in the middle of the foyer. Norton stepped in, closing the door behind him. He knelt close to Josh and grabbed him by the collar, pulling him off the floor as he stood up. Josh's feet barely touched the floor when Norton slammed him hard against the wall.

"You and I have a little somethin' t'talk about," said Norton between his gritting teeth.

Josh felt Norton's knuckles push against his throat. He couldn't breathe. Instinctively, he grabbed onto Norton's wrists, trying to relieve the pressure by pulling them away. A cold wave coursed through his body. Norton had come to kill him.

"What's tha matter boy? I can't hear ya'," said Norton as he increased the pressure on Josh's throat.

Josh kicked wildly, hoping to hit Norton's testicles, but he had no leverage for a good kick. Norton pinned him to the wall with his huge body.

"Try and get outta this one, ya' skinny dipshit!" Norton had lost all control by now. This time was going to be the last time.

Josh closed his eyes tightly, concentrating his strength on his own fingers, squeezing tighter and tighter on Norton's wrists. His eyes squinted together so hard, a shower of bright colors displayed within his pupils; more so as his oxygen supply dwindled in his lungs.

Then a final effort of self-preservation tensed his whole body. The prickling sensation of a beast struggling to escape from inside him growled through his throat. Suddenly, Josh heard something crack. Norton cried out in pain, forcing him to release Josh.

"You goddamn sonofabitch," cried Norton bending over as he fell on his knees.

Josh, wasting no time to wallow over his pain, swiftly cocked his right leg, kicking Norton hard on the ribs.

Norton rolled, hitting the kitchen table, but he wasn't one to stay down for long. His football training usually gave him the edge in any type of street fight. He was up on his feet before Josh had time to wind up for a second kick. Charging like a bull, he knew that if he tackled right, he could break Josh's back; but he missed and hit the wall with his head. Josh had easily sidestepped him, managing to administer another swift kick in the ribs as Norton slid to the floor, unconscious.

✦◦✦◦◦✦◦◦✦◦✦

Josh sat quietly by the kitchen table massaging his bruised neck. He looked at Norton lying there on the floor, wondering how he'd been able to subdue him, and wondering about this newly found strength. He sighed, then went to the kitchen sink, and poured water into a bucket.

"Come on you jerk," said Josh as he stood over Norton, discharging the cold water over his face. "Get up and get out of here."

Norton stirred. He opened his eyes slowly. He pulled himself into a sitting position; his arms folded over his stomach.

"I said, get out!" repeated Josh, nudging him on the leg with his foot. Norton looked up and was about to say something when Josh grabbed him by the collar, managing to pull him up to his feet. It was easy. He picked him up with no sweat, no effort.

Norton's eyes opened wide, half-surprised, half-afraid. "I don't get it, Pin," said Norton, "I don't get it."

"My name isn't Pin, you piece of shit." Josh still had him tight by the collar.

"I... I don't know your name." His sweaty hair covered his eyes. He looked like a wet chicken.

Josh smiled as he let go of him. He fixed Norton's collar, then patted his cheek. It was almost a slap. "That's all right. You can call me Master," he said, quickly grabbing Norton by the seat of his pants, pushing him like a reluctant poodle towards the front door.

He stood by the door, and watched Norton turn the street corner. *This shithead will never bother me again. In fact,* he thought, *nobody would.*

TEN

Josh stepped out the front door with a feeling of accomplishment. He wasn't sure about this little episode with Norton, but he had kicked his ass and knew he could do it again. He smiled. Janet had to hear this. He was about to cross the street when he looked down the block and saw Laura working on her garden. Turning in her direction, he walked over, and stopped behind her. Trinket sat next to Laura, almost like a garden statue, watching Josh's approach. She did not wag her tail.

"Hello, Josh," said Laura casually while continuing with her garden work. She patted some earth over a newly planted row of pink Azaleas.

"Good morning, Laura."

"Good for you, perhaps," she replied as she stood up with difficulty. It took her a bit to bring herself to a full upright position. "I'm glad it's almost over. I've done nothing but work, work, work, and my back is killing me." As Laura spoke, Trinket tried to hide between her master's feet.

"Trinket!" Laura scolded the dog when it almost managed to trip her.

"How's my favorite dog today?" Josh, squatted to Trinket's level with arms extended to receive her, but she shied away. She looked at him nervously from behind Laura's protective territory.

"What's wrong with Trinket?" asked Josh. "Is she sick?"

Trinket whimpered. She didn't bark or growl at Josh, but she was certainly shivering. Laura looked down at Trinket. Picking her up, she held her close to her face, cradling her in her arms like a baby. "What's the matter, honey?" said Laura in a mushy, baby-talk voice.

The dog kept staring at Josh.

"Come on, now. You can tell mommy," she continued. Laura brought the dog to her face and kissed her on the nose. "Look at her," she said to Josh. "She can't stop shivering." Trinket wouldn't keep her eyes away from Josh, no matter how Laura turned her.

"Maybe she's sick," said Josh with concern.

"She sure seems so," Laura turned towards her house. "I think I'd better call the Vet. See you later." She changed Trinket's position when she walked away from Josh, holding her over her shoulder, just as she would an infant who needed to be burped. Trinket's eyes did not blink away from Josh for an instant.

Suddenly, a prickling sensation swept over Josh. An alien wave of thoughts and sensations poured into his brain. It was fear. A deep feeling of fear emptied out the pit of his stomach like a sponge. Then, when Laura closed the front door behind her, it went away.

Walking the rest of the way to Janet's house in a daze, he tried to understand what just happened. He knew what he felt - fear was something he was very familiar with - but these were not his feelings. They came from the dog.

As he neared Janet's home, a new sensation came over him, a powerful sadness. He was about to cry. The closer he got to Janet's house, the worse it felt, almost making him turn back. He didn't want Janet - or anyone, for that matter - to see him cry. It wasn't the manly thing to do. Stopping several yards away from the front door he tightened his fists, and imagined his hand moving towards a light switch. He flicked the make-believe switch, and turned the feeling off.

With a stupid expression on his face, he wiped the tears that had swelled in his eyes. Then he walked to her porch, and knocked on the door. No one answered. He knocked again. Finally, the door opened.

Janet greeted Josh, but none too happily. Her eyes were swollen with crying.

"Hi, Janet," said Josh somewhat timidly. "I came to pick up my bike."

She nodded sadly as she lowered her eyes.

"Are you all right?" said Josh.

She bit her lower lip, and then nodded again. Josh took a step forward trying to get closer to her, but she moved away from him.

"No, please don't; please. Don't look at me."

"Oh, I'm sorry," said Josh stepping back outside, but not before he noticed that Janet had a black eye. He felt anger at the thought of anyone hurting her. "What happened to you? Who did this to you?"

"Please," pleaded Janet. "Go away. My father, he..."

"Your father did this?" he interrupted with surprise. "But, why?"

"It's nothing, really. It's nothing. Just go away, please." She tried to close the door on Josh, but he would not allow it.

"Was it me, Janet? Was it because of me?"

"No, no," she insisted. "Not because of you." She moved closer to him lowering her voice; as if afraid her father might hear what she was saying. "It just happens sometimes." She looked at Josh and saw the concern written in his eyes. "Look, I'm used to it, so don't worry about it... please."

Josh looked at her in silence.

"Your bike's in the back yard," she said, trying to change the conversation.

Josh couldn't care less about the bike at this moment. He wanted to hold her, to comfort her, to let her know how much he cared. "Are your parents here?" asked Josh not knowing what else to say.

"No," replied Janet. "They're out working."

"Are you grounded?"

"No."

"Then we can talk."

She looked at him and seemed to think it over for a moment. "Okay," she finally said, "but only on one condition. I don't want to talk about this." She brought her right hand up to cover her swollen eye as she turned her face away from him.

He made a move to walk inside before he checked himself, and then took a shy step back towards the porch.

Janet studied him closely then smiled. "Come on in, you big dope."

"Look, I don't want to get you in trouble."

"What's the worst that can happen?" she asked.

"That's what I'm afraid of," he said, nodding towards the street. "Come on, let's go walk around for awhile."

"The hell, you say. I'm not gonna' let anybody see me this way." She opened the door wide to allow him in. "If you want to talk, then we talk in here."

He hesitated for a moment before she stretched her hand out and gently pulled him in by the shirt. She closed the door behind him.

"Damn!" he said as he looked towards the living room. "Some party you must have had here."

"Yeah," she said. "Dad likes to rearrange the furniture whenever he gets into one of his moods." She walked to the sofa, which was upside-down in the middle of the living room. "Here, help me straighten this one out so we can sit down." She stood at one end of the sofa, as if waiting for Josh to go to the other end. "I don't know how he does it. Maybe the booze makes him feel extra strong and brave."

Josh stood there, just looking at the mess of disarrayed furniture in the living room.

"Come on, what are you waiting for?"

He moved to the other end of the sofa, but before bending over to pick up his end of it, he said, "wait a minute."

"What?"

"Let me do this alone."

"Oh, come on, Josh. Stop the macho bullshit!"

"No, I'm serious. I just want to try something. A lot of funny things have been happening to me, and I..."

She looked at him as if he were testing her patience, then, dropping her arms to her side, she said, "sure, sure. Go ahead." She moved aside and smirked.

Smiling weakly, his eyes froze on the sofa as if it was some wild beast. He bent down, cradled his arms around the sides, and then lifted it without much of an effort. The sofa flipped upright as he put it down. "Care to sit down?" A wide smile covered his face.

She stood there looking at him without saying a word.

"You look silly standing there with your mouth open," he said, sitting down.

"Sorry," she said shaking her head, sitting next to him.

"You know, I really came to thank you for saving my life."

Janet was distracted with her own thoughts, trying to make sense of what she just saw.

"If you hadn't told me yesterday about the mirror in my closet..."

"Josh," she said, her eyes fixed upon him.

"When I woke up this morning..."

"Josh," she said again. This time, a little louder.

"I was clean! Do you know what I mean? Clean!"

"JOSH!" she finally shouted somewhat upset.

Her sudden tone of voice startled him, but it had the desired effect. He shut up.

"How the hell did you do that?" she continued, indicating the sofa.

"Well, that's what I've been trying to tell you. I have changed." He stood and walked to the window, then paced back towards her. "I have been going through changes that I don't fully understand... like... like suddenly knowing

I'm stronger." He sat next to her once more. "It must have been happening a little bit at a time but never had a chance to find out until I was forced to defend myself against Norton this morning."

"What about Norton?"

Then he told her about Norton.

◆━◆━◆━◆━◆

Janet sat next to Josh on the sofa; they faced each other. Her left arm draped over the backrest as the tip of her fingers barely touched his shoulder.

"You know," she said, "if I hadn't seen you lift that sofa the way you did, I'd be kinda' hard pressed to believe you."

"I know, but you've seen me do other things. Remember that day at school, when I opened Norton's locker without knowing the combination?" He slid closer to her. "How do you think I opened that?"

"I don't know," she said.

"It came to me, Janet. The combination came to me as if I was picking it right out of Norton's brain." He sat straight, turning his side to her. "But today was the weirdest. I think I'm receiving, not only thoughts, but feelings as well."

"What do you mean?"

"I saw my next door neighbor on my way here, and her dog was scared shitless of me. The funny thing is that I felt it. I felt the dog's fear as if I was feeling afraid myself." He turned to face her again. "Then, as I approached your house, I felt like crying. I didn't know why, cause I had no reason to cry. That is, until I saw you crying." His right arm moved over the sofa's backrest, and then he placed his hand over her shoulder. He never dared touch her before, but it felt wonderful to be close. "I was reading your feelings."

"If what you say is true, then there is something that bothers me." Her expression registered Josh's closeness with a childish nervousness. "Why would a dog that - as you say - likes you, be suddenly afraid of you? What is that dog seeing in you, that no one has yet noticed?"

Josh knit his eyes together wondering why the question hadn't occurred to him. Then, he felt an unpleasant rush course through his body. He winced.

"What's wrong, Josh? What's the matter?"

"I don't know. I think we're being watched," he said, instinctively turning his head towards the hallway.

Janet's father stood there.

She followed Josh's eyes. When she saw her father, she stood up immediately, as if a spring in her body had been released.

"Dad," she said, her voice breaking with terror, "what are you doing here? You're supposed to be at your office." Her voice trailed off the last few words.

He rushed towards her with the determination of a charging bull. "I'll show you what I'm doing here, you little floozy!" He angrily shoved Josh aside making his way towards her. Before she was able to raise her arms in self-defense, he slapped her face so hard that her knees bent, sending her in a quick trip to the floor.

Josh saw, with horror that the man was about to kick her in the face. Extending an arm towards the man, he managed to grab the traveling foot, pulling it back with all his strength. Janet's father lost his balance, falling backwards against one of the sofa's armrest. Josh quickly stood up and ran towards him. He grabbed him by the neck, and then extended his arms upwards, bringing the man's body clear off the floor. The man was choking.

"Josh, wait," screamed Janet as she raised her head from the floor. "Stop!"

"No," he replied without turning his burning eyes away from the man. "He deserves to die."

The man's eyes widened as he heard Josh's words. "Please," he pleaded, hardly able to say the word through his heavily constricted windpipe.

Janet stood up as fast as she could, pulling on Josh's arms, but unable to move him. "Josh, no! Listen to what you're saying!" She kept pulling on his arms. "Look at me, Goddammit!" she yelled.

He turned his head to meet her eyes.

"Please, let him go," She said, gently bringing her hands to his face.

"Why should I?" he said dryly.

"Because he's my father."

"You call this a father?" The man desperately held on to Josh's arms to avoid breaking his neck with the dangling weight of his own body.

"Let him down, please," she repeated softly.

His eyes regarded her serenely, but his grip on the man remained just as strong. Janet's father had just wet his pants.

"Please," she said searching into his eyes.

Josh released him. The man slid against the wall until he landed on the floor; he coughed and rubbed his neck. "I want you to listen to me," said Josh bending down to the man's eye level, "and pray to God you never forget. If you lay a hand on her again, I'll kill you!"

The man looked at Josh, but immediately turned his eyes away.

Josh was about to stand up, when his mouth took an unpleasant twist. He clenched his teeth and said, "you'd be wasting your time." He was obviously talking to the man.

"I didn't say anything," said the man cowering away from him.

"Oh, really? I thought you hated his guts."

The man's eyes widened.

"Anyway," continued Josh nonchalantly as he straightened up, "he's dead."

"Josh," interrupted a puzzled Janet, "What are you talking about?"

"Your father thinks he can call Ratface and have him beat the crap out of me."

"Jesus!" said the man looking at Josh with raw fear on his face.

"Yeah, you're right, old man." Josh gave him a wicked smile. "I can read your mind. But you don't have to worry," he continued as he walked to the front door, "as long as you leave her alone." Turning the doorknob, he opened the door. "Understand?" he finally said, looking back at the man. He waited for a reply.

The man nodded nervously.

"Come on, Janet," said Josh, "Let's go outside."

She stood fixed to the spot with an astounded look on her face.

◆◆◆◆◆◆◆

After a while, she walked outside with Josh. They sat on the porch and remained silent. Her face remained expressionless, almost solemn.

"You're worried, aren't you?" he said, almost apologetically.

"I'm just trying to figure this whole thing out."

"Figure what out?"

"Dammit! You want to act as if you don't know what the hell happened?" She suddenly exploded with a broken voice. "I still can't understand what you turned into back there. I mean it wasn't like you. I was watching you behave like some comic book monster or something."

"Jesus, Janet! I was only putting on an act," he said defensively.

"An act?" She raised her voice. "You mean, like pretending?" There was almost mockery on her face.

"Yeah."

"Stop it!. No one lifts a man twice his size, twice his weight, then just says he's putting on an act."

"I don't mean that. I was talking about the way I behaved."

"I know what you meant, believe me." She sounded angry, but Josh knew she was upset because she was afraid, not of him, but of facing her father again.

"Don't you see, I had to do it that way? I had to make him dread what might happen if he touched you again." Gently touching her shoulder, he hoped she wouldn't recoil from him. She didn't.

"I thought you'd gone mad," she said lowering her voice, as if his touch had produced a soothing effect in her soul. "I thought you were going to kill him."

"Then I had you both fooled. I knew all those nights of role-playing would come in handy someday." His face twitched with amusement.

"I'm glad someone's happy," she said sadly.

Forcing a smile, he touched her cheek tenderly. "Hey, don't worry about him. He won't bother you again. Believe me."

"How can you be sure?"

"He'll avoid you like the plague." His hand moved under her chin and lifted her face. "Come on, give me a smile." She blushed fiercely before finally smiling. He turned his face close to her and kissed her softly. They both blushed as they smiled nervously at each other.

"Did you really read his mind?" she asked.

"I don't understand it very well, but I, sort of, heard his voice, although I didn't see his lips moving. I took a chance on it." He moved his head thoughtfully. "I also felt something in the pit of my stomach that I couldn't put my finger on."

"What was that?"

"I don't know, but it felt like a combination of anxiety and very strong hunger pangs."

"Hunger pangs?" she asked as if she hadn't heard right the first time.

"It's the best way I can describe it," he said raising his eyebrows.

There was a brief silence between them before she said, "can you read my mind?"

"No. For some reason, I can't seem to do it consciously." Josh could have sworn he saw a twinkle in her eyes.

"Thank God," she said moving closer to him.

"How stupid of me," said Josh, suddenly rushing towards the front door.

"What is it?" cried Janet.

"Your father's got a gun and he's loading it!" Upon entering the foyer, Josh heard, to his left, the clicking sound of a cocking gun. He dived to the floor as the first bullet grazed past him, missing his head by a few inches. Janet entered the foyer right behind Josh. The second bullet also missed, but the splinters from the wood paneling chipped off straight into Janet's neck and shoulder.

Josh didn't wait for the sound of the third bullet. He grabbed a flower vase from a table and threw it straight at Mr. Phillis's face. The man tried to avoid the missile, but it smashed into tiny pieces against his arm. It was all Josh needed. Before the man could recover from the blow, Josh rushed him and pushed him hard against the wall. The man pulled the trigger one more time as he hit the wall, but the bullet ended up in the ceiling. By the time he fell to the floor, Mr. Phillis was unconscious. Wasting no time, Josh moved towards him and took the gun away.

"Are you okay, Janet?"

"Yes," she replied. She cried. "How could he do this to me?"

"It's a miracle he didn't." He approached Janet and held her in his arms. "I'm calling the police."

◆◈◦◦◈◦◦◈◦◦◈◦

Mr. Phillis was under arrest within the hour. Josh and Janet were a little shaken by the experience, and perhaps none the wiser. Mary Ann showed up at police headquarters to pick up Josh. Janet's mother took her to the hospital.

ELEVEN

Malcolm sat by the kitchen table. His conscience picking at his lack of principles. All the years at playing these con games never prepared him for anything like this. Abandoning Josh the way he did made him feel ashamed. He was a coward at heart, and if he ever doubted it, last night proved him wrong.

All along he believed this 'chakras and Kundalini' business, the spiritualism, the telepathy, was pure hogwash. Then Josh had to come along to turn his life upside down. How could he continue knowing what he knew? How could he live with himself?

There had to be something he could do to help. He couldn't stand idly by, and do nothing. Yet, he had no 'real' experience with the occult. He knew all the right things to say, and knew the necessary background to make people believe, but it was all a show, a way to a quick buck. He never expected anything like this to happen. *Who was this creature?* he wondered. *What was she a ghost, or a demon? How do we get rid of her? She seemed strong; yet, she had to have some weaknesses.*

He needed to compose himself, to gather his thoughts. The night before last went by too fast. *Josh said she was a prisoner of some kind, and not human. If so, then, what is she?*

No, speculating won't do, he thought. *I must call Josh, and hope he's still willing to talk to me.*

He went to the telephone and dialed.

※◆◦◆◦◦◆◦◦◆◦◆※

"Oh, it's you," replied Josh when he picked up the telephone. He had an edge in his voice. "Look, Malcolm, you don't need to worry about me. I took care of the problem without your help. And by the way," he continued, "don't call me again. I don't need you."

"Wait, Josh. Wait! Don't hang up!"

"WHAT?"

"I want to see you again, please." He paused. "Look, I'm sorry I acted like a coward. I know it's no excuse, but I was scared to death. Please, let me back in. I want to see this through."

"I thought you were my friend, but you certainly showed me, didn't you?" Josh was clearly upset.

"I am your friend, Josh. I may be scared, but I'm still your friend."

"Right now, I have other problems. What you want to discuss is over. Lilitu didn't show up last night."

Malcolm chewed on this for a moment. It didn't make much sense. "What makes you so sure you're heard the last of her?"

"It's a long story and I don't have time for it."

"I want to hear it, Josh. I really want to see you."

Little by little, Josh lost his edge. He was not one to hold a grudge for long. "So you're apologizing, huh?"

"Absolutely. You've got to believe me."

"Okay. Apology accepted, but I don't think I can come over, anyway. Something serious happened today. Mom probably won't let me."

"What happened?" asked Malcolm.

Josh told him about Norton and Mr. Phillis.

"Is Janet all right?"

"Yeah, she's a little shaken, though. I called her at home a while ago, and she'll be okay."

Malcolm took a deep breath. "Josh, what's happening is too important. I need to talk to your mother. I'm sure I can talk her into letting you stay with me for the night."

"You're welcome to try," said Josh. "Let me get her."

Malcolm waited for Mary Ann to come to the telephone.

❖⟡❖❖⟡❖❖⟡❖

At Nine o'clock that evening, Malcolm parked in front of Josh's house honking his horn. Mary Ann came out.

"He'll be out in a moment," she said leaning on the door. "Malcolm, I really appreciate this. I know he's a little rough in the edges, but he's really a good kid."

"No need to worry, Mary. It's not the first time I've had to deal with a little rebelliousness." He smiled reassuringly.

"Yeah. So far, you've been a blessing to me. Thanks again." She sighed. "Let me get him or he'll make you wait here all night."

Just as she turned towards the house, Malcolm called her. "Mary."

She turned back to him.

"Don't worry," he continued. "Everything will be all right."

She smiled and nodded, then went into the house.

Josh came out two minutes later and got in the car. "I have no idea what you told Mom over the phone," said Josh as he threw his backpack on the backseat, "but it must have been good."

"There's nothing like sprinkling a little guilt here and there," replied Malcolm with a smile and a conspiratorial wink.

"I hope you didn't give her details." When Malcolm didn't answer, he added, "did you?"

"I didn't need to. She loves you too much and only wants to help. As far as she knows, you're going through some adolescent emotional problem."

"I wish," said Josh.

"Well, I asked her if you could stay overnight for a hypnosis session and some fatherly advise. I wasn't too far from the truth, anyway." Malcolm glanced at Josh and extended his right hand towards him. "Still friends?"

Josh took his hand. "Yeah."

"You said over the phone that the creature didn't show up last night. Why do you think that is?"

"Remember that experiment I did with the mirror? The Rosicrucian experiment?"

Malcolm glanced at Josh and noticed something different about him. He couldn't put his finger on it, but it was perceptible. Maybe he just hadn't paid attention before.

"Well, I believe," continued Josh, "the mirror was, somehow, the connection between her and me. Last night I painted it black, trying to close the link." He leaned back on the seat and placed his hands behind his head. "It must have worked, cause she didn't show up."

"Sounds good, but we still have too many unanswered questions. That's why I want to hypnotize you tonight. Maybe we can find out what she may have left inside that little brain of yours."

Josh's smile, as he looked at Malcolm, revealed his approval. The rest of the ride went silently.

◆◇◆◇◆◇◆

The lights in Malcolm's living room were turned down. The only illumination came from a small nightlight, making the shadows move within an intimidating chiaroscuro. It was the type of ambiance that, in the past, Malcolm created to conduct spiritualist sessions. It helped loosen the pockets of some of his customers. He stopped doing that sort of thing a long time ago. The intensity of most people seeking contact with the spirit world was more than he could take. Although it was a con game for him, it always drained him emotionally.

Josh sat on the sofa chair with his hands resting on his knees. His eyes were closed, as he was already deep in trance. Malcolm sat on a chair next to Josh.

"What do you see?" asked Malcolm.

"I see something, but it doesn't look like her."

"What do you mean?"

"It looks like the creature that I found under the tarpaulin when she locked me in that awful room."

"That may make more sense than we realize. It certainly explains the presence of the creature inside that room. What you see might be the way she really looks," said Malcolm. "I want you to get into her mind, the part of her that she left in your subconscious. Then we'll go back in time. Back as far as we can go." Leaning closer to Josh, he lightly touched his forearm. "Are you okay?"

"Yes, I'm fine."

"Good. Now relax. Concentrate on that body and imagine you're floating into her mind. Go inside her."

"Yes," said Josh, his eyebrows knitting together. "I'm inside. It's like walking into some dark labyrinth."

"Go deeper. Penetrate her thoughts and go back; back to her earliest memories. Let's find out what she meant when she said 'the beginning'. You are looking for her past. It's in there and we are going to find it. Come on now, look deeper." This was uncharted territory for Malcolm. As old as hypnosis was for him, this was a new reality.

"I see blackness. It's very dark." Josh's voice sounded hesitant.

"Can you see anything at all?"

Josh moved his head sideways, as if making an effort to penetrate the haze of a foggy night. "Yes, I can see Lilitu."

"What is she doing now?"

"She's waking up."

MESOPOTAMIA –
1.5 MILLION YEARS AGO

TWELVE

As Lilitu opened her eyes, she heard them arguing. It didn't matter much. They seemed to argue constantly, and by now, listening to them was as listening to crickets in the night.

The Igigis argued about work and they had come to let Enlil, their overseer, know of their discontent. It upset Enlil to hear the same arguments repeatedly. Although they complained almost daily, today they were on the verge of mutiny.

The Ancients divided their society into two classes: The Igigi, workers that labored in the fields, and the Anunnaki, which were their leaders. Enlil, the second most powerful Anunnaki, was the founder of Nippur, the first settlement of the Ancients.

Enlil was born in, what the Anunnakis referred to as, 'the house in the heavens', but as soon as he became of age, Anu, his father, appointed him 'Overseer of the Lands'. After that, Anu rarely, if ever, bothered to intervene with Enlil's decisions. Today was one of those special occasions in which intervention was necessary. Enlil, trying to avert a disaster, asked his father to mediate.

Anu did not live in the settlement. He preferred to live the rest of his days in comfort and away from conflict. All the bickering and fruitless arguing never got them anywhere, so he gave up his rule. Instead, he put one of his sons in charge. It was a good plan. If anything went wrong, he still kept the best weapons at his, and only his, disposal. Retirement was good. This he was able to do by making sure his home was hard to reach. Very few Anunnakis, and much less the Igigis, had the means to go to 'the house in the heavens'. Normally, Anu waved away any involvement with the settlements, and if there were a need for him to intervene, the leaders would usually convene at his house. Except this was an emergency and his presence was needed.

Enlil was not one to take arguments easily. His temper flared for the slightest transgression, but the Igigis, this time, did not take 'no' for an answer and their tempers also threatened to flare.

The meeting began in the courtyard, behind the laboratory. As soon as Anu entered, there was a sudden silence. Enlil acknowledged his father's presence and immediately invited him to approach. Everyone looked in awe of him as he slowly walked to the podium.

Anu sat for a while and listened to the Igigis' arguments. Now, it was his turn to speak. He walked to the front of the podium and brought his hands behind his back, holding one hand against the other. He cleared his throat, allowing his eyes to roam the whole courtyard. He finally addressed the group. "You complain your work is too heavy, and we know it is." His voice was deep and his delivery paused and calm. "You complain your burden is unbearable; that, too, is true. But I ask you, my friends, what do you want us to do?"

Enki, who also had a seat in the podium, stood and asked permission to speak. Anu granted it. He acknowledged the Igigis' concerns, and he believed he had a solution.

Enki, considered the third most powerful Anunnaki, was their lead scientist and Anu's second son. He was the founder of Eridu, the second most ancient settlement in the southern part of Mesopotamia. Eridu was situated on a large lake, surrounded by reed-lands and marshy areas; today's meeting was held in Enki's estate, a domain befitting an important nobleman. The property was more than a family dwelling. It was built around stables, workshops, banquet rooms, a large garden including a menagerie, and of course, the laboratory. Enki's living quarters stood at the center, whereas the workrooms, kitchen, and other sleeping quarters were crowded together to the south of the laboratory. A tall sun-baked brick wall surrounded the complete area. A large gate protected the residence from unauthorized entry.

The rivalry between Enki and Enlil was legendary. Enlil was a strict disciplinarian, and Enki was a wise scientist, but the thirst for power was great in both of them.

"My Lord," said Enki to Anu, "the Elohim and I, have been working day and night to create a primitive worker to alleviate their work, and I know we are on the verge of a breakthrough."

"A breakthrough?" said one of the Igigi with laughter. "So far all you and your scientists have created are freaks. The worst one had wings, but as hairy as an ape, and worse to look at than a bat. A most intimidating creature, to say the least."

Enki was surprised at this outburst. Normally, the Igigis knew their place and dared not challenge any Anunnaki so openly. "Given the poor equipment we have been forced to work with, we have done wonders. Besides, scientific experimentation isn't easily predictable," replied Enki, obviously upset.

"Well, I could have predicted the freaks you created. A creature with two heads, others with goat feet, horses with an Igigi's torso." The Igigi spoke passionately. "You can't go about mixing our essence with horses and goats. It isn't right."

Anu, trying to avoid more arguments, turned to Mummu. "What do you think, Mummu? Can we create some primitive worker with enough intelligence to toil for us?"

Mummu was the eldest female amongst the ancients, yet the Igigis, as well as the Anunnakis, looked up to her as their spiritual mother. "I'm sure we can, given enough time," she said. "Our Elohim are very skilled, but they need time."

The Igigis did not like the answer. "We have given you more than enough time already," said the Igigi leader. "We don't want any more freaks. They are unruly and uncontrollable. Besides, they are too stupid to learn."

One of the Elohim stood up. "I believe I can speak for the rest of us," he said, referring to the rest of the Scientists. "We understand the need to create a worker with the proper physical characteristics and intelligent enough to take over your chores. I am sure we can do this, but we need to be careful with the kind of creature we create; otherwise, we may have a worse time controlling it than any other we have created so far. This is not a simple assignment."

"Careful?" asked Mummu. "In what way?"

"They must be smaller and weaker than us, and they must have a limited life span," replied the Elohim spokesman.

Another of the Elohim stood up and said "If we make them in our image, after our likeness, it will make our job simpler and will yield faster results."

"But that will make them even harder to control, if they believe they are one of us," said Enlil.

"That," said Anu, "can be properly channeled."

"How?" asked Enlil.

"As the Elohim suggested, we limit, not only their life span, their strength, and even their size, but we must also limit their access to knowledge. We give them only the tools they need to toil the fields; then we feed them, and nothing else. If we also limit their contact with us, and never treat them as our equals, we should easily control them."

"They will grow to hate us," said Mummu.

"Not if we teach them fear. We will be as their gods and will not dare oppose us," replied Anu. He looked around at each one, waiting for a counter suggestion. None came forth. "Then it's settled," he continued, knowing the argument was over. "If you'll bear with us and our scientists for just a while longer, you will get your wish."

"Our wish, if you want to know the truth, is to go back home," shouted another of the Igigis.

"You know that is not possible," replied Anu. "We have made machines good enough to allow us to travel within the boundaries of this world. We all know that. But we lack the raw materials and equipment to provide us with the necessary power for our journey back."

"Will we ever go home?" asked Enki.

"We can always dream, but let us not dwell on such things," replied Anu. "This world is our home for now, and we must take care of our immediate problems."

The Igigis murmured in protest, reluctantly agreeing to give the scientists more time. For the moment, a mutiny was averted.

Lilitu heard everything, but had no idea she was one of the freaks they referred to. *What was all this talk about not wanting to work?* She was a slave, and cared not about their stupid talk. For her, there was no choice. Work was all she was born to do, and all she needed to know.

◆━◆◆━◆◆━◆◆━◆

Leaving the straw bed, she yawned while stretching her body and wings. The reflection on the mirror showed her wings had not atrophied yet. In spite of never had taken flight, she secretly exercised them every evening, before turning in. Her room, small as it was, allowed her enough headroom to remain aloft for a few minutes at a time. The Elohim forced her to wear a small harness and could only take it off for sleeping. If she ever were caught outside without the harness, she would be executed. She was not ready for flight yet. For now, escape was out of the question. They could catch her in no time, and she knew it. Besides, she had no idea what was outside these walls surrounding Enki's domain. She wouldn't know where to hide. The only world she knew, since the day she was born, was this borough.

Looking out her window, towards the courtyard, she watched the crowd leave. They were not easy to read, these Anunnaki. It took her awhile to know when they were pleased with her, which was seldom. Knowing when they were displeased was much easier. Their tempers flared up at the slightest provocation or mistake. Today might prove to be a day for her to watch her step. Controversy and arguments always brought out the worse in them; in all of them.

Mummu, who helped raise her, was the kindest, but that was not saying much. For the most part, they were not even kind to each other. The best thing Mummu did for her was take her out of her cage and trust her with some menial work. Otherwise she would be, either dead, or wallowing in her own feces. At least for this she could be thankful.

Putting on her restraining harness, she hurried out to the garden. After plucking a couple of Apples from the nearest tree, she headed towards the laboratory to start her daily routines. The lab smelled strong. It looked clean, but the chemicals and the smell of fear were overwhelming. Nothing compared to the back room, where they kept all the creatures. The animals, if they could be called as such, were filthy. They were forced to defecate and urinate inside their cages, and oftentimes, on top of each other. When Lilitu walked into the back room, she avoided their eyes. Their typically sad condition reminded her of the time she was in her own cage. Some, the most aggressive ones, were invariably destroyed, usually in front of the others to set an example. This made them all the more nervous, but it brought most of them down to manageable levels. Fear, she learned, is a powerful incentive. A few minutes later, she began to clean the cages.

❖◦❖◦❖◦❖◦❖

For the next few months, life seemed no more than the same everyday routine. She had no way of keeping time, since the use of a calendar was unknown to her. While Lilitu's main duties mostly included keeping the cages and the laboratory, a few times she was burdened with helping the Elohim destroy some of the creatures; specially the dysfunctional ones. This was the most distasteful of her chores. Regardless of how much she tried to detach herself from their pain, it was useless. Even behind the most horrible faces and disfigured bodies, she could see their unimaginable suffering. Those eyes would haunt her for days after the slaughters.

Then came the worst part; disposing of the bodies. By this time, the urine and excrement of the other creatures did not bother her. Even touching their feces did not daunt her. It was handling their lifeless corpses that proved unbearable.

The Elohim laughed every time she cried. Often, while in the process of their slaughter, they were purposefully cruel, just to see her reaction. Try as she might, she was unable to hide it. Many times, the thought of wringing the Elohim's necks, just as they did to the creatures, crossed her mind, but she had seen them use their thundersticks. Fire must be fought with fire, and she could not fight that with her bare hands.

Since she became aware of a meeting called early one morning by the Enki and the Elohim, Lilitu knew something was afoot. There was excitement in the air. Inside the laboratory, she sneaked behind one of the windows facing the garden and looked. Had she dared walk outside while the Anunnakis were assembled, she would have been punished. And when you were punished, they made sure you would not forget. She already bore enough scars to remember.

The Elohim kept the garden full of animals, all kinds of animals, yet most of them had no names, as far as she knew. In fact, she knew the names of very few things; they never bothered to teach her much of anything. She was taught only what she needed to know. Some of the animals were eventually used in the laboratory, and some were kept simply as pets. But the animals in the garden were beautiful and healthy; the creatures in the laboratory were not.

Aside from the animals, everyday, a group of Igigis came to the garden to maintain it, to toil in it and break sweat; and she observed them carefully, yet she knew nothing about them.

As the group gathered around the podium, Enki spoke. "I know this may be premature, but I believe we are ready to show you the initial results of our work." He asked them to sit as he slowly moved back and forth in front of them. "We are well on our way to our goal, and we feel this will meet with your approval." He waited for a bit, almost enjoying the suspense created, and then stepped closer to the curtain behind him The Elohim stood next to Mummu with a proud smile upon their face.

'*What were they up to?*' thought Lilitu.

"This," said Enki as he held the edge of the curtain with his left hand, and parted it to the side, "is the Adapa."

A naked Anunnaki stood behind the curtain; a much smaller version with a hairy face, but without a doubt, an Anunnaki. It shivered nervously; his eyes stared at the floor.

As Lilitu got a better look at him, something stirred inside her. The goose bumps on her skin pricked from the inside out. It may have resembled an Anunnaki, but it was not. This was a new creature.

"If it works out as expected, we will have your primitive worker. Now we need to see how well it can be trained. After that, if you find the results acceptable, we will make more." Enki wore a proud face as he spoke.

❖─❖─❖─❖─❖

For the next few days, Lilitu kept to herself, dutifully following her routine, apparently oblivious to the new acquisition; but she watched.

The new creature, the one called the Adapa, was clumsy. Enki accompanied him every waking moment, for the most part, teaching him the basics. Walking was the hardest part, and it took him the longest to learn. It was the most fragile looking thing she had ever seen. Even now, after days of practice, he would often trip on his own feet and fall flat on his face. She wondered how long it would be before they tortured him, like they did to the rest of the creatures they created.

After the Adapa learned to walk somewhat steadily, Enki took him out to the garden. He tried to teach things to it, but the creature seemed unable to concentrate. It had the attention span of a child. In many ways, that is exactly what he was.

It was most unexpected when Enki, seeing her looking out from the laboratory window, called out to her. She immediately hid behind the wall, but Enki called her a second time.

"Lilitu," he said, "I know you are watching us. Don't make me call you again."

She peeked out, barely showing herself, and replied in a shy voice. "Yes?"

"Come out here!" he ordered.

Normally, when an Anunnaki or the Elohim called her, it was for punishment. She approached Enki cautiously.

The Adapa was naked. She had never seen a naked Anunnaki, and this new creature was beautiful. Every living thing she had seen roamed about naked, except the Anunnaki and the Igigi. But there was something about the Adapa that made her uneasy. She noticed the appendage that dangled between his legs and wondered if the Anunnakis had such an organ.

Enki plucked an Apple from the nearest tree and asked her, "what is this?"

"I do not know, Master," she replied cowering from him. She waited for the slap, but it never came.

Enki took a bite at the fruit and showed it back to her, saying, "this is an apple."

"Yes, Master."

"Now, say it," he ordered.

"What would you have me say, Master?" Her voice was a murmur. For no reason would she dare raise her voice.

Enki rapped her on the head. "What is this?"

"What is this?" she repeated. It was a dumb thing to do, but it was a survival device. If they thought her stupid, they thought her harmless.

The Adapa stood silently looking back and forth at their exchange.

"Are you trying to make me believe you are so useless?" said Enki. "Perhaps I can arrange to have you destroyed. We have no use for stupidity."

"Apple," she said almost immediately. "That is an Apple, Master."

"Good," said Enki pleased with himself. "Now we can get some work done." He turned towards the Adapa and looked at him from head to toe. "I want you to teach him words. You are to be with him night and day and will talk to him until he understands what you are saying."

"Master?" she said with her eyes turned downwards. "What about my work?"

"This is your work from hereon. It will be arranged for an Igigi to take over your duties until I deem it convenient."

"Yes, Master."

"I will arrange for another bed to be placed in your room; for the Adapa. You will do nothing but what I just ordered. Is that understood?"

Lilitu nodded, but dared not raise her eyes to meet Enki's.

Enki turned to the Adapa and grabbed his hand, then placed Lilitu's hand over it. "You will stay with Lilitu now."

The Adapa looked at both; not quite understanding what Enki wanted. When Enki began to walk away, he tried to follow, but Lilitu held him back. The Adapa, feeling her strong hand on him, turned around and whacked her hard on the head. She whacked him back even harder. Now she knew she was going to hate him as much as she hated all Anunnakis.

Enki could not help but smile as he entered the laboratory.

THIRTEEN

There was much more to the Adapa than simply teaching him words. The first few days, he urinated and defecated wherever he felt the urge. So, the first word he learned was '*no*'. Since it usually came accompanied with a strong blow on the head, it didn't take him long to understand its meaning. Basic cleanliness was also of the utmost importance; the Anunnakis demanded it. Lilitu taught him that water had uses other than for drinking. The first few words he learned were '*no*,'*yes*', '*eat*', '*drink*', and '*sleep*'. After that, things progressed quite fast.

The only time that Lilitu almost got into trouble because of the Adapa was the day she showed him the laboratory. She knew Enki did not intend her to teach him the goings on inside that building, yet he never mentioned it. It was a risky thing to do, and just in case, she waited until the day's work was done and the place was empty. If the Adapa was to learn, he might as well find out who his creators really were. They entered through the service door. She held his hand, but when she tried to walk inside, he pulled her back shivering with fear.

"What is it, Adapa?" she asked, not realizing the smells coming out of the laboratory were alien and intimidating to him.

"Bad. No," he said while trying to let go of her hand. Had she released him, he would have run away, but her grip on him was strong.

"Look," she said pushing the door wide open, "there's nothing to be afraid of."

The Adapa saw several tables full of beakers and other implements. "Please, no go." He continued to pull away.

Lilitu moved closer, wrapping her arm around his waist. This was something he was going to see, whether he liked it or not. She lifted him easily, and carried him inside. Before putting him down, her right leg pushed the door close behind them. The lab looked perfectly clean, but to the Adapa, there was something threatening. His eyes suddenly fixed upon the back door on the far side of the laboratory.

"Ah," said Lilitu. "I see you discovered my favorite place. Come," she said grabbing his hand again. "Let's see what's in there."

The Adapa stood his ground refusing to move.

"Don't make me drag you, Adapa. You know I will if I have to."

His pleading eyes met hers, but it was useless to resist. As they approached the back door, a low moan escaped his lips. She released him and opened the door. He remained frozen to the spot as she walked halfway through the threshold.

"These are some of my friends," she said. Her arms extended wide, indicating the rows of cages. The Adapa slowly entered, nervously looking ahead. His hands grabbed the frame of the door, in case he needed to leave quickly.

"Come. I want you to meet them."

Several of the creatures moved closer to their cage doors, curious about their visitors. Others cowered towards the back of the cage as far as it would allow them. Lilitu approached the first cage.

"What do you think this is, Adapa? Can you try to guess what kind of animal it is?" The cruelty she showered upon him betrayed her disdain for the Adapa.

His face went from the creature's face to Lilitu's face as his body swayed left and right. "Chicken?"

"No, not quite. Too big, don't you think?"

The creature's mouth opened and closed frequently, as if its breathing was hard labor. The Adapa looked closer, seemingly recognizing a human face somewhere in that deformed head. His heart skipped a beat. Suddenly, from the cage behind them, a creature that may have been an ape with horns threw a large piece of feces at him. It hit him on the head and rolled down his neck. His stomach convulsed with the repulsive smell. The creatures began getting excited. As the front door opened, the Adapa threw up over Lilitu's legs.

"Is anyone here?" asked a voice from the front entrance to the laboratory.

Lilitu quickly grabbed the Adapa and whispered, "Come, let's get out of here." She ran towards the back door, pulling him behind her.

The Adapa slipped a few times as they silently ran through the courtyard, but she managed to hold him up. When she opened the door to her bedroom, he slipped one more time, but this time she let him fall and crash against the wall.

"You smell," she snarled at him. "Go wash yourself."

"You smell too," he replied defiantly.

They never went back to the laboratory after that night. That lesson was over. He never mentioned it again, and neither did she.

❖❖❖❖❖❖❖

Time passed faster as the Adapa learned from Lilitu. Within a few weeks, he grasped the use of speech and his motor coordination was much improved. Enki came out occasionally to check on their progress and to add some words to Adapa's vocabulary. Lilitu also benefited from Enki's visits, since he did not dismiss her. They both learned the names of many other animals and things, and of people too. As the Adapa learned, so did Lilitu.

"I believe," said Enki one day, "that it is time to give him a name." He turned to Lilitu. "Don't you think, Lilitu?"

She lowered her eyes and nodded. This was a first for her. No Anunnaki ever asked her opinion, although she was sure Enki didn't expect an answer. She gave him one anyway. "Is not his name Adapa, Master?"

"No," replied Enki, somewhat amused. "Adapa is a word with unknown meaning to you because you had no reason to learn it. Adapa means 'model'. He is but a model, or a mold, if you will."

"I don't know the meaning of those words either, Master."

"Never mind. I have a name for him, with which you will call him from now on." Enki looked at the Adapa and smiled. "We will call him Adamu."

❖❖❖❖❖❖❖

At night, whenever they got ready to go to sleep, Adamu was usually at his most talkative; tonight was no exception. This new name was quite unexpected. He was already used to being called Adapa, and had a hard time responding to Adamu.

"I do not understand," said Adamu while he lied face up on his straw mattress. "Why did he name me Adamu? What does it mean?"

"The Master already told you it means 'man of the earth'." His stupidity exasperated her. This intolerable assignment tested her patience to its limits. All she knew was to obey, and now she was giving orders; at least to this incredibly dense creature.

"But earth means soil, does it not?" he asked

"Yes."

"How can I be made of soil?"

"Look, I don't care if you were made of mud! Can we go to sleep now?"

Adamu felt a bit afraid and a bit hurt. "You are always rude to me. Why?"

"I am rude to you because I can. Have you seen me be rude with any of the Masters? No. You know why? Because I want to live."

"You do not care for me, I know."

"Care? What is that? No one cares for you, or for me. And I care for no one either. Why should we? We were both born to be slaves." She tried to keep her tone down, but was unable to. "Open your eyes, Adamu. Have you not seen that he with the biggest whip gets the most respect? If they can hit you hard, they will. If they can hurt you, they will. And there is nothing you or I can do about it, except be humble in their presence and accept our fate."

"Well, I can see why you should feel like that. You are not one of them."

"Neither are you!" she replied.

"You keep telling me that," he said, "but I look like them."

"You think you look like them, but you are not! I know that to be true." She came closer to him and whispered, "believe me, if you were, you would not be sleeping here, nor would you be under my care. Now keep quiet and go to sleep." Lilitu turned on her straw bed and faced the wall.

"What do you know? You're just an animal," said Adamu.

"Really? An animal? Like what? Like the ones in the garden? Perhaps like the ones in the cages? You and I, both came from the laboratory, in case you didn't know. I don't know what that makes us, and I don't care. The only difference between all of us is what's up here," she said as she pointed at her head with her index finger. "But before you go show them how smart you are, I suggest you practice running as fast as you can."

"Running? Why?"

"Because they will kill you. They will kill you if you are too smart. They will kill you if you are too dumb. They will kill you if you are too strong, or perhaps if you are too weak. And, believe me, they will kill you simply for fun."

"I don't believe you," he said in confusion.

"That suits me fine."

There was a long silence between them. From within the darkness of the room, however, she could sense his agitation.

"What are we, Lilitu?" he asked softly.

"What do you mean?"

"The Masters have a name for every creature, except you and me."

"Of course we have a name. You're Adamu and I'm Lilitu."

"No," he said emphatically. "Not that kind of name. I mean a name, like when you see a dog, any dog; you know what it is. When you see a peacock, you know what it is. I know you are not a Lilitu, because there is no such thing. Lilitu is not what you are. It is who you are. I know the difference now. But I still do not know what I am. You and I are unique. There is only one of you and only one of me."

She lowered her guard for a moment and felt sympathy for him. This and many other thoughts had been on her mind since she began to think. "I don't know, Adamu. I wish I could tell you, but I don't know."

"Maybe I should ask Master Enki," he said softly.

"Maybe you should." There was a moment's pause before she added, "just be careful."

For the rest of the evening, they kept quiet until both fell asleep.

❖❖❖❖❖❖❖

The next morning, as Lilitu and Adamu walked out to the courtyard, Enki approached them. As usual, they faced Enki with their eyes lowered.

"Adamu, your time here is over," he said. "You are to be taken to our orchard in Edin."

"What is Edin, Master?" he asked. Adamu, of all the Anunnaki's creations, was expected to ask questions. At least, for now.

"Its near 'the house in the heavens', where our Lord Anu lives."

"How long will I stay there, Master?"

"You are to live in Edin from this day on." Enki smiled.

"But why, Master? Why do I need to go? Have I not behaved?" asked Adamu apprehensively.

"You will like it there, so do not look so worried. It is a good place to live, not a punishment. You will enjoy its warm, breezy climate. The soil is good. You will learn agriculture and horticulture, and the cultivation of orchards." Enki to talk to himself.

"Horticulture, Master?" Adamu nervously swayed his body from side to side.

Enki reacted to the question as if coming back from a dream. "It's just one of many things that you will learn to do. Do not worry about it now. Only know that it is what you were born to do." His eyes then turned to Lilitu. "You have done well, Lilitu. Perhaps one day I may compensate you."

"What is to become of me now, Master." Her eyes never left the ground.

"You will go back to your chores, of course." It was a matter of fact reply, said with no malice, but also with no forethought. "You may go to the laboratory now."

Adamu watched Lilitu walk slowly towards the laboratory. A great sadness overpowered him. For the first time, a tear fell down his cheek. This was also the lesson for the day.

Lilitu had never grown attached to anyone, but she missed Adamu so much it hurt. Her thoughts wandered constantly towards him. One day, she hoped, she might see him again. By then, he surely would be able to teach her a few things. She went about her chores mechanically; efficiently, but mindlessly.

A couple of days later, Enki called upon Lilitu. She was to be taken to Edin also. Adamu, said Enki, refused to eat or do anything but sit under a tree. No one had been able to get him to work either. If Lilitu could not help him, he was to going to be destroyed.

Enki walked her outside, past the gates. She had never been outside Enki's Estate. A guard walked next to her, nudging her towards a strange vehicle. She had seen one such as this fly above the Estate before, but never expected to come this close to one. The wind around the vehicle rushed around like a whirlwind as it roared, almost warning her to stay away. The guard took her arm, and pushed her inside. Enki climbed in behind her, closing the vehicle door as he indicated to another Anunnaki sitting in front, that they were ready to leave.

They were airborne almost immediately and a slight dizziness overcame her.

"Just sit back and relax. You have nothing to worry about." Enki patted her on the knee as if she were a dog. "You'll soon see Adamu."

"Why are you taking me to him, Master?" Her eyes never left her window as she saw the Earth down below and the clouds flying past them.

"We don't know what has come over him. He does nothing of what we ask. You must talk to him; make him react, somehow."

Had this been any other creature, she thought, *he would have been tortured to death. Why not Adamu? Had Enki, perhaps, grown partial to him?*

They did not speak for most of the trip. All she did was look out the window and wonder at the greatness of what she saw. Yet, the more she saw, the more her resentment grew. There was so much more than that hellhole of a laboratory she was forced to clean day after day. As they approached their destination, she turned towards Enki, and looked him in the eyes.

"What's so special about Adamu? Why have you not destroyed him for his transgression?" She half expected to be slapped down on the spot. This was the first time she addressed an Anunnaki without using the word Master, and the first time she did not lower her eyes.

Enki returned her gaze and seemed ready to have one of his outbursts. Instead, his face softened, for a brief moment, forgetting their differences. "In a way, he's my son," he whispered. This time, Enki lowered his eyes.

To Lilitu, the word was meaningless, but something about his demeanor made her feel sad for him. This heartless beast may have had feelings after all.

As they began descending, the garden looked as expansive as she had never imagined. The trees were tall and robust, and had all kinds of fruit. Some she recognized, some she saw for the first time. Many new animals, graceful and beautiful, ran freely amongst the trees. Her eyes swelled with tears, not only for what she saw, but also for what she realized she had missed all her life.

Enki opened his door. "Go now and find Adamu. Help him, Lilitu. Help him." This was not an order; it was a plea.

She almost smiled, but instead nodded, then left the vehicle.

"I will be back tomorrow," said Enki as the vehicle took flight again. He looked at her from his window as it flew back to Eridu.

There seemed to be no one else in the garden. It might take her days to find Adamu, she thought. She called out his name several times, but got no reply. This was just a temporary reprieve from her slavery, and she knew that as soon as Adamu was back to his senses, so would she go back to the laboratory.

It was now or never. Her hands flew to her harness, undoing the buckles. The harness fell to the floor with a soft thud. That was the sound of freedom. Perhaps Enki suspected what she would do, perhaps he didn't, but it mattered not. As soon as she found Adamu, if he didn't want to escape with her, she would escape alone. They would probably find her, and there would probably be no place to hide, but now she was willing to die.

"Adamu," she cried aloud. "Adamu!" For almost an hour, her calling continued as she walked about the garden. Then, finally, she heard her name.

"Lilitu!" He called back running towards her. His laughter filled the garden as he jumped on her, almost making her lose her balance. Her wings flapped instinctively, helping her keep her balance. This was the first time she heard laughter, but without realizing it, she herself began to laugh. It was the strangest sensation.

A while later, their conversation had simmered down to a whisper.

"I have walked the whole of Edin," said Adamu, "and escape is impossible. They have guards all over the perimeter. Even if I wanted to join you, I cannot fly."

"And I probably cannot carry you either," she agreed. "My wings may not be strong enough for the two of us."

"Then you go, Lilitu. Live free for the both of us."

"I cannot leave you here," she protested sternly. "You will be destroyed."

"Not if I cooperate with them. I will do as they ask. In the meantime, you can find a place out there, and maybe later we can find a way to be together again."

She had no words of comfort. She liked him, more than any animal she had been close to. But escape was inevitable. It was either freedom, or death.

She waited for the blanket of darkness, and flew out into the night. Adamu cried once more as her saw her leave. Lilitu also cried as she looked back towards the Black Forest.

FOURTEEN

The exhilaration of flying made her feel powerful. Looking back, the dark silhouette of the distant garden stood out in the horizon. The image of Adamu, sadly sitting under a tree, came to her, but now, there was no time to think. Exhaustion forced her to land. Cautiously hovering a few feet above the ground, she slowly allowed her bare feet to touch down in the cold, sandy patch of a riverbank. It lay just a few yards away, and she badly needed to quench her thirst. She drank deeply from its clear, inviting waters, yet she also needed to appease her hunger. A cold breeze blew over her head and, for the first time, knew there was no comfortable bed to sleep in either, no blanket to keep her warm. It made her feel vulnerable. The temptation to fly back to Edin crawled under her skin with every passing minute.

Where could she hide when they came looking for her in the morning? Assuming she could survive this ordeal, how was she going to get Adamu out of Edin? Was all this worth the sacrifice?

Yes, she thought. She had to survive. Until today, her life seemed pointless, but now, she had a reason to live. Although rescuing Adamu was a small part of it, all those other creatures – those other souls - in the laboratory needed her also. The more she thought about the Anunnakis, the angrier she felt. For now, however, she needed a place to hide. With night already upon her – out here in the open - things might even get downright dangerous.

She looked back towards the garden. Most of the trees in Edin were tall and had thick enough branches to hide in, and all she needed was a way to keep from falling off if she fell asleep. Her discarded harness was just the thing. After a short rest, she took off, heading back to Edin.

Flying into the garden was easy. The cloak of night provided her cover; besides, the guards would never suspect an intruder from above. She found the harness still on the floor, exactly where she dropped it. Adamu slept nearby, next to a tree. Without waking him up, she whisked up to the tallest branch above, and then tied herself to the trunk. It was uncomfortable, but it would have to do. In fifteen minutes, she was fast asleep.

The next morning, the din of a flying machine woke her up. It was bright morning, she noticed. Not only was it beautiful, but also cool and breezy. She watched the machine land nearby, and a figure walking out towards Adamu.

"Master," said a startled Adamu when Enki approached him.

"Where is Lilitu?" he asked. There didn't seem to be much concern in his voice.

Adamu lowered his eyes and said nothing. He had the habit of shuffling his body from side to side whenever he felt nervous.

"Well?" said Enki. "Do you plan to answer or did you lose your tongue?"

"No, Master, I still have my tongue," answered Adamu quietly. "She is not here."

"I can see that. Where is she?" Enki's voice had a slight edge.

"I do not know. She is gone."

Lilitu waited for Enki's reaction. The branch she sat on shook slightly, but not enough to attract Enki's attention. Her body tensed.

"She left? How could she leave? There's no way out," said Enki, raising his voice. Suddenly, his expression changed. "Of course! The ungrateful freak simply flew out of here," he drawled, grinding his teeth with frustration. "I will hunt her down and make her know what it means to disobey me."

Adamu reacted nervously. This unexpected outburst from Enki had him shaking. "Please, Master. Do not punish her. Punish me. I am to blame for this. I am to blame. Please." His hands went up to his own chest, beating it like a drum, as tears trickled down his cheeks.

"You're to blame?" asked Enki glaring at Adamu. "How?"

"I raised my hand at her, Master." He cowered slightly as he spoke.

"Why did you do such a thing?"

Adamu hesitated. "When you brought me here, alone, I observed the animals roaming about. They all had a mate. They all had a mate except me, Master."

"So?" Enki's anger turned to curiosity.

"I tried to force her to lie with me, but she refused."

Lilitu could not believe her ears. Adamu was lying, and she never taught him to do that. Did Adamu see her as a potential mate? She never looked at him as such, yet the thought of it did not repulse her.

Enki moved closer to Adamu. "What do you know of these things? Who taught you this?"

"You gave me eyes to see," replied Adamu cautiously taking a step backwards.

"Then you should also use your eyes to also see that she is not like you. I did not create you to debase yourself with animals."

At these words, Lilitu almost fell from the tree. Enki considered her lower than Adamu. As painful tears of rage raced through her eyes, she felt lower than the low. He was her maker too, someone she once feared, and now was learning to hate intensely.

"Then, who do I debase myself with, Master?" continued Adamu. The sentence sounded sarcastic, but Adamu was incapable of it. He knew not the meaning of the word 'debase' either, although he used it in the right context.

"Not with her," added Enki with emphasis.

"You say she is not like me, but you never told me what I am." Adamu tried to meet Enki's eyes, but looked away immediately. "Please, Master. Tell me what I am. Why do I look so much like you?"

"You are Man, and although we created you after our likeness, do not believe, for a moment, that you are one of us. You were only made to serve us." Enki raised an eyebrow and continued. "Never forget this, lest you wish to be destroyed."

"I was created to be your slave?"

"To serve us, to do our menial work. You will till the land and take over much of our hardships. This is your destiny, your purpose." Enki's face softened as he placed his hands over Adamu's shoulder. "But do not worry, Adamu. You will have your mate. I never intended for you to live alone. Lilitu, however, is not what I had in mind." His eyes remained on Adamu for a moment. "Wait here." Enki headed back towards the vehicle.

Lilitu lay still. Adamu stood by the tree waiting, nervously swaying his body from left to right, then back again. A few minutes later, Enki returned holding a small bag in his right hand.

"I said you were going to have a mate," said Enki, nonchalantly, "and I will keep my word." He opened the bag, taking out a small bottle. "I want you to lie down."

"Here, Master?" asked Adamu, meekly indicating a patch of grass on the ground. He had no idea what Enki was about to do, but as always, felt compelled to obey. He had never done otherwise.

"Yes," replied Enki. "That will do fine."

Adamu complied as Enki opened the bottle, pouring its contents into a piece of cloth. Carefully, closing the bottle, he placed the cloth over Adamu's face. A short while later, Adamu was unconscious.

Lilitu had seen this before, in the laboratory. Sometimes, the Elohim used this liquid to make the creatures helpless before they proceeded to destroy them. She poised herself to attack. If Enki threatened Adamu in any way, she would kill him.

Enki reached into the bag again, this time, grabbing a syringe. This was unexpected. The Elohim never used a syringe for destruction. Their preferred method was dismemberment. She watched Enki closely as he softly plunged it into Adamu's left side, near the lower rib.

Why did Enki take a blood sample from Adamu? She thought. *This is not the laboratory and there is no equipment nearby.*

"There, my friend," said Enki to an unconscious Adamu. "You will have your mate before long." He stood up, allowing his eyes to roam the garden. "As for you, my little Lilitu," he whispered, "I will send my messengers after you. You will remember me for all eternity, mark my words." Without looking back, he returned to his vehicle. He made a signal to the pilot, and before long, they took off, flying away, into the horizon.

As soon as the aircraft disappeared from view, Lilitu hovered down towards Adamu. He was still unconscious, but she patiently sat next to him and waited.

An hour later, still disoriented, Adamu awoke. Slowly the effect of the drug began to wear off.

"What are you doing here?" he asked with surprise.

"I was here all along," she replied, pointing with her index finger. "Up there."

Adamu looked up. "Oh," he said.

"I heard your conversation with Enki. You told him you tried to force me to lie with you, why?" Her tone was soft.

"I did not expect him to ask so many questions. What should I have said?"

"I have no idea," she said looking into his eyes. "But I know I never taught you to lie."

"I know you never taught me." Adamu shifted his weight nervously. "Why didn't you?" They talked on totally separate wavelengths.

Something in his demeanor told her what he had in mind. "No, Adamu. When I say *lie*, I mean something other than the truth." Her impatient tone changed when she looked down, and saw the appendage between his legs. It was engorged and erect. A warm rush of blood came over her face.

"I want to debase myself with you," he said softly.

Her eyes slowly moved up until their eyes connected. She never felt this before. "It seems to me you still have a lot to learn, Adamu." Her hand reached towards his erection. "But I think this time, perhaps we can learn from each other."

That day, Lilitu gave herself to Adamu.

MARY ANN'S
DILEMMA

FIFTEEN

It was now early morning and the sun was out. As much as Malcolm wanted to continue, he was dead tired. His notepad was almost full. It was time to bring Josh out of the trance. He had a lot of research to do if any of this had any basis in truth, but for now, they needed to get some rest.

Malcolm allowed Josh to transition to a natural sleep, and then he dozed off in his chair.

◆◆•◆•◆•◆•◆•◆

The telephone rang near noon, awaking Malcolm. Josh was already in the kitchen making coffee. He picked up the telephone as Malcolm walked to the bathroom.

"Hi, mom," said Josh, holding the telephone between his head and his shoulder. Two slices of bread jumped out of the toaster. He opened the refrigerator to get butter. "No, everything's fine. Malcolm's in the john right now. You want him to call you when he comes out?" He waited for an answer. "Okay, I'll let him know. Bye… What? Yeah, I'll see ya' at dinner." Josh hung up, and then opened the cupboard to get a small plate for the toast.

Malcolm walked into the kitchen. "That coffee smells good."

"I hope you don't mind the toast. It's a little burned," said Josh as he sat on the chair opposite Malcolm's usual spot.

Malcolm sat and began having breakfast.

Josh calmly waited, but after a few minutes, he blurted out with an impatient "well?"

"I was wondering how long you'd wait before exploding." He laughed as he put the cup down, taking a long-winded breath. "If anything, it was a very interesting night."

"Well, you'll have to tell me, cause I can't remember Jack-shit."

"I must remember to give you a post-hypnotic to make sure you remember next time." Malcolm then proceeded to recount the events of the night.

◆◆◆◆◆◆◆◆◆◆

Josh leaned back on his chair. "Wow!"

"Yeah," replied Malcolm. "I couldn't have said it better myself."

"So what do you think?"

"I need to do some research. Many of those names ring a bell, although I can't quite place some of them. Some of the names did strike a strong chord."

"Mention one, cause I certainly don't recognize any of them," remarked Josh.

"How about '*Elohim*'. Ever heard of it?" asked Malcolm.

"No. Should I have?"

"Have you read the Bible?"

"No," replied Josh. "Never. I'm sorry."

"No need to apologize," said Malcolm leaving his chair and walking toward his bookcase in the next room. "Mythology, modern or ancient, always makes interesting reading."

Josh followed right behind. "I've never heard anyone refer to the Bible as mythology."

Although the shelves were packed with many books, Malcolm knew exactly where each one was. "It all depends from whose point of view you look, doesn't it? *Every* religion is the *only religion*, and all the others are referred to as mythological falsehoods." He grabbed a thick book from one of the shelves, and then sat on a lounge chair next to a small wooden table with a lamp. He held the Bible on his lap. "Come here," he said, pointing to a chair next to him. "Sit down and listen." He opened it to the first page of Genesis and read aloud. *"In the beginning Elohim created the heavens and the earth."*

"Whoa! That's probably just a coincidence."

"Maybe," said Malcolm seemingly deep in thought. "I need to find more about this." He closed the Book as he stood and placed it back on the shelf. "Why don't I take you home and let me see what I find? I'll call you when I have more to go on."

"Okay," said Josh.

◆◆◆◆◆◆◆◆◆◆

Later that afternoon, Malcolm returned from dropping off Josh. In a way, he was relieved that Mary Ann was still at work, although he was certain she would call him before the day was over. The whole thing was incredible and there was no way he could explain it to anyone. Who would believe him?

He turned on his computer and double clicked on his Internet connection. A search for some of those names was called for. One of them, however, was too obvious. Adamu. Now, that was a name to conjure with. He was the first man mentioned in the Bible. The Elohim, at least in the context of Lilitu's story, were Scientists, but in the Bible, Elohim was the name of God. Strange, because the word Elohim is a plural word. If Lilitu's story really happened, then it makes sense how the facts were distorted as it passed from one generation to the next. But how many millennia ago was Lilitu born? Who were some of these people that created Lilitu and Adamu? The legends of Man are full of anthropomorphic gods. What if they were real people and not gods at all? Even if he discovered the truth, who would listen? He didn't care. It was enough for him to know.

Mesopotamia was the logical place to begin his search. The Sumerians founded the first city-states, and most likely invented writing. But that was only 5,000 years ago. This must have happened way before the Sumerians, which meant that the place to look was not in history, but in mythology.

As soon as the Internet connected, he went to his bookmarks and selected google.com. He searched for the name of *Enki*. Several sites came up. He used one referencing "Sumerian Deities".

Enki: god of water, creation, and fertility.

If Enki was a mythological god, then the rest of them were, most probably, gods also. Things were getting interesting.

"Enki created man from the heart of the clay over the Abzu. The Abzu means watery abyss, but it is also the word for semen. He was the keeper of the 'old tablets'."

What tablets? he thought. *The Ten Commandments?* He wondered how many parallels to these gods could be found in other legends. He kept scrolling down the document until he came to the name of Enlil.

"Enlil was the god of earth and king of all the lands. He lorded over all the rest of the gods, except Anu. A strict disciplinarian with a very short temper. The creation of man in response to the Igigi's complaints forged upon him an almost instant dislike for Man. He quickly grew weary of the noisy humans and released several disasters upon them. No sooner would Man recover from one catastrophe, he would release a new one. He appointed one of the lesser gods to terrify mankind,

and sent all kinds of disasters to afflict him, including disease, flood, drought, and the great flood."

Great flood? thought Malcolm. *Is this the flood mentioned in the Bible?* He looked for 'flood' further down the document.

"Enki refused to flood mankind on Enlil's orders, but he was finally coerced. He had no choice but to accede. Enki then goes ahead with the flood, only after advising Atrahasis to build a boat in which to weather the flood."

This was a clear reference to Noah. If he understood correctly, there seems to be a lot of Sumerian mythology in the Bible. This was exciting stuff. He scrolled up the screen and found the name Anu.

"Anu was the god of the sky, father and king of the gods. He lives in heaven. His 'kishru's (shooting stars) have awesome strength."

Those shooting stars, thought Malcolm, *must refer to some sort of weapons, equivalent to Zeus's lightning bolts. How does Lilitu fit into this picture?* He tried another search, and several sites popped on the screen. He clicked on the first one in the list.

"Lilitu was the Sumerian name for Lilith, who according to the Jewish Talmud, was Adam's real first wife. One of the legends says that God created Adam and Lilith as equals, but when Adam wanted to lie with her, she was offended. She refused to lie beneath Adam. Because Adam tried to force her into sex, Lilith, in a rage, flew away from the Garden of Eden. Adam complained to God that Lilith deserted him. God then sent his angels, Senoy, Sansenoy, and Semangelof, to fetch her back. They found her by the Red Sea, a region that was full of demons. They arrived too late, for she had already mated with them.

The angels ordered her to return to Adam, to which she refused. "How can I return to Adam after I have given myself to these demons?" God punished Lilith by ordering her demon children destroyed. Lilith vowed to destroy as many human children as she could. She vowed to seduce sleeping men, during which time she would suck their blood and eat their flesh, taking many forms, including that of 'frightening wolves'.

The name Lilith may have derived from the word 'layil', meaning night. Often she is described as appearing at night as a hairy monster. It is said that Solomon suspected the Queen of Sheba to be Lilith because of her hairy legs."

So much for Gina Lollobrigida, thought Malcolm with amusement.

"After the angels returned with the news that Lilith was not returning, Adam then complained to God that he was lonely. God then created Eve. After the expulsion from Eden, Adam returned to Lilith for a time, since he blamed Eve

for the 'fall'. This short reunion between Adam and Lilith gave birth to demons. Eventually, Adam reconciled with Eve and returned to her."

What had they stumbled into? He had just heard a first hand account; an incredible story of what may have been the real birth of humanity. But it was incomplete. Only Josh could fill in the rest. This was the discovery of a lifetime.

He logged off the Internet and shutdown his system. Doing more research was not going to get him any further. The telephone rang almost immediately. It was Mary Ann.

"Hi, Malcolm," she said. Her tone was amiable but he could sense her apprehension. "I know you're kinda' busy, but I wonder if you could come over for dinner tonight?"

"Is anything wrong?" He believed he knew what she wanted, but asked anyway.

"I just want to talk about Josh and, well… what's been going on."

"Sure. In fact, I was going to call on Josh anyway. What time do you want me to be there?"

"Seven thirty?"

"Fine," he agreed. "I'll see you then."

◆◆◆◆◆◆◆◆◆

The three of them sat awkwardly at the dinner table. No one broke the ice. Malcolm and Josh seemed to be waiting for Mary Ann to say something. Finally, she did.

"I know that there is more going on than either of you is willing to let on, but if you guys won't talk, then I will." Her nervousness betrayed her.

Both Josh and Malcolm tried to put on a *'what are you talking about?'* kind of face, but what Mary did next was unexpected. She went out to the laundry room and came back with a bundle of clothes.

"These," she said as she placed them on the table, "were white blouses, which for some inexplicable reason, are now pink." She stepped back a bit from the table and crossed her arms. "Do you guys want to tell me why?"

Malcolm had no idea what she meant, but Josh knew exactly the cause. He didn't say a word either.

"I also noticed," she continued, "that the clothes washer was not draining properly, so I moved it to take a look at the drain pipe. The floor was wet back there, but it wasn't water." She dug her hand into the bundle and produced plastic bag. From inside the bag, she took out a towel drenched in sticky, clotted blood. Her hands shook uncontrollably. "I used this to wipe under the drainage." She looked at them accusingly. "I know it is not my blood, and it is not Josh's either." Their reaction told her she discovered something important, and they were going to tell her one way or another. "Now, one of you is going to tell me what's going on, or do I need to run away before something happens to me too."

Malcolm and Josh looked at each other. Malcolm leaned forward, placing his hands on his forehead. "Oh, boy," he exclaimed.

"Oh, boy what?" she almost exploded. "Is it, 'oh boy, she found us out?' or is it, 'oh boy, this woman is crazy?' or what?" She pulled back her chair and sat. Leaning forward, she brought he face close to Malcolm's. "I'm waiting," she drawled.

"Mom," said Josh stretching his hand to touch her. "It's complicated."

"Complicated?" Her face turned red, almost as if suddenly her hopes of neither of them knowing the answer were dashed. "Nothing explains this amount of blood without a dead body. Have you killed someone?" she asked Josh. "I'm well aware that if the answer is yes, I'd better start saying my prayers."

Malcolm lowered his hands, opening them in front of him, "wait, Mary Ann. I know you deserve an explanation, and you will get one."

"Oh, I'd better get one fast." Now that she knew they were covering up for something, her tone got more demanding.

"There is a situation here that is going to be hard to explain, and much harder to believe," said Malcolm.

Josh jumped from his chair. "She's not gonna' believe us, man. She never..."

"Josh," said Malcolm raising his voice. "Sit down! Let me handle this."

After a moment of silence, Josh calmed down and sat again. Mary Ann did not say anything. Instead, she decided to let them play it out.

Malcolm looked Mary Ann in the eye. "Something incredible has happened. When Josh came to me with the problem, I didn't believe him either."

"I'm listening," she said nervously.

"Do you know what Astral Projection is?" he asked.

"I've heard of it, but what has that got to do with this?" she nodded towards the bundle of clothes.

"It's got everything to do with this."

Malcolm began to tell Mary Ann of the recent events, but almost halfway through it, when he began to explain the reasons for the blood, she exploded.

"Stop!" she ordered. "You can stop right there! I'm not going to sit here and listen to this bullshit. You think I was born yesterday?" Standing up, she backed away from them. "What crazy ideas have you been feeding my son?"

"Believe me, Mary. If I had known this was going to happen, I would never have even suggested…"

She interrupted him. "I want you to leave my house, now." Her left arm stretched towards the door as she pointed. "Now!"

"Please listen to him," pleaded Josh.

"Listen to some stranger that tells me my son is a murderer?" she yelled.

Josh reacted from the gut at her emotional outburst with emotions of his own as he stood flailing his arms upwards. "NO!" he yelled back with an impossibly deep tone of voice. Her demeanor registered the change as she watched his arms move down fast against the heavy mahogany dinner table. For a second, she saw his face visibly distorting. The force of the blow broke the table in two, as the thundering noise of the breaking wood shocked Mary into immobility. She looked into her son's eyes and they had lost their pupils. They were the deep, crimson eyes of an alien.

Mary Ann fainted.

SIXTEEN

As Mary Ann regained consciousness, she looked at Josh. He was kneeling next to her. Her breath and heartbeat accelerated wildly while she slid backwards on the kitchen floor trying to get away from Josh. The wall behind stopped her feeble attempt at flight.

Malcolm approached her slowly, so as not to upset her further. "It's okay Mary. It's okay. You have nothing to be afraid of." He opened his hands as if to show he meant no harm. "Look, it's only us."

"That creature I saw was not my son," she stated firmly. Then, her eyes fixed on Josh. "Who are you?"

"It is me, mom. Please believe me." He lowered his eyes. "Something has happened to me that's hard to explain. You must listen."

Malcolm offered her his open hand. "Come on, Mary. Let's go to the kitchen and talk."

She hesitated while she looked back and forth from Malcolm to Josh.

Josh moved closer to help her up. "Come on. I'll make you some coffee while you get your bearings."

Her mouth twitched. "I'd rather wake up, if you don't mind." Lifting her arms, she allowed Malcolm and Josh to help her up.

For Mary, nothing could be the same again. Until today, she had all her bases covered and knew what to expect from life, now suddenly her world was torn apart. *What was going on? Who was this monster she thought was her son? It talked like him and looked like him, but was it him?*

They helped her to the kitchen and pulled out a chair from the breakfast table. Looking towards the dining room, she saw the dinner table, split in two over the floor. What had just happened wasn't a dream.

"I want you two to sit away from me," she said.

"Sure Mary," replied Malcolm as he backed away. "Josh, why don't you start the coffee?"

Josh hesitated. He seemed lost, rejected.

"Go on," whispered Malcolm between his teeth. Josh reacted. "Now, Mary try to understand the situation. It's important we stay calm."

"Okay," she said. "What the hell happened back there?" She tried not to look at Josh as she continued. "Is he my son?"

"Yes. I assure you he is." He tried to use his most reassuring tone. His years of experience as a hypnotist taught him well enough how to seduce with his voice. "Let's start over; from the beginning," replied Malcolm. "But this time, listen closely and keep an open mind."

⬥◆⬥◆⬥◆⬥◆⬥

The evening passed slowly. Although the night seemed serene, there was turmoil inside the home of the Sebastians.

"I need more coffee," said Mary Ann.

Josh jumped from his chair to get the pot from the stove. Mary Ann observed him intently as he poured her a fresh cup. It made him uneasy.

"Please don't stare at me," said Josh.

Immediately taking her eyes away, she said, "sorry. I couldn't help it." Her left hand combed her hair in a backward motion as she sighed. "So where do we go from here?" she asked them.

"It all depends," replied Malcolm. "If Lilitu never shows up again, then we're home free."

"Not quite." Mary Ann had already lost most of her fear and distrust of them. "He's already a different person, and we don't even know how much more he's going to change."

"Please don't talk about me as if I wasn't in the room," complained Josh quietly.

"Sorry." Her hand stretched towards his hand until they touched. "But I'm worried that there may have been changes in you that you don't even suspect."

Josh squeezed her hand gently. "Well," he turned to Malcolm. "We can continue what we started last night."

"At this point, I think we should let your mother decide."

Josh and Mary Ann looked at each other for a moment. The truth crossed between them in a flash of understanding.

"This is not her decision," said Josh looking back at Malcolm. "We need to find out how far this has gone."

"And how much further it will go," she added in obvious agreement.

"I was hoping you'd both say that," said Malcolm enthusiastically. "When do we start?"

"Right now. Let's move to the living room. Josh can lie in the sofa," said Mary Ann.

"I'd much rather he use a chair. I want him to be comfortable, but not too much."

"That's fine," replied Josh standing up. "Let's go."

◈–◈–◈–◈–◈–◈

Ten minutes later, they had turned off most lights in the house, except for the dim night-lights shinning from their sockets. Mary Ann sat uneasily on her easy chair; Malcolm sat directly across from Josh. Soon, Malcolm began his hypnotic chant on Josh, and before long, he was deep under.

Suddenly, Josh's body shivered. "She's here!" he said nervously.

"What? That's impossible," said Malcolm. He looked up at Mary; his face clearly said *I don't get it!* "Show me Josh's room, quickly," he told her. Josh remained hypnotized in his chair.

Mary Ann stood and walked briskly up the stairs. "This way." She opened Josh's bedroom door and hit the light switch.

Malcolm slowly studied the room until his eyes came upon the closet door. He opened it. The mirror, propped against the wall, was covered with a pillowcase. After some hesitation, Malcolm pulled the mirror out of the pillowcase. The mirror was covered with paint, just as Josh said he did. They looked at each other somewhat perplexed. He placed the pillowcase back over the mirror and closed the closet door. Mary Ann turned off the bedroom lights before they went back downstairs.

Malcolm entered the living room first, and then sat across from Josh. Mary Ann remained standing.

"Josh, what makes you think she's here?" asked Malcolm.

"I feel her presence. Don't you? Can't you feel the cold?"

He had not noticed it before, but Josh was right. It was colder than usual. "I'm going to ask you to open your eyes and look around the room. If she's here, you will see her, but you're to remain calm. Do you understand?"

"Yes," answered Josh in a monotone.

"Good. Now, slowly open your eyes."

Josh looked behind Malcolm. His face retained an impassive expression as he said, "she's standing behind you."

Malcolm shifted uneasily in his chair, but resisted the temptation to look over his shoulder. "What is she doing?"

"Nothing," said Josh. "She's just looking at me and smiling."

Mary Ann, who stood just behind Malcolm's right shoulder, moved away, closer to Josh. This was alien to her, and it felt like a scene from The Exorcist.

"That's all she's doing?" asked Malcolm.

"There's not much else she can do," continued Josh. "As long as I occupy my body, she can't use it."

"Try to speak to her."

"What do I say?"

"You need say nothing, Josh," said Lilitu. "Only you can hear me, but I seem to be interrupting something." She approached him and caressed his face. "Now what are you up to, if I may ask?" Her tone was playful, as a cat playing with a mouse.

"We want to know more about you," he answered.

"Josh," said Malcolm. "Can she hear us as well?"

"Your friend must be stupid," she said to Josh. Turning towards Malcolm, she stood next to him and shouted in his ear, "of course I can hear you, you dumb ass."

Josh said nothing.

"Well," asked Malcolm again. "Can you ask her if she can hear me?"

"She just yelled the answer in your ear. Yes, she can hear you."

"Good. Then why are you here, Lilitu?" he said, talking to the air.

"Oh, he knows my name." She slowly walked around him, her hand lightly touching his shoulder. "What else does he know?"

"We have been looking into my mind. You left part of yourself in me."

"Looking for what?" she asked casually.

Mary Ann moved further away from them, and sat on a chair across the room. Her eyes fixed on Josh.

"Did she answer?" asked Malcolm.

"She wants to know what we are doing?" replied Josh.

"There's so much we can learn from you. Perhaps we can help each other if we know why you're here," said Malcolm, again addressing the air.

"Tell your friend where I'm standing so I can feel he's looking at me while he talks," said Lilitu.

Josh looked at Malcolm and repeated her instructions as he indicated where she stood.

"It's a shame he can't see me," she continued. "I'm sure he has never seen someone quite as desirable as I."

Josh repeated her words to Malcolm.

"We can try," said Malcolm, a bit unsure, but ready to do what needed to be done. "There's no reason why I can't go into self- hypnosis."

"He's brave. Specially after what I did to him the other night." She moved closer to Malcolm and sniffed his neck. "Hmm, hmm. I think I like him. He's good enough to eat too."

"What did she say, Josh?" asked Malcolm.

"I don't think you want to hear it," said Josh.

"There's an even better way I can talk to him face to face," she said turning to Josh. "Why don't you leave your body for a bit? Let me be the driver so I can show him what a wild ride I can be."

"We already know that," said Josh. "The answer is no. I'll sleep during the day for the rest of my life if I have to." Josh looked at her beautiful body, but was unmoved. He had savored more of her than he wanted; besides, he now knew she was a shape-shifter, and this was only a false outward appearance "I want to know how you got by the paint in the mirror."

"The paint in the mirror? What mirror?"

"The one in my closet. The one you used as a gate to come to this dimension."

Lilitu laughed. "Is that what you thought?" It was a restrained laugh, but her face showed her amusement. "Do you believe I come from another dimension?" she asked. "My dear Josh, I was born here - in this world - before any of your kind, and I'm flesh and blood, just like you."

"No. Not like me."

"I never used the mirror. All I used was simple astral projection, as you call it. I can go anywhere I want. I can see anything I want."

"But you can't do anything you want, is that it? Unless you can actually use a living body, you are nothing but a wandering spirit."

"True. So true."

"Josh," interrupted Malcolm. "What is going on?"

"Wait, Malcolm," said Josh. "I'll tell you in a moment." He continued talking to Lilitu. "Why didn't you come to me two nights ago?"

"Because I wanted a rest, and you needed a rest. Your friends, the ones that came to kill you…"

"You mean Ratface?" interrupted Josh.

"I believe that's what you called him, yes." She smiled wickedly. "They provided more food than I needed for one night. After such a feast, I like to rest."

Josh's hopes of being rid of her were dashed. The mirror solution was too good to be true.

"Josh," continued Lilitu. "Do you know what symbiosis is?"

"Yes, I know what it means. Why don't you try someone else?"

"I told you why I can't. Someone like you only comes around every hundred years or so, if I'm lucky. You'll do fine."

"I'll never let you."

"You think that by never sleeping at night you'll keep me away? Don't be a fool. Eventually you'll forget, and I'll be back in charge. You don't want to make me angry. I can hurt the people you really care about." She looked towards Mary Ann and showed her teeth. "But, if we come to an agreement, I will stop forcing you to go back to the dungeon, and I'll do whatever I need to do far from here. You may even come with me if you like. You might enjoy some of my little idiosyncrasies."

"And how do I live with my conscience with the deaths of all those innocent people you destroy."

"Innocent people? How many *innocents* have I killed so far?" She turned her eyes towards him and looked deep into him. "Think, Josh. How many? Tell me."

Josh remained silent. Innocence was a relative term.

"Well, do we have a deal?" she asked nonchalantly.

Josh brought his hands to his face, as he rested his elbows on his knees.

"What's wrong, Josh? What's the matter," asked Malcolm with concern. Mary Ann stood and crossed her arms as if a sudden current passed through her.

"I need to think about it," said Josh without raising his head.

"Think about what?" asked Malcolm.

Josh stretched his right hand forward and motioned with a *'wait'* gesture to Malcolm.

"I cannot ask for more than that," said Lilitu. "I have been patient for millennia. I can be patient for awhile longer." She looked at Malcolm and Mary Ann. "They seem overly concerned. Tell them not to be."

Her smile was not comforting. Maybe Josh saw more than there was to see, but it didn't make him feel any better.

"I find it strange," continued Lilitu, "that you would rather find out about me using this crude method, when you can simply talk to me."

"If we talk to you, we'd have no way of knowing if you were lying."

"I see you mistrust me still. Then go ahead, do it your way."

"You don't object?" said Josh somewhat surprised.

"I have no choice. You will find an eternity of lifetimes in your subconscious. Probe all you want. It will only show you who I really am. Perhaps then, you will learn to trust me more."

"Perhaps," said Josh. "Can you leave us alone now?"

"I have nothing else to do, but if you insist."

Suddenly, Lilitu's presence, as well as the cold, was gone.

Malcolm looked directly into Josh's eyes. Although he looked perfectly alert, he was still under the trance. "Do you want to continue?"

Before Josh replied, Mary Ann interrupted by turning the lights on. "I'm not sure that is a good idea. This is too new for me and my nerves are about to go to hell, assuming I'm not there already."

Josh reacted to the sudden lights by closing his eyes, but he remained sitting perfectly still.

"We still have a few hours left before sunup," beseeched Malcolm. "Josh can't, under any circumstances, go to bed. We might as well take advantage of the moment. The longer we take, the worse it can get."

"I'm not used to these hours. I'm ready to drop."

"If we allow Josh to fall asleep, it may be the last night for us. We need to find out as much as we can about Lilitu." There was urgency in his request.

Mary Ann didn't take long to consider it. Her own safety did not concern her. Josh needed help and she knew she couldn't stand in the way. She turned down the light switch and went back to her chair.

Malcolm nodded at her, and then turned back to Josh. They began the regression.

LILITU ESCAPES FROM EDIN

SEVENTEEN

Lilitu could ill afford to lower her guard. Until the right time came to help Adamu escape, she kept her eyes and ears open. In the meantime, whenever she needed sleep, she would fly up to a tall tree and rest. Several flight excursions took her to far away places. There was a tall mountain some distance away she decided would be the place to settle, assuming she could manage to release Adamu. The mountain still needed further study since she found a few caves that might prove useful for shelter, but other than that, she had no doubts about the area. At the beginning, she flew out every night, however, once the escape route was settled, there was no reason to visit the site until the moment was right.

The patrolling guards of Edin were not always in full alert, but she could not take the chance they might shoot her down. And that was the problem. Adamu was too heavy to carry; most certainly, he would not be able to simply walk out. Her biggest worry was to get Adamu to the new shelter, while being pursued. She could fly there and avoid detection, but Adamu had to walk through open desert. The prospects of success were slim.

Adamu adapted well to his chores. Every day, for the last six months, small groups of Igigis showed up to till the land and teach Adamu. Adamu was a good pupil. The more he learned, the less often the Igigis came by, until one day, they didn't return. Only the guards moved about to make sure that Adamu did not waste his time sleeping. They watched him, but not close enough to notice Lilitu, just enough to ensure he was aware of their presence.

Enki came by every seven days to talk with Adamu for an hour or two. The only day Adamu was allowed rest. Perhaps because Enki wanted his full attention or perhaps because Enki felt sorry for all the hard labor Adamu was forced into. The Anunnakis may have been capable of compassion, but they rarely showed it. Adamu counted the days by marking by the ground with a stick. When the seventh mark was due, his heart pumped in anticipation.

Seeing Enki was not particularly unpleasant, at least Enki did not treat him badly, but on the seventh day, he could do whatever he wanted. Rebellion never entered his mind. Although Adamu toiled daily from sunup to sundown, and was growing stronger every day, it mattered not. Using brute force against the Anunnakis was inconceivable.

Enlil – Enki's hated brother - on the other hand, seldom came to Edin. From the beginning he disliked Adamu, and spoke harshly to him whenever the fancy struck him. If Enlil had a reason to visit Edin – something he seldom did - it would be to confer with his father Anu, who lived at the peak of a nearby mountain to the east.

For Lilitu finding a place to live, away from the Anunnakis, was only part of her plan. Liberating Adamu was the first step, but finding her way back to the laboratory was of the utmost importance, and that could mean a long wait. Those poor creatures would suffer no more. Of course, the plan might only succeed the first time. After that, the Anunnakis would be on their guard. This meant she had to free as many as she could in one risky undertaking. For now, the cover of night, as well as her timing, was crucial.

⟡◆⟡◆⟡◆⟡◆⟡

Today - the seventh day - Adamu expected Enki, who usually came around in the early morning. Yet nightfall was only a few hours away and he had not come yet. Lilitu hated Enki's presence. He stole precious moments from them. To her, Enki was an unwelcome intruder of the worst kind. Their best moments, the ones she enjoyed the most, were Adamu's days of rest. No one bothered them, except for Enki's short morning visits. Once he was gone, they spoke for hours, made plans, and made love. They waited all day for Enki, while anticipating his early departure, but maybe he was not coming today.

As the sun began its slow descent to the horizon, the loud din of the flying machine stirred them to attention. As always, Lilitu flew to a tall branch from a nearby tree and observed. This time, Enki was not alone. There was another with him, another as naked as Adamu, and just as beautiful.

A few things seemed familiar about the creature that walked alongside Enki. Its resemblance to Adamu was great, but this was a female. Carefully shifting her position on the tree, she lowered herself slightly for a better perspective on them. Adamu pretended to sleep.

"Wake up!" commanded Enki as he approached. "I have brought you something."

Adamu stood, looking immediately at the female. His face turned red when he saw her.

"This is your companion." Enki brought his arm behind the female and pushed her lightly towards Adamu. "You may call her what you will."

Lilitu observed Adamu's reaction very closely. His appendage slowly swelled, just as it did when they lay with each other. It enraged her to see this.

"It is of the utmost importance," continued Enki, "that, from now on, you take care if ever my brother visits Edin."

"Why is that, Master?" asked Adamu, his eyes not leaving the female for a second.

"You must learn to hide your desire for her when he comes. And I guarantee you that he will visit you." Enki paused. "Adamu, look at me when I speak!" he commanded.

Adamu reacted as if he had just been slapped. Enki did not usually raise his voice.

"When Enlil found out I was making this female for you, he was not happy." Enki walked closer to the tree and leaned against it. "But the Elohim are under my command, not his."

"Do you mean that Master Enlil does not know?"

"He does, yet that is not your concern. She is here to help you with your work, and will do whatever you teach her. Whatever else you decide to do with her is unimportant."

"May I lay with her, Master?"

The female simply stood there. Most of what they said was beyond her comprehension. One thing she did seem to understand. Her eyes fixed themselves upon Adamu's erect penis.

Lilitu felt uncontrollable anger overwhelming her.

Enki smiled wide. "Of course. She knows what to do. Just don't let Enlil know you did, don't let him see you excited, and least of all, that I said so." He straightened himself and began to walk away. "You must never forget he does not like you."

Lilitu closely followed Enki with her eyes. She could ill afford to climb down the tree until he was gone. The moment she saw Enki enter his vehicle and fly away, she looked upon Adamu and the new female. Without wasting a moment, Adamu already laid with the creature.

A primeval scream escaped from Lilitu's entrails. The shrillness of her voice reached the perimeter, alerting the guards to her presence. The sound of the guard's boisterous approach through the trees and shrubs told her how little time there was to escape. Now that Adamu betrayed her, Lilitu had no reason to stay. She wanted to fly away and never return. Yet there was still something she needed to do. Crouching to position, her wings extended outwards. A low growl escaped her when she pushed herself downwards. The growls' intensity moved up in pitch as her wings caught the air giving direction to her glide. As the surprised couple looked upwards, she dove faster and in a swift maneuver, defecated on their faces. The expression on Adamu's face as it was splattered with her copious discharge, somehow compensated for the pain he caused her.

By now, flight was second nature to Lilitu. She quickly swooped upwards and northwards, towards the perimeter. As the guards spotted her above the treetops, they shot at her, but it was easy to avoid their fire. Using a slight side-to-side variation in flight pattern she got away. Before long, she was out of sight.

It was getting dark and it became imperative to put her second plan in motion. Until now, the Anunnakis had no idea where she was. After today, they would surely go into high vigilance.

Once she disappeared from the guards' view, far in the horizon, she turned ninety degrees west, towards Enki's laboratory. There were some friends that needed her help.

The complex that comprised Enki's property was quiet. A few guards were stationed around key areas of the enclosure - outside, there were two by the gate, and one on each corner; an identical arrangement on the inside. Some of the guards dozed off on their posts, which suited her fine. If she could manage to steal away all their experimental animals without making a sound, the guards would be put to death, which suited her fine also. Several lampposts around the enclosure, one located near each of the guards and one between each post, made it easy to see anyone trying to get in by foot, but no one expected an intruder from above. Flying in was easy. The problem was that not all the creatures she planned on liberating could fly. She needed to prepare their way out in advance.

Behind the laboratory – outside, near the wall - large containers and empty boxes could be used to jump over. Silently, she moved a few of them around, until they formed easy steps to climb over. Then she quietly flew to the nearest lamppost and disabled it. Quickly hiding on top of the wall, she waited for a reaction from the guards. None came. They slept soundly through their watch as she snickered at their stupidity. Everything was ready for their escape. The darkness of the night would cover their tracks.

'Some gods these are,' she thought with amusement.

The laboratory itself was usually unguarded and unlocked. There was no reason to, since no one living on Enki's property would dare do anything out of place. Lilitu slid down the wall, approaching the back door. Now was the crucial moment. If the creatures reacted excitedly, the plan would explode in her face. Without turning on the lights, she slid inside and whispered towards the line of cages. The words were unimportant, since the majority of them did not speak her language. Her manner was the key. She was well aware of the tones they used amongst themselves; the whisper of secrecy was one they all knew well.

Some of the cages rattled slightly. They were awake. Lilitu knew many of their sounds, and learned some of their basic communication while she herself was caged. Emitting a low growl, followed by a purring sound, she got their attention. Slowly, Lilitu approached one of the windows, opening it slightly, enough to allow some moonlight inside the laboratory. They creatures held on to their cage doors; something was up. Most of them were new to the group, but some of them still remembered Lilitu. She was not one of their hated torturers.

From that moment, their communication was pure body language. The creature in the first cage near the door, held on to the bars by the lock. It sat quietly, closely observing Lilitu's every move. As Lilitu unlatched the lock, the creature – which looked like a small simian with short red horns – touched her hand. Lilitu stopped to look at it. Their eyes met for what seemed like a long time. She smiled compassionately; the creature smiled with reverence. Somehow, they all knew what she was here for.

The simian climbed down from its cage. Moving very quietly, and without verbal communication, each one released moved on to the next cage to free another. Before long, they all huddled near the door, waiting for a cue from Lilitu. Their number counted over one hundred, and none made a sound.

Lilitu slowly opened the back door. Bringing one finger up to her lips, she tiptoed backwards as she indicated to them the universal signal for silence. With hand signs, she indicated what she wanted them to do next; they quickly understood. As the first few jumped over the wall, Lilitu flew up and over.

The escape route was clear in her mind, but they had to act fast. Herding close together at the other side, they followed her lead walking towards the east. It was a long trek, but the safest one. Soon, hills and mountains would help cover the group, and quite a group it was. All sizes and shapes stuck together like glue, as a fellowship of sorts emerged among them. The stronger ones would carry the smallest and weakest when their step faltered.

❋◆❋◆❋◆❋◆❋

Several hours later, shortly before the sun was up, they reached the shelter of a small cave. Lilitu decided to stay there for the rest of the day. If anything were certain, the Anunnaki soldiers would be out in a frenzied search for the rest of the day, and a few night guards would be executed.

The one thing she forgot was food. Fruit was the only food they knew; yet these mountains were bare. They could survive for only a short while, unless she found them a source of food and water. None of the creatures, however, complained once. They cuddled against each other and slept as best they could throughout the rest of the day. Although the sun shone bright outside, inside the cave it remained cool.

Occasionally, they heard the din of their flying machines. They flew back and forth from east to west; awaking some of the creatures, but the intensity of the pursuit only strengthened their resolve to escape. Nightfall came, and for a short while longer, the machines continued their search. Lilitu enjoyed every second. The Anunnakis underestimated every other living creature so much, that she was sure they must have been totally lost as to their whereabouts. An hour after nightfall, the search was called off.

It was time to get food. She selected the strongest and biggest of them that could fly for a short excursion to Edin. If each one could carry three or four fruits, there would be enough to feed them all, at least for the night. Once their hunger was taken care of, she would take them to their final destination. Talking to the group in short phrases, she hoped that soon they could communicate more thoroughly.

A selection of about thirty-three - including Lilitu - flew in a somewhat disorganized formation, somehow managing to keep out of each other's flight path. Once they reached Edin, she took them to the most fruitful parts of the orchard to eat their fill. They were quiet, going about their meals quickly. Lilitu was careful not to let them make a mess, since she was sure this was not going to be their last time. If the guardians suspected their presence, they might not survive the next meal. For a weak moment, Lilitu thought about Adamu. Then she remembered his betrayal. She needed to put him out of her mind. While the group ate their fill, she kept busy by scattering the seeds they dropped.

Their flight back was uneventful, as each creature carried enough food for the ones that hungrily waited. But time was of the essence, and before the middle of the night, the group left the cave, continuing to move towards the spine of mountains that would be their home. By air, Lilitu could get to their destination in two hours; on foot, it could take a couple of days. The ones that could fly took turns forming an air-guard several feet above the group. The next stop had to be scouted ahead of time, so Lilitu selected the most communicative of the flyers and pointed out the general direction they needed to follow. It was a mid-sized bat-like creature with a six-foot wingspan. The creature understood her signals perfectly as it proudly took their temporary leadership while Lilitu flew ahead.

❖◆❖◆❖❖◆❖

The moon shone over the mountains, giving Lilitu enough light to determine their next stop. If they could get there before sunrise, they would be safe for another day. She flew down, towards the entrance to a cave that seemed safe and well hidden. Her landing was soft and quiet. Cautiously, she stood outside the entrance looking in. There was something inside the cave, and that something looked back. Its eyes shone from the darkness, staring, unmoving. They needed this shelter, and she could not allow losing it; yet, fear was getting the best of her. The creature inside also smelled of fear. This was a standoff. Not able to see inside the cave, Lilitu stepped closer, but not too close. She needed room to react, in case the thing suddenly lunged at her.

A low warning growl reverberated inside the cave. Not a good sign. Signs of labored breathing came from the cave; perhaps it was wounded. Bending slowly, Lilitu picked up a rock; one way or the other, she had to force it out of the cave. It was a matter of survival, the life of one against the life of all the others she felt responsible for. Taking careful aim at the floating eyes, she threw the rock with a full swing. It hit home as the thing inside roared in pain. The reaction froze her to the spot. The sound of suffering was too familiar, making her feel dirty and cruel. She was no better than the Anunnakis.

Lowering her head in shame, she decided to fly away. As she turned away, the creature jumped out and attacked her; its mouth displayed its long fangs when it went for her throat.

EIGHTEEN

The force of the creature's body slammed her against the ground. The creature bit hard, but Lilitu grabbed its mouth before its fangs tore her throat apart. This was a struggle for life and every muscle in her body strained to get the upper hand. Each second seemed endless. The creature countered with its claws and talons. Lilitu, however, had weapons of her own. On its first attempt to dig into her, as it missed, her knees turned upwards, catching the creature's belly. She pressed hard, digging deep. Tearing downwards, her talons caught its penis and testicles, taking them clean off. The creatures' jaws opened with a cry, dropping its weight on top of her. Although it pinned her to the ground, it was already too disabled to continue the struggle. Its blood and guts spilled over from its opened stomach.

Lilitu was badly hurt. Blood seeped slowly from her jugular. Her body was also severely cut. If she wanted to survive the night, getting out from under the creature's heavy carcass was imperative. Only her left arm and leg were free. The creature still breathed, panting slowly, laboriously.

Trying to push the creature off, she reared her free leg, but a sharp pain shot through her; she was more hurt than she thought. Her breathing grew worse, since the weight of the beast pressed hard on her right breast. Moving sideways, she faced the front of the creature, placing her left hand over its chest. This was going to be tricky. To free herself, she had to push it away with her left arm as she pulled the right arm from under it.

The moment her hand pushed at its chest, the creature let out its last breath. A hot, humid blast of foul air escaped its lungs straight into Lilitu's face, but its body weight shifted slightly, giving her the chance to pull away from under it. As she did, a stronger explosion of pain rendered her unconscious.

❖◆❖◆❖◆❖

She woke up inside a cool, dry cave. When she tried to get up, a soft hand pushed her back on an improvised leafy bed. Several pairs of eyes hovered above her. Somehow, she assumed, the creatures she helped escape had found her. She tried to sit up one more time, but was too weak to move. A hand, or what looked like a hand, softly caressed her face. As she looked up, she saw a creature with a long nose that resembled a bird's beak, but this was no bird. Its eyes, set to the front, had very expressive eyebrows. It smiled at Lilitu, managing to disarm her desire to get up.

"How long have I been...?"

Bringing a finger to her lips, the creature shushed her. It took a piece of fruit from an empty coconut shell, and placed it in Lilitu's mouth. Her hunger took over, making her forget any other questions or considerations. The creature shooed away the others that milled around the makeshift bed, then continued to feed Lilitu.

Days went by before Lilitu was finally able to sit. The bird-like creature continued to nurse her as she lost and regained consciousness.

"I want to thank you for taking care of me," said Lilitu when the creature offered her a fresh piece of fruit. Lilitu looked into the creature's eyes trying to find a link of understanding. The creature, upon feeling Lilitu's scrutiny, lowered its eyes. "What I am saying is probably gibberish to you, isn't it?" continued Lilitu. She stretched her hand towards the creature's face, touching it tenderly.

The creature closed its eyes, enjoying Lilitu's touch. "I understand," it said.

Lilitu's withdrew her hand in surprise. "You understand what I just said?"

"Some," replied the creature. "I have good ears. Masters talk much while in cage."

Of course, thought Lilitu. She underestimated them also, just like the masters did to all creatures. A mistake she would try not to repeat. "You have a name?" She asked with a smile.

"Azazel."

"Azazel?" asked Lilitu.

"Master Enki name me that. He say it means 'creature from the wilderness'. Said I belong in wilderness and promised one day to take me there."

"Master Enki spoke to you?"

"When you left, I help in laboratory."

"When I left?" Lilitu looked towards the entrance of the cave. It was day. "Where am I?" she asked.

"Inside cave where you almost die," replied Azazel.

Lilitu sighed, remembering the struggle with the beast. A slight pain in her neck brought her right hand to touch it. Something was wrong. Her neck was bandaged. She looked at her body, noticing one of her legs and the right side of her torso were also bandaged. For a moment, she felt panicky. Did any of these creatures fly back to the laboratory to get bandages?

"Where did you get these?" asked Lilitu indicating her dressings.

Azazel fidgeted, hemming and hawing while shifting on her feet. She was hiding something.

"Don't tell me you risked going back?" she said leaning forward. "Don't you know they're looking for us? They'll destroy the whole lot of you when they do."

Suddenly, someone stepped from out of the shadows and approached Lilitu. "Some of us are not as bad as you think, Lilitu."

She looked up and almost fainted at the sight. "Master Enki!" When she recognized him, her eyes instinctively avoided his gaze.

"I see you're feeling better now," he said with satisfaction.

Her adrenaline system took over as she readied herself for another fight – in her present state however, it was a fight she would surely lose. But she was not going to be a slave any longer and was willing to die for it. Raising her eyes to meet his, she defied him. "Are you here to take me back or to kill me outright?"

"I am here to do neither," said Enki a bit upset at her boldness.

"Master Enki take care of you," interrupted Azazel. "Me not know what to do. He come and cure you."

Lilitu's eyes narrowed with suspicion as she looked from Azazel to Enki. "Why?" she asked. "And where are the rest of my people?"

"Your people, is it? Is that what you call them now? Your people?" Enki approached Lilitu's leafy bed and sat next to her. "Your people are safe. Some of them are here, since they did not want to leave you."

"And the rest?"

"The rest continued their journey to wherever it was you sent them. They are establishing a colony of sorts, but are waiting for you to join them. As soon as you are well enough, of course."

"You still haven't answered my first question. Why?"

"There are many things that my brother and I disagree with. By challenging him, I have become his Satan. In a way, I am on the verge of becoming an exile, just like you."

"His Satan?"

"His adversary. He considers me his enemy."

"That means he wants to kill you too."

Enki laughed. "Not, not yet. But the way things are going it may soon come to that. When that happens, I need to know if I can count on you."

"You want me to fight on your side?"

"You catch on quickly. Yes, when the moment comes. For now, you need to recover. Get your strength back," he said as he stood up. "It's beginning to get dark now and I must be going. We can't risk their knowing where you are."

"I don't hear their flying machines."

"They gave up the search a few weeks ago."

"A few weeks ago?" asked Lilitu surprised. "How long have I been out?"

"Quite awhile now. It took a lot of effort to bring you back from the dead, if you know what I mean. You had lost a lot of blood by the time I found you, and I couldn't very well take you back to my house lest they kill you."

"I lost blood?"

"Ah," said Enki. "That is the secret of life. Blood is life; the precious liquid that runs inside you as red and bright as the passions that make you what you are." He paused at the cave entrance and approached her again. "By the way, why *did* you leave Edin? You could have had it good there."

"Life as a slave is not good. Not even in paradise."

"I thought you liked Adamu."

"He betrayed me," she said with anger.

"Betrayal is such an ugly word. I gave him a powerful drive to procreate. Too powerful, now that I think about it." He laughed. "Well, anyway, he's no longer there, either; he's now wandering in the desert."

"What do you mean?"

"Enlil expelled them from Edin."

"Why? How?" asked Lilitu in disbelief.

"It seems my brother suspected I was up to something since he has been against this project from the beginning. He ordered me to make sure they would not be able to procreate. I agreed to comply with his wishes, but my mind was already made up."

Enki knelt to Lilitu's eye level. "Now why did he think I would do such a stupid thing? Man was my creation. I made him with my own two hands. What possible reason did Enlil have to forbid such a thing? He hates Adamu, for he carries my genes; he also hates all my creations. He hates all of you. Now, he hates me too. You can all procreate and there's nothing he can do about it."

"Yes he can," replied Lilitu. "He can kill us all."

"And I'm sure he'll try. But you should have seen his face," Enki said laughing again. "He asked me to accompany him to Edin just to check on Adamu – he must have suspected something. When we got there, Adamu was in the middle of intercourse with Eve. He was aroused, so he tried to hide."

Enki went into storytelling mode as he pompously imitated Enlil.

"Where are you, Adamu? Why are you hiding? asked Enlil."

"I'm here, Master, Adamu replied from behind a bush."

"And where is Eve? continued Enlil."

"She's here with me, Master."

"Come out where I can see you."

"Master, said Adamu, *we are naked."*

"Now that was funny. We are naked indeed!" continued Enki, obviously amused.

"Did you lie with this woman? Who said you were naked? asked Enlil as his patience grew thinner."

"Adamu then went crazy with fear as he pointed a finger at Eve."

"She did, Master. She did."

"Then Eve turns around and points towards me. I'm just standing there listening to all this and can't believe my ears."

"You don't deserve my confidence, Enlil said to me. *From this day on you shall grovel at my feet. I shall soon see you crawl before me. Count on it."*

"Of course, he didn't dare destroy them or attack me right then and there. I had my personal guard standing behind me – a precaution I always take where my brother is concerned. Then he turned to Eve."

"I hope every child you have from this day on will cause you excruciating pain. And you, you ingrate, he said to Adamu, *do you believe you are one of us? I am your god and will not be disobeyed. Take your woman with you and leave this place at once. Let's see you try to grow anything in the desert. You'll water the plants with the sweat of your brow and I'll be there to enjoy every minute of it. And if you try to come back, I'll make sure my guardian angels kill you."*

At this moment, the sun came out from the East. Mary Ann was fast asleep. Malcolm allowed Josh to continue into natural rest and went to the couch to lie down.

LILITU'S REQUEST

NINETEEN

"Well, Josh," asked Lilitu. "Did you find what you were looking for?"

Josh reacted nervously. "What are you doing here? I thought you couldn't venture out in daylight." He was asleep, but his astral body floated near his feet in the middle of the living room. Lilitu stood naked in front of him.

"Only when I'm inside a human body," she said nonchalantly. Her face wore a slight smile as her eyes surveyed the living room. "I can't stand the sun then."

"So, some of the vampire legends are true."

"Perhaps. However, there is a disease among humans called Porphyria, which is probably closer to the truth. Or it could be a reaction of the human body attempting to reject my alien presence. I don't really know, but it's a horrible sight when the sun triggers the effect that kills my host."

"But not you."

"But not me." She smiled wickedly.

"What do you want now? Can't you leave me alone?" This game seemed to have no winner except Lilitu.

"You interest me." As she spoke, she floated towards Josh's mother, apparently not paying much attention to Josh's replies.

"Tell me something I don't know." Josh kept his eyes on her, worried about Malcolm and Mary Ann, but knowing there was nothing Lilitu could do while in her astral form. "I want to know how to get rid of you."

"I have been in a state of living death for too long and seen more about humans than I care to see. I need your help."

This was an unexpected turn. Was she playing games? He needed to find out. "Go ahead. Talk."

"For someone so young, you have managed to impress me." Taking her eyes off Mary Ann, she looked at him. The room was in semi-darkness, which made her flaming-red eye sockets shine brighter.

"If I didn't know you had all the time in the world, I would say that you waste your time trying to butter me up." Josh didn't trust her, and his attitude clearly showed it.

"I'm not trying to - as you say - butter you up." Josh's imagery amused her. She floated away from Mary Ann, moving closer to Malcolm. "Of all the humans I have dealt with, you're the first that does not care about what I have to offer."

"And that is?"

"An extended lifetime, for one." Her left hand rested over the easy chair Malcolm occupied.

"Oh, haven't you heard, the whole reason why I got into this mess to begin with? I'm depressed and sick of life."

"Yes, but only because you were powerless, but that time is past. You have only seen a small part of my gift. I can give you so much more in exchange for a favor."

"You say I'm the first that is not interested in what you have to offer. I can't believe that."

"It is true. Power is difficult to resist, and that, my dear Josh is something all humans want." Her hand slipped over the chair's headrest, lightly combing Malcolm's hair.

"Except me?"

"Maybe." Lilitu floated closer to Josh, but avoided touching his astral body. "Humans are a plague to this world. A virus. An infection. You are worse than the pus oozing out of a diseased lesion. Your kind destroys. There is no cohabitation between you and anything else that lives. You don't allow for it. Even within your own species, hate is a way of life. Your history books are not of good deeds, but of deaths and wars. You have refined blood spilling to a fine science, or worse yet, a religion. Your history books venerate the worst offenders of all. The Hannibals, the Alexanders, the Hitlers, the Stalins, the Duvaliers, and those are only some of the obvious ones. For the most part, it's a petty species. Most humans contemplate upon the altar of human sacrifice – as long as it's someone else's sacrifice – then you have the gall to pray for trivialities. While other humans suffer tortures and hunger, you pray for some god to come fix your miserable little life for you. What do men in power do? Nothing, except spill more blood, preferably the blood of your own kind. But the rest of you, the little people, what do you do? Even less. Hurting your fellow humans in any way seems good enough for most."

Josh moved slowly away from her.

"You are the image of your creators," Lilitu continued, "inheriting their worst genetic attributes. Man has always wanted to know the nature of the god or gods that created them. Don't look any further than your own souls. You are what you are because you came from someone exactly like you." She moved back towards Malcolm and touched his head with both hands. "You believe this man is good, don't you? He might be, but chances are that given the right circumstances he would jump at the chance for power. Power he would use to destroy and dominate others. The same power I offer and you so easily dismiss."

"Why don't you give it to him?" asked Josh.

"Because I can't," she said letting go of Malcolm. "I cannot jump into any body I choose. My choices are limited. The same way you cannot indiscriminately transfer blood from one human to another, or transplant a body part to another, I cannot transfer my essence. I could not force it if I tried a hundred times. It would only hurt my intended host enormously, and me specially."

"You mentioned a favor."

"I want to die." Her eyes looked straight into Josh. There was no way to read her expression. This might have been a poker game and Josh would end up losing.

"I thought you were dead. I have seen your body and it looks plenty dead to me."

"The Anunnakis did not kill me. When the war of the 'gods' began, I reluctantly took sides with their adversary. I don't know why I decided to help him, because I hated him then, and I hate him even now."

"You mean Enki?" asked Josh.

"So, you have unlocked more of my secrets. That's very good. Should I assume that you know everything?"

"No, just part of the beginning."

"You have no idea of what you believe you have discovered. How many lifetimes do you think I have lived? Fifty? A hundred? A thousand?"

"I suspect you want to tell me," said Josh.

"One lifetime in this pigsty of a world is more than any creature should be subjected to."

"Why didn't you ask any of your previous victims for help?"

"Unfortunate word, victim. None of my hosts saw themselves as such. That's why you intrigue me. I did ask, however, and it was always a waste of time. Well, not always. I almost convinced one of them; at least I thought I did, but he fooled me. I should have known better than to trust such a one."

"So, if the Anunnakis didn't kill you, then what?"

"They imprisoned me. You may have seen my inanimate body, but I am not dead. Your gods were crueler with me than with most others. Can you imagine what it is like to be entombed alive for eons, not able to live or die?" Her rage showed through the brightness of her crimson eyes. "The mind, however, has no bounds. I escaped." Her tone lowered, drifting away to a whisper.

"Not quite," said Josh with some sarcasm. "You're still a prisoner."

"Yes!" Her voice boomed bitterly. "I am still a prisoner, but I am also here."

"As a helpless roaming spirit. You call that escape?"

"You do not want to upset me, Josh," she warned. "I asked for your help, but not because I am helpless. All it takes to make your life miserable is a moment of carelessness on your part. I would destroy everything and everyone you ever cared for; and after that, I would stand in the sun and let your body burn."

"That would kill you too."

"Unfortunately, no; I tried it long ago with a specially loathsome host that never should have been born. My astral body cannot be destroyed. But yours would roam the Earth for eternity. No peace or death for you." Her aura changed to a light pink as she continued, "but I do not want it to be this way. You must believe me."

"You said one of them fooled you. In what way?"

"Why do you ask? Do you believe you can outsmart someone who has managed to survive several million years? You pathetic little creature."

"Someone has already done that. It seems we are not so dumb after all."

"Yes. Once, and only once. There was a part of him I was never able to read. He was cunning, that one."

She revealed more than Josh expected. If she did it on purpose remained to be seen. "Since I can go back into your life, why don't we save time," said Josh. "Tell me."

"I can be just as selective with what I leave in you. Nevertheless, there's not much to tell. I revealed the hiding place of my physical body to this human monster with the promise that he would destroy it. Instead, he took it to his castle and kept it there."

"Human monster?"

"Is there any other kind?" she added.

"I don't understand. What keeps your body preserved?"

"The chamber. He did not just take my body. He took the glass coffin and buried it deep under his castle - the glass enclosure is what keeps me alive. Upon exposure to air, my body will decompose rapidly. I would finally die. Now, there's no easy access to my entombed body. He took care of that."

"Why didn't you punish him as you continually say you'll punish me?"

"He kept promising he was going to help, but not until I bestowed him with all my powers. I eventually grew tired of waiting, so one day, while I was still in his body, I stood outside and waited until the sun came out."

"You killed him."

"He is still around," said Lilitu as she faced Josh. She wanted to see his reaction. "Oh, not in body, but in spirit. He avoids me, of course, because I can cause him excruciating pain if I feel like it. Occasionally I look him up for my own amusement. He thought he was a Tiger and I showed him he was a pussycat. I have not looked him up in the last hundred years. Perhaps I should pay him a visit."

"Where is this castle?" asked Josh.

"You are going to do as I ask?"

"If I do decide to help you," said Josh hesitatingly. "And I'm not saying I will, you must promise me not to continue murdering people."

"That," replied Lilitu, "I cannot promise. I need sustenance for my form to take expression when I possess you. Manifesting through another body is the only relief I get for my solitude. Otherwise, I will be damned to live an eternal state of simulated death. No, I cannot promise you that. But I am willing to compromise."

Josh listened quietly as she spoke.

"Since I can remember, I have been quite selective in my meals."

"Please," pleaded Josh. "You're going to make me sick."

"For a species as cruel and inhuman as yours, you want to deny the most basic instinct of living." She studied Josh for a moment, realizing that it was crucial to get her point across without upsetting him. "Very well. If you insist, but I don't know how else to put it. When I said selective, I meant not to simply choose the first human I see. The ones that my host perceives as their enemies are my first choice. It seems to make things more palatable." She smiled lightly at the unintended pun. "And I don't need continual sustenance either. For me it's always been a matter of survival; for my hosts, it was always for pleasure; theirs, not mine. If I told you some stories about my previous hosts, you would soon see who is the monster."

"You told Malcolm that you have written much of our history with no one the wiser."

"If you dig deep enough, you can discover all of me and all of my hosts. They are part of you now, as I am. Even after you destroy my body, we will be with you until the day you die."

"Then I will never be rid of you."

"No. You will be rid of me, but my memories will always be with you. As you gain my powers, you will become more like me. How monstrous you turn out to be, is up to you – it will only be your kind that suffers. Evil is not part of my equation. That is something humans bring with them."

"So you think killing is not evil?"

"When you eat a cow, do you feel evil? It certainly feels that way if you happen to be the cow."

"That's all we are to you. Cattle."

"I am not human - although I show more respect for other species than your species shows even for its own - and I only try to eat bad cows. Unfortunately, so far, all of my hosts have been good examples of human excrement. The things they did were never under my control."

"Yes, but you gave them your powers."

"I gave them nothing. I simply happened. As it is happening to you."

"Will I end up looking like you?"

"No, but you will be able to shape-change as you please long after I'm gone." She paused as she observed his face. "I see you like the idea."

Josh turned away from her stare. "I can't make this decision alone. I need some time."

"You want time to think about it? Why?" She was perplexed.

"Look, trust doesn't grow on trees, and to be honest, I don't trust you."

"I am not going to allow your lack of confidence to upset me," she said with a frown.

"From the looks of it, I'd say you are upset, but we are not going to let that get in the way, are we?" Josh saw his mother get up from the couch. She walked towards the kitchen. "I don't want you back until tomorrow. I'll let you know my decision."

"Very well. I'll go."

"And don't try to sneak in because I can feel your presence."

"Josh. Do not push me," she said as she left the house.

The smell of fresh coffee and toast awoke both, Josh and Malcolm. It was two-thirty in the afternoon.

TWENTY

Josh and Malcolm sat at the kitchen table, while Mary Ann stood by the kitchen sink. Not much of a conversation passed between them. Lilitu's proposition was tossed around for a while, but they had decided it was a bad idea to allow Lilitu back in. Nothing in Josh's regressions showed them she was not what she claimed, but caution was necessary. It was better to keep using hypnosis until they were sure Lilitu could be trusted. Maybe they could find a way out of this without allowing another possession.

Mary Ann looked out the kitchen window. "Josh," she said. "Your girlfriend is outside." She turned back to Josh. "Do you think it's wise to have her here?"

"Mom, she knows what's going on."

"How come I'm always the last to know anything about you?" she said as she threw the dishwasher towel in the sink.

"Don't get upset again. When we tried to tell you last night, you didn't react very well. Remember? You want me to trust you with my secrets, you must learn to trust me."

Mary Ann looked sadly at Josh. "Yeah. I guess you're right." She approached Josh as he got up from the table and embraced him. "I'm sorry."

Josh kissed her cheek. "Let me get the door," he said as he moved towards the foyer. He hesitated a bit before opening. He wasn't sure he wanted to jeopardize any more lives. He finally opened it.

"Hi, Josh," said Janet. "Can I come in?"

"Sure," he replied as he opened the door wider. "You look much better."

"Yeah. I feel better."

"How are things at home?"

"Well, mom's not doing real well. We've put a restraining order on dad, but you know how those things work. Anyway, he'll be out of our hair for a bit. Mom's a frail little woman, and is deadly afraid of what dad can do to her."

"But he's in jail, isn't he?" asked Josh.

"Sure, but they'll have to let him out sometime. That's what's got us worried. We've decided to move out, change our names." Janet leaned against the doorframe bringing her hands up to her face as she began to cry. "I don't know what to do?"

"Okay, okay," said Josh as he took passed his arm over her shoulder and nudged her inside. "Let's go to the kitchen and have a cup of coffee or something. Mom and Malcolm are here."

"Oh, I should go home then."

"Don't be silly. It's okay. Come on."

They shuffled their way into the kitchen. Janet did her best to clear up her tears.

"Hello, Mrs. Sebastian."

"Hi, Janet. Hey, are you okay?" she asked concerned as she approached Janet.

"I'm fine. I'm fine," replied Janet with a weak smile.

"Would you like a soda or maybe coffee?" asked Mary Ann.

"Soda will be fine, thanks."

At this point, Malcolm said, "I'll be going home for a quick shower and some research. I'll be back tonight."

"Malcolm," said Mary Ann. "Under the circumstances, you should feel free to bring some clothes and stay with us. We have a spare room you can use."

"Okay. Let's try that route. I'll be back around eight."

"You're welcome to come for dinner if you like."

"What time, then?"

"Seven-thirty?" she said.

"Good. I'll see what information I can find that might be of use to us. Can you stay up late again tonight?"

"I have to call my office Monday morning. I have some sick days and some week's vacations I can use. I'll give them some excuse so they don't expect me."

"Excellent," said Malcolm as he prepared to leave. "Nice meeting you, young lady," he said as her stretched his right hand towards her. "I've heard many good things about you."

"Thanks. I've heard about you too."

"Good things, I hope." Without waiting for an answer, he walked towards the door and left.

Mary Ann Looked at Janet and said, "make yourself at home. I have a few errands to run, so I'll see you guys later." She walked upstairs for a quick change of clothes, and then came back down again. "All right, I'll be back in an hour."

GILLES DE RAIS

TWENTY-ONE

Lilitu felt curious about her previous host, the one who liked to call himself *The Black Baron*. She had not tried to find him for the past hundred years or so. Maybe it was time to check on him; give him a little something to remember her by for the next few years.

Astral travel is extremely fast. All she had to do was think about where she wanted to go and her astral body would traverse the distance at several times the speed of sound. Lilitu was no scientist and not one to be curious about irrelevant details. If something worked, it's all she needed to know. No philosopher, she, although she met with some of the greatest; no intellectual, yet she had talked with the best. Opinionated fools all of them, wasting their lives away on useless pursuits and stupid ideas.

A few minutes after she thought about Gilles' castle- if such it could be called - in the French Alps she was transported there. It was worse than she remembered, gloomier, more menacing. This was the reason why she avoided the area where her body lay; it was a lifeless, depressing place.

The castle stood at the top of a crag. On the north side, the sheer drop from its walls to the bottom of the cliff measured over four thousand feet. On the south side, the drop was a little less, but it ended in a flowing river. The only way to the fortress was via a sister cliff, using a spiraling narrow road. At the end of the road, a drawbridge connected both cliffs to the fortress gate. The place was in ruins and unused for centuries, forgotten by history and shunned by man. A gloomy mist usually covered the top of the cliffs, and the only things living there were bats, rats, and an occasional wolf. Somewhere deep inside that crag lay Lilitu's body, and the only way in was through the citadel itself. Even in its prime, it was never a spectacular work of architecture, but it served its purpose.

Once one of the richest men in Europe, Gilles clandestinely had this hidden shelter built for an emergency; knowing his lifestyle of witchcraft, necromancy, and human sacrifice could not be kept secret forever. He managed to build it as far from Rennes as possible, on a mountain in the Southern Alps of France, a long trek away, but a necessary one. After the authorities caught him on October 25, 1440, he was excommunicated; the following day they marched him to the gibbet, and there garroted. After that, his corpse was placed on a pyre; but his relatives were allowed to remove his body before the flames reached it. Most were lead to believe he was interred in the nearby Carmelite church. The truth is he did not die that day.

Much of the fortification was carved out of the mountainside. The inner ward – or courtyard – was small, as well as the gatehouse. Once the drawbridge was up, no man or beast could get across. Although not a fortification made for defense, its impregnability was guaranteed by its sheer inaccessibility and secrecy.

As Lilitu drew closer to the gate, she noticed some unusual activity, human activity. What she saw transported her a few centuries into the past, when men walked by the light of the moon and carried gas lamps instead of flashlights. They were Gypsies, as far as she could tell. In her past, some bands of gypsies served their masters well, none of them ever knowing when they spoke to Lilitu or her host. It mattered not, since she never needed their service. She had no use for most humans, other than the occasional sustenance. However, someone or something had brought them here.

The courtyard was busy with approximately ten to fifteen men moving about. Some tended their horses and some carried food from their wagon to the dilapidated kitchen that was now in use, given the smoke coming out of the flue. *What was going on? What reason would anyone have to bring these ruins to life?* Her eyes wandered until they fixed upon a small light coming from one of the higher windows of the inner keep. Their leader had to be there.

Floating up, towards the light in the window, she looked in. A tall man sat on a high chair, with his left leg dangling over the armrest. His right hand worried his teeth with a makeshift toothpick as he spoke to a gypsy woman sitting by his feet.

Suddenly, he stopped speaking and sat straight. His startled eyes looked around wide open.

"What is it, my master?" asked the female.

"I'm not sure," he whispered slowly. "There's something I have not felt in a long, long time." He stood up suddenly, almost knocking her to the floor. "Call Zgeza, quickly," he commanded.

The woman left the room, but not before looking back at the man. His rugged, handsome face turned pale, as if something scared him to death.

Lilitu did not recognize the shell of the man that stood in the room, but recognized his mannerisms. *This was no gypsy. It was Gilles. Was he alive again? Had she neglected him for too long? How could she have been so careless? No, he wasn't alive.* He was as she. She should have known it was only a matter of time before he discovered the secret of soul transference.

The man nervously roamed the floor sniffing at the air like an animal. Lilitu remained by the window observing him closely.

A tired old woman came through the door. Her parched and dry skin contrasted against her razor-sharp penetrating eyes. She did not exude wisdom, but pure evil. An evil as old as time and man himself.

"Zgeza," said the man. "There's someone here. I can feel it. Is it her?" His frowning eyes threatened her for an answer.

Zgeza, turning her back to him, walked towards a small chair and sat. Climbing stairs always took the wind out of her. "There's only one way you can know for sure," she said. "Go back to your spirit form."

"What! Give her the satisfaction of torturing me again? No, woman. You tell me or I will break your neck." He raised his fist, showing his anger.

Zgeza was unmoved. "There's not much more you can do to me now, my son. I don't expect you to be grateful either. I conjured you out of hell, and hell is exactly what you have brought us."

"Stop pestering me with your babble." He seemed about ready to explode. "Tell me what I ask. I command you!"

"You command?" She smiled and coughed lightly. "Then I presume I must obey." Straightening her body on the chair, she closed her eyes and took a deep breath.

Lilitu observed with amusement, until the moment the woman opened her eyes and looked straight at her.

"She stands by the window, my son."

The man reacted with a start, tumbling over the high chair that stood behind him. He fell backwards with a loud thud.

The loud noise of his fall attracted the young woman back into the room. "What is it my master?" she asked as she rushed towards him. "Are you hurt?"

He looked at the young woman disdainfully. Quickly, he brought himself back to his feet while grabbing the girl on the back of her neck. Her pulled her straight as he would a rag doll, his right hand squeezing her neck strongly.

"Master, please," begged the girl. "You're hurting me. Laslo…!"

The man's nails slowly extended outward, turning into sharp claws. Pulling her head back to expose her neck, he turned towards the window where Lilitu stood. Bit by bit, his ears stretched upwards, like a bat's, and his nose began to flatten horribly as his nostrils flared. By now, any resemblance to humanity had disappeared. He made it a point to look exactly towards the spot where the old gypsy indicated.

"You believe you have come to torture me, Lilitu? Not anymore. You will never know how grateful I am for what you did. Thanks to you, I can live forever." Opening his mouth wide, he brought his teeth to the young girl's throat, taking a small bite out of her. "Ah, that was sweet," he said as the girl now cried and begged for her life. He placed his free hand under her neck, as if to catch the flow of blood from falling on the floor. "But this liquid is the best part. After the meat, comes the juice of life. Do you not care to partake?" He brought his bloodied hand up to his cheek as he made a mocking face. "Oh, how rude of me. I forgot you have no real substance right now. I can wait for you while you get some body… Oops. I forgot again. We can't just use anyone, can we?" The girl managed to lightly hit his face in a weak struggle to free herself. "Excuse me for a moment," he said to Lilitu. "My food is begging for me." He raised her neck up to his teeth once more, and took a large bite off her throat.

The old woman sat unmoved, staring at the floor as the monster dropped the dying girl on the floor. "May I leave now?" asked the old gypsy.

"Don't you move!" He shouted, looking back towards the window. "Tell me, old woman, is she still there?"

Zgeza looked back at Lilitu. "Yes. She's still there."

"I hope you come to dinner again. I'll make sure to prepare a feast worthy of you. You will find me to be a gracious host." He looked down on the girl and knelt down to her level. "Or would you like a bite tonight," he said, exposing her throat to Lilitu. "Unfortunately, all I can offer you are a few leftovers. How about a little snack, for the road? Something to tide you over, perhaps? Tell me, Lilitu. Are you still partial to bone marrow? I can save you a few scraps. Don't forget we still have some unfinished business. I *have* been taking good care of your body, but I need you to tell me what you want me to *do* with it." His mouth curved into a sardonic grin.

Lilitu looked at him with renewed abhorrence. This was the second time he managed to outwit her. He was going to place a definitive damper on her plans. Now the complications grew exponentially. If Josh were to keep his word and destroy her body, he would now have to go through this monster.

True, she could allow Gilles to complete their original bargain, but she was not prepared to give him the satisfaction. She had a change of plans; Gilles must die first... painfully.

The creature was behaving like a raving maniac. His continual ranting was hard to take. Lilitu looked at the old woman. For a brief moment, their eyes met. Maybe the intensity she saw in her eyes was not pure evil, but pure hate – hate for the monster she had to serve. Lilitu did not stay to ponder the matter, and in a split second, flew away.

"She's gone now, my son," said Zgeza.

"Who in hell asked you!" he growled at her. "And what is this 'my son' shit? This shell may have been your son, but I am not. Leave me now. And get someone to clean this up."

TWENTY-TWO

"So what happens now?" asked Josh.

"I don't know," replied Janet. "The hearing is today, and the judge is expected to set bail. I just hope he realizes the danger to us, if they let him out."

"Why didn't you go to court?"

"I went this morning and had a meeting with the judge. He saw my face but didn't seem much moved. I told him there was no way I was going to sit in court and face dad again. If he gets out on bail, mom and I must leave tonight. He'll kill us next time."

"I want you to call me if you need me in any way. I helped you once, and I can do it again."

"Josh, this might be our last time together. If we leave, I'll miss you incredibly. I wish…" Her voice trailed off.

"What?" asked Josh in disbelief.

"Will you make love to me?"

"There's nothing I want more in this world, Janet…"

"But?" she said as her eyes searched his. "But what?"

"I didn't say 'but'."

"You didn't have to say it," she replied. "I can see it in your face."

"Look, things are complicated for both of us as it is. Let's not do something we might be sorry for."

"I see." She looked down sadly. "I understand." Her eyes glazed over as she held back a tear.

"No, you don't see. You don't really understand even if you say you do. I can't afford to allow myself any distractions right now. It's too dangerous for everyone, including you."

Janet looked up to meet his gaze. "But I do understand. Believe me, I do." She sniffled lightly and smiled as she touched his cheek.

He brought his hand up to touch hers and smiled back. "I'll be here if you need me. Just call me and I'll rush over. He won't know what hit him."

"Okay. I'll do that," she weakly acknowledged. At that moment, Mary Ann's car came up the driveway. She was back from the supermarket. "I gotta' go," she said standing up.

"Okay, but promise me you'll call if you need me."

"I will," she said as they walked towards the front door.

⬥⬥·⬥·⬥·⬥·⬥

Malcolm, Mary Ann, and Josh were finishing up dinner. Malcolm had already set himself up in the guestroom. It was a small by Malcolm's standard, but under the circumstances, it would have to do. The guestroom had been in disuse for a long time. Mary Ann had it set up as an exercise room, but after she bought the treadmill and the weights, neither she nor Josh ever got around to using it. At least not after the first few times when they realized exercising required large doses of commitment and lots of sore, hardly used, muscles. Until today, the exercise machines were little more than expensive clothes hangers.

"I've been seriously considering our alternatives," said Malcolm. "Although this doesn't mean I'm admitting defeat, I am at a loss as to where to go from here. Most books and information I have been able to get my hands on regarding spiritualism, demonic possession, and esoteric matters, show me that most of it is pure bunk. The Bible, The Koran, The Talmud, and every other mythological or religious concept man has ever written, only seem to contain a distorted seed of the truth. The real story will never be known."

"What do you mean?" asked Josh. "What about Lilitu? Isn't that the real story?"

"How do you know she hasn't planted those stories? How do you know that all this has not been lies also?"

"I don't know that," replied Josh. "But somehow I believe her."

"We're going back to the problem. You believe because you want to believe. That's not good enough to get us out of this hole. We need to *know*, not believe."

At this moment, Mary Ann jumped in. "Then what do we do? I'm not one to just sit around and mope."

"What do you think, mom? Do you trust Lilitu?" asked Josh.

"Yes and no," she replied with uncertainty. "I'll be honest with you. If you weren't my son, I'd be hard pressed not to act. If it is true, that she's been alive for so long, I can see why she wants to rest. Heaven knows I've been there myself, and I've only lived one lifetime, but the main thing is to get rid of her. Doing what she asks solves our problem too."

"Then that settles it," said Josh.

"Wait!" jumped Mary Ann. "I was just talking. No, there's got to be a way other than surrendering my son to a demon."

"But is she a demon?" asked Malcolm. "Is there really such a thing?"

"And Lilitu is not proof enough that demons exist?" asked Mary Ann.

"No. If Lilitu's story is true, then everything we thought we knew goes out the window. Look at the story and compare them to some of the legends and Bible stories. Anu sounds like Zeus to me. Then look at Anu, and Enlil, and Enki. Those three combined are the God described in Genesis. Remember the name Azazel, the one that nursed Lilitu back to health?" Malcolm looked around as if searching for something. "Do you have a Bible here?"

Yes," replied Mary Ann. "Let me get it." She went to the living room and quickly returned, handing it to Malcolm.

Malcolm opened it to Leviticus 16:1 and read: **Leviticus 16:6-10 RSV** *"And Aaron shall offer the bull as a sin offering for himself, and shall make atonement for himself and for his house. Then he shall take two goats, and set them before the LORD at the door of the tent of meeting; and Aaron shall cast lots upon the two goats, one lot for the LORD and the other lot for Azazel. And Aaron shall present the goat on which the lot fell for the LORD, and offer it as a sin offering; but the goat on which the lot fell for Azazel shall be presented alive before the LORD to make atonement over it, that it may be sent away into the wilderness to Azazel."*

"Why would they make an offering to God and another to Azazel?" asked Josh perplexed. "And who was Azazel?"

"Ah," replied Malcolm. "Well, I looked it up in the Merriam-Webster's Collegiate Dictionary. It said it is an evil spirit of the wilderness to which a scapegoat was sent by the ancient Hebrews in a ritual of atonement. I can see giving an offering to God, but why make an offering at the same time to an evil spirit?"

"It strikes me of devil worship, or at the very least, of polytheism," commented Mary Ann.

"Sounds like that to me too. By the way, this is where the word 'scapegoat' came from. The second goat was an appeasement to an evil spirit," continued Malcolm.

"But what we've heard from Lilitu's story," interrupted Josh. "Azazel was neither a devil or an evil spirit. She was just an innocent trapped between two factions. Not being human does not make you a demon."

"Perhaps not," said Malcolm. "But we don't know the rest of the story."

"Do we want to?" asked Mary Ann with concern.

"We must," said Josh as he stood and walked towards the living room. "We've already wasted too much time talking. Let's get this over with."

Mary Ann felt in no position to protest. In a way, she also wanted to get it over with, but she had mixed feelings about it. It was in moments like this when she missed her husband the most. He would take the bull by the horns and… Who was she kidding? She thought. She loved him, but he was no heroic figure. He was a man, plain and simple, but she needed him now more than ever. She needed an anchor for her drifting soul.

Malcolm followed Josh into the living room and waited for Mary Ann.

"I'm ready," said Josh sitting on the chair they had set up for the session.

"Mary," said Malcolm. "Will you get the lights, please?"

THE WAR OF
THE GODS

TWENTY-THREE

By now, Lilitu had settled with her friends to the East of Edin. They carved living quarters out of existing caves and fissures, managing to interconnect several of them, constructing a maze of rooms large enough to accommodate the group. There was room enough to grow into, since the caves were part of a spine of mountains that strung together like a string of pearls. These interconnected caverns were their underground city, where each creature happily did his part for the good of the rest. One side benefit of their digging was the resulting minerals and metals they could use to make weapons and shields. Enki secretly came around once a week to help them with their organization and education. He showed them metallurgy and other practical things necessary for their survival.

The Anunnakis - the ones that sided with Enlil - unaware of their exact whereabouts, referred to them as daemons. At the beginning, Enlil, in his wrath, sent several messengers out to destroy them, but to no avail. The messengers never found them. After awhile, they seemed to ignore them. It was peaceful for the moment, and the creatures preferred to keep it that way. Lilitu was happy.

Some time later, Adamu came begging her forgiveness, and she took him in for a short time. His disappointment with Eve was short lived, however. After Eve's beauty, it was difficult to look at Lilitu. Lilitu had wings, a hairy face that resembled a humanoid bat, and her body was no comparison to Eve's; besides, Eve was pregnant with his child. Clearly, they did not belong together. When Adamu left Lilitu for the second time, she decided it would be the last. She wanted nothing more to do with the human race.

Her happiness was short lived, however. One day, the creatures heard some explosions far away, coming from the Anunnaki settlement. Before long, the ships arrived. It was Enki, a few soldiers, and some of his Elohim. Mummu was also with them. Most of the creatures figured something was terribly wrong when they saw Anunnakis coming out of the ships. Some were bleeding; some were hurt very badly. Enki was the first to step out. He met Lilitu by the entrance of the main cave.

"Quickly," he said to Lilitu. "You must help us hide our ships."

Lilitu looked at him with distrust. "Why do you need to hide your ships?" She no longer called him Master.

"We are at war with Enlil. He must not find us before we can regroup."

"But why do you bring their wrath upon us. We want no part in this."

"You are the reason we are at war. They want to destroy the whole lot of you and we refused to help them. Don't you see? Together we both may have a chance." His eyes pleaded. Enki never pleaded before.

Lilitu studied him closely. She was well aware of Enlil's volatile temper and had no doubts about these two factions getting at each other's throats. Nevertheless, the Anunnakis were a deceitful people. On the one hand, Enki may be lying just to get the refugees to back them up. On the other hand, it was a fact that Enlil's forces had conducted a thorough search in an effort to exterminate them. The creatures would follow her lead regardless of what she decided. It was her decision, good, or bad. Either faction was just as bad, but Enki did help them before and never revealed their hiding place.

"Very well," she agreed reluctantly. "There is a large hidden cavern behind this hill, further east. Have your men follow me."

"Some of us need to stay now. They are too hurt to continue," added Mummu. "May we remain here with your people while our pilots hide our ships?"

Lilitu nodded to Azazel, who immediately reacted by getting some of the creatures to help with the wounded.

"You go to the main ship," Lilitu ordered Enki. "I will glide upwards to see if you have been followed. At my signal, stick to my tail."

"Very well," said Enki, as he returned to his ship.

This is an epic moment, thought Enki. *One that history will sing and write about for millennia to come.* Enki's most trusted lieutenants, Beelzebub, Moloch, and Belial, piloted three of the largest ships. Their wounds were not serious enough to stop them from following Enki's command.

Lilitu's swift flying was no match to the speed of the Anunnaki ships, but her maneuverability on the air was incomparable. She could fly rings around any Anunnaki pilot.

The cavern Lilitu guided them into was, in fact, much bigger than Enki expected. The three large ships fit adequately, leaving enough room for the other ten smaller ones. After the ships were safely on the ground, Enki surveyed the cavern.

"This will do very nicely," said Enki with satisfaction. "Very nicely, indeed."

Just at that moment, the roaring noise of Enlil's ships passed overhead. Lilitu hoped her companions had taken cover.

"Good," continued Enki. "It seems we have been able to elude them."

"For the moment," interrupted Lilitu with a strained voice. She approached Enki menacingly. "I want you to get one thing clear…"

Moloch and Belial, who had just stepped out of their own ships ran towards Lilitu and grabbed her by the arms pulling her away from Enki.

Enki reprimanded them. "Let her go this instant," he commanded. Moloch and Belial released her. "I'm sorry," he continued, this time addressing Lilitu. "This is no way to appreciate your hospitality. You were about to tell me something?"

She rubbed her arms, as if trying to shake fleas off her body. Lilitu could have taken both of them without much effort had she wanted to. "We will help you recover from your wounds, and hide you for as long as you need. Do not expect us to fight your fight for you. We have had enough suffering among our people."

"I am a bit disappointed. This is not my personal fight. You are involved also, whether you want it or not. If you sit passively, to simply watch us fight each other, they will come after you next. My small group cannot possibly win this alone."

"My group are not fighters either," added Lilitu.

"You have managed to survive. Besides, we do not have to fight a confrontational war. We can fight surreptitiously. Take them down a bit at a time. Some of the ones on their side will end up joining us too. I know."

"This is too much for me to decide. I will need to call an assembly."

"Good. I ask no more."

"Very well," said Lilitu. Her heart felt heavy with sorrow. This matter would divide her people. Death was inevitable. "Let us get your soldiers taken care of."

"Should we not wait for the enemy ships to stop their search?" asked Moloch.

"We have managed to connect many of these caverns. There is no need to step outside. You can reach the center of our compound through that tunnel over there," said Lilitu pointing towards a dark opening on the wall.

"Is there another cavern such as this one?" asked Enki.

"Why do you ask?" she said stopping midway to the tunnel.

"We need to have a meeting where both our peoples can discuss what to do next."

"Yes. There is another. A little smaller, but large enough to accommodate us all. I will show it to you after you have rested."

●◆●◆●●◆●●◆●●

The meeting began early the next morning. All the rebellious Anunnakis, including most of the wounded and all the refugee creatures were present at the cavern. Enki spoke first. Beelzebub, his second in command moved forward asking for silence. Several times he repeated his request, until running out of patience, he took out his thunder stick and released a shot in the air. The crowd went silent in a second.

"I want to thank you all for being present at this historic meeting," said Enki. "I also want to thank Lilitu for providing us with this opportunity to speak to you. I have much to say, and little time. It will not be long before Enlil's forces find us. I know this is a terrible position we have placed you in, but it had to be done."

The low murmur swept the crowd.

"It had to be done," continued Enki, slightly raising his voice to drown out the murmurs, "because Enlil is set on destroying us all."

Lilitu, who stood at the front of her group, interrupted. "Why do you include us when you speak of destruction?"

"It is complicated, but I'll try to explain. In our efforts to create a primitive worker for the Igigis, we created you all. Enlil tried to force me to destroy you, and for a time, I had no choice. True, my Elohim sacrificed some of you, but not without regret."

Lilitu remembered otherwise, but allowed Enki to continue.

"For the few of you that suffered under our hands, I most regretfully apologize. During those days, I was buying time. I recognize it was a terrible choice to make, but Enlil forced my hand. He considers you all an abomination he is not willing to tolerate. Once we created the perfect worker they needed, he ordered me to stop our experiments – which meant destroying all of you - and enter full production. We, of course, refused. A confrontation was imminent, when, to my relief, you managed to escape. As you well know, they looked for you for many months until, in frustration, they gave up. My many visits to your compound did not go unnoticed, however. Enlil insisted I reveal your whereabouts to him. I refused, and… well, here we are." He paused for a moment, sweeping the congregation with his eyes. "You have as much a right to live as any of us. I say let us give them hell. Are you with me?"

The crowd roared their agreement loudly. There was nothing Lilitu could do to control the situation. They all agreed with Enki wholeheartedly, the Anunnakis, as well as the creatures. Emotions ran deep, yet she had serious doubts about the *real* reasons behind their war. She lived long enough under the Anunnaki's boots to know better. Some of the things Enki said made no sense.

"We will give them more than hell. We will show them the meaning of pandemonium."

The meeting soon adjourned. Azazel assigned Anunnakis their rooms, but Lilitu personally chose Enki's sleeping quarters. She needed to see what they were up to. A small hole in one of the walls of Enki's room would allow her to hear his conversations.

She saw Beelzebub and Moloch enter Enki's chambers.

Beelzebub seemed worried. "I am with you, no matter what you decide to do, but we are overpowered. How are we to win this rebellion?"

"You worry too much, my friend. Why do you think I befriended these misshapen creatures? I told you one day they would be useful to us."

"What do we do when we run out of cannon fodder?" asked Moloch.

"That's when we press our attack." Enki smiled.

"But they will all die. I thought you liked these creatures," said Beelzebub.

"Did you really?" Enki's face wrinkled with an indescribable expression of disdain.

Lilitu had no time to react when Belial approached her from behind, knocking her hard on the head. She lost consciousness.

◆◆◆◆◆◆◆◆

When she came to, she was inside a glass enclosure. Enki stood outside, looking at her. She tried to force the glass walls open, but it was hermetically sealed. "You goddamned son of a bitch!" she screamed. His lips moving, but she could not hear him.

Enki reached with his right hand to a switch on the glass box. "Can you hear me now?" he asked.

"You are evil, just like all of your kind."

"Perhaps, but do not forget I am also your creator. I have a right to use my creatures any way I please."

"Let me out of here!" she screamed.

"Sorry. I cannot do that."

"What is this? What are you going to do to me?"

"This is a stasis chamber. We used things like this on long journeys to other god-forsaken planets. It kept us in suspended animation for as long as we needed to. It will not kill you, but it will allow you to dream away for the rest of eternity."

"My people will kill you for this."

"Your people will believe what I tell them," said Enki with confidence. "I will tell them you valiantly volunteered on a secret mission to scout Enlil's compound, and was discovered." He leaned forward, resting his elbows on the glass top. "You struggled, but it was an impossible battle. Your last words were '*tell my people to avenge me*'." Enki acted out every word, savoring the drama of his words. Lilitu knew he could fool her children easily. They never learned the art of Anunnaki deception. "My men tried desperately to recover your body, and they did, but it was too late; you were already dead. With a heavy heart, they brought you back, to display your heroic remains in this glass container. We will build you a shrine. Now, our battle has a greater cause, not only for justice, but also for revenge. I will stand in the great hall as I kneel and cry in front of your corpse, and say to them: '*we will not allow Lilitu's death to be in vain. She fought for your right to live, and we will make you free, even if we die trying.*' They will continue to attack and attack, until I have won."

He moved his hand again to another button. A loud hiss was felt inside the chamber as cold gas enveloped Lilitu. "Goodbye, Lilitu. May eternity be kind to you."

✦◆◦◦◆◦◦◆◦

The loud, unexpected sound of the telephone startled Malcolm and Mary Ann.

TWENTY-FOUR

Mary Ann answered the telephone, looking towards the grandfather clock that stood near the dining room. It was ten past two in the morning. "Hello," she managed to say before a desperate voice interrupted her.

"Please, help me," Janet whispered over the line. "He's here. He's outside and I'm afraid. I don't want to die."

"Who's this?" asked Mary Ann. "Janet, is that you?"

While Mary Ann spoke over the telephone, Lilitu was trying to recall Josh from his regression. "*Josh*," she commanded. "*Listen to me. Come back to the present and listen.*"

"Yes?" was Josh's response.

Malcolm sat immediately on alert, watching Josh like a hawk.

"*Janet is in danger*," said Lilitu. "*She needs your help, but you will never get there on time. Let me use your body. I can get to her house faster. I can fly.*"

"No," replied Josh.

"Josh?" asked Malcolm with concern. "Who are you talking to?"

"Calm down," whispered Mary Ann over the telephone. "Hang up so I can call 911."

"There's no time," said Janet, raising her voice louder at every word. "He's already at the door. Oh, God!"

A loud crash came over the line. Mary Ann growing desperate began to lose control.

"*Josh*," demanded Lilitu, by now, upset. "*You must trust me or your will forfeit your friend's life.*" This was the perfect opportunity to get Josh to open to her, and she intended to milk the moment. If she was going to win his trust, this was it.

All the time in the world, thought Josh, *yet now he had none. No choices left.*

"Malcolm," cried Mary Ann. "It's Janet. Her father just broke into her house!"

Before Malcolm reacted, Josh ran towards the door.

◆◆•◆•◆•◆•◆•◆•

A warm evening breeze caressed Lilitu's face. She was back in control. The clothes over her back split apart as her metamorphosis began. Leathery wings that had flown the skies so many times spread wide. From a low crouch, every muscle in her body strained to get the needed spring, setting her wings close to her body just before jumping.

Now airborne, navigating the air currents, she kept a steady and effortless course. Soon, Janet's house came into view. Silently, she surveyed her surroundings, but saw no one.

The man must already be inside, she thought. She noticed the open attic window, and dove straight for it.

Thousands of years of flying gave her options undreamed of for any human. Quietly, she landed near the window. She had to decide whether to shape-change back to Josh, or remain in her natural form. No one must be able to trace violence back to Josh, but her survival depended on not revealing herself.

For now, she decided against the transformation. Inside the attic, she slowly approached the trapdoor, and opened it. With great caution, she dropped to the second story hallway. She heard their voices coming from below.

"You two little bitches thought you could just turn me in and I'd play dead?" said Janet's father. He was drunk. "Don'tcha know how easy it is to get out? Judges don't give no shit for ya'. No one gives no shit 'bout nothin'."

Lilitu quickly moved down the stairs. The whole house was in darkness, except for the living room desk lamp – where the voices came from. Janet and her mother, cornered on the floor, hugged each other. Both their faces showed bruises; blood flowed from Janet's left eyelid. Her father sat on a nearby easy chair with a kitchen knife in his right hand, and a bottle of whiskey in the other.

"If I'm goin' a jail, it might as well be fer somthin' worthwhile," he said, taking a swig off the bottle. Leaning forward, he stood up and approached the women. They pleaded for their lives while attempting to melt into the wall. He spread his legs as he stopped, looming in front of them like a giant, and said, "Okay, ladies. Who's on first?"

Lilitu timed it carefully, waiting for the right moment. As the two women hugged each other, hiding their faces from the man, she sprung. Without wasting a second, she swiftly closed in, grabbing him by the neck. To Lilitu, he was as light as a kitten. So strong was her grasp, that not a sound escaped his lips. She was already out the back door, dragging him like some discarded rag, before Janet and her mother saw what happened.

The police were just arriving at the front, and here she was, standing on the back yard with a struggling human at the end of her claws. If they saw her, they would shoot her down without hesitation. She shape-changed back to Josh, and then jumped the fence towards the next house. The man hung from her right hand like a puppet.

He badly wanted to scream, but Lilitu's grip on his throat was too strong. "What should I do with you?" said Lilitu. "Josh warned you the last time, but it didn't scare you enough. People like you do not learn. Your kind only understands one language. Treat evil with evil, I always say. It works for me." She sniffed at the air like a wolf. "I think we should find a more secluded spot. We do not want to be discovered, do we?"

The man continued to grunt as he attempted to release her grip from his throat, but to no avail. She pulled him with her from one fence to the next until they reached the underpass of a rarely used bridge. Lilitu released him.

"This looks like a nice, quiet place to have a meal, don't you agree?"

"A meal?" whispered the man. His sore throat did not permit him to speak beyond a whisper. "Whatcha' talkin' 'bout?" he said coughing.

"Well, maybe I shouldn't say this, but you are the main course. Is it not exciting?"

"What? You're a cannibal now?" His sarcasm betrayed his fear. This kid was crazier than he thought. *And why are his clothes all tattered?* He thought.

"Actually, I have consumed humans for a long, long time." She sat next to him, crossing her arms across her raised legs. She looked at the stars and sighed. "As old as I am, I have not been able to understand one thing about your kind. For all your mental capacity, you seem to dwell only on the bad things. Most times, it seems to me that there's no brain inside that skull of yours."

The man tried to move away, but she grabbed his arm and pulled him down to the floor, making him fall hard on his ass. She patted his head as if he were a small dog.

"There," she said calmly. "Is that better?" Turning her eyes back to the stars, she continued. "I usually do not make a habit of playing with my food, you know. It is bad taste."

"Are you nuts or somethin'?" he asked as he massaged his arm. When she pulled him down, she almost pulled it out of its socket. "Why are you dressed like that?"

"Never mind," she replied with a smile. "Now, tell me, why did you think it was fun to torture your wife and daughter?" She maintained her smile as she looked at him. "I'm just curious."

"I… I didn't torture 'em. They were misbehavin', that's all. They needed to be taught."

"Oh. It was an educational process."

"Yeah! That's it!" he said, trying to smirk.

"Then you are a teacher?"

"Uh-huh. You can look at it like that."

"Are you still drunk or has the night air cleared your head a bit?"

"I'm okay, I guess."

"Good," she patted his leg. "It is important you keep a clear mind. We have important business at hand." Lilitu then moved her face closer to him and spoke as if betraying someone's confidence. "You know, when you asked them *who's on first,* you had me worried for a moment. I thought you were going to harm them."

"Really?" he replied as if he had just played a prank on Josh and he had fallen for it. "Ya' really thought that?"

"Yes" said Lilitu. Her smile widened.

He tried to force a laugh, but it came out choked. "Nah, nah! Nothin' like dat at all."

"You think you're speaking to Josh, don't you?"

"Is that yer' name?" he said as he stretched his hand towards hers. "Pleased to meetcha'."

Lilitu shook his hand. "I must be honest with you. I don't usually do this, you understand. As I said before, I don't enjoy playing with my food, but humans like you intrigue me."

"Ya' like me, huh?"

"No, the truth is I dislike you very much." Lilitu turned to face him. "Look at me carefully. What do you see?" Her tone sounded a bit playful.

"I see a nice boy that'd make a good son in law."

"Well, that *is* interesting. I like it." She paused for a moment, moving closer. "You know, there is one thing that you need not worry about. Your wife and daughter will never miss you, and no one will even know or care about what became of you."

She began a gradual metamorphosis, a slow one, just to study his expression. His eyes opened wide. Before he could move away, she placed her right hand behind his neck and with her left hand, held him in place. "You like what you see?" she asked. By now, Lilitu was in front of him in all her glory. "Would you mind very much if I kissed you?" She took a small bite from his neck. This was going to be a long, savory night.

ZGEZA AND LASLO

TWENTY-FIVE

Zgeza had no one to turn to. A lifetime spent delving in black magic with no visible results, and the single time it worked, only brought her an uncontrollable demon. When her son Laslo died, her world collapsed. He was the only person that provided her with any degree of comfort, and was all she had in her insignificant life,

Before his tragic death, she lived as a fortuneteller and spiritualist; she was good at it too. People came to her for all sorts of things, from love potions to contact with the spirit world - superstition was a lucrative business. While she took care of the *customer,* Laslo found his way into their pockets.

Many times, the marks – as she liked to call them - gave away their money with little prompting. Other times, she asked them to bring large amounts of cash, which she would put away in a box and bury in her backyard. If the spirits took the money, then their *customer's* fortunes were about to change. It worked every time - getting the money, not changing their fortunes. A change of luck could bring anything from a new job to a new love. It varied from mark to mark, but the results were always the same.

For the most part, however, she lived simply. She had no choice; society shunned gypsies, no matter where they went. Although the council of Europe approved the use of Rroma to refer to gypsies in their official documents, she preferred to use Romani instead, but it made no difference. Luxuries were something she never knew or wanted, but for Laslo, it was different. He loved the sound of gold too much, which was why she helped him out whenever he asked.

Feeling rejected throughout his life, he made it a point to reject back. He met discrimination the first day he went to school. Given that he was gypsy, they made him sit in the back row. Sometimes, the parents of the other children protested, and he ended up alone, in special-education classes – that is, when Zgeza could afford it. Many times, they tossed him out of school – not for bad behavior, but for defending himself. Other children and teachers frequently ostracized and insulted him. As he grew old enough to work, he could not find jobs. When their neighbors abused them, the police ignored their complaints. They always lived as second-class citizens, but never gave up because of it. Being a gypsy was painful, which is why he developed talents of his own to survive.

One day, Laslo met someone who failed to appreciate his talents. He promised a man he would meet the *love of his life* if he brought him five thousand francs in cash. It was the old *bury the money* trick. When the *love of his life* failed to turn up a few months later, the man came after Laslo, shooting him to death in a fit of anger.

He might as well have buried a knife deep in Zgeza's chest, for she lost her heart that day. She could have died together with her son, but fate had her at the supermarket buying groceries when the man shot him. By the time she came home, a few from the crowd gathered there, told her what had happened. Yet, even with all the evidence they had against the man, the police never arrested him.

Revenge was her only reasonable alternative. After all, her son was dead, and for anyone who had eyes to see, so was she. After Laslo died, his Romani relatives and friends came to ask for forgiveness. It was an old custom to prevent that person from coming back as an evil spirit. Zgeza did not allow it. They begged her to plug her son's nostrils with wax, so evil spirits would not take his body. That too, she refused. Zgeza wanted him to come back as a muló, a living dead to seek revenge on anyone who harmed him during his life. Her friends warned her, but she refused to listen.

His burial was quick and simple; no fanfare, no embalming, no fancy coffin. A simple wooden box was more than enough for the likes of him. From the beginning, she had other plans, but the authorities would have none of it. She went along with all their rules and regulations except for the embalming. After some arguing, she convinced the coroner that it was against her religious beliefs to profane his body with embalming fluid.

That night, after the burial, Zgeza and a couple of well-compensated drug addicts, slipped into the cemetery to exhume his body. It was later, during an invocation over Laslo's body that she got the shock of her life, almost dying of fright because of it.

When the two men carried her son into her flat, everything was ready. All her furniture had been moved out of the living room, and replaced with a hand-painted large pentagram in the middle of the living room. She instructed the men to place his body in the center of it. Laslo fit perfectly inside the circle. She dutifully paid the men their dues and dismissed them. No need to worry about them. They were too preoccupied with getting their next hit to care, as if digging out a body from the cemetery was not strange enough.

The pentagram consisted of an inverted (one point down) five-pointed star inside a large circle, made to resemble the head of a goat. Each tip of the star touched the circle at measured points within its circumference. The circle was for her protection. The pentagon at the center of the pentagram was the gateway for Laslo's spirit. If anything other than Laslo took form, the circle would keep it at bay, in which case, Zgeza would immediately perform a banishment ritual. Carefully, she placed an unlit candle on the first four tips of the star. Later, during the ritual, she was to light each one, chanting a different invocation.

With the fifth candle in hand, she reached for the box of matches, and then turned off the light switch. The flat went black. Kneeling in front of the first point of the pentagram, she recited the first invocation while placing the candle on the tip of the pentagram. She slowly moved to the second candle, repeating the invocation. Nothing happened yet, and expected nothing to happen until she completed the ritual. Yet, by the time she started on the third candle, the flames began to flicker. Suddenly, before the third invocation ended, a strong breeze smothered the flames, leaving her in total darkness.

Zgeza shuddered at the cold feeling unexpectedly invading her bones. Her right hand went immediately to the box of matches lying on the floor by her feet. Taking one match out of the box, she struck it against the side. To her utter shock, Laslo sat staring at her in the middle of the pentagram. His pale face leered triumphantly while the flickering lights played a macabre dance with the shadows, making it seem like little demons celebrating around her in a circle.

Laslo's eyes spewed hate. That much she expected. He was back for revenge. Recklessly, she approached him, but he pushed her back hard.

"*What are you doing, woman?*" he said to her.

It hurt. It cut deep. Her son did not recognize her. And why did he call her '*woman*'? Then, she knew her mistake. This was not her Laslo, but an evil spirit, a demon as cruel as she could ever imagine. Expecting protection from the pentagram and the circle, she instantly moved away. She began the banishment ritual, but Laslo laughed intensely.

"Stop this ridiculous dribble, woman," he said walking towards her. "Do you think you can get rid of me with such stupidity?"

Yes, she was stupid, and realized it much too late. That was then, and this was now. Yet, after all the years of doing this fiend's bidding, she had but one goal in life, to banish him. She felt sorry for Piotra. The girl adored the dirt he walked on, and he paid her with murder; Zgeza could do nothing for her now.

The spirit she saw by the castle window a few minutes ago might be the answer to her prayers. The monster inside her son was deadly afraid of her. She could try to invoke her spirit, but it was nothing she dared to try again. One evil spirit was more than she cared for.

Walking down the dark, dank circular steps of the keep, she thought about telling the gypsies in the kitchen that Piotra was dead, specially her father. This would be no easy task. Two women and a boy moved about in the kitchen preparing food for the group. Mircea was outside with the rest of the men. Zgeza called the boy and asked him to call two of the men to the kitchen, but to make sure Mircea was not one of them.

Two men walked in and she told them what happened upstairs. They reacted with fear, but had learned to restrain their response. This was nothing new, and knew what they needed to do. Lowering their eyes, they sadly went up the stairs to fetch Piotra's body. Zgeza then called on the boy again.

"Go fetch Mircea," she ordered in a monotone. She walked to the cupboard and served a large amount of whiskey in a ceramic flagon.

Soon after, Mircea came walking in with a smile on his face. He used a dirty rag to clean some axle grease from his fingers.

"Yes, Zgeza. What does he want now?" he asked referring to the many errands he ran for Laslo. Mircea disliked Laslo as much as he feared him. Even when the beast took a liking to his Piotra, he dared not protest. The beast was too powerful, and sometimes even seemed to have eyes behind his back. He served the man and kept a close watch on his daughter.

"Sit down, Mircea," she said, indicating a chair near the kitchen table while extended the flagon to him.

"What is this?" he asked with a smile. "What are we celebrating?"

"Drink!" she ordered. "Drink it all, and we'll talk."

Mircea suddenly had a bad feeling. He looked into Zgeza's eyes, but was unable to read anything. He downed the glass quickly, but Zgeza waited.

"Are you planning to tell me now or should we wait for sunup?" A smile was no longer upon his face.

The pain of losing a child is the worst of any man's nightmares, and Mircea's nightmare came alive the moment Zgeza told him of Piotra's fate. His shrieks of pain contrasted Laslo's sardonic laughter as both voices echoed in the keep. A symphony of horrors best left unheard.

Mircea's cries attracted some of the men working in the yard. Rushing into the kitchen and hearing from up close the cacophony of pain and mockery, they arrived just in time to keep Mircea from going up the stairs to confront Laslo. Zgeza, although too weak and old to do anything but comfort Mircea, knew she had an ally who would do anything to destroy Laslo. Maybe a plan of some sort was in order.

The two men came back down empty handed. Piotra's body remained upstairs.

"Where is my Piotra?" cried Mircea. "Why didn't you bring her to me?"

The two men looked at each other and shrugged their shoulders in unison.

"She wasn't there," said one of them.

"Laslo told us she was not dead," said the other, somewhat perplexed.

Mircea jumped from his chair, incredulous. "What? Where is she, then?"

"We don't know." The first man swallowed. "But Laslo said she was only a bit hurt, and was going to make her well again."

"Did he say when I can see her?" His pain subsided considerably as he asked with swollen eyes. All of them feared Laslo to the point of hysteria.

"He said he'd call you up to his chambers. He will let you see her when she's ready." The second man lowered his eyes and sympathetically touched Mircea on the shoulder. "Everything will be alright, my friend. We must go back to work."

The four men walked out with drooping shoulders. Mircea fell back on the chair with a sigh of relief.

"We need to talk," said Zgeza.

"Why did you lie to me?" Mircea asked angrily.

"I do not know what Laslo has in mind, and I do not wish to make you unhappy, but I tell you what I saw." Maybe this was not the right moment. There was no doubt in Zgeza's mind that Piotra was dead. She decided to let Laslo play his hand. The only thing she could think of was that the monster had figured out a way to call another spirit demon into Piotra's body. Yet, that was impossible. A demon cannot summon another demon. Besides, Piotra's body was too damaged. "I hope things turn out as you expect, Mircea, but if they don't, then I want to talk to you alone." Zgeza felt sorry for Mircea. *What new cruelty did Laslo have in store for him?* She wished she could spare him the pain. "Come to my chambers later," she finally said as she walked towards the stairs that led into the bowels of the mountain.

The women preparing the food tried to continue with their work, but they were just going through the motions. Their hands trembled. The boy stood behind Mircea, frozen to the spot. As Zgeza walked past him, she rustled his hair a bit, but she wished she had not done it – it only managed to startle the boy further.

Then, just before Zgeza reached the first mossy step to the next level down, where she slept, she heard Laslo's voice calling.

"Oh, Mircea!" His playful voice stretched every syllable with a singsong. "Someone wants to see you. I think it's your daughter."

Mircea looked towards the stairs leading to Laslo's chambers, at the top of the keep. He bit his lower lip, and stood slowly, faltering.

Zgeza froze by the threshold. "Mircea. Stay here. Don't…."

"Be quiet, woman!" Mircea growled.

Suddenly, the voice of Piotra called. "I'm here, father. Please come to me." It sounded distant, indistinguishable.

The gas lamps flickered, forcing the shadows to play against the wall. The threshold leading upstairs looked foreboding. The decaying walls and the mold stuck to them giving the impression of grotesque paintings moving about to the sway of the dim lights.

Mircea shuffled up to the first step and looked up. The stairs were dark, and only a faint light came from the top chamber, Laslo's chamber. Zgeza held back the impulse to pull Mircea away. She wished he did not have to see whatever it was Laslo wanted him to see.

"Father?" echoed the sweet distant voice from the walls of the keep.

The two cooks and the boy slowly cowered away towards the door leading to the courtyard. Their breath was agitated.

Zgeza walked towards Mircea, who was petrified by the doorstep. His eyes tried to penetrate the darkness within the flight of stairs.

"Mircea," Zgeza said as she touched his shoulder. "Leave now. You must not go."

He flinched and shrugged his shoulder away.

"Are you coming, father?" The seductive tone carried danger behind every syllable.

Mircea pushed Zgeza aside. "Leave me be. I must go. I must see for myself." He reached for one of the gas lamps and began to tread upstairs. The musty smell inside the keep was one of death and corruption. Carrying the lamp near the walls, he staggered up, noticing that what looked like mold, was dried blood; old, moldy dried blood. *These walls must have seen a lot of death in their time,* he thought.

He stopped midway, bringing his lamp towards the center. The diameter of the tower must have been thirty-five feet across, each step being five feet wide. That left a gap of, at least a twenty-five feet diameter. The spiral went up all the way to Laslo's chamber, but it also continued downward to unknown depths. The best way not to fall was to hug the walls.

This tower always made him nervous, so he stepped carefully. As he neared Laslo's chamber doorsill, the soft light coming from within snuffed out.

"Please lower the light, father," said the voice so softly. "It hurts me."

"Is it you, Piotra?" He stopped on his tracks.

"The light, father." The voice repeated.

"Yes. Yes, of course." He lowered the light to a bare glimmer and moved closer to the doorstep.

"Come in," was the bare whisper he heard.

The glowing moon sliced the room into segments of shadow and light. Squinting, he tried to locate his daughter.

"Where are you, Piotra?" he asked.

"I'm here," was the whisper from the corner, near one of the windows.

Mircea turned towards the voice and barely saw a figure. It looked like a woman, but could not quite make her out.

"Are you well, my darling?" His voice quivered. "Come out where I can see you. Why all the mystery?"

The figure moved out of the darkness allowing the moon to paint a misshapen silhouette behind it. The figure was too tall to be Piotra.

"You may turn up the lamp now," whispered the figure.

Mircea's unsteady hands turned the lever on his lamp. When the light hit the figure that wore his daughter's clothes, he saw the impossible. His daughter's face hung loosely from Laslo's head. The rest of her flayed skin covered his body.

"Hello, father," said Laslo, mimicking Piotra's voice.

TWENTY-SIX

Laslo sat on his high chair, peeling away Piotra's skin from his body, munching on a few pieces before discarding the rest. He eagerly waited to hear Mircea's wail of pain the moment he revealed himself, but instead, the asshole fainted. A pity. It would have been a sweet song.

Maybe it was for the best. Uncontrollable laughter always came upon him when hearing humans cry and he needed his wits now that Lilitu knew about him. He remembered reacting like this when he was alive. His orgasms were so intense he usually laughed himself out of control.

Then he discovered the passion of blood. The sight of it gave him convulsive fits of pleasure. Joining *The Maiden*, in their war against the English was the best thing that ever happened to him. He was free to kill and enjoy it openly, every kill, an orgasmic pleasure. After all, war is war, and killing is the natural thing to do. Nevertheless, he savored every drop of blood through the edge of his sword, and many times, after a battle was over, he tasted the precious liquid in private.

Then the war ended, and a miracle happened; Lilitu. A miracle that, as it turned out, was also his demise. It certainly took her a long time to find him. He was midway through his life when he first saw her in a dream. She seduced him. She was his Succubus, his private pleasure machine. Yet, she brought him more than the pleasures of the flesh, she brought him the power to do what he wanted when he wanted. He could have been a little more discreet, but he did not care. When they discovered his antics, he was prepared. He allowed them to take him to trial and he even confessed. No one suspected that he bribed the executioner. Once they thought him dead, he could operate in the background, unseen, unsuspected. He built this hideaway in the mountains because he had foreseen all of it.

His mistake was to underestimate Lilitu. Just as he manipulated everyone else, he thought he could manipulate her. He should have destroyed her, when first she asked, but no. He wanted it all, every drop of power she had to give.

Now, he constantly thought of condemning her to the same eternity of undeath he lived in, but then, he would NEVER get rid of her. Laslo's body was not going to last forever; when the need to abandon it came, Lilitu would surely be there to torture him worse than before. No, that route would backfire. If he destroyed her body, he needed to make sure her spirit was in it, otherwise he would never be rid of her.

Maybe, now that he had found his way back to the physical world, he could negotiate with her, he thought. Make her an offer. She might accept. It was certainly worth a try. He stormed out of his chair and called Zgeza.

"Zgeza! Come to me now!"

Mircea's unconscious body lay near the door, and for a moment, he was tempted to throw him out the window. "You have been useful to me so far," he whispered to the man. "Let's see how you repay my leniency."

Knowing he would not have to call her twice, he paced back to his chair and waited.

❦◆◦◦◆◦◦◆◦

Zgeza, expecting to see Mircea's body flying down the tower at any moment, held on to the amulet on her neck. When Laslo shouted his orders, the two men that had previously gone upstairs, Zurca and Fonso came back inside. She signaled at them to follow. They assisted her up at a slow pace. The last twenty years, since she brought Laslo back to life, had taken a toll on her bones. Now, what little strength left in her, she swore to spend on Laslo's destruction.

"If Mircea is still alive," she told them as they helped her upstairs, "take him to my room and stay with him until I arrive."

"Yes, Zgeza," they both replied, almost in unison.

When they entered Laslo's chamber, they saw Mircea lying unconscious on the floor, and Laslo covered in blood. A bundle of skin and hair was on the floor, near Mircea's shoulders. The men gasped as they looked at the skin and recognized it for what it was. Zgeza held their arms, squeezing lightly, indicating with a nod to pick up Mircea and get out quickly. This they did.

Zgeza looked at the bunch of skin on the floor and spoke without raising her eyes from it. "Why did you call me?"

"Is there a reason why you're not looking at me?" asked Laslo.

"It offends you when I do." Zgeza thought about Piotra's bones. They probably ended up at the bottom of the ravine, where Laslo usually threw his leftovers.

"Your very presence offends me," said Laslo.

"Then why not do away with me?" she asked in anger, slowly raising her eyes to meet his.

"Tempting, very tempting, but not yet. I still have use for you." He lowered his right foot from the cushion of the chair and leaned forward, resting his arms on his legs. "I want you to summon Lilitu for me."

"I cannot."

At this response, Laslo stood and shouted, "YOU REFUSE?"

Zgeza, as always, did not allow herself to be intimidated. Although she lost her fear of death a long time ago, this was one of the reasons why Laslo had not killed her.

"No," she said. "I do not refuse. I simply do not have the power to summon her at will."

"You summoned me," he lied. Her ritual had been pure nonsense and it had nothing to do with his presence, although her pleading voice attracted him that night. A happy accident that led him to try her son's body on for size. A chance in a million. It was as Lilitu said, once every hundred years or so. "If you did it with me, you can do it with her," he insisted.

"I must prepare and see what I can do."

"When?" he asked with anticipation.

"Be patient. I will let you know."

"Make it soon, Zgeza. Make it soon." He made it sound like a threat.

"You need a bath," she said indifferently.

He licked his bloody arm, as a cat would. "Care to join me?"

Zgeza ignored his attempt at humor. "May I take Piotra's remains for burial?"

"The skin is my favorite part, but I've had my fill already. If you insist, you may take it." He began to take his clothes off. "Have someone bring me water for my bath. It will be daylight soon, and I want to be clean for my rest."

"Very well," replied Zgeza as she placed a tablecloth on the floor to gather Piotra's remains. She could have ignored his commands if she wished, but his form of retaliation for her non-compliance was by killing her Romani friends. At least this way, he spared most of them – as long as they served him.

❖❖❖❖❖❖❖❖

Zgeza never discovered Laslo's daylight resting place, but if she could communicate with this 'Lilitu spirit', she might get the help she needed. The thing that occupied her son's body was more than an evil spirit; it was some sort of ghoul. Symbols and amulets had no effect on him, but his fear for the sun was good enough for her. If the sun failed to do the trick, then a little fire might do it. Whatever his weaknesses, the first step was to discover where he slept, if he slept at all.

As she came back into the kitchen, she called the boy - Kore - to her. "Get me Belo. Tell him I need him." She looked at the boy rush out of the kitchen, and felt sorry for him. She knew the child would not live for long, given this monster's preference for young boys. What she lacked was not the courage to save him - of that she had plenty - but that the others would suffer dreadfully if she tried such a thing.

She turned towards the two women in the kitchen and added, "you, take water upstairs to Laslo. He wants his bath. Go quickly."

The two women reacted as Kore ran outside calling for Belo.

Belo, a tall, strong-looking man, walked into the kitchen. Kore stood behind the man, awaiting further instructions.

Zgeza asked Kore to go water the horses, and then turned to Belo. "I want you to make a coffin for Piotra. As soon as it is ready, call me. We will have a funeral today."

"Where is her body?" he asked sadly.

Zgeza handed him the bundled tablecloth and said "Here. These are her remains."

Belo stood aghast by the kitchen door, with the bundle in his hand, as Zgeza walked down the stairs to her room.

❖❖❖❖❖❖❖❖

The air inside the castle walls was unhealthy. If she walked too fast, she would end up wheezing for hours. When she finally got to her bedroom door, she heard Mircea wailing inside. He was drunk.

"Why did you give him so much to drink?" she asked Zurca. There was a frozen expression on her face.

"How else could we keep him under control?" he asked, uncomfortable with the fact that he may have not handled him well.

Zgeza ignoring Zurca's reply approached Mircea. She tried to speak to him, and all he did was cry. Taking a deep sigh of despair, she threw her arms up. "Very well," she said to Fonso and Zurca. "Give him all the drink he can handle, then let him sleep it off, but I want you to stay with him; do not leave him alone. You may take turns sleeping if you need to."

"Where will you sleep?" asked Fonso.

"Today, I'd rather stay with the horses," she said.

TWENTY-SEVEN

Malcolm and Mary Ann tried reaching Janet over the telephone, but were unable to. Mary Ann got ready to go out there and find out what happened, when Josh sauntered down the street.

Mary Ann ran towards him, and held him. "Josh, are you alright?" she asked, obviously concerned. "God, Where have you been? You're soaking wet and your clothes are all torn."

"I needed to wash off," replied Lilitu in Josh's voice.

"Come on, let's go inside before you get sick," said Malcolm, leading him by the arm.

Lilitu stopped and looked at them solemnly. "You are not talking to Josh." She waited for their reaction.

Both Malcolm and Mary Ann jumped back, startled.

"I must get these wet clothes off." She continued towards the house and stopped by the door. "Are you going to stand there the rest of the night?"

"Where's my son?" demanded Mary Ann walking towards Lilitu.

"He will be with you soon," she said turning back towards the house. "I will change in a moment. Wait in the living room."

Mary Ann and Malcolm waited downstairs. Before long, Lilitu came down and sat next to them. She still wore Josh's form.

"I will leave Josh's body soon and you may talk to him directly. For the moment, you need to know there are new complications."

"I don't…!"

"No interruptions," said Lilitu cutting short Mary Ann's outburst. "What I have to say is important." She paused to make sure they understood. "There is a serious problem now."

"You mean, worse than you?" said Mary Ann.

"I said, NO interruptions!" Lilitu raised her volume with a deep tone while allowing her eyes to take a crimson shade.

Mary Ann was taken aback. She swallowed hard and bit her lower lip.

"What is done is done," continued Lilitu. "There is no purpose in idle arguments." She lay back on the chair and crossed her legs. "I found one of my previous incarnations to be alive, and he is the problem. He does not yet know his potential, but he must be destroyed before he realizes how far he can go. He has allies that will make it difficult to get to him, although even without them he can manage very well."

Malcolm asked Lilitu to stop with a hand movement. He had felt her anger before and did not want to risk it again, but he had to interrupt before she continued.

"Yes," she said impatiently. "What is it?"

"I don't want to sound disrespectful, but why is that important to us?"

"He is not impotent to harm Josh, just to get at me. Similarly, no one close to Josh is impervious to him either. That includes both of you."

"I thought you didn't care?" asked Mary Ann sarcastically.

"I don't care what happens to you, one way or the other. I care what happens to Josh. If Josh dies, either by the hand of this monster or by one of his agents, I'll roam this Earth as a disembodied spirit for another century. I cannot endure one more lifetime."

Mary Ann took another chance and spoke. "For someone who is so insistent upon our help, you certainly have a rude way of asking."

Lilitu looked straight at Mary Ann. The impulse to explode violently came upon her, but she held it in check. For all the millennia she observed and interacted with humankind, in very few instances did she feel one was worth the effort. Even Adamu, the only man she ever loved, betrayed her. Yet, there was something different about Josh. Very few humans impressed her, and very few she liked, for she found most to be petty, repelling.

"And for someone in such a vulnerable position," she finally said, "you are much too brave. You should learn to check your impetuousness or one day you may live to regret it. The monster I speak about will not be as forgiving, and you may count on it that he will, eventually, come after you."

Malcolm knew he needed to intervene for Mary Ann. She reacted as the mother hen protecting her chick, but completely ignored whom she was dealing with.

"Very well," said Malcolm lightly touching Mary Ann's hand. "What should we do now?"

"At the moment, I am not sure. An ocean separates us, which neither can cross alone. The sun would always catch up with us in mid-flight, but if any one of us has the advantage, it is he. He flies with the sun, I fly against it."

"We must, then, go to him," added Malcolm.

"No!" blurted Mary Ann. "We... we can't." She turned to Malcolm. "I thought you wanted to help us and you agree with this... this thing?"

"We must take the offensive before he does," Lilitu said, ignoring her insult. "I can spy on him, but he dares not do the same."

"Why not?" asked Malcolm.

"If he leaves the body he now occupies, I can prevent him from entering it again. He cannot allow that to happen. It puts him on the defensive."

"Why doesn't he simply wait until you're not around?" asked Mary Ann.

"That is a chance he cannot take. If he is out of the body and I catch him, he is done for."

"Can you destroy him? Can you destroy his spirit?" Malcolm was curious. He always thought a soul was indestructible.

"I have never tried. I can hurt him badly, but I have never tried to destroy him. Perhaps I enjoy torturing him too much."

"Why does that not surprise me?" asked Mary Ann with disgust.

"You are quick at judgment," said Lilitu. "As I have said to you before, there are humans that deserve that, and more. This man, while alive, was an abomination of nature. If this answers your question, I enjoy giving back to your fellow humans what they so easily dispense."

"Yes," continued Mary Ann sarcastically. "Only, you decide who deserves it, right?"

"Such matters are not hard to understand. I will counter evil with evil. There is no other viable alternative. Do you believe a child torturer is material for rehabilitation? Do you even want to understand their motives? In nature, a Lion may eat a deer because he is hungry, but man is the only beast that does it for pure pleasure. Yes, I can easily recognize evil humans because I have seen too many of them." Lilitu leaned forward towards Mary Ann. "I will tell you something about the man that is now alive again. In his time, he was garroted for killing and maiming over 300 children. They misjudged him. In reality, he tortured over 800 of them. Do you know why he did it? For pure sexual pleasure. He would make a cut in their bodies with a sharp knife and use the bleeding opening as you would a female sexual organ. Then he would sit on their body and have an orgasm inside the cut as the child screamed with pain. Is that good enough for you? I can tell you more. Much more." Lilitu saw Mary Ann's paling face. "But I can see you have heard enough."

"So," inquired Malcolm, "if he was garroted, why did his spirit survive?"

"When they garroted him, he did not die. He had inside help, you see. Even when they were about to burn him at the stake – after the garroting - his immediate family managed to convince the authorities to allow them to cut him down before the flames reached his body. No one suspected the truth. Once everyone thought he was dead, he secretly retreated to his mountaintop castle to continue his depravities there. He was careful, however, not to build his retreat anywhere near Rennes – his place of origin. He moved closer to the Center of France, near the Southern Alps, where the jagged landscapes are very impressive. It is quite difficult to get to his crude-looking castle, and unless you know what you are looking for, you will never find it.

How he managed to keep such a place a secret was his greatest accomplishment. Fear does wonders when you need to keep a few mouths shut. In his case, terror is a more accurate description. The place was never truly finished, and as it neared completion, he killed most of the workers. With such a man, I should have known better than to think he would keep his word to me. You see we had a covenant, he and I. He promised to release me if I revealed my hiding place. Not that I wanted to keep it secret. It was simply difficult to figure out without my help. Alas, it was not to be. After he promised to destroy me, he defaulted on his word. He kidnapped my body, moved it to his secret mountain, and extorted me for more power. It was then that I decided to put an end to us both by exposing him to the sun while I still occupied his body. I had never tried this before, but I wanted him to die, painfully, if possible. At least that part of it, I achieved. His body burned to ashes slowly, agonizingly. However, my plan backfired, for I survived the ordeal and his soul did not die either. All I managed to do was to condemn him to an eternity of nothingness. He should have remained a disembodied soul forever – a fitting punishment indeed - but now he has found a way to reincarnate."

Mary Ann had heard enough.

"Does this man have a name?" asked Malcolm.

"Presently, he goes by the name of Laslo. When he was alive, however, he was known as Gilles de Rais."

"Why does that name ring a bell?"

Lilitu looked at the grandfather clock. "I believe it is time for me to leave."

"The name is familiar to me. Why? Who was he?" pleaded Malcolm.

"He was the right hand man of your 'Saint Joan of Arc'."

TWENTY-EIGHT

Lilitu flew straight to Gilles' castle. There was something in that old gypsy woman that caught her attention. By now, Josh must be telling Malcolm and Mary Ann all they needed to know about the situation. It would save her the time and patience of having to explain things to mere mortals. Strange that she thought of humans as *mere mortals*. She was as mortal herself, and hoped, one day, to attain her eternal sleep. Before that, however, she had to find a way to destroy Gilles completely and irrevocably. That might prove hard to do.

Although daylight was just beginning in Linden Town, Florida, in France it was closer to noon. Laslo would be in his hiding place, but he was not whom she wanted to see. It was Zgeza.

Lilitu floated above the keep, trying to sense Zgeza's whereabouts. Her eyes suddenly focused on the stable. The woman lay there asleep. Gliding towards the stable, she stopped by the gypsy's feet.

Zgeza seemed to sense Lilitu's approach as she shuddered slightly. Sitting up, she looked around; her hair was covered with straw.

"It is you," she said, not quite determining Lilitu's location. "I believe I know why you came, but we need privacy. I must not go into a trance out here." She stood and walked towards one of the gate-towers. It was small and square, with a door at the middle of the bottom story, but no one used it anymore except the occasional spider. Zgeza opened the door and entered the guardroom. The only other accesses to the tower were the murder hole and two arrowslits – nothing to worry about with those, since they faced the ravine. The other gate-tower, at the opposite side, contained the machinery to operate the portcullis. Zgeza closed the door behind her and sat on a small stool by the northeast corner of the guardroom. Lilitu observed closely as the gypsy woman went into a trance.

Zgeza opened her eyes, looking directly at Lilitu, and spoke. "Why have you come to me? What is it you seek?"

"I want to know why you serve this man?" asked Lilitu.

"I have no choice. If I don't serve him, my people will pay with their lives."

"How did he find you?"

"The shell he occupies used to be my son." Zgeza lowered her eyes in shame. "I was a fool. When my son, Laslo, was murdered, the authorities did nothing. So I tried to bring him back from the dead."

"And got him instead," Lilitu interrupted.

"Yes." Zgeza looked back at Lilitu and, after some consideration, decided to speak her mind. "I wish him destroyed. Can you help me?"

Lilitu smiled. "I was hoping you would say that. Can we count on any of the others?"

"I'm not sure. I had hopes for Mircea, but Laslo slaughtered his daughter last night and I worry for his sanity." Her mind seemed to drift for a moment. "The rest of them fear him too much. They may betray us."

"Do you know where Laslo sleeps?"

"I have searched for his lair, but with no success. It is something I must do with great care, since he can sense my presence. I can only search during those times when he leaves the castle."

"Perhaps I can find it. Where is Mircea now?" asked Lilitu.

"He's in my chambers sleeping away a few pints of whiskey."

"Where are your chambers?"

"Below the kitchen. Go down the steps near the wood stove to the next level. The first door is my room. I'll be there."

"Very well. Go to Mircea and check on him. Is he strong?"

"Physically he's a bull."

"Good. We may be able to destroy Gilles after all. I will nose around for a bit and come back to you later."

"What did you call him?"

"That is his real name. Gilles," said Lilitu as she left the gate-tower and began to sense her way around the inner ward.

Gilles' astral trail was weak. This meant he must be somewhere deep in the vowels of the mountain. A spectral hound could not have done a better job of sniffing him out, but she had to deal with the residual traces of his comings and goings within the castle. The strongest pulses came from the keep, so she moved upward and entered his chambers. An inhuman rage permeated every crack in the walls. The door leading towards the circular steps in the keep pulled her in that direction. In her astral form, not only could she see and hear, but she could also smell. The stench surging up from the bottom of that pit unexpectedly threw her backwards. The smell of death was not foreign to her, but this reminded her of other times; times she would much rather forget. What poison did the Anunnakis carry in their blood that they passed on to humanity? What disease drove humans to so much meaningless bloodshed? At least for her, blood was food, but for these *animals*, killing was fun. She had no answer, and expected never to find one.

She moved back inside the tower and looked down. It was totally dark, but her astral vision permitted her to see all the way to the bottom. The depth of the tower continued for approximately 200 feet below the kitchen door, with a few additional doors scattered throughout different levels of its length. The scent got stronger the deeper she moved down the pit. As she passed near the kitchen door, she became aware of a large Iron Gate spanning half the diameter of the tower, with a gap of several steps on the way down. The gate would stop anyone from trying to walk down the steps, and the gap was a further precaution against intruders. It had been so long since she explored this place, that she had completely forgotten. Somewhere down there lay her body. She hurried down to the bottom. There was no visible door, but she knew there was one. Then she felt his presence. He was on the other side of the wall.

"I know you are out there, Lilitu," said his muffled voice. "I was waiting because I have a proposition for you."

She had no way of answering that he could hear. Suddenly, the wall shifted. He stood naked next to the glass coffin where she lay. He did not wear Laslo's shape, but a counterfeit of Lilitu's inhuman form. It was a strange sensation to see someone - other than herself – that looked like her. After seeing her own reflection on the mirror millions of times, it unnerved her. None of her previous hosts had advanced to this point. *'Give humans a little power,'* she thought, *'and they think they can conquer the world.'* They always forgot that, even with their newfound power, they were still vulnerable.

"You must excuse me," he said, "but I like to feel comfortable. Clothes bother me when I rest. If you stand by the door, I will know where to address you." He rubbed his hairy hands together, his mouth drooling with expectation.

Lilitu did not move, waiting for him to continue.

"Now, let's get back to business, shall we?" he said talking to the door. "Many years ago you asked me to help you, and being the fool that I was, I tried to take advantage of you – that is a transgression that I hope you have forgiven. Now, however, I am in a position to do your bidding. Think of it, all

I need to do is push this little button here, and I will set you free." His huge clawed hand caressed the button on the glass coffin. "I know you want it, so what do you say?" Smacking his lips, he savored the moment. "You need not say anything, for I cannot hear you, but if you agree to my offer, I will know. All you need do is reenter your body and I will feel it." He looked towards the door, and then towards the coffin. "I am waiting."

Lilitu knew exactly why he was willing to help her. He needed to get rid of her to guarantee *his own* freedom. Besides, if he destroyed her while she was out of her body, he knew she would torture him without mercy until the end of time. The man was no idiot, and neither was she. He was her only living mistake, and it was time to remove it.

He began to speak again, but she had heard enough. She traveled up toward the kitchen to find Zgeza while Laslo cursed aloud when he realized she had turned her back on him. Lilitu smiled, leaving him behind.

The gypsy woman sat in a trance by the straw bed where Mircea still lay unconscious from his drunken stupor. Other than Mircea, Zgeza was alone.

"Have you found him?" asked Zgeza.

"Yes," replied Lilitu, "but I know not how to open the door. Yet, even if I did, neither Mircea, nor anyone here, will be a match for him."

"Then all is lost."

"Perhaps not."

TWENTY-NINE

Malcolm did not know what to make of the information he discovered from his research. Not that he doubted Lilitu, but there were many controversial things about Gilles de Rais. He found several detractors to the fact that the only proofs for the man's depravities were the confessions of his servants; most of them extracted by torture. With the exception of Gilles himself, who confessed without going to the rack, there was not much hard evidence; but his confession was fairly damning. He confessed, not only to the 140 children his ecclesiastical accusers charged him with, but also to the murder of, at least, 800 more.

Malcolm found all sorts of essays and articles regarding the man, starting from an effective and logical defense by Alester Crowley. Unfortunately, Alester Crowley, a well-known charlatan and self proclaimed Satanist, did not fare well in the credibility department. H.G. Wells, in his book "Crux Ansata", condemned Gilles, but failed to consider that there was good reason for the Church to fabricate a case against the man. He was a challenge to their power over the king and his court, and if found guilty, the Church stood to gain his considerable lands and properties. Gilles had been, during his lifetime, one of the richest, if not the richest man in Europe.

If he was the threat Lilitu claimed, then their lives were, indeed, in danger. One thing gnawed at him, however. Although Josh corroborated her story about Gilles, unless this monster was a mind reader, how could he know Lilitu had found a new host? There were many unanswered questions. If he dared not leave his new host, how could he make it over the Atlantic Ocean? Just to harm Josh? Unlikely. Either way you looked at it, the man could not win. He decided to confront her tonight.

❖◆❖◆❖◆❖◆❖

Josh had made up his mind, and at this point did not much care for arguments from either Malcolm or Mary Ann. His main concern was to get Lilitu out of his life as soon as he could. She had no hidden agenda other than to die, but this new wrinkle, however, complicated matters quite a bit. Even if she managed to destroy Laslo, his spirit would live on, even after the Sun had gone supernova. This meant that if left unimpeded, Gilles would most certainly hasten humanity's downfall. The point was not in destroying Laslo – that was just a body - but in destroying Gilles. Lilitu, in spite of her scorn for humanity, refused to leave this legacy behind, although she was convinced mankind would, sooner than later, obliterate the planet.

"I have no choice but to help her face Gilles," said Josh as he paced back and forth in the living room. "She has a plan, I'm sure."

"There's only one way you can help her, and that is by airplane," added Malcolm.

"Well, I'm not paying," interjected Mary Ann. She was too worried for her son's life to think straight. "I don't want to mourn both you and my husband for the rest of my life."

Josh approached Mary Ann and knelt in front of her chair, resting his elbows on her knees. "Look, I am well aware of how you feel. I don't look forward to the confrontation either, but I have to do this."

"What, for the sake of humanity?" Mary Ann brought her face close to Josh. "I don't want a dead hero. I want my son."

'That is exactly why I must do it. I don't want Lilitu around me for the rest of my life. If I don't do this, you will never know when you are speaking to me or her."

Mary Ann sighed with frustration as she leaned back on her chair.

"You have no idea what this monster can unleash on the world," continued Josh. "I do. I have seen it in Lilitu's memories. She is right. Besides, if I don't accept this now, eventually he'll learn about us and no one close to me will ever be safe."

Mary Ann's eyes were swollen and tearful. She avoided looking at Josh. "If this can't be avoided, then you're not doing this alone."

"I was hoping I could count on Malcolm to…"

"I meant I'm coming with you," she interrupted, still avoiding his eyes.

"No! I will not put you at risk." Josh stood and, with his right hand, forced her to face him. "That is final."

Mary Ann saw her son as if it was for the first time. He did not behave like a kid anymore. He handled himself differently. *What did Lilitu do to this child?* She thought.

"She did nothing to this child, mother," replied Josh to her unspoken question. "At least nothing I'm not grateful for. I carry with me thousands of years of experience. I now understand and see everything in a different light. Mother," he said, kneeling down to her once more, "I am so much wiser and stronger. You're right. I am not the same Josh anymore, and you should start getting used to it. Don't treat me like a kid, please."

She could do nothing but look at her teenaged son, and realize that he was not there anymore. Trying to hide her face with her hands, she cried.

"That's alright, mom. I understand why you're crying. Believe me, when this is over, we'll both sit and cry together." He held her close.

Malcolm waited for the moment to pass, and said, "well, now that that's settled, we need to get things rolling." He stood and began to walk to the kitchen. "I need some coffee."

Mary Ann looked at Josh and smiled. "Well, you may think it's settled, but you're wrong about one thing."

"What do you mean," asked Malcolm.

Josh answered for her. "She's coming with us."

They looked at each other and laughed nervously while going towards the kitchen.

❖◦❖◦◦❖◦◦❖◦❖

For the good part of an hour, they made plans regarding the purchase of plane tickets, packing, clothing, and all the rest of the things that a long trip usually entails - including passports, which they all had. Mary Ann would have to take an extended leave from work, and Malcolm would have to cancel his calendar appointments for the next month or so. If this was not resolved within a month, then they would probably all be dead by then.

Mary Ann began by calling the airlines to get schedules. Their expenses, as well as the tickets, they agreed, would be a shared venture. A flight was available for France, two days away, and they made their plans accordingly.

Malcolm was about to go home to get his things ready for the trip, when he turned around at the door. "Don't you think we'd better let Lilitu know?" he said to Josh.

Josh returned his gaze and smiled as he said, "she knows."

THIRTY

Almost like clockwork, exactly at sundown, a naked Laslo went into the kitchen screaming for Zgeza. One of the cooks pushed Kore to go fetch her, and the child ran down the stairs to her room. The two cooks and some of the men that were eating at one of the tables froze on the spot. It looked like a freeze-frame picture from a video movie. Laslo excitedly paced around the kitchen until Zgeza finally showed at the door.

"Why did you summon Lilitu before I was ready?" he asked tersely

"I did not summon her. She simply came." Although she was not lying now, Zgeza knew, perfectly well, how to lie to Laslo. He never realized she could hide things from him.

He punched one of the tables, managing to break it easily. "Did she tell you why she came here?"

"I thought you knew that," replied Zgeza defiantly.

Laslo looked at her wickedly. "Why must you constantly confront me?" he asked as his eyes roamed the kitchen. He eyed each of the gypsies in the room. "I am sure you appreciate that Piotra need not be the last." None would dare run away, even while he slept. The few that tried died horribly.

"It is no secret to you that she wants to destroy you," said Zgeza moving closer to him, standing between him and the gypsies. "Why do you torture us with this?"

"There are only two ways she can try to eliminate me. Either she has an accomplice - perhaps several of you - or she has found…" His eyes narrowed and hardened as he saw the truth. "Yes, that's it! Why did I not think of this before? She has found a host."

"I don't know if this is true. She didn't tell me."

"She didn't have to. I know," he said, walking out to the courtyard, laughing.

Zgeza stepped as far as the threshold, observing him with apparent indifference, but she visualized his death a million times a day. One day, her dreams would come true, even if she died trying.

"I want to feed tonight. Don't wait up for me, mother." Laslo changed his shape in clear view of the gypsies. It was no secret to them he was the devil incarnate. "Are my clothes ready?" he asked.

Zgeza took a leather bag from a hook by the kitchen door and threw it towards him. Laslo hung it from his neck, and then walked to the bridge just outside the portcullis. Stretching his wings wide, he plunged down the ravine in search of humans.

He enjoyed the freedom and the feel of fresh air on his face, as he silently glided between the twin-mountains. His flight pattern and destination varied from night to night so as not to arouse undue suspicions on any of the towns he visited. They may have been his hunting grounds, but it was important to avoid discovery. Sometimes, he simply followed the roads, plucking his food like Apples from a tree. Other times, lonely cyclists practicing for the 'Tour de France' - or some other cycling event - would be his prey. The trick was to prevent predictability; a mistake he made during his previous life, and would not repeat again. This is why he made an extra effort to leave no evidence of his feedings. Although just yesterday he fed on Piotra, the hunt satisfied him immensely; one weekly feeding was all he really needed.

The thing he missed the most about his past life was his good looks. He remembered frequently standing in front of the mirror, taking pleasure in his reflection. This body, however, was not attractive by any means, and even the smell was foreign to him. Occasionally he used fragrance, but it was no use. Laslo's smell would still be there. It was good he was now a changeling. Although he could not improve his looks, the enjoyment of watching his victim's faces when they saw him change into an inhuman beast, was heaven. Heaven, indeed. The screams, the smell of fear, and the flavor terror added to their meat.

Is there such a thing as Heaven? he wondered. If there was such a place, he knew he would never see it, but he knew about Hell. He was in it and Lilitu was his tormentor. Was this his personal Hell? If it was, then why wasn't he the King? How many Hells were there?

No, he concluded. *There is no hell and there is no heaven. What happened was an accident. Lilitu's intention was to kill me, but she had no idea of what ended up happening. Now, trapped in this nowhere-land forever, I finally found a way out to make my existence bearable.* There had to be a way to make Lilitu accept his generous offer.

Tonight was specially windy and cool, particularly for summer. On weather like this, he could glide through the sky forever.

He skirted the *Croix de Fer* pass, up to the summit where it joined the *Col du Glandon*, and saw no one. On many occasions, the scenic route of the Alps provided him with all the nourishment he needed, but tonight, the fruit was not there. The next town on his schedule was *Ville-Madeleine*, a small, quaint town, full of superstitious, amusing rabble. Some of his meals attempted to keep him at bay with their crosses and amulets. What hilarious idiots!

Wasting no more time, he changed course and flew directly to the village. There was more to life than eating, but for him, human cuisine was out of the question. The few times he tried he got convulsions. In his past life, his favorites were *Foie Gras, Magret de Canard*, and anything cooked with garlic. Now, garlic was poisonous to his constitution. Even wine was not to his taste any longer. A one-course dinner was all fate left for him.

As he approached the edge of *Ville-Madeleine*, he landed near the road, and then changed to his human form. He hid behind a large rock, and pulled out some clothes from the leather bag. For these outings, he normally used exquisite clothes, to give the impression of wealth. When he walked into town, as far as anyone could tell, he was nothing more than what he appeared to be; a generous, affluent human.

One of the things he wished to have in his castle was electricity; an incredible convenience, and luxury. Night seemed to turn into day with these wonderful lamps, but he knew that, for his refuge, it would never be. The castle, however, was too remote, and he would much rather keep its location a secret even if it meant putting up with oil lamps. In his astral form, light, or the lack of it, was of no consequence, but ever since he possessed this body, he dared not abandon it. In human form, darkness was almost unbearable.

Ville-Madeleine had a little *café en plein-air* by the main plaza, which he usually frequented. These sidewalk cafés were quite convenient, for they allowed him to observe and select his prey without attracting attention. Whatever libation he ordered ended up in the shrubbery next to his table. Obtaining money was not a problem. A few Francs were all he needed for his nights out, and his victims, as a rule, provided him with enough for the next outing. Besides, he had amassed more than enough wealth in this new lifetime, to carry him over any emergency.

His favorite dish was young boys. He fancied them before, and he fancied them still, but they were not usually available at night. Young male prostitutes were a good second choice; if one disappeared, no one would miss them. On a small town such as this, however, male prostitutes were scarce. Females, if he had no other choice, would do in a pinch.

Then, there was the next best thing. This particular café had the convenience of a club directly across from it, frequented by homosexuals. This was new for Gilles. Now they were called gay, a new name for an age-old institution. He remembered when the word gay simply meant 'happy'. How ironic. In his time, no one dared openly proclaim sexual preferences. What a good thing, this was. Window-shopping at its best.

Tonight he got lucky. A handsome young man caught his eye just before he entered the club. The young man looked at him, flirting openly. Laslo smiled as he beckoned at him with his index finger.

Pointing at himself the young man mouthed the word *"Moi?"* Laslo nodded, and the boy sashayed across the street.

"Good evening," said Laslo in a deep seductive voice.

"Good evening yourself," replied the young man eyeing Laslo from head to toe.

"Won't you join me?" said Laslo as he pulled out the chair next to him, softly patting the seat.

The young man sat. "Can I have anything on the menu?" he asked.

"Whatever your heart desires."

"Are *you* on the menu?" he flirted tentatively.

"Are *you*?" Laslo asked back.

"Hmm. We'll see." The young man took the menu and pretended to study it.

"I presume you have a name."

"Phillipe." He replied with apparent indifference, without taking his eyes away from the menu.

"Well, Phillipe, you look delicious to me. When can I have a sample?"

"Buy me dinner first, and then we can go for a walk. This is a very special night for me." Phillipe's hand lightly touched Laslo's thigh.

"And why is that?" asked Laslo pretending to be interested.

"As if meeting one as handsome as you weren't enough?" Phillipe raised his left eyebrow and giggled lightly.

Laslo nodded gracefully.

"When I left home, I had a feeling about tonight. I don't know. Call me romantic." His hand, much bolder this time, grabbed at Laslo's crotch. "Please, let's make it special." His voice whispered the words, almost pleading.

"I promise you, it will be."

THIRTY-ONE

All the preparations for the trip were behind them. It was now a matter of going to the airport the next day to catch the plane to London. From there, they would connect to Geneva, take a train to Chamonix, and finally on bicycle to an old abandoned hamlet near the foot of the cliff where Gilles' castle was located. Josh knew the final destination; Malcolm took care of the route. After that, it was Lilitu's hand.

A feeling of loneliness gnawed at Josh, especially after seeing Janet. Although he promised her he would be back, she cried for him. Aside from his mother, no one cried for him before. He felt sorry for her, and felt sorry for himself. Nevertheless, Janet would get over it. Of that, he was sure.

What worried him the most was Mary Ann. She had no business going on this trip; even Malcolm should stay too. They would only get in the way of things, although both had their reasons for tagging along. Malcolm felt responsible for this situation, and his mother wanted to protect him. Nothing he could do would persuade either of them to stay.

◆━◈━◈━◈━◈━◆

The 747 flight from Miami to London was to leave at 7:30 p.m. and arrive at 9:10 a.m. the next day; the airline typically overbooked the flight. After an hour's delay at Miami airport, it finally departed. They had three seats next to the left wing. Josh sat by the window, Mary Ann in the middle, and Malcolm in the aisle seat. Sardines in a can had more room than they did. Josh, who was the smallest of the three, could barely move. An hour after departure they had, what some people may call, dinner. Malcolm got engrossed in a book on mysticism he brought along, and Mary Ann flipped the small television screen forward and watched a movie. They agreed not to talk about their plans during the flight, or people might think them crazy.

Josh tried self-hypnosis to try to contact Lilitu, but had no luck. Either she was elsewhere, or somehow the vibrations during the flight caused a disturbance. He tried astral projection, but that also failed to work. The best thing to do was to sleep the time away.

◆–◆–◆◆–◆–◆◆–◆–◆

The flight arrived in London at 10:15 a.m. They brought two carry-ons, each with enough clothes for a week or two. The five-hour layover forced them to wait in the main lounge of the airport. Mary Ann browsed around the shopping area, while Malcolm and Josh sat it out, discussing trivialities; again, purposefully avoiding the topic of Lilitu or the purpose behind the trip.

The connecting flight to Geneva, Switzerland, scheduled for 3:35 p.m., had another delay for which they waited an additional hour by the gate. At 4:45, the 757 finally took off.

Geneva, located in the far southwestern corner of Switzerland that juts into France, was a short hop away from Chamonix, France. Although it was summer, the temperature was around 64 degrees Fahrenheit; they brought some light, but warm clothes. A mistake Mary Ann thought they might regret once they tried hiking up to Gilles' castle; it would be much colder up in the mountains, without a doubt. She would have to buy a few extra pair of long johns once they got to Chamonix. The flight arrived in Geneva at 7:30 p.m.

The Geneva airport was small, with only one baggage claim area. Beyond that, there were two exits, one in front of the baggage area leading to the Swiss side, and one to the left, leading to the French. They took the left exit, where they passed through the airport police and customs. Ahead of that, there was a small room for car rentals and telephones. Exiting to the parking lot, Malcolm made inquiries on the shuttle bus to the train station. Mary Ann, about to drop with exhaustion, was grateful there were no more busses or trains leaving until the next day. It forced them to stay the night at some hotel.

To Land in Geneva and not take the time to see the city bordered on lunacy, thought Mary Ann, but this was not a pleasure trip. So far, outside of the flight delays, the trip went without a hitch.

The city lies at an elevation of 1,230 feet, located at the southwestern end of Lake Geneva, in the center of a natural basin encircled by mountains. Enclosed from the west by France, on the north by Germany, on the east by Austria and Liechtenstein, and on the south by Italy, Switzerland is landlocked amid the mountains of central Europe.

A local taxi took them to a quaint little hotel near the train station. For the moment, after discussing the possibility of taking separate rooms, they decided to go for adjoining accommodations and leave the connecting door open; a safety precaution that, under the circumstances, was necessary.

Their only plan, so far, was to get to their destination. They assumed that Lilitu would take charge once they got there. Up to now, however, she had mysteriously, remained silent. They felt apprehensive about that, but figured she would reveal her strategy soon. After a quick bite at the hotel restaurant, they went to their room to sleep. No big discussions, no planning, only rest. Malcolm, who knew enough French to get by, did most of the talking and translating.

❖◦❖◦❖◦❖◦❖

Josh knew Lilitu would come to him that night. It was not long after he fell asleep that she called to him.

"It's was about time you showed up," said Josh in his astral form.

"I have been busy."

"We're all a little nervous here. What's the plan now?"

"I'm not sure yet," she said hesitatingly.

"Please tell me you're pulling my leg," he replied in despair.

"Pulling your leg?" She thought about that one for a moment. "No. We will discuss things more thoroughly after you are all settled in Chamonix. In the meantime, I want you to come with me."

"Where?" asked Josh.

"Let us see the battlefield. I want you to see what we'll be up against."

Lilitu floated out of the bedroom, pulling Josh with her. She still had the power to control him.

As they flew to their destination, Josh noticed a difference between Lilitu's astral body and his own. Lilitu had no umbilical cord. This cord, also known as Ariadne's thread, connects to the physical body during astral projection by an infinitely elastic and very fine silver cord, a cosmic umbilical cord. Josh also wondered why he had not yet seen any other astral bodies floating around. There must be thousands of wandering astral bodies, and he should be able to see them. Then a horrible thought came to him. What if all those disembodied spirits get tangled, or confused with each other and end up returning to the wrong body? Was this some sort of hallucination, or some bad connection in his neurons?

Lilitu pointed out the town of Chamonix as they quickly flew by. It lay in a large valley, but they went by too fast for Josh to get much detail about it. They continued for a long stretch, which in astral time was insignificant.

She stopped for a moment at what seemed to be the abandoned hamlet they planned to use as their center of operations. It looked haunted and creepy. The moon shone over the deserted buildings, giving the impression that werewolves and ghosts frequented the place. Josh detected some movement inside some of the houses, but to him, it felt more like a few fleeting images seen with the corner of the eye, than a solid mass.

"This is going to be our first obstacle. Once we get this far, we will convert it into our camping ground." Lilitu turned to look straight at Josh. "Are you afraid?"

"Yes, very much afraid. You said *obstacle*. Somehow, that makes me nervous. What awaits us here?"

"This is only a *watch tower* for Gilles, sort of speak; an advance warning system. It is nothing we cannot deal with, but we must be careful." She pointed towards some of the buildings. "You must have noticed some movement inside the houses."

"I thought it was just my imagination. What was it?" asked Josh.

"A few gypsies, but they are armed and dangerous. Come let us see," she said as she passed by one of the windows and pointed out a couple of men sitting inside. One slept while the other kept watch. "They have no reason to fear us. While in this state, there is nothing we can do to harm them. Besides, they cannot see us."

"I should have insisted on leaving Malcolm and my mother behind. They are of no use to us, and I don't want their deaths on my conscience."

"It is too late for lamentations now. We can, however, make good use of them."

"Good use!" interrupted Josh with anger. "For God's sake, Lilitu, these are not disposable persons."

Lilitu waited for Josh to calm down. "I am well aware of what they mean to you. I will protect them as much as I can, but once you see the monster that is up there," she said pointing to a distant peak, "you will understand why this must be done." She did not remember another host such as Josh. He was about to put his life on the line, yet his thoughts were about someone else's safety. "For the moment, I want to begin the process of weakening their defenses."

"How?"

'It takes a lot of effort and taxes my resources quite a bit, but if I can make them see me, they might get frightened enough to leave without a fight."

Josh stood by as he watched Lilitu shape-shift, then slowly begin to take a more solid appearance. Her real form could make any man die on the spot; a werewolf with the face of a bat and the wings of a demon. No wonder she always appeared to him as a beautiful human female. This apparition could seduce no human in his right mind. It made him wonder about Adamu…

Lilitu walked towards the gypsy and emitted a low, menacing growl.

The startled man dropped his rifle and ran out of the house screaming. The noise woke the sleeping gypsy. When he saw Lilitu, he also ran out. Josh could not help but laugh at the whole thing.

"Josh," she said. "This rifle will be useful to us later. I can call on a limited amount of solidity, so keep your eyes sharp and let me know if they are coming back." She tried to grab the rifle, but it kept slipping through her hands – it was too heavy. Josh could hear the men talking excitedly to each other within one of the other houses. Before long, some of them would come back to investigate.

Lilitu looked at Josh and said, "I must make a stronger attempt, but there is a price. Doing this will weaken me. The only way to get my strength back is to feed tonight."

Josh closed his eyes and nodded.

Lilitu's eyes flared with red fire as she finally picked up the rifle and flew outside with it. Soon after, a group of three armed gypsies carefully entered the house.

They argued amongst themselves, and surprisingly, Josh could make out most of what they said. This was another one of Lilitu's gifts; her knowledge was his.

A heavy-set bearded man, who must have been their leader, shouted at the two guards that were here before. "What you saw was probably Laslo, you stupid fools. What are you? Scared rabbits? I see no one here!" He then shouted to them, "find your rifle!"

They frantically looked around the floor. Two other armed guards stood behind the bearded man. After a short search for the rifle, they stopped and faced the leader with an expression of wonderment. Suddenly, their faces turned pale. It was just before the man shot them dead. "Search the area!" he growled to the men behind him, his rifle still smoking in his hands.

Josh began to understand Lilitu's attitude towards humans. The man did it so cold-bloodedly, so casually; it shook him to his foundations. He left the house looking for Lilitu and saw her floating towards him from one of the foothills. Her previous semi-solid form had reverted to her astral body; her inhuman shape still apparent.

"We now have a weapon. I hope Malcolm will have no problem using it if it comes to that." She saw a strange expression on Josh. "I notice my appearance bothers you."

"I'll get over it," replied Josh.

"Good. Now we have less of them to worry about. We must now continue our journey. I want you to see the castle."

THIRTY-TWO

"We have tarried long enough." Lilitu turned around to face Josh as she flew backwards. "See that string of mountains behind me?"

"I see them," replied Josh.

"That is where we are headed. There is a narrow pass through the rocks at the foot of the largest peak. The road leading up to the castle begins there."

"Wait, wait," said Josh suddenly realizing why she was showing him the area. "I thought *you* were going to take him on, not me." He stopped in mid-air, a sensation of desperation swept over him.

"We must plan for every contingency. If it comes to your having to do the deed, then you and your companions must know how to get to him quickly."

"If you can't handle him, what makes you think any of us will?"

"I have not tested his strength, nor have I had to face my own power turned against me. If we reach an impasse, it will come down to you having to finish him off during his most susceptible time, daytime. Remember, I am not invulnerable, and neither is he."

"And neither am I!" He felt stunned by her coldness. "If he hurts you while you are in my body, I will be hurt as well. Why is it that with every passing second I feel worse about this?" Josh stood his ground, not moving either way.

Lilitu moved closer to him, looking down at him intensely. "Josh, he made me an offer to destroy my body. I could accept if you so desire, and you will be rid of me. Is that what you want?"

"And the meek shall inherit the world," he said with sarcasm and bitterness. It was pointless to deny her logic.

"What stupidity! The meek will never inherit the world," she blasted back in anger. It took her a moment to regain her composure. "But I knew you would understand," she continued, turning back towards the mountains. "You worry too much. Whatever will happen, will happen."

Josh began to move with her. "I don't get it. You have to be much stronger than he is. You must see that."

"You are probably right."

"Then why don't you simply go up there and kill him?" asked Josh, completely dissatisfied.

"That is exactly what I intend to do, but not before I am ready; not before I am certain of the outcome. Nothing is simple, and it is foolish to assume anything about the enemy. When I finally go to the castle, everything must be in place in case I fail. That is where you and your companions come in. First, I need to eliminate Gilles' allies. We already got rid of two; tonight I intend to come back to clean up the hamlet."

"You intend to kill them all?" Josh was aghast. He still had mixed feelings about killing.

"We have an ally at the castle, and I will spare those that she persuades to abandon their futile cause. It will be a matter of who they fear the most." She struggled to control her curtness. Not used to having her decisions questioned, this conversation annoyed her.

"But they don't know you from Adam. How do you expect them to fear you?"

"Don't use that name in my presence!"

"Sorry," said Josh. "I forgot."

"After tonight, they will have ample reason to fear me. Now," she continued after a short pause, "we must sweep the path leading to the castle to see what else we find. If we do this right, at the end, it will only be him against us."

"There's a problem," said Josh as a disturbing thought came to him. "If we set up camp at the hamlet, my mother and Malcolm will be there alone. How do you know that when you go up there to confront him, he's not going to slip by you? He can easily fly down and kill them."

"I have considered it." She stopped once more, determined to put to rest Josh's fears. "Trust me, I will not leave them unprotected. If all goes as expected, they may not have to stay at the hamlet at all."

"If you are thinking of bringing them up to the castle, you're crazy," said Josh, boldly meeting her eyes.

"Can you think of anywhere safer for them to be, than with me?"

Although it made sense, Josh stiffened at the possibilities. If anything happened to Mary Ann or Malcolm, he would never forgive himself or Lilitu.

"Tonight, after we go back to your hotel, I must possess you to take care of as many of his allies as I can. We cannot set camp in the middle of enemy territory unless we get rid of them first." Looking at him with intense determination, she continued, "Josh, we must be prepared for any eventuality. Your companions came with you; it is too late to go back on that now. Believe me, I will take all possible precautions. I will not be careless. For the moment, Gilles has no idea where you are or that you even exist. He can only suspect that I have found a host."

"Don't refer to me as an object. It makes me feel used." He felt deflated, humiliated.

"What should I call you then?" She tried to suppress a smile, but her eyes betrayed her amusement.

"Forget it," countered Josh, slightly angry. He was about to say something else when he saw a large figure gliding down one of the peaks. It looked like a giant bat from a distance. "Look…over there" he managed to say.

"That must be our friend, Gilles," said Lilitu turning towards the mountains. "This is better than I expected. If he is no longer in the castle, I may have time to speak to Zgeza." She waited for the figure to disappear and pulled Josh with her towards the pass. "This may not look like an easy route," she said as she showed Josh. "But looks can be deceiving. Gilles caused a huge landslide after he finished the castle, to discourage the curious, but he left a way through. If you look behind these large boulders, you will notice there is a path, large enough for a horse and wagon."

"Clever," remarked Josh.

"He is no idiot. I will not make the mistake of underestimating him twice." She then pointed towards the path, as it seemed to go up and around a tall peak.

Josh looked up and noticed he was in a large crevice between two cliffs.

"The path goes steeply up this cliff, encircling the mountain a few times, until it reaches its midpoint. Then, the path abruptly ends, connecting with a drawbridge to the castle on the adjacent cliff; when retracted, the chasm is too wide to attempt crossing by foot. At the end of the drawbridge, you will find an iron portcullis that only opens from the inside of the tower to the left. Our allies may come in handy with that also, assuming Gilles does not first kill them all."

Josh could not believe the grandeur and intimidating feel of the place. A light, but permanent fog covered the area. The path disappeared into the fog, and from behind it, the occasional howling from some unknown beast cut into his fears. *What manner of place was this?* He thought.

"I can feel your anxiety," asked Lilitu. "Try to control it, for he can smell it."

"I will do my best," replied Josh as casually as he could manage.

"Good. Let us continue, then."

"What other surprises can we expect?" he added, not really expecting an answer.

Lilitu looked at him, not quite understanding the alarm carried by his voice and demeanor. For most of her lifetime, she never had cause to fear much of anything.

As their astral bodies floated up the path, their sight cut through the fog most efficiently. Human eyes had no such advantages. They encircled the mountain once, before finding an outpost. It was a small shack, large enough for a four-person guard. Lilitu looked inside. Two men guarded the path while two others slept. She was convinced these men would not dare fall asleep on their watch, or Gilles would torture them to death. Fear does not make for good allies, but she could take no chances. She would dispose of them also. Encircling the mountain once more, they reached the end of the path. The drawbridge was retracted, and the gate was down.

"Let us go inside," said Lilitu confidently. "There should be only handful of people in there."

Gliding inside behind Lilitu, Josh saw that it was true. The four men in the courtyard went about their business, and as they glided through the kitchen, two women and a child labored away. All of them seemed oblivious to their presence. Josh followed Lilitu down a set of dank, dark stairs. When they approached the next level, Lilitu melted into the female human form Josh was accustomed to see.

"Why did you change?" asked Josh.

"The one we are about to see, it is important she not see my real form, lest I frighten her away. We need her on our side."

Suddenly, an old woman's voice called to Lilitu from behind one of the doors.

"I am here," Zgeza said in a monotone.

Josh had seen plenty of horror movies, and none came close to the disturbing atmosphere permeating these walls. In fact, the whole thing, from the hamlet to the castle, gave him an eerie feeling. The abandoned hamlet, the fog, the howling, the cliffs, and the putrescence of the castle; it was like a living nightmare. This time, the difference was in him. He was the ghost.

Lilitu entered through the door, followed closely by Josh. Zgeza looked at him as if his astral body was still solid.

"She can see me?" he asked Lilitu, looking at her in surprise.

"I can see you and hear you as well," countered Zgeza with apparent disinterest. She then addressed Lilitu and asked about Josh "Who is he?"

"He is…" She was about to say the word host, but Josh interrupted her.

"I'm her host," he said in her language. It came out natural and effortlessly. He surprised himself as the foreign words came out instinctively. "How is it you are able to see me?"

"I am a medium. In a trance I can see things," she responded.

"What have you to tell me?" asked Lilitu impatiently.

"Mircea will not be of much use to us. He is almost catatonic. He sits in his room swaying back and forth, whimpering his daughter's name over and over."

"What about the rest?"

"Laslo has a group of Romani waiting in the hamlet down by the foot of the mountains. They are an evil bunch that will follow him blindly. I will not even try to sway them."

"You are aware that those you cannot persuade, I must destroy," said Lilitu

Zgeza nodded.

"What about the ones here, in the castle?" Lilitu asked.

"They fear him greatly, but they will follow me if I could lead them to safety. There are several guards on the mountain path, and we cannot get past them without Laslo knowing it."

"Worry no more. After I get them out of your way, including the ones in the hamlet, I will let you know. Then, when the sun comes up, you may leave in peace. I strongly advise you to leave before next sundown."

"Very well," she said with a sigh. "I will not talk to my people until after sunup. If they decide to stay, they may betray me to Laslo. Once the sun is out, there is nothing they can do – unless they decide to kill me themselves."

"Why would they want to stay, for heaven's sake?" asked Josh.

"They fear him more than they fear God," Zgeza replied with shame. "He repays faithlessness with torture; long, painful torture." She lowered her eyes. "I don't blame them."

"You may warn them that if they harm you in any way, I will take special pleasure with their deaths." Her warning was firm, final.

"I am prepared to accept whatever they want to do with me," Zgeza said determined to atone for her sins. "I brought this curse upon them."

Lilitu suddenly reacted as she looked towards the ceiling of the small room. "Quiet," she whispered a bit startled. "I feel his presence. I wasn't expecting him back so soon." Looking at Zgeza, she said, "I must leave, but you will hear from me soon."

Josh suddenly felt himself violently pulled out of the room, passing through walls until they reached the outside of the castle. Lilitu continued a fast downward trek towards the base of the cliffs. It was a brief but confusing feeling.

Passing through solid rock made him feel disoriented and nauseous, with an absolute loss of reality. While inside the solid material, he had no awareness of direction or movement. It gave him chills just to imagine himself trapped inside a mountain without knowing how to break out.

"Why the hurry to leave?" he asked Lilitu as they reached the foot of the cliffs.

"He might take it upon himself to murder Zgeza or another of the gypsies, just to spite me. Besides, I didn't want to risk having him discover you."

"He can see me too?" asked Josh.

"No. Not like Zgeza can, but he may be able to feel your presence. His men are alert, but they won't be ready for what I have in store for them." Lilitu pressed her flight back to the hotel.

"When you take my body again, are you sending me back to that awful dungeon?" He stiffened at the thought of it.

"No. I don't see a reason for that now. You may stay with me if you wish, and observe, if you feel up to it."

"No," he replied tersely. "I am not up to it, but I want to make sure nothing goes wrong. Too much is at stake for me to take the easy way out. Can I communicate with you once you take over my body?"

"Yes. We are in tune with each other. I will be as aware of you as if you were in your solid condition."

"Good. Then I will be the eyes behind your back."

She smiled, with satisfaction.

<hr>

The visit to the hotel was short. Mary Ann slept in the twin bed next to his. A slight snoring came from the adjoining room, where Malcolm slept soundly. Lilitu wasted no time in entering Josh's body.

For Josh, it was a bizarre spectacle to see his body up and about, while he stood by and watched. The feeling did not last long, however, as Lilitu shifted to her real appearance. The change was brief, but not instantaneous. She went from a human to, what looked like a werewolf. Finally, her wings emerged. Josh looked at her with fascination. She reminded him of a creature best described in the Mayan mythological epic, the *Popul-Vuh*; the beast called 'the Camazotz', a human-sized, vampire-bat-god of the underworld.

Lilitu smiled as she heard Josh's thoughts. "I was the Camazotz," she whispered casually. Then, with extraordinary swiftness, she opened the window and flew towards the hamlet. Josh followed right behind her.

THIRTY-THREE

It was not long before Laslo burst through Zgeza's bedroom door. She expected to find him in his perpetually foul mood.

"Was she here?" he asked, studying her with curious intensity.

Zgeza knew better than to lie this time. She was well aware he had sensed Lilitu's presence. "Yes, she was," she replied; only giving him what he asked for; no more, no less.

"You are plotting with her," he growled. His eyes blazed with anger as he extended his right hand towards her neck. He pulled her up until her eyes came to his level, while squeezing her throat firmly. Zgeza held on to his arms, her feet dangling in the air.

"Would you kill the only one that can help you?" she managed to croak through her constricted windpipe.

Laslo relaxed his grip, putting her down again. Zgeza coughed convulsively, attempting to get her breath back. Almost tripping over the chair behind her, she managed to hold on to its backrest.

"So you presume I believe you to be on my side?" he asked humorously.

"How do you expect anyone to be on your side if you constantly threaten them?" she said as she slowly managed to sit. Her hands massaged her throat.

"Fear is the only thing humans value, so I let them know how much I understand their dilemma." He placed both hands on his hips and slowly paced the room. "Every once in a while, I give them a token of my appreciation. Take you, for example. Did you not experience, just now, how much you wanted to help me?"

"Yes, of course."

"You lie," he said indifferently.

"You know I cannot do that. If I lie, you can tell."

"Oh, ho! No, not with you. You can lie impudently and get away with it." He brought his face to her level, just inches from each other. For effect, he took his voice down to a deep growl, showing her his large canines. "This would not be one of those times, would it?" His hand lightly touched her chin, forcing her eyes to meet his. "Well...?"

Zgeza met his gaze with an equally defiant intensity. "If you don't believe me, then kill me now."

"Ha!" was his mirthful reaction, as he straightened up again. "That's what I like about you. One of these days I'm going to open those legs of yours and find the largest balls I have ever seen." He continued to pace the floor. "Now, what did she want this time?"

"She came looking for you."

"Did she say anything about her host?"

"She came alone, and said nothing about a host," replied Zgeza with a stone face.

"That means her host must still be far-off, otherwise, she would have killed my men at the hamlet. Instead, she just tried to frighten them. What a fool she is to show me her hand." The thought froze as he stared at the wall. He could not make the mistake of forgetting how powerful an opponent Lilitu was. "I took the precaution to find another sanctuary before she physically gets here. This castle is not safe any longer." His hands brushed the hair off his face.

"Where is this new place?" asked Zgeza, wondering if he was baiting her.

"There's no need for you to worry about it. You will know when I am ready to tell you."

"Should I begin packing?"

"There's only two ways you are leaving this god-forsaken place, dear mother. Down the cliff, head first, or with me, as my companion. It all depends on how you play the game." He stopped mid-stride, slowly turning towards her. "I will ask you once again, are you on my side?"

"And I will repeat my answer: you either kill me or trust me."

He turned to the door and left.

◆◆-◆◆-◆◆-◆◆-◆◆

Gilles knew Zgeza hated him, and would betray him as soon as she had the chance. Killing her was his only option, but not yet. If he could fool the old woman into giving Lilitu false information, it might be worth keeping her alive a while longer. True, the possibility of moving to a new sanctuary was now a reality, but he was not ready. For the moment, he secreted his lair to a deeper recess within the mountain. There, he could hide, hoping that Lilitu would believe he was gone. Of course, this meant the old gypsy would have to die once she passed her information to the enemy. He flew up to the crown of the Keep and kept his eyes open.

If he were lucky, he would be set for life in less than two weeks, and all it took was a little restraint when the opportunity presented itself. A wealthy Londoner he met at the gay bar in Ville-Madeleine fell in love with him, unwittingly revealing his assets just before Gilles was about to strike him dead. Gilles enjoyed having his victims perform fellatio on him, before killing them. Doing it right after the orgasm intensified his pleasure tenfold.

Nevertheless, this man talked continuously. Unintentionally, he talked his way out of his own death. The man lived in London and needed to return the next day on business, but not before he begged Gilles to come live with him, to be his lover. The man owned a castle and a few other properties. Gilles knew he was not lying. This, he understood, was his ticket out.

He explained to the man that he was allergic to sunlight. Travelling in daytime was out of the question; to which the man jokingly asked: "You're not a vampire, are you?" They both laughed it off, and the man promised he would figure a way to get him to London. The next day, Gilles had one of his gypsies rent a mailbox in the town of Ville-Madeleine, then sent the man a perfumed letter with his return address. That would be his point of contact. This was six days ago, and Gilles expected to hear from him soon.

His new life was good, enjoying it with almost perfect freedom – until Lilitu found him again. His mistake, once he found his host, was to continue using this old hideout. After all the years of Lilitu getting a kick out of torturing his astral soul, he discovered that she never came back to the castle, so it turned out to be a good place to hide. Yet, once he possessed Laslo, he should have found some other sanctuary. This was stupidity itself, and he had never been a stupid man.

Suddenly, out from the distance, he heard the faint sound of repeated gunfire. His eyebrows shot up with surprise as he sat attentively. The sound, as far as he was able to determine, came from the abandoned hamlet. This must be Lilitu' doing. His first impulse was to fly down and investigate, but caution was called for. It was time to put his plan into action.

Hurriedly, he flew down to see Zgeza. He opened her door and feigned extreme nervousness. "Lilitu is now at the hamlet," he said from the door with a touch of alarm on his face. "I must fly to my hideout." He hesitated at the door, and then addressed her again. "I will come for you later." With that, he closed the door and flew away, laughing all the way down to his usual lair within the bowels of the mountain.

THIRTY-FOUR

Lilitu, now in full body, approached the hamlet silently. Josh, in his astral form, observed, acting as a backup warning system. Her ability to see in the dark was limited, since now she saw through Josh's physical eyes. The dilapidated state of the houses now exuded a more substantial, mustier odor. Many of them had lost half their roofs, so she could look from above and determine if there was someone inside.

After a careful reconnaissance, she determined there were four houses posted with two men at each corner of the hamlet. In addition, a building near the center served as headquarters for their leader and his three bodyguards. If these men kept watch all day, then there must have been a group of replacements sleeping somewhere; or perhaps they came from a nearby village to replace the night shift.

The first house Lilitu decided to attack was the furthest away from the castle, the northwest corner. Flying over the caved-in roof, she easily saw the two men inside. With careful positioning from above, she suddenly dropped between them. They never had the chance to react. She grabbed each by their throats, squeezing hard and fast. The only sound heard was a short gurgle, and a pop from one of the men's eyeballs as his eyes fell on the floor.

Josh stayed outside, watching for stragglers. He did not hear much, since Lilitu caught the men's rifles before they touched the floor, but he heard their necks breaking. He shuddered at the sound.

The center building was strategically within sight of every house in the hamlet. At one time, it must have been the village meeting place. Josh wondered about the possible reasons for the original owners to abandon this place. If Gilles re-awoke some 40 years ago, then he probably wiped them all out. Maybe there were legends around the region. A village does not simply disappear without people speculating and gossiping about it.

Lilitu interrupted his reverie by moving on to the next house, at the southwest corner. This one had a full roof and she figured she had to enter through the front door. On this one, she had no way of determining how many men were inside, or their exact location. She hesitated, deciding to skip this one, moving on to the next, by the northeast. As easy as the first round, she dispatched two more men in similar fashion. Four down, eight to go.

She exited the second house the same way she came in, through the roof. As she took wing, a man came out of the center building; he pulled out a cigarette, and lit a match. He looked straight at her.

Calmly, the man took a long drawn out drag from his cigarette, leaning his head to the inside of the building.

"Hey, Yoska," she heard him say, "Laslo is back." He turned once more towards Lilitu, and waved to her while flicking the match to the ground.

Freezing in mid-air, she landed softly and crouched, but kept her eyes on him. She did not wave back. As soon as he took his eyes away, she took off towards the next house. She had to act fast.

Palko flapped his arms against his body, trying to generate some warmth for his muscles. Looking at the moon, he allowed a mouthful of smoke to escape his lungs. He was not oblivious to her presence, but rather expected her to approach. When next he looked in her direction, she was gone. *Strange*, he thought. *Laslo always comes to speak directly to Yoska. What's going on?*

He threw the cigarette on the floor and called to Yoska.

"What is it now?" said the burly man as he walked out with a glum face.

"I just saw Laslo, right over there. Did he tell you he was coming back tonight?"

"He never tells me these things," Yoska growled with irritation. "If he shows up, he shows up."

"Yeah, but weren't we supposed to be on the lookout for strangers?"

"And how many do you know that look like him, huh? Tell me that."

"I don't know. I don't like this. He always comes straight to you, then leaves. I've never seen him walking around."

"All right," said Yoska as he cocked his rifle. "Go look."

"Me?"

"I'll cover your back you stupid idiot. Now go on!" Yoska butted him with the rifle, egging him on.

Both men walked closer to one of the houses Lilitu had attacked, and called out for the men inside. No one answered. They called again. The only sound came from the hoot of a distant owl as the clouds covered the moon on and off.

"Okay, Palko" whispered Yoska. "There's something strange here. Go inside and find out what the hell's going on."

Palko mumbled a curse deep inside, but complied. He approached the house slowly, his rifle at the ready in front of him. Stopping at the threshold of the door, he looked back at Yoska and shrugged. "They're gone," he whispered.

Yoska waved his arm ordering him to go inside and look.

Palko swallowed hard, turning back into the house. "Hey, guys…" Taking a step inside the house, he stepped on something; but before he determined what it was, Lilitu tore out his vocal cords.

Yoska waited outside for Palko. "Palko," he whispered. "Where'd you go, you big coward?" After calling him a few times, he knew the man was dead, and whatever killed him was still in there.

Alone in the darkness of night, he panicked. This was trouble. He shot a couple of rounds in the air to call out however many of his men might still be alive.

Two men inside his headquarters came out, guns in hand, as well as two men inside the house by the southwest corner. They ran towards Yoska.

"What is it, Yoska?" asked Ferka, his main bodyguard.

"Get ready. The enemy's here." He pointed towards the house that Palko just entered.

"Where are the others?"

"I think they are dead," Said Yoska.

Lilitu stood inside the house, with Palko's body by her feet. She knew Yoska and four more men were outside. Five men with rifles were more than she could handle openly. Then she heard Josh speak to her from outside.

"I'm standing right next to them, Lilitu. They're all facing your position, but they're not making a move."

The men heard nothing, although Lilitu heard him clearly. It gave her an idea. She spoke out loudly, changing her voice to sound like Josh, "if you surrender now, I will spare your lives." Right after she said it, she jumped out the opposite window and took flight to a high altitude.

"Why it's just a kid," said Ferka.

"Yeah, a kid that just killed half my men," replied Yoska.

Suddenly, from the sky, Lilitu flew towards them. "Stop," she ordered in as deep a tone as she could. "What is the meaning of this disturbance?"

The men waited for her to land next to them. Yoska addressed her.

"The enemy has arrived, Laslo. We have him cornered in there." Yoska moved aside, allowing Lilitu to stand in the center.

Knowing Gilles, Lilitu knew exactly what to do. "You fools! Why are you just standing here?"

Yoska studied Lilitu closely, his probing eyes bored into her.

"Lilitu," she heard Josh say. *"You have blood on you."*

Six armed men surrounded her and she had to think fast. "I will take care of this," she growled, pushing them aside, running inside the house.

"NOW, I HAVE YOU WERE I WANTED YOU," she shouted out deeply.

"NO, PLEASE DON'T KILL ME!" she replied in Josh's voice. She scuffled inside, took Palko's rifle, and fired a shot against the wall. Then, smearing blood on her body, she threw body parts all over.

Finally, coming back outside, she feigned exhaustion, faking wounds on her arms.

"Get me some water," she ordered Yoska. "And you," she said to the rest of them, "don't just stand there. There might be more of them around. Keep your eyes peeled and go to your posts."

Yoska turned to his main man ordering him to get a pail of water and some bandages. The others, he told to scatter to each corner of the hamlet. They all jumped at his command. When Yoska heard Lilitu's low, but persistent laughter, he turned to face her. It was difficult not to laugh as she picked them off one at a time.

Tonight she fed well.

❖—❖❖—❖❖—❖❖—❖

Lilitu looked towards the castle in the distance. This part of the plan took her longer than expected. Dawn was fast approaching, and it was time to return to Geneva. The men on the mountain pass would have to wait. Entering one of the houses, she picked up some bloodied clothes from one of the dead men, and then quickly ran towards the well near the center building. After washing them with water, she gathered all the scattered wallets. Altogether, there was enough money to spend the night somewhere.

"This is for you, Josh. We may not have time to return to Geneva."

Josh certainly did not want to suffer Gilles' fate, roaming the world for eternity as a disembodied spirit. In his astral form, he could get to their hotel swiftly, but she was not in her astral form. When they reached Chamonix, Lilitu flew lower to avoid the burning rays of the sun. The surrounding mountains helped keep her somewhat protected, but it was time to stop.

"Josh," she said, "Let us find a place to stay in Chamonix."

THIRTY-FIVE

The town of Chamonix, located in the center of a valley at the foot of Western Europe's highest and most spectacular peaks, was a large, but quaint town, with a total population of approximately 10,000. To Josh, the whole area made him feel as if he had stepped into Disneyworld; only this was real beauty, not artificially created make-believe.

Lilitu landed a bit past the town, deciding on a group of lodges devised for hikers and mountaineers. Although not a place for the average tourist, it was appropriate for the night. From there, she surmised, the group could rent bikes and any other equipment they might need – the hamlet was not within easy reach, and a car would not be appropriate. She stopped near the chalet 'La Maison Volante', which was close enough to downtown and had telephone facilities. Transforming back to Josh's form, she altered his appearance enough to look ten years older. She put on the clothes from the dead men at the hamlet, and then checked in at the lodge.

Explaining her lack of passport, luggage, or identification turned out to be an overwhelming ordeal. The man at the front desk was stubborn, and disagreeable. He begged to die, and Lilitu felt tempted to comply. In one of her previous incarnations, she might have torn his heart out on the spot. After some arguing, and money under the table, the clerk felt satisfied Josh would have his papers by tomorrow. The clerk finally gave her a room but had no idea how close he came to dying. If she had the time, she would teach him a lesson he would never forget.

The room was small, with no bathroom. The bathroom was outside - one bathroom for each floor, known in Europe, as the W.C. - a short term for "water-closet." Without a moment to waste, Lilitu lied down - allowing Josh back into his body - and left quickly. She had to warn Zgeza about the men still in the pass.

◦◆◦◦◆◦◦◆◦◦◆◦

Shortly after, Josh awoke and opened the bedroom window; the air smelled different here. It was as if he had never known what fresh air smelled like. The sky just began to get light, when he looked outside. The spectacular view showed a valley rich with green forests and meadow paths. An early morning cable car carried a few passengers up to a high Chalet ski station. In the distance, you could see the town of Chamonix.

He grabbed the telephone and spoke to the operator. While comfortable with his newfound, foreign language abilities, he forgot and spoke in English. The operator replied in kind. After a few descriptions, and some vague recollections of the name of the hotel in Geneva, she managed to connect him.

"Mom?" he said into the speaker. He dropped his eyes, waiting for the worst.

"For heaven's sake, Josh. Where are you? I've been..."

"Look," he interrupted before it turned into a lecture. "I know you're worried, but I'm fine. I'm in a hotel in Chamonix."

"Chamonix?" she reacted with shock. "How the hell did you end up over there?"

"It's a long story. I'll fill you in when you get here." His voice was firm, unwavering. "Take the next train over and ask a taxi to bring you to the 'Maison Volante' hotel."

"Alright," she said, still coming through the line as quite upset. "Malcolm is outside looking for you, but he said he'd be back in time to take the eight o'clock to Chamonix if you came back. Promise you'll wait for us."

"I promise," he said before hanging up.

Josh placed the telephone back on its cradle, then went to his bedroom door, and locked it. Lilitu had left for the castle, but he wanted to be there as well. There was no point now in trying to stay away from Gilles. Once he heard of what happened at the hamlet, he would realize Lilitu's host had to be near. Hypnotizing himself once more, his astral body took flight towards the castle.

◦◆◦◦◆◦◦◆◦◦◆◦

Lilitu approached the fortress in time to catch Zgeza getting ready to leave. Zgeza hesitated for a moment, staying her hand as she placed an amulet inside a small, dilapidated leather suitcase. Her eyes roamed the room. "You are here," she said, "but I get a sense of urgency in your presence. Must I assume that things did not go as planned?"

Lilitu passed her hand over Zgeza's face, to which the old woman reacted. She closed her eyes for a moment, then looked directly at Lilitu.

"I did not have time to get to the men at the pass," said Lilitu warning Zgeza of the situation. "The rest have been taken care of."

"Then I must remain here," replied Zgeza, obviously frustrated. She closed the small bag, and placed it next to her bed. "I will not be allowed access beyond the pass."

"Was anyone else leaving with you?"

"I expected to take Mircea, but only because he has lost all contact with reality. I have not spoken to the others." Zgeza's remorseful eyes turned downward. "I am concerned for them, but they fear Laslo too much to leave. I cannot place my trust in them." She smoothed her face with both hands, muttering uneasily. "There is one more thing. I believe Laslo has found another place of safety."

"How do you know? Did he tell you so?"

"Yes."

"What else did he say?"

"He promised to take me with him if I didn't betray him. I do not look forward to that, for I think he plans to kill me. Promise me that you will destroy him if I die before he does."

"My plans are to destroy him regardless, but I'll kill him before it comes to that." Pensively, she looked out to nowhere. "This hiding place, did he say where it was?"

"He doesn't trust me. He'd kill me for sure if he knew I found out."

"Yes. I guess he would." She touched her cheeks and her muscles seemed to tense. "But I think he is lying."

"What makes you believe that?" asked Zgeza.

"He wanted you to tell me, to throw me off his track." There was a cold edge in her voice. "But I sense he is still here. I know him too well," she said with certainty. At this, she turned around to face the door. "As well as I can sense you, Josh. Come in, you might as well join the conversation."

Josh slipped in through the door, and looked at Zgeza. She nodded; he nodded back. He looked at Lilitu uneasily. "I'm worried about her," he said referring to Zgeza. "She has to leave now."

Lilitu stared at him in silence.

"I cannot get past the guards at the pass," said Zgeza with conviction. "They have orders to stop any of us from leaving."

"I know it's not going to be easy, but I fear for your safety," added Josh.

"It seems to me there's something on your mind. Come on, out with it," demanded Lilitu.

"Well, here's the plan," continued Josh, then turning to address Zgeza. "If you leave now, when you get to the outpost in the pass, you tell the men you have a message from Gilles..."

"Laslo," interrupted Zgeza.

"What?" asked Josh

"Laslo. The men know him as Laslo," she said shamefully.

"Laslo, then," Josh agreed. "Tell them you need to talk to Yoska - you must be very firm with this and not let them dissuade you. They will want to either accompany you to the hamlet, or let you continue on your way. If they let you continue, you're home free."

"Home free?" asked Zgeza.

"Safe. I mean safe and out of here," explained Josh. He looked at Lilitu; she had a wide grin on her astral face.

"And if they accompany her to the hamlet, which is more likely," said Lilitu finishing the thought, "they will probably panic and run away, leaving Zgeza free to leave." She wondered if the plan might work.

"What if they fail to panic?" asked Zgeza.

"They will, if you prepare them first," added Josh. "Be creative. Come up with a scary story, like telling them that Laslo's enemies are here, that they are very powerful demons. I'm sure you can come up something frightening enough to worry them out of their wits. Then, by the time you get to the hamlet..."

"I won't need to make up a lie," interrupted Zgeza with a glint in her eye. "What Laslo has shown them is terrifying enough. They've already seen a demon."

Lilitu was all for it. "You have a vivid imagination," she said to Josh." It is a good plan."

"I'll get Mircea," said Zgeza.

"Leave him," ordered Lilitu firmly. "He will only give you away."

"Don't you see?" continued Josh. "If you go down alone they will not suspect."

"I cannot leave Mircea," said Zgeza, holding her emotions in check. "He is…"

"I promise you," interrupted Lilitu, "I will try my best to see that no harm comes to him. He is of no consequence to Laslo now. If you decide upon doing this, you must hurry. Time is essential."

"But where will I go?"

"Take a horse from the stable, suggested Josh. "Once you're out of the grasp of Laslo's men, you can ride to Chamonix and join our group."

"I will never get there before dark. I am old and can't ride very fast."

"I understand," said Lilitu, "but by the time Laslo figures out what happened, I will be close enough to escort you the rest of the way. He will not come near you if he thinks I am close at hand."

"You underestimate him," said Zgeza, her expression stilled.

"Perhaps, but it is worse to stay here and wait for him to kill you." This time, Lilitu's voice showed concern; something she had not allowed herself to feel for a very long time.

"Very well," relented Zgeza. She got up, walked to the edge of the bed, and grabbed her small suitcase.

"You must leave that behind," said Josh. "I'll bring it to you when this is over."

"All I possess is in there," she said sadly.

"I will bring it to you," Josh assured her. "I promise."

⬥⬥••⬥••⬥•

Zgeza walked outside, approaching the stable slowly.

The horses did not react to Josh or Lilitu, but just in case, they both remained some distance away. They could not afford to have the horses panic now.

Zgeza took the reins and a saddle from a row of hooks on the wall. Her horse neighed slightly, stepping backwards as she approached him. She talked softly to it, managing to calm him down. After saddling the horse, she slowly pulled him towards the gate. She was halfway to the portcullis when Belo called out to her.

"Hey, Zgeza," shouted Belo from the threshold of the dilapidated hall, his voice reverberating on the walls. "What are you doing?" He had a piece of cloth on his hands and was scrubbing them dry.

Zgeza turned around with her index finger on her mouth, indicating silence. Belo approached her a bit guarded. "What's going on?" he whispered loud enough for her to hear.

Conspiratorially, she waved him over. Belo looked around the courtyard, as if half-expecting to see someone hiding behind the walls. When he got near her, she spoke low, but more naturally.

"Laslo sent me to the hamlet. I need to warn the men to be on the lookout for his enemies."

"But they already know that," he said trying to understand. He gave her a side-glance.

"Of course they do. We all know that," she said impatiently looking over her shoulder. "But last night, when Laslo went out to scout, he discovered a group on their way to the castle from Chamonix."

"Well, why didn't he take care of them right there? He's strong enough to take care of an army." Belo had seen Laslo in action too many times, and was well aware of his capabilities.

"That he is," agreed Zgeza. "That he is, and more…"

Then?" Belo's eyes turned icy. "What are you trying to do, Zgeza?" He stood over her, boldly intimidating. "You're not trying to get away, are you?"

If Laslo was never able to intimidate her, she was not about to allow Belo to try the same on her. "If you don't believe me, then come with me," she answered, shaking her head in utter contempt.

"I don't know about this," he said, his hand moving to grab a hold of the horse's reins. If she was bluffing, he was not buying it.

Zgeza pulled the reins away from Belo. "Stop me from doing Laslo's bidding and you will suffer the consequences." Zgeza glared at him angrily. She seemed to growl as her features hardened. "Laslo may be strong, but the *men* coming after him are just as strong. We must be ready before they reach the castle tonight."

Suddenly, Belo turned pale. His brows drew together. "What do you mean, as strong as he?"

"What? Do you think Laslo is the *only* one of his kind?" she drawled with mockery. "The demon that came from the depths of hell and entered the shell of my own son fears no human." Her hands flew to her waist. "And believe me, I know he is very much afraid."

"They arrive tonight?" His eyes clouded with visions of death. "Are you sure of that?"

"You are nervous?" she asked defiantly, knowing she now had the upper hand.

"No, of course not," he replied, his voice quivering slightly. He looked behind him to see if anyone else was listening, then changed his tone to a whisper. "Listen, Zgeza, perhaps you should not go down there by yourself. I should be with you to protect you."

Zgeza confidently rejected the idea with a derisive, but gentle laugh.

"Please," he entreated her once more. "Let me go with you."

She looked at him from head to toe. "What are you trying to do, Belo? You wouldn't be trying to get away, would you?" she said, throwing his same lines back at him. Her eyes narrowed to a slit.

"No, no. I'm… I'm just concerned about you."

"Very well," she said with a sigh. "Bring your horse." She reacted as an impatient mother finally acceding to a child's pleas.

"Yes!" His eyes brightened. "Thank you, Zgeza. Thank you." Belo hurriedly went to the stable, managing to put on his horse's bridles and saddle in record time. Zgeza looked on with veiled amusement.

They went through the portcullis and out to the bridge, mounting the horses only after crossing the chasm. The view was impressive enough to make man or beast nervous. They rode slowly down the pass, going round the mountain twice before reaching the outpost. Predictably, two men came out to meet them.

"Hold it," said Luciano. A cigarette dangled from the left side of his mouth. He had a wristband on his right arm. "Where do you think you're going?"

"I have orders from Laslo to talk to Yoska," she said with authority.

"Tell me what it is and I will tell him myself. I have orders not to let anyone leave," replied Luciano. The second guard, standing next to Luciano, kept his rifle at the ready, but said nothing.

"What I have to say is for Yoska alone, but you may come with me if you wish."

Luciano looked at Belo inquisitively. "And you, what are you doing here?"

"I am here to protect her," replied Belo a bit nervous, but keeping it under control.

"From what?" asked Luciano. "From us?"

"There was trouble at the hamlet last night," said Zgeza. "We need to talk to Yoska now or there will be hell to pay when Laslo wakes up."

The men were well aware of Zgeza's privileged status where Laslo was concerned. All of them knew he often called her 'mother', although he did it facetiously.

"Yes," continued Luciano. "We heard the shots."

"And you didn't investigate?" asked Zgeza with a reprimand.

Luciano was temporarily taken aback at her sudden verbal attack. "Why… no. I…"

"You fools," she scolded the men. "Get your horses and come with me," she ordered.

"Why? What is it?" asked Luciano with great concern.

Belo decided to cut in. "The enemies that Laslo spoke about, they are his own kind. They are inhuman, demons." Belo seemed to be losing his composure.

"Quiet, you coward," yelled Zgeza. "Get behind me and do as you're told. You came to protect me, not to cry like a baby."

Luciano's eyes narrowed as he looked at Belo.

"Well?" demanded Zgeza. "What are you waiting for?"

Luciano nodded to the man behind him. He lowered his rifle and moved to get the horses. In a few minutes, they were on their way to the hamlet. Luciano and the other man rode behind Zgeza and Belo. So far, things went as planned.

Lilitu and Josh watched for a distance. Lilitu felt amused by Zgeza's daring, Josh, was terrified for her safety.

They rode at a brisk pace from the foot of the mountain, not fast enough to exhaust Zgeza, but fast enough to get them to the hamlet within twenty minutes.

Belo was the first to see the blood and the body parts strewn all over the hamlet. His horse bolted at the outset, probably due to the nervousness conveyed by his rider. Belo did not fight the horse's reaction and began to ride away. Luciano, not yet aware of what Belo had seen, cocked his rifle, and shot him, throwing Belo of the horse. He killed him instantly.

"You fool," said Zgeza, placing her hand on the barrel, forcing it to point down. "Why did you do that?"

"He was trying to escape," explained Luciano. He turned to the side trying to get his partner to back him up, but the man had turned pallid. "What is it, Pitti?"

Pitti did not reply. His eyes turned teary red and his mouth filled with spittle. He would not stop looking towards the hamlet.

Luciano turned around and finally saw what bolted Belo's horse; the streets littered with blood and body parts. He almost fell of his saddle.

"Quickly," said Zgeza, "you must go back to the castle and warn the others. I will look after Belo."

The horses nervously shuffled sideways, threatening to rear them off their backs. The riders could not stop staring at the scene.

"Go quickly," ordered Zgeza forcefully.

"Yes. Yes, of course," said Luciano uneasily. He turned his horse around, kicking his heels hard into the animal's side. Pitti followed him closely.

Zgeza observed them riding halfway to the pass then saw them suddenly turn towards the east, escaping into the horizon. She had a good belly laugh at the expense of two of the bravest cowards she had ever seen.

Then she remembered Belo. She went to him, but it was too late. The man was already dead. With a deep emotional sigh, she turned her horse east, riding towards Chamonix.

THIRTY-SIX

Josh and Lilitu followed Zgeza for a while, when suddenly, Josh felt a strong pull. Involuntarily, his astral form was drawn back towards his hotel room. For a moment, it felt like he was falling off a cliff. It was the dizzying sensation of his physical and his astral body being abruptly pulled together. As he awoke, a loud knocking attracted his attention to the door of the hotel. It was Mary Ann and Malcolm. He sat up and walked from his hotel bed to open the door.

"Hi, guys," said Josh casually, while bringing his left hand to scrub his eyes.

Mary Ann waltzed in, still in a fluster. Malcolm came in behind her, attempting to maintain his neutrality.

"Did you check in?" asked Josh.

"Now, what kind of question is that?" snapped Mary Ann dropping her handbag on the bed.

Malcolm turned back to the door and was about to walk out. "I think I'd better go to the front desk. I left my passport…"

"You stay right there!" she ordered, pointing her finger at the spot he stood on. Withdrawing her hand, she quickly faced Josh again. "I thought this was going to be a team effort. What you did is totally unacceptable and I hope you have a good explanation for this."

Josh looked at Malcolm, almost as if asking for support. Malcolm raised his eyebrows, shrugged his shoulders, and sighed loudly. It was easy to see on his face that the whole train trip had been a nightmare of temper flares.

"Stop looking at him," she said. "Look at me."

"If you're willing to listen, I'll tell you; but you must calm down."

"Calm down?" Her voice went a notch higher.

"That does it," interrupted Josh in anger. "I'm going out. I'll be back later, maybe."

"Don't you walk away from me!" she growled.

"Look," said Josh suddenly turning on her and growling back. "I didn't ask you to come here; neither of you. What I have to do, I must do alone. There is no team here." He came closer to Mary Ann and looked at her straight in the eye. "Now sit, and listen," he said pointing directly to his bed.

Mary Ann felt, for a moment, that her husband stood there. Something about her son reminded her of the man she still loved. She looked startled, and did as he asked.

"If you want to tag along, then don't treat me like a child." He softened his voice, but not his purpose. "This is an extremely dangerous undertaking, and there will be moments where I will not have the time or be able to tell you what I need to do. In the last twenty-four hours, I have seen more than twelve men killed; and will probably see more death before this is over. Heaven knows I will have to do things I do not care for, but I have already resigned myself to the inevitable. I have memories of things and of lifetimes neither of you will dare dream about." He knelt in front of her and took her hands in his, softening his tone even more. "I am your son, and I love you; nothing will ever change that, but I have changed, and for the same reason, our interaction must change. If you want any part of this, it will not be to tell me what to do."

Her eyes glittered with hurt. "I was upset because I thought I'd never see you again."

"It will not come to that. I have faith that Lilitu will do her best to keep us safe, but this is not going to be easy. There is extreme danger, and I would feel better if this was as far as you came." He stood and looked at Malcolm. "Both of you."

"No," she pleaded; she suddenly realized her control of the situation was illusionary. Now, a rush of panic overcame her. "I'll behave. I promise I will, but don't leave me out. Please."

'This has nothing to do with behaving. Right now, Gilles has no idea where I am. That is to our advantage. I can move around as I please. If you come with us, it may be all he needs to turn the tide against us."

"What if something happens to you? What if you get hurt? Or worse? How will I know? Do we stay sitting in this hotel forever?" She rejected the idea of staying behind as obviously absurd.

"I can't promise nothing will happen to me but, at least, let me try to keep you safe."

"Alright," she said, as she stood and walked towards the window. She glanced outside. "I will agree to change my behavior. I will stop being the mother-hen, and talk to you as an adult." Her hands shook with restrained emotion. "Let us turn the tables for a moment. What if it was me going on a dangerous mission. Would you let me go alone if it was in your power to help me?"

Malcolm saw both sides of the argument. Coming to this part of the world, then sit at the hotel, to wait for things to happen, was unfair. He knew that both he and Mary Ann could get in the way, but he also figured they might be useful in a pinch. "May I say something?" he interrupted.

Mary Ann nodded. Josh turned to him.

"I agree with both of you," he said walking fully into the room. "Yet, we must be sure we are making the right decision for the right reasons." Sitting on the bed, he said to Josh, "You know what you have to face out there, we don't. Heavens knows I have felt Lilitu's powerful grip." His right hand went to his neck, remembering when he first met her. "If Gilles is as powerful as she is, then there's not much we can do to help."

Josh inclined his head in agreement. Mary Ann turned towards the window, consciously making an effort not to interrupt.

"But you have told me that, powerful as she is, she in not invulnerable. That means she can be killed – meaning you. Gilles then, must be just as vulnerable." He placed a hand on the bed and leaned forward. "Most important, you said that you have seen over twelve men killed. This means that Gilles has allies, human allies. Those, if there are more around, we can help you with. I may be older, but I am not helpless."

"Neither am I," said Mary Ann quietly, without taking her eyes from the window.

Josh sighed with frustration. Maybe he was being unfair. "Okay, you win."

Mary Ann's reflection smiled softly.

"But just because Lilitu and I have to do something, you will not necessarily be included. For the moment, we have been clearing the way; we may not yet be done with the task."

"You can, at least, keep us informed, right?" asked Malcolm.

"Yes, of course."

"Fair enough. What's next? Then?" Malcolm was satisfied.

"There is a woman," continued Josh, approaching Mary Ann from behind. He placed a hand on her shoulder in a conciliatory move.

She looked at his reflection on the window, and took his hand.

"Her name is Zgeza."

"Laslo's mother?" asked Malcolm.

"Yes. She is coming here this very moment. Lilitu is with her, but we don't know if they'll get here before nightfall. I must be ready to let Lilitu take over. She will need to be protected, at least until she can join us."

"What do we do in the meantime?" said Mary Ann, swinging her head around.

"I need something to eat, so let's get breakfast." He nodded towards the door. "After that, you can do whatever you want. You may want to find out where you can buy supplies, like flashlight, blankets, canned food, and the like."

"You're not coming with us?" asked Malcolm.

"Only to get breakfast. I must return to my room as fast as I can."

Mary Ann stopped at the door. "Why?" she asked.

"Now, mom," Josh also stopped. "You promised."

"I want to know," she added with new objectivity. "You just agreed to keep our communication channels open, didn't you?"

He regarded her pensively, and then nodded in agreement. "I must project back to Lilitu and Zgeza. Although Gilles has his hands tied during the day, I can relieve her from watching over Zgeza as she rides to meet us. Gilles may have gone into hiding, so Lilitu needs to go back to the castle to find out if he's still there."

"What if he's not?" asked Mary Ann.

Josh's eyes met hers, analyzing her reaction. "Then we have our work cut out for us."

❖──❖──❖──❖──❖

Josh finally rejoined Lilitu as they rode towards Chamonix. The old gypsy woman looked tired and frail. She kept the horse going at a steady gallop. He wondered how long Zgeza could keep it up.

"Is everything alright?" asked Lilitu.

"Yes. So far so good," he replied. "You should be on your way back to the castle. I'll watch over Zgeza from here on."

She regarded him with amusement. A sort of gentle camaraderie was beginning to form between them. "Very well," she said with great satisfaction. "Keep your eyes open. Make sure you occasionally fly ahead. If you see anything funny, come back and tell her. She will hear you."

"What do you mean 'something funny'?"

"Just report to her what you see. She'll know if it's safe to go on, or if she needs to take another route."

"Will do," he assured her as he kept his eyes on the road ahead. "Now go. Make sure you find that son of a bitch."

She looked at him intently. Her eyes shortly beamed her approval, but the expression was fleeting. Josh never saw it. Without further talk, they parted company in opposite directions.

THIRTY-SEVEN

As Lilitu neared the hamlet, she looked down. The mess of body parts down there called her attention. The hamlet may not be the best place for camping after all. Mary Ann and Malcolm would surely turn back upon seeing this carnage, although, in the end, that might be for the best. Doing a quick dive to the village, she glided in and out of the abandoned buildings. No one had discovered the bodies yet, although this was not surprising - the hamlet was not a frequented place. Maybe people avoided it because of its remoteness, or because of the evil surrounding it. She felt no sorrow for these men, no sorrow for what she had done. She countered evil with evil, and if that made her wicked, then so be it.

Throughout her existence, she had studied humankind. A very ingenious species, indeed. Yet, man placed himself above all other creatures, slowly strangling the planet, and every other human along with it. They were their worst enemy, always manipulating, always stepping over others of his kind, from the highest to the lowest. Then there were the ones that claimed "God" was on their side, while at the same time, causing more death and destruction - in "His" name – than for any other reason since creation. Every religion was the "only" religion; all others would fry in Hell, all others must be eradicated. The genes of the Anunnaki were a sickness impossible to stamp out, short of destroying humankind. Still, she did not have to worry about that. Man had never been this close to extinction before.

Nonetheless, here she was, worried about a man such as Gilles. Why not let him accelerate humanity's destruction? Why not accept his proposal and allow him to have his way? After death, there was no caring, no love, and no hate – after death it would be impossible to care, one way or the other. Was it humankind she hated, or their foulness? Was the whole of nature itself, wicked? The natural world thrived upon one species devouring another. Was that evil? Nature was, neither good nor bad; it simply was. But why the brutality? She had lived longer than the whole of the human race, and up to now no one had found the answer – not the greatest philosophers, the simpletons, nor her own creators. Persons such as Josh only clouded the issue. She was tired of her own thoughts; tired of her own existence.

Leaving the hamlet, she headed for the castle. If Gilles were there, she would find him. Astral flight allowed her to reach places faster. From the hamlet to the pass, a galloping horse might take twenty minutes; in astral form, she could do it in seconds.

There was no one at the outpost. It seemed abandoned. This simplified things, if it remained so. Wasting no time, she flew up to the fortress, finding the courtyard empty. Perhaps everyone had panicked and walked out on Gilles. *No,* she thought. *They wouldn't have had time.* Just then, the noise of a falling utensil came from the kitchen. She flew closer. Three men, two women, and a child sat around a table. Mircea was not among them. The two women and the child cowered while staring at the floor; the men shouted at each other. They argued on the merits of staying or leaving. It did not matter, the men would probably kill each other, or Gilles would do it for them.

Ignoring them, she continued over to the circular stairs that lead from the kitchen to the tower. The darkness within the walls did not phase her, but the disagreeable smell of decay always did. *A strange reaction,* she thought, *for, what humans would categorize as, an angel of death.* It was not as odd as it seemed. Humans were *'angels of death'* as well, yet the smell of decaying flesh revolted most of them. Centuries of dried blood caked these walls and perhaps the souls that died here could only scream through the stench, giving their pain an undeniable physicality.

When she reached the bottom of the stairwell, she noticed something that had previously escaped her attention. A dark, mud-like, crust covered the floor; judging from the few bones and skulls strewn around, it must have been three inches thick. Disregarding everything, she went through the wall until she reached the prison where her physical body lay. This time, Gilles was not there. Going through walls and solids was a disorienting experience that she preferred to avoid. Advantageous as it was, she only used it when there was no other choice.

She should have been more observant when Gilles built this place. When he was alive, she despised his presence intensely, so she only came to him when it was time to feed; and even then, he always received her in his chambers. His thoughts were repugnant to her; consequently, although she had access to them, it was easier to completely block him out.

She left her prison and flew up the stairs to the next level, two stories below the kitchen. A platform stood in front of a dilapidated wooden door. On the other side of the door was an old, mostly rusted out, torture chamber. Upon entering, she noticed the torture rack and an iron maiden; those were the stellar pieces. The floor, littered with human bones and thick with dirt, contained all sorts of rusted paraphernalia meant to inflict pain - pincers, prongs, finger presses, foot presses, and knives. A metal grate in the center of the room revealed a reservoir beneath it – caked with congealed blood - which drained out to the stairwell. Another door to the back, led to a large closet. Nothing there.

The next level up, directly under the kitchen, but on the opposite side, had a solid metal door with a huge, recently oiled lock. The reason for the oil on the lock may have been to throw her off. It was too obvious. Unlike the previous door, this one had no cobwebs or dust on it. If Gilles was in here, she needed to figure out a way to get in, once she was in Josh's body. The door was too solidly set in the rock for her to break it down.

Again, she braced herself and passed through the door. The other side revealed a narrow passage with an unlit oil lamp hanging near the end of the passage. A flurry of footsteps suddenly called her attention. Large spiders and rats ran freely; some of the spiders had a span of almost a foot. On each side of the passage – carved into the stone - were two sizeable niches covered with thick webs.

In her astral form, she had no reason to fear anything. In her physical form, it would be foolish not to. She remembered, in one of her incarnations, when a spider bit her. The pain was so severe, she immediately left the body, allowing it to suffer and die. Such an act of indifferent abandonment never bothered her, since that host was the typical human power monger, but she never forgot the experience. This kind of spider, she had not seen before. If Gilles was here, then they were harmless or he had somehow learned to keep them away from him. The dust on the floor indicated that no one had been in here for a long time.

Pressing on to the other end, there was a thick, wooden door. This one had no lock, only a latch. She passed through and found a big room with a large, rectangular dining table in the center. The room had been in disuse for centuries, as could be ascertained by the thick, mostly undisturbed, layer of dust throughout. There was an occasional faint footprint here, and there. On top of the table, lay the skeletal remains of a male child with some of its bones cracked open. It reminded her of Gilles partiality for bone marrow. No other openings, doors, or windows were apparent. Yet, there had to be some connection to the hall upstairs or to his chambers at the top of the tower.

Circling the room a few times, she was about to leave, when she noticed some of the footsteps leading towards a set of tapestries. Behind the tapestries, a staircase led up. She followed it, and ended in the Great Hall. Improvised as a sort of barracks for his gypsy servants, it looked more like a messy campground than a Great Hall. The stairs continued towards Gilles' chamber in the tower, and the Hall led only to the courtyard.

Full of frustration, she glided up towards Gilles' chamber. The neatly kept room had some sparse furniture; a few chairs - some knocked to their side - and a round table. A throne-sized chair stood almost by the center and to the left of an extra-large bed. On the other side of the bed, there was a tub. At least Gilles bathed occasionally. Other than that, there was no sign of the monster.

Her senses told her, however, that there was more to this than met the eye. She felt it. Gilles was here, somewhere in the castle.

Redoubling her efforts, she started back in the kitchen. She had forgotten the stairs that led to Zgeza's bedroom. The men in the kitchen stopped arguing, and it seemed they reached an agreement to leave. Come tomorrow morning, they would be gone. *If Laslo doesn't kill them first,* she thought.

Down by Zgeza's room, were two doors. One lead to Zgeza's bedroom, and the other, still occupied by Mircea. She wondered if the plans of the gypsies upstairs included taking Mircea with them. The man just sat by the edge of his bed, staring blankly at the wall. There was nothing else here except these two rooms and a man whose mind had gone. Another dead-end.

Perhaps Gilles did have another place to go, but her instincts kept nagging at her. If he was getting ready to hide elsewhere, then time was of the essence. She went back to the courtyard to think. One way she could discover his secret would be to wait until sundown. Although she might not discover the hideout, she could convince herself that, at least, the man was still here. Yes, but that would accomplish nothing, not if the actual hideout remained secret. If he had been anywhere near the areas she checked, she would have felt his presence. She missed something; of that, she was certain.

Slowly floating back towards the Great Hall, she checked the stairwell again. That is where his imprints were strongest. She stopped precisely at the point where the steps led up to the tower, or down to the Dining Room. A slight instinctive sensation pulled her downwards. This time, she did a thorough search, touching almost every brick on the way, until finally, she reached the Dining Room again.

The moment she inadvertently touched the wall at the end of the stairs, she felt the faint imprints of her prey. His disagreeable smell came through the walls.

Now, it was time to go back to Josh. No sense in alerting Gilles of her discovery.

◆◆◆◆◆◆◆◆◆

"You're back," said Josh. Zgeza rode her horse directly below them. "What did you find?"

"You have made good time," she observed. "Good."

"Yeah, yeah!" said Josh. "I asked you a question."

"I found his hideaway," she said with a side-glance. "I just hope I did not make my discovery known to him."

"So what's next?" asked Josh.

"I need you to go back to Chamonix. Instruct Malcolm or your mother that I need to get a pick and a shovel."

"What for? You're not planning to take my mom up there, are you?"

"No, but when I come after Gilles tonight, if he sees me and goes back into hiding, I will have to break a wall or two."

"What about Zgeza?"

"I will stay with her as far as the hotel."

THIRTY-EIGHT

Zgeza would have given anything for a little energy, but she was already out of steam. Her body slumped forward every few paces, until she pulled the reins to slow down. Lilitu flew down to her side.

"What's wrong, Zgeza?"

"I'm too tired. I can't go on." Out of breath, she finally came to a full stop.

Lilitu looked around. "We are not far from Chamonix. You can rest until sundown. I will return then to accompany you the rest of the way, but do not be startled when you next see me."

"Why should I be startled?" asked Zgeza.

"What you now see, is not my real form."

"After seeing the thing my son has turned into, there isn't much left to surprise me," said Zgeza, calmly stepping down from the horse. "Do what you must do. I will wait here."

Lilitu grinned at the irony of her words. Coming from some other, she might feel offended. "You believe I am an angel, a messenger from God. I am no such thing. And you must understand that what took possession of your son is not a demon either."

"He looks and acts like one," countered the old gypsy.

"Zgeza," said Lilitu pausing for a moment. "I am not human. I may seem to be, because I do not care to frighten you. Gilles, on the other hand, was human; yet he would rather look like me for opposite reasons."

"Like you?" gasped Zgeza, clearly surprised.

"When Gilles was alive, I did to him what he did to your son."

Zgeza sat upon a rock by the road, trying to grasp Lilitu's words.

"I cannot explain now. When you see me return, I will be in Josh's body, but I will look…"

"I don't understand," said Zgeza, shrugging to hide her confusion, "I only know you want to destroy him. That's good enough for me."

Lilitu nodded, and then flew away.

❖◆•❖••◆••◆•❖

Zgeza was not about to let disappointment take a hold of her. Her faith had to remain strong. Whatever the outcome, God would prevail. She knew not who or what Lilitu was, and she didn't care. Lilitu *was* an angel, even if she denied it. It had to be true, for she desperately needed forgiveness, desperately needed redemption.

In the eyes of God, she had sinned, and by His will, she could now atone for it. If this angel looked like the Devil himself, she cared not. Blessing Lilitu, she made the sign of the cross, and sat on a rock by the wayside. Judging from the position of the Sun, the wait would not be long.

Gilles rested peacefully, gathering his strength for the events to come. Tonight, he would know if Lilitu swallowed his story. He missed the liberty his astral life gave him, but he dared not leave this body. In the first place, if Lilitu caught him out, she would torture him mercilessly. Nevertheless, he had a greater concern; the fact that Laslo was not alive when he took control of his remains. The only thing that kept the body going was his astral life force. He artificially enabled the heart to beat again, virtually willing it to keep going. If he left Laslo's body, even for a second, he feared it might decompose rapidly. Other than that, life was comfortable, and the food was good.

Sitting on his comfortable bed, he stretched a bit. He slept totally naked and usually got dressed after leaving his lair. A small oil lamp remained dimly lit on a small table by his bedside; he disliked total darkness. Letting out a loud yawn, he picked up a box of matches from the table. Lazily, he walked to a larger oil lamp that hung from a hook on the wall. He lit it, took the lamp in hand, and then walked up a narrow tunnel that led to the Dining Room level.

Before opening the sliding partition, he placed the lamp on a hook near the door. With his face and hands pressed against the wall, he tried, not to *hear* if anyone was on the other side, but to *feel* if anyone was. This was necessary for his survival. After a few moments, he released the latch, opening the partition.

Tonight, he planned to go into *Ville-Madeleine* to check his mailbox. Perhaps there was news from his British friend, but first, he needed to attend to Zgeza. He walked up to the Great Hall, after closing the door behind him.

Zgeza usually arranged for one of the Romani to receive him by the top of the stairs with a fresh bundle of clothes. To his disappointment, he found no one. His eyes wandered around the room. The Great Hall was in total disarray.

Damned slobs, he thought as he continued towards the courtyard. *One of these days…*

He stopped short of the kitchen door, noticing two of the horses missing. "ZGEZA!" he shouted without taking his eyes off the stable.

Djivan came out cowering from the kitchen; his hands held one against the other, almost as if in prayer. He shook visibly. "She's gone Laslo."

"WHAT!" Gilles reacted by stretching his right hand towards the man and pulling him by the neck. "And you let her go?"

Djivan tried to reply, but the power of Gilles' grip precluded the possibility. He gasped for breath while trying to talk, holding on desperately to the crushing arms that held him.

Finally, Gilles released him. "Idiots. Useless idiots, all of you," he said pushing the man aside with his foot. "Where are my clothes?" he asked the two women standing in frozen horror near the stove.

"Here," said Pesha, the eldest, handing him a sack while avoiding looking at his manhood. She was the one that usually prepared his clothes, and had the presence of mind to do it now, despite their plan to escape.

Gilles took the bundle from the woman, and smiled wickedly. He looked at all of them as he spoke. "I suppose you expect me to believe you are still here because you are loyal to me?"

Djivan stood and moved into the kitchen, where they all huddled together. Kore, the boy, held on tightly to his mother's aprons.

"I know of your plans," added Gilles as he stepped into the kitchen. "I can read your intentions. You would kill me if you dared."

"No, Laslo, no. You must not say such things." Djivan threw himself in front of Gilles. He knelt, he begged, he cried. "I have served you well." He turned towards the others, moving his arms to include them. "We all have." His watery eyes glanced back at Gilles, pleading for mercy.

The supplications pleased him, but their cowardice was irritating. Cowards were useless to him. "If you are not with me, then you must be against me," he continued while slowly going into his metamorphosis. "How dare you even think of leaving me? I have feelings too, you know," he said in a playful singsong tone. Whenever Gilles got humorous, it was time to take cover. His face now looked somewhere in between a large bat and a human. His claws grew out like sharp black knives.

"Run, Kore, run!" said Pesha as she pushed him toward the door. To her horror, Gilles' clawed hand stopped her child cold. When she saw Kore's still beating heart in the hand of the monster - before fainting - she rendered an ear-piercing shriek. The rest of them froze on their tracks, too frightened to move away, trapped in the web of terror Gilles spun around them.

"Hmm, delicious," said Gilles with glee as he squeezed the blood from Kore's heart into his extended tongue. His metamorphosis was complete. "They say that at moments like this, it does a soul good to let out some steam. Feel free to scream if it makes you feel better. No one will hear you."

◆◆◆◆◆◆◆◆

No use in going after Zgeza, thought Gilles as he washed the gypsies' blood away. At least he fed well and would not need nourishment for a few days, but he couldn't go to *Ville-Madeleine* with blood on him. *Lilitu is probably protecting her. Besides, the men at the hamlet, and possibly the outpost are dead too. But, why didn't she come for me last night? What is she waiting for?*

If everyone was dead, it meant he was on his own. Not that it mattered against an adversary such as Lilitu. No man could stand against her, but he was no pushover either. After milking her for all her power - he was convinced - he was as strong as she; surely she knew that. If push came to shove, he could take her on, and probably defeat her, too. He wondered if Lilitu knew how to handle a rifle. Would she use one if she did? Then the question popped up again: *why did she not come for him last night? What held her back? Lilitu never postponed anything in her life. Her decisions were, always, quick and deadly.*

Many unanswered questions preyed his mind. He left the bathtub, and looked out the window as he dried himself, wondering at the future. "All right," he said, wrapping the bundle of clothes around his neck. "Time to check things out for myself." He jumped out the window and took wing.

When he passed the outpost, he saw his men were gone. Similarly, he figured the ones at the hamlet would be gone too. Continuing his flight, he approached the village, the smell of death announced what he already suspected. They were all dead.

"Son of a bitch!" he yelled in anger. *The gall of this female! How she dared insult him this way. She came so near, yet she did not come to confront him. Why?* There was only one possible conclusion. *She is trying to protect someone, and it is not her host. Surely, it must be Zgeza.* Then he thought about it some more. *Had it been Zgeza, she would have attempted to attack me last night.* There must be others. If this was correct, then Lilitu has turned weak. She never cared for a human before. *No, it cannot be true,* he thought. *It is so unlike her, yet... She is being too cautious. There is someone else, and this is a weakness I will exploit!"*

He sniffed the air, and felt a gentle pull towards the East. Cruising near the ground, he looked for fresh horse tracks. Zgeza might still be useful, after all. If she were riding towards Lilitu's new host, then he would have the upper hand.

A few feet from the hamlet, he found Belo's corpse. A bullet had killed him, not Lilitu. And there, leading away from Belo's body, were the hoof marks he expected to find. With renewed optimism, he followed the spoor left by Zgeza's horse.

THIRTY-NINE

Zgeza heard a familiar flapping of wings above her. Her heart froze with thoughts of Laslo's demon. Fleeing was not an option, for with Laslo, there was no place to hide. She remained quiet, hoping he would fly past her.

"Zgeza," called Lilitu flying above her. "Don't be alarmed. It is I, Lilitu. We must continue our journey."

Nervously, Zgeza looked up into the sky, and saw her silhouette, dark against the moonlight. Her driving need to see her was stronger than her fears. "Come down," she said anxiously. "Let me see you."

"We are wasting time."

"Let me see you, Lilitu" she repeated, softer this time as she pushed herself to a standing position. "Please."

"No human, other than my hosts, have ever seen me and lived," growled Lilitu.

Zgeza sighed and threw up her hands. "Lilitu, stop putting up this silly barrier. I have seen my Laslo at his worst. Nothing about your appearance will change my mind about you. Now, come down and let me see you."

The woman was not about to take 'no' for an answer. Lilitu looked upon her, softening her somber expression. Zgeza was not afraid. As intolerant to humans as Lilitu was, occasionally some managed to make an impression on her. She glided down to the old woman. *Old,* she thought. *How ironic. She's nothing but a baby compared to me.*

Zgeza, never taking her eyes off Lilitu, she looked straight into her eyes.

"Well, old woman? What have you to say now?" Lilitu gave her an expressionless look.

"You carry much pain," said Zgeza, moving closer to caress Lilitu's cheek. Lilitu reacted with an instinctive flinch.

"Don't turn away," she added sadly.

"I do not want this," said Lilitu, gently moving her face away.

"You don't want what?" asked Zgeza mystified at the reaction, before she realized the truth. This creature was a stranger to kindness.

Lilitu turned her back on Zgeza. She could hear her thoughts clearly. "You are right, woman. I *have* known little kindness, and I do not crave it either. For what kindness I have shown, betrayal has been my reward. That is the poison of your people." She turned back to face Zgeza, when an involuntary tear rolled down her left eye. "Stick to your 'revenge' against Gilles. It will serve you better."

Zgeza smiled softly, a warm glow flowed from her face. "Very well," said Zgeza. She was about to get on her horse, but stopped herself. "I will never betray you," she added, lightly touching Lilitu's hand.

Gilles saw Lilitu's silhouette fly upwards, her wings contrasting magnificently against the full moon. Flying low, to avoid attracting attention, he followed her. Her flight path was slow; at times, she simply hovered in place as she looked all around. There was no doubt in his mind that Zgeza was riding below, and he was the reason for her precautions. He kept his distance. It was too big a risk to fly too close. Even if she could not see him, she might feel his presence.

Nearing Chamonix, Lilitu flew down and shape-shifted. Now Gilles knew what her host looked like. From that point on, their step slowed considerably as Lilitu led Zgeza's horse by the reins. It made his job of tracking them much easier. He was about to fly closer, when he felt the presence of Josh's astral body hovering above them. This was a dangerous undertaking, but one that could pay off in spades if he didn't get careless. The three of them remained under his eagle eye all the way to the lodge, and they never knew it.

An attractive woman and a slightly overweight man received them by the steps of the lodge. He wished he could have heard their conversation, but it was too risky to try to get closer. Hiding on the limb of a nearby tree, he settled and observed.

❖〰❖〰❖〰❖

Zgeza and the two strangers walked inside as Lilitu ran to the back of the lodge, sprouted her wings, and flew towards the castle; Josh followed close behind.

This was much easier than expected. He overestimated his opponents. Now was the time to strike. After Lilitu and Josh disappeared on the horizon, he came down from the tree. After changing to his human form, he put his clothes on. A new confidence coursed through him as he walked into the lodge. From the door, he watched them go up the second floor and into one of the bedrooms. He waited for a moment before entering the lobby.

There was some activity in the lodge. Summer attracts mountain climbers, cyclists, and nature lovers to this area. A convenient arrangement, for he never ran out of food. During summer, he had the mountaineers, and bicyclists; in the winter, it was the skiers.

He passed the lobby and reached the stairs unnoticed. Although he already dined, the smell of humans moving about felt appetizing and tempting. Maybe after today, he would have no reason to move to England – if everything went well.

At the landing, he turned left, stopping at the second door. He knocked. An appealing woman opened the door. Smelling of sweet blossoms, her delicately carved face was arresting.

"Yes?" said Mary Ann as she stood by the half-open door.

"Please excuse my intrusion," said Gilles softly. "I came to find my mother." He pushed the door open, forcing himself in. With his right hand on the door, he closed it behind him. "There you are, my dear," he said leaning back against the door. A wave of electricity filled the room.

Zgeza, who sat on a chair by the window, gasped. "Laslo!"

"Why don't you introduce me to these kind and hospitable people? I didn't know you had such good friends." He chuckled nastily while acting very much the gentleman. "Who are you, for example?" His finger moved slowly up to Mary Ann's face, lightly touching her under the chin.

Mary Ann slapped his hand away. "Don't touch me," she ordered with authority.

"My, my, my," he reacted smiling. "What lovely disposition, coming from such a beautiful woman."

"Laslo," said Zgeza, approaching him defiantly. "I will go back with you, willingly. Let us leave these people alone and be gone."

Gilles gleamed with self-satisfaction. "What manners! I came to thank you, dear mother, for showing me my enemy's lair." His smile waned and his pitch lowered. "Now, I asked you a question. Who are these people?"

Malcolm stood nervously. "My name is Malcolm, and this is my wife, Mary Ann." Mary Ann's eyes opened wide at Malcolm's unexpected answer.

"Wife, my ass," said Gilles derisively. He turned his head towards Mary Ann. "Your feelings betray you, my dear. The only thing I could ever read out of Zgeza was her motherly instincts. I read the same from you." His left hand moved over her head, as if caressing her hair, but not touching it. "And whose mother might you be?"

"I'm nobody's mother, you son of a bitch," she drawled, attempting to move away. Gilles caught her by the hair, pulling her against him. Mary Ann flinched in pain.

"Leave her alone!" Malcolm attempted to move towards Gilles, but Zgeza held him back. The eyes of the monster suddenly glared bright red. That alone would have stopped anyone cold.

"You're Lilitu's mother... or should I say, her host's mother, aren't you?" He guffawed loudly. "This is perfect!" While holding Mary Ann in his grip, he looked at Zgeza. "I need you to do one last thing for me, dear mother. When Lilitu gets back - unless I see her first - tell her to find us at my home. I believe we can conduct our business now." He pulled Mary Ann towards the back porch door and opened it. "I will attend to our little disagreement, later," he said to Zgeza.

Mary Ann struggled wildly, resisting Gilles' attempt to pull her outside. Malcolm tried to rush him, but Gilles rammed him back with such force, he flew clear across the room.

"I can tear your arm off its socket if I want to, you stupid woman. I will do it unless you stop resisting me." His left hand tensed against her shoulder while he held her by the neck with the other.

"Do as he says," said Zgeza, her mouth thinning with displeasure. "He will crush you if you defy him."

Reluctantly, Mary Ann stopped struggling.

"I am not used to carrying anyone, but you seem small enough. Let us see." He pushed her against the railing and held her there as he took his clothes off.

"What are you doing?" asked Mary Ann beginning to panic. His nakedness intimidated her.

"Do not worry," said Gilles, giving her body a raking gaze. "We will have plenty of time for fun, but now, I need to spread my wings." On that note, he distorted quickly, showing them the horror of his bestiality. His hairy hand drowned Mary Ann's scream. Very slowly, his lips came near her ear. His husky voice whispered, "Should I snap your neck now, or are you going to keep quiet?"

She closed her eyes tight and nodded, but could not hold back her sobbing.

"Very well," he said. Holding her firmly in his arms, he jumped into the night.

◆◆◆◆◆◆◆◆◆

Lilitu approached the castle cautiously. She wanted to make sure Gilles could not slip by her. There was only one way in or out of the castle, so in a way, although it may have been easier to defend, in reality, it was also a death trap. Josh flew ahead of her as an advance patrol while she visually covered every bush and rock. When she reached the courtyard, she saw a setting as devastating as the one she left at the hamlet. It was an unanticipated sight, since she expected the gypsies to be up in arms awaiting her arrival. Instead, they were all dead. Quickly, she flew to Gilles' chambers at the top of the tower. It was also deserted. A couple of lit oil lamps filled the room with a yellow, flickering light. The bathtub was full of bloodied water.

"He bathed," said Josh. "After he killed his own men, he bathed! Why?"

Lilitu jumped out to the courtyard then entered the Great Hall. A few lit torches hung from the walls, but there were no dead bodies. Without much thought, she took a torch, and then ran down to the Dining Room. She felt no vibrations, no indication of his presence anywhere, not even behind the secret wall.

"Josh," said Lilitu. "Go inside and check."

Josh slipped through, almost managing to get lost inside the walls. His sense of direction steered him left then right. A sense of panic started to take hold of him, when he finally came out the other side. Gliding down, he searched the room.

"It's empty," he shouted, turning back toward the secret door. This time, he built up speed, hoping the force would carry him through the wall faster. He passed the wall, but the momentum shot him straight through Lilitu also. A sharp pain shook both of them, knocking Lilitu backwards.

"Ouch!" said Josh as his astral body threw sparks into the air.

"Now you know why our astral bodies cannot touch," she said getting up from the floor. She was about to scold Josh, when she suddenly remembered Mircea. *If he's still alive, he might know something.* "Let's go see Mircea."

She looked to the door at the other end of the Dining Room. Through there, she could go across the small passage connecting to the kitchen. Taking a step in that direction, she remembered the spiders and the rats. In her physical form, it was too great a risk to try. "I can't go through there," she said to Josh.

"I can. I'll wait for you on the other side," he replied.

With the torch still in hand, she ran back to the Great Hall, then out to the courtyard. When last she saw Mircea, he sat on his bed in a catatonic state. As she entered the kitchen, she carefully walked around the bodies; blood could be as slippery as soap. Reaching the flight of steps leading to Mircea's room, she dashed down and opened the door; the man still sat there. Crying no longer, he stared at the wall.

"Mircea," she said. "Can you hear me?"

Mircea's face ran a full gamut of emotions as he saw Lilitu; in his eyes he saw, not Lilitu, but Gilles. His features twisted from a stony indifference to bewilderment, and finally to an uncontrollable anger. Without warning, he jumped on her, his strong hands going straight for her throat. As Lilitu stepped aside to avoid him, Mircea met the wall with his cranium and slumped on the floor. The crack on his head was not enough to render him unconscious, but he was dazed. Moaning with pain, his hands went up to massage his head.

"I guess you can hear me now," said Lilitu, realizing Mircea had nothing to tell her. She turned around to leave, but Mircea tried to jump her again. He grabbed on to her legs, trying to tackle her. Lilitu lifted him easily and threw him against the bed. "Sorry, old man. You are attacking the wrong monster."

Mircea groaned as he hugged his knees. "You murdered my Piotra. Kill me, or I will not rest until I kill you. Go ahead, do it now." He rocked himself back and forth, expecting the final blow that would end his life.

"Goodbye," she said, darting up the stairs. Mircea did not follow.

"Perhaps we're too late," said Josh, following behind her. "If Gilles was already in his new lair, this whole thing has been a waste of time. Unless…"

The possibility of Gilles following her into Chamonix never entered their minds, until now. Suddenly, with reckless desperation, Lilitu took to the air, and dove straight down the mountains towards the valley below.

Josh flew ahead at astral speed to meet with destiny.

FORTY

Gilles, expecting Josh or Lilitu to cross his path somewhere along his way to the castle, purposefully took a route closer to the mountains – it would be easier to hide from them. Eventually they would realize how he fooled them. It must really grab Lilitu's craw, to know that on every one of their encounters, he managed to deceive her. This one promised to be his crowning moment.

Mary Ann, still in shock, remained quiet in his arms. She had no previous idea what this monster looked like until she saw him change. Now, she understood the danger.

As he approached the castle, he felt Josh soar past him. He hid behind a foothill - knowing Lilitu followed close behind - and waited for her to pass. They would soon be back, of that, he was sure. The breather did him good, as he had never carried anyone before. Mary Ann was small, but this extra weight stressed his wings too much.

"What do you think of all this, my dear," he asked Mary Ann, lustfully measuring her body, his hand moving slowly up and down her leg. "How does it feel to be bait?"

She avoided his face while uselessly trying to stop him from touching her legs.

"You don't want to look at me?" Her reaction amused him. "No need to worry. When we get to my bedroom, I will show you how good I really am. I promise." He looked up and waited a few seconds longer, until he was sure it was safe to continue.

A few hours before sunup remained, and if Lilitu did not come to visit him tonight, it would give him a whole day to consolidate some sort of plan. For the moment, he was certain Lilitu's host would not allow this woman to die. Lilitu would have to comply with his demands. *Yes, that's exactly what it was, a demand. No more asking, no more pleading.*

He took to the air once more, reaching the castle shortly after. The stakes were too high to take chances with any attempted rescue, so he brought Mary Ann directly to his bedroom, below the Dining Room.

"This should hold you until it's time. Once I get rid of Lilitu, who knows? You may want to join me?"

"I'd rather die!" she said, her eyes flashing with outrage.

Gilles dropped her hard against the bed, and then sat next to her, his right arm resting across her body. "I can help you with that one too, but not until I grow weary of you – or you grow weary of me – whichever comes first." Moving his face closer to her face, he whispered, "is that not a nice prospect to look forward to? Do you want to come first, or shall I?"

"Get away from me," barked Mary Ann, pushing his face away.

"Ha, ha! I like it! There's nothing like a woman with courage. We may get along after all." He stood and pulled her towards the wall opposite his bed.

"What're you gonna' do to me?" she said, her body stiffening at his pull.

"I just want to make sure you feel comfortable, my dear. I will simply tie you to these lovely shackles. They should keep you under control. Oh, and whatever you do, do not pull too hard on them."

"You expect me to stay put while you leave me here?"

"Well, you may be right, but…" He grabbed the chains, and standing apart from the wall, gave them a hard tug. Several rows full of long iron spikes flew out of the wall; anyone held by the chains would certainly be impaled.

Mary Ann's eyes opened wide with terror.

"I see we understand each other," he continued as he reset the spikes, then pushed her against the wall, attaching the shackles to her ankles and wrists. The short chains allowed little movement; she could only sit by leaving her arms outstretched towards the ceiling. "By the way, if our negotiations don't go well, I can control the spikes from the outside, so I suggest you pray to whatever god you think appropriate." He walked up the narrow tunnel, leaving Mary Ann alone. Outside the room, he set the lock to trigger the spikes; if they figured out how to open the door, they would surely kill her. If he died before reaching an agreement with Lilitu, this woman would, either rot inside the cell, or die by their hands when they triggered the device.

◆◇◆◇◆◇◆◇◆

Josh returned from the hotel, meeting Lilitu on her way to Chamonix. She stopped in mid-flight.

"We must go back to the castle!" said Josh, his voice rising an octave. "Gilles took my mother."

Lilitu turned around instantaneously. "What about Zgeza and Malcolm?"

"They are okay, but a bit shaken. Malcolm rented a four-wheel drive and they are on their way." He turned around towards Lilitu as he flew backwards. "I can't stay with you. I must go on ahead."

"Go on. I'll catch up." She looked ahead, as Josh rocketed towards the castle; her heart lurching madly. *Why did she feel worried? What was the life of another human being? They meant nothing to her; Josh was just one more host from a multitude she had used.* Forcing her wings to its limits, she picked up speed; her arms pulled straight ahead of her like an arrow flying to its target.

⬥⬥⬥⬥⬥⬥

Gilles waited in his chambers, sitting on his usual high chair, when Josh approached him. He straightened immediately as he felt the presence.

"I can almost smell you," said Gilles with glee. He was in control of the situation, and enjoyed it to the hilt. "It's a shame I cannot see or hear you, but you are most definitely not Lilitu. I know her too well." He lowered his right leg from the armrest, turning to raise his other leg over the opposite armrest. "You must be the new host. What a pleasure it is to have you here. I assume Lilitu will be along any moment now." Reaching towards a nearby table, he grabbed a cup from it and swished it in front of his face a few times. He took a deep drink, and then smacked his lips loudly. "Oh, how rude of me, I forgot to offer you some libation. Why don't you have…Oops, I forgot. You cannot drink as a spirit, can you?" He placed the cup back on the table and made a face. "It's for the best, anyway. This blood has spoiled a bit; too thick for my taste." His lips dripped with the viscous liquid as he delicately pulled out a dainty handkerchief and dabbed his face. He looked at the handkerchief with a sigh. "Not a good crop at all. How mortifying; it must have been a bad year." Bringing the handkerchief up to his face, he giggled and flirted effeminately at the unseen Josh. Looking over the hankie, he said, "I know what you're thinking, but you're wrong. She's perfectly safe. Not a scratch on her… yet! Oh, and if Lilitu has any idea about hurting me to get me to free her, I'll make sure she really dies slowly. It's in your best interest to stop Lilitu before she tries anything against me. She is so impulsive."

⬥⬥⬥⬥⬥⬥

Josh left the tower to find Lilitu before she got to the castle. As he flew downwards, Gilles' sardonic laughter reverberated behind him. Josh reached Lilitu nearing the outpost, flying up faster than he had seen her fly before.

"Wait," he shouted desperately.

"Did you find him?" She stopped in mid-air.

"Yes, but there's a problem. Whatever you do, you must not hurt him."

"Josh," replied Lilitu, her face a glowering mask of rage. "Pain is the only thing this fiend understands."

"He's too confident. He knows something we don't. Let me find mother first and try to assess the situation. Can you wait by the outpost?"

Lilitu was about to ignore Josh's request and got ready to continue towards the castle. Her eyes glared with fire.

He placed himself directly in front of her. "Lilitu, please. If there is any compassion in you, show it to me now. I promise Gilles will be all yours once we get mother out of his grasp."

Lilitu, barely able to control her emotions, stopped in her tracks. "Very well. I'll do as you ask. I'll wait at the outpost, but remember, daylight will be upon us in a few hours."

At this, Josh turned back to the castle and disappeared from view.

◆◇◆◇◆◇◆◇◆

There was only one place Mary Ann could be; the hidden chamber. Flying through the kitchen, he crossed the circular staircase in the tower, hoping against hope that Gilles would fail to sense him. It amazed him how, even in total darkness, his eyes could see the spiders and the rats; it was as if the small hallway was illuminated with neon. The light, if it could be called as such, manifested itself in a pale, clear blue, and all colors within the spectrum bathed with a touch of it. He passed both doors, reaching the Dining Room. The gloominess inside gave him a sense of horror, yet no nightmare came close to the reality of this god-forsaken place.

As he approached the sliding wall, he felt Mary Ann's presence. He had no doubt in his mind now. Closing his astral eyes, he took a step back, then lunged against the wall. He came out the other side quickly. Moving down a short tunnel, it led him to the smallish chamber; Mary Ann was kneeling on the floor with her hands stretched upwards by the pull of the chains. His approach went unnoticed, however. He spoke, but got no response. Mary Ann, although wide-awake, remained unaware of Josh.

How can I make her know I'm here? he thought. Suddenly, he remembered the last time he crossed the door exiting this very room, when he bumped into Lilitu. The sensation was a bit disturbing, but very real. It was worth a try. Coming closer to Mary Ann, he thrust his hand into her shoulder. Mary Ann flinched with a short outburst. With a startled look on her face, she scanned the room. The dim light of the oil lamp showed her she was alone.

Wrong approach. He only managed to startle her. Concentrating as hard as he could, Josh brought his hand close to her face, caressing her softly. The effect was electrical. A sudden chill ran over her.

"Oh, God. I hope this is who I think it is," she whispered, suddenly bursting with hope. "If this is you, Josh, listen to me," she continued, kneeling upright, squinting her eyes trying to see what she could not. "These chains are not what they seem. They are rigged to kill me in case anyone tries to free me. If I pull on them, a row of sharp spikes coming from the wall will impale me. Gilles also has a way of setting them off from outside, but he didn't say how." She leaned a bit forward. "If you can hear me, please touch me again."

Josh caressed her face with both hands.

She closed her eyes as she leaned her head to the side as if caressing his hand with her cheek. "You must go now."

Slowly, he moved his hands away. He looked at her for a moment, then left.

FORTY-ONE

Mircea desperately needed to release his revenge. He was well aware of Laslo's powers. After all, he was his right-hand man for longer than he cared to remember - but to let this fiend live was out of the question.

I should never have allowed this creature to pollute me, he thought. *Yet, I have no one to blame but myself. Assisting and participating with Laslo to carry out his vices was not enough; I gave him, not only my unswerving loyalty, but also my most precious treasure - my Piotra. And for what? For the measly crumbs he threw at me, to rape children and lie with dead bodies, I behaved like a beggar.*

No, Mircea's sins went further than that. He enjoyed the torture and death of other humans, and then sold his soul to a demon. No cause touches a man deeper than the one that hits him in the heart. Until Laslo killed… no, until he *ate* his Piotra, Mircea thought nothing of his actions or their consequences.

Zgeza never knew of his eager involvement in Laslo's wantonness, yet she was the one that should carry the blame. This nasty piece of work was her son, and he would have to take care of her too. As the son goes, so goes the mother.

If he knew something about Laslo, it was his vulnerabilities; his deadly fear of the sun, and the fact that he was sure he could kill him.

He tried to lead us all to believe he was an eternal, but I know the beast can be hurt. I have seen him bleed before, and if it bleeds, it can die.

He kept a few weapons in his closet. Being Laslo's handyman was only one of the many things he did - in fact, getting this pigsty he calls a castle, into some livable condition, was his first job. For a while, before he got used to the awful smells, he puked everyday – at least for the first week. But he cleaned the place enough to make it livable, repairing doors and greasing them, fixing the stable, the kitchen, the well that took water from the melting ice, the pump… not anymore. It was time for payback, and Laslo was going to go to meet his maker, whoever that might be.

When he finally found the courage to go back upstairs, it did not surprise him to find his gypsy friends dead. He was not stupid enough to believe any of them would end up otherwise. The dead bodies were unrecognizable; they were more 'dead parts' than corpses.

If Laslo thought he was a weakling, he had a surprise coming. With two rifles, a gun, and a large hunting knife, one way or the other, he *was* going to get him. No more fainting for him; now it was time for action… and for death. And if God allowed it, for atonement.

Laslo would not be able to hide from him. He was the only one that knew about Laslo's secret chamber. When he restored the locks, he left himself a little insurance, in case he needed to rescue Piotra from his claws. Now, saving his daughter was not an option, but catching Laslo in his lair, was.

Tiptoeing over the blood and body parts in the kitchen, he moved out to the courtyard. A light in the tower, from Laslo's chamber, reflected outside.

Good, he thought, as he tiptoed towards the Great Hall. *Laslo's in the Castle. I will stay out of sight until sunup. If Laslo remembers I'm alive, he'll never look for me there.*

He quietly entered the Hall. It was empty, but he heard voices carrying through the gloom. Laslo was down by the Dining Room, and he was not alone. The words were indistinguishable, but he definitely heard a woman. He inched closer to the staircase, when the familiar sound of the trap went off. The bastard had a prisoner! He knew Laslo well, and there was no other reason for him to trip it.

Laslo enjoyed the look on their faces when they saw what would happen if they tried to escape. Some of them never made it either. They would eventually grow too tired, and die. That was fine with him; they were only his meal, anyway.

Once, Laslo invited him to watch. They sat there, as a beautiful boy impaled himself. But that was not for him. He would rather enjoy the sex and leave the killing to Laslo.

Not that Mircea was a constant partner to Laslo. It had been a random invitation that only happened as 'compensation' for a job well done; an infrequent event. Laslo was not one to appreciate anything or anyone. Hell only knows why he did it.

A short time later, he heard Laslo close the sliding door of the chamber then set the trigger device. Mircea silently moved back into the shadows, to hide behind a large bureau. Laslo walked up to the tower, chuckling to himself. For a brief moment, Mircea felt curiosity about the prisoner, but the thought left him as soon as it came. He was there to kill Laslo, not to fiddle with trivialities.

Maybe waiting for him to go back to his lair was not such a good idea. His prisoner would probably keep him awake, making it impossible to break in unnoticed. There was no time like now, he concluded, quietly cocking his rifle.

Just as he was about to go up the steps, he heard Laslo speaking again. This time, whomever he spoke with, did not reply - Mircea only heard one voice. Kneeling softly by the steps, he tried to listen. Laslo spoke of a spirit and some person called Lilitu. What was going on? Moreover, who *was* the prisoner downstairs? Why was Laslo bargaining for her life? He never bargained; he took. Mircea also noticed something in Laslo's voice; a certain nervousness that had never been there before. It was fear.

Was it possible the woman downstairs was a hostage? Why? What if he snatched her away? It was worth a try. Maybe it would distract Laslo enough to get in a good shot or, at least, a chance to stab him in the heart – even if it cost him his own life.

The conversation upstairs was over, but Laslo's typically sardonic laughter was absent this time. Mircea moved back behind the bureau and waited for Laslo to come back downstairs; he did not. *What a shame*, he thought. He would have caught him from behind with a clean shot between the shoulder blades.

Slowly, Mircea approached the staircase, and walked down to the Dining Room. As he reached the last step, the gun slipped from his belt, making a loud thud when it hit the floor. His heart skipped a beat; his blood ran cold. He had nowhere to run or hide.

Stepping away from the stairway and into the middle of the Dining Room, he cocked the rifle and waited. Surely, if Laslo heard him, he would be down here soon.

Then he waited some more. Nothing.

With a deep sigh, he lowered the rifle and slowly approached the staircase. Before he could react, Laslo stood next to him with a wide smile on his face.

"Looking for someone, my friend?" said Laslo, quickly yanking the rifle away from Mircea.

Mircea backed away. There was no time to ready the second rifle hanging from his shoulder, not before Laslo would tear him to pieces. "Y... yes. I... I found everyone dead, and I thought…"

"You thought…?" For every step Mircea took backwards, Laslo took one towards him. He brought the rifle to a shooting position, and pointed it at Mircea. "Do you know how to use one of these?"

"It's loaded. Please, Laslo," he pleaded.

"Yes, I know, but there's no need for you to worry. I will not use this against you. It is such an impersonal way to deal with problems, don't you think?"

"Wha…what do you mean?" He continued to back away, but Laslo kept moving closer.

"Let's see." Laslo gazed at the ceiling, as if in deep concentration, while his right hand flew towards Mircea's throat, holding him in a tight, vice-like grip. "If I shoot you, I will not feel the pleasure of your terror dissolving into my hands, will I?"

Mircea could only gurgle with incoherent words as Laslo's mouth opened wide, displaying a set of long, sharp teeth.

"Do not worry, my friend. You shall live a while longer. I want you to feel this." Laslo sank his canines into Mircea's shoulder, taking a large chunk of flesh along with part of his clavicle.

FORTY-TWO

Lilitu entered the Dining Room the moment Gilles attacked Mircea. This was the right moment to pounce on him. If Gilles had a way to trigger the trap from the outside, he could not do it while feeding on someone. She jumped him from behind, pulling him by the wings, managing to tear the membranes that gave him the power of flight. Although she had the advantage of surprise, Gilles was no stranger in hand-to-hand battle. He released Mircea on pure reflex, as his hands stretched in front of him in an attempt to protect his fall.

Straddling his body with her legs, she held on to him like a horse. Both her hands grabbed on to his wings, pulling hard in an effort to break them. Gilles reached back, attempting to pull her forward by the hairs on her head, but she kept her face away from him. Giving up on that, he then tried to untangle her legs from his waist.

Mircea dropped to the floor, bleeding profusely. He could not believe his eyes when he saw two Laslos fighting each other. Both looked equally terrifying. He tried to crawl away from the struggle, but his bleeding shoulder made his efforts impossible. His strength abandoned him, negating his attempt to pull the second rifle out from under his body; the rifle limited his movement as it dug deep into his ribs. The gun lying in front of him, however, was well within reach. He picked it up, his vision blurring rapidly. Turning the gun towards the struggling beasts, he cocked it.

Which one do I shoot? The gun weighed a ton, but if his strength lasted just a bit longer, he could kill them both.

Suddenly, Mircea felt a cold, clammy hand touching his arm. It was as if a ghost tried to pull his hand away. He thought of Piotra and his mind wandered towards her. *It cannot be*, he thought. *My Piotra would want me to kill Laslo. Why is she trying to stop me?* The cold hand felt stronger now. Gathering his strength as much as possible, he spoke aloud: "This is for you, my daughter. Let me be your avenging angel."

With that, he squeezed the trigger, hitting one of the monsters squarely on the shoulder. The strong recoil of the gun threw his hand backwards, throwing the weapon behind him.

One of the beasts fell with a loud, painful cry, releasing the other from under it.

Gilles struggled to get up, his wing membranes completely torn; one of his wings hung loosely to the side. Lilitu's left arm had a gaping hole where Mircea's bullet had struck.

"Well," said Gilles, catching his breath. "It seems I have friends in high places." No sooner did he finish saying it, than he kicked Lilitu hard on her bleeding wound. "That should keep you down for a bit." With his right hand massaging his disabled wing, he then glanced towards Mircea. "I'm not quite sure why you did this, but you will be handsomely repaid." He turned again to Lilitu, kicking her hard on the face, managing to split her upper lip. "Why didn't you listen to reason? I made you a reasonable offer, did I not?"

"We can still negotiate," she whispered between coughs.

"I think not. If I kill your host now, I'll be rid of you for a long while."

"You may be right, but you can believe me when I say that I will never leave your side. And when destiny finally hands you over to me, eternity will not be long enough for the torture I will put you through. I will do as you ask, if you let these people live."

"What? Is this the same Lilitu I have always cherished? I'm touched." He brought his face near hers, his breath polluting her nostrils. "I didn't know you cared."

Their eyes held each other for a frozen moment. Lilitu could have bitten his nose off, but kept the impulse under control.

"Very well," said Gilles with a wide grin. "I will let you go. Save your host, but I will keep the mother."

"No," growled Lilitu. "She leaves with my host."

Gilles was amused. He enjoyed the cold sparring between them. "It's only a small guarantee. Once you have fulfilled your part of the bargain, I will fulfill mine. I will let her go."

"Tell me how to unlock the trap to release Mary Ann."

"Oh, is that her name? She is such a desirable woman. I'm impressed." Gilles stood as straight as he could; his broken wing caused him undue pain. "I'm sorry, that knowledge will remain with me until we conclude our business. I did give you my word, you know."

"Worthless. Your word is worthless, but you give me no choice." With great difficulty, Lilitu pushed herself up, her left arm bleeding freely. "Allow me to put some distance between you and my host's body; I will return in astral form to finish this."

"Nothing will please me more. I will wait for you at the bottom of the tower. You may go now."

Holding her left arm while trying to stop the bleeding, she walked towards the staircase.

"Oh," said Gilles as an afterthought, "I must remind your host that if he tries anything, anything at all, his mother dies."

"He heard you," said Lilitu.

"I know he did. I can almost feel his breath on my neck." He turned to the general direction where he sensed Josh, and said, "wait for your mother by the outpost. I will release her soon." His hard, cold-eyed smile held a note of mockery.

Lilitu left. Josh followed close behind.

❖◈◦◦◈◦◦◈◦

Gilles limped slowly towards Mircea, towering over him with eyebrows raised inquiringly. *Lilitu's legs around my waist must have dislocated something,* he thought. "And you, my friend. I do not know what to make of you. I feast on your daughter, almost got to kill you, and yet you decide to save my life." With great difficulty, he knelt in front of Mircea. "Are you friend or foe?"

Mircea could hardly breathe, but his eyes still held an intensity hard to characterize. "F… friend."

"Are you?" He patted Mircea's cheek. "We shall see. I'm a bit curious. I shall attend to you later. Perhaps you shot Lilitu by accident. Perhaps not." Bringing himself back to a standing position, he limped towards the staircase. Before climbing up the steps, he addressed Mircea once more. "If you want to join the party, you'll have to cross the passageway behind you, since I'm too weak to carry you." In spite of the pain, he burst out laughing. "If you can survive the spiders and the rats, that is."

❖◈◦◦◈◦◦◈◦

Lilitu stopped by the Great Hall. She tore a piece of material from one of the bedspreads and wrapped it around her left arm, managing to stop the bleeding.

"Josh, go down to the outpost and keep a watch for Malcolm. Wait for me there."

"It's almost daylight. You must hurry." Josh's misgivings increased by the minute.

"I am well enough to fly. I'll get there before the sun comes out." She waved him away with her hand, "Now, leave."

"Why can't you give me back my body now?" asked Josh.

"Because *you* still do not have the power to fly. I want you as far from here as possible."

Josh did not argue, and flew away, reaching the outpost in a few seconds. From the distance, he saw Malcolm's four-wheeler rental approaching the foot of the pass. If the car could make it through the boulders, they would soon reach the outpost.

❖◦◦❖◦◦❖◦◦❖

Gilles reached the courtyard just in time to see Lilitu fly away. *What a fool,* he thought. *Once I get rid of her, I will be the king. Then, what sweet meat that Mary Ann will be. I will taste her flesh right down to her precious marrow. I will then be free to build an army, to conquer the world I was born to subjugate.*

As he entered the kitchen, the flesh strewn about was beginning to rot. Not that it bothered him, but perhaps he could get Mircea to clean up a bit – if he survived. Pity, though, that he lost his temper in such an unfortunate manner. Killing all his servants was a bit over the top. Next time, he would try to control himself.

Tiptoeing over the body parts, he crossed the kitchen, and reached the tower door. Pulling a lit torch from the wall, he stepped inside. The way down was dangerous. No normal human would risk his life attempting to cross the chasm created by the missing steps.

A difficult task to jump to the next level, he thought, *now that my wings are disabled, but getting rid of Lilitu is well worth the effort.*

The crumbled steps evidenced a slipshod construction, yet given the difficulties of building in such a forbidding place, he could not ask for more. Cautiously, he measured the distance, and made the jump. Miscalculating his weak physical condition caused him to misstep his landing, almost falling down the deep well. An old grating on the wall saved his life when he grabbed on to it with his claws. He pulled hard, until the grating nearly came off, but it held. The torch fell a few steps below - that much was fortunate.

His shoulder hit the wall as he pulled himself in, when a sharp pain shot through his body, making him yell loudly. He looked up to the kitchen door, and knew he had a bigger problem now. With his wings clipped, he would not make the jump back up to the kitchen, and the only other way out was through the passageway to the Dining Room. The last time he opened that door – some years ago - a spider bit him. The poison almost killed him, forcing him to lie in bed for a week. Not that the stale air inside this tower was any better. Nevertheless, he was not about to worry about spiders now. First things first. He reached for the lit torch on the floor, and with it, he lit a second one stuck to the wall, next to the passageway door.

Going further down the steps, he reached the next level, the torture chamber. He pushed the door open and looked inside. A bit of nostalgia overwhelmed him. As soon as Lilitu was gone, he proposed to restore it to its previous glory. Smiling to himself, he continued down the steps with smug delight.

Finally, he reached the bottom of the tower, stepping over the slush of old, coagulated blood. The smell was appalling, but he ignored it. Turning towards the East wall, he felt elated. Finally, his victory was near. He looked up to make sure he was alone, and then pulled the brick that gave him access to the door latch.

Inside the chamber, he sat next to Lilitu's glass coffin, and waited.

FORTY-THREE

Josh waited impatiently. Lilitu did not reach the outpost quickly enough for him, and the sun was about to come out.

Finally, she arrived.

"Listen to me, Josh," she said. "I must go back in my astral form now and find Gilles. Once I do that, I will try to distract him long enough to allow you to return to the Castle."

"Return to the Castle? Why the hell did you ask me to come all the way down here for?" asked Josh, infuriated. "That's a long walk!"

"Because, if he even suspected we did not do as agreed, he would have killed Mary Ann. There was a reason I damaged his wings. Once he is down in the tower, he will not be able to climb out. That gives us some advantage to work with."

"Is he that dumb?" asked Josh incredulously. "Will he go down there, knowing he can't climb back up?"

"He is smart, but his biggest problem is that he is impulsive. Getting rid of me has been his dream for centuries and to do that, he has no choice but to climb down. I know he will not think straight, and will realize his predicament after it's too late."

"What do you want me to do?" asked Josh.

"Go to the Dining Room and get a gun. I have an idea on how to get your mother out safely."

"What's your plan?" asked Josh, nervously looking out the window. The sun was beginning to show its crown.

"In a way, you showed me," she said with satisfaction. She lay down on the floor. "Now, let me give you back your body. I'll tell you the rest on the way up."

Josh stood in the Dining Room, looking at Mircea. The man's breathing had stabilized somewhat, but he doubted he would survive the night. Mircea ranted Piotra's name repeatedly. Under other circumstances, he would stop to help him, but time was of the essence. A rifle lay next to Mircea, and the gun lay just behind him. Carefully, Josh slung the rifle on his right side. His left arm was practically useless because of the bullet wound that still needed a doctor's care. He then checked the gun. It was a revolver. The closest he had been to any weapon were the toy guns he used as a child. It did not matter; there was no science to handling something like this. Checking it for bullets, he found five in the chamber, and hoped it would be enough.

"Sorry, old man," whispered Josh. "If I make it out alive, I'll come back for you." Turning around, he ran up the stairs, past the Great Hall, and into the courtyard.

When he tried to walk into the kitchen, a strong, disagreeable smell pushed him backwards. The stench of the decomposing body parts and the blood weighed him down.

"Shit," he said aloud. Hesitating for a moment, he was about to take a deep breath to go through, when he heard the sound of a car outside, by the edge of the pass. There was hardly any room to maneuver on that steep, narrow road. If they survived this, that car only had two ways to go down again: in reverse, or over the cliff.

"Josh!" called Malcolm rushing out of the car. Zgeza stepped out from her side with a much slower pace. "Are you alright?"

Josh bought his index finger to his lips, telling Malcolm to lower his voice. "Go with Zgeza to the Dining Room – she knows where it is – and tend to Mircea. There's another rifle lying there on the floor. Hold on to it, just in case."

"Where are you going?" he asked anxiously.

"Don't worry about me now. Do what I asked and wait there." Zgeza heard part of it when she finally got closer to them. He told them to go on with a motion of his head.

Malcolm turned to the old woman. "Zgeza," he said, "where's the Dining Room?"

"This way," she replied in her broken English as she grabbed Malcolm by the arm, continuing down the courtyard into the Great Hall.

Josh turned back to the kitchen. He took a deep breath, and briskly walked towards the staircase in the tower. Some sunlight entered the kitchen, but by the threshold of the staircase, there was little light. Only the torch on the next level, and a faint light at the bottom, illuminated the inside.

"Okay, Lilitu," Josh whispered to his unseen companion. "I'm ready if you are." A wispy breeze touched the hairs on his arms, and she was gone.

After a few seconds, Gilles' voice boomed over the walls. Although Gilles could not see or hear Lilitu, Josh knew he sensed her. He must have been speaking to her. Sound carried incredibly well inside the tower.

"Hey, Gilles," shouted Josh from the edge of the kitchen level. "Can you hear me?" Three stories down, the light at the bottom of the pit moved, then he saw Gilles appear from one of the sidewalls with a torch in hand.

"Who the hell are you?" asked Gilles, barely distinguishing the figure at the top of the steps.

"Oh, we've met…" Josh moved his head from side to side. "Well, kinda'. You've got my mother locked inside your cozy little room."

"I told you to wait by the outpost, but I see you do not care what happens to your mother," he said in a harsh, raw voice.

"I hope I didn't piss you off," replied Josh, teasingly. "Listen, I need you to tell me how to disable the trap. Can you do that for me?"

"I thought we had a deal. You have no word, no honor."

"That's a good one, coming from you," said Josh with a cool voice. "Tell me, how do you plan to get out of there? I don't see how you can do it with your wings broken."

"That is not your concern," growled Gilles.

"Oh yes, it is. You see," he continued playfully, "I have no plans of letting you come out alive unless you tell me what I want."

"THEN THE DEAL IS OFF!" he shouted turning back towards the chamber. "Say goodbye to your mother and to Lilitu." When he tried to enter the chamber, a strong jolt cursed through his body, reeling him backwards. "What the hell!" He fell ass backwards into the bloody sludge behind him. It felt as if he had hit an electrified wall.

"Ooh, that must ha' hurt," yelled Josh, mockingly, from his vantage point. "I forgot to tell you about Lilitu. She's my little helper. You didn't know she could do that, did you?" He chuckled with scorn. "Bummer!"

Gilles wobbled, his body glistening with perspiration. Standing up in anger, he roared like a frustrated Lion, his dignity and pride hacked to pieces. It took him a moment to reorient himself. "You think you are very smart, do you not? Well I know something about this little trick that even Lilitu does not know." Saying that, he dived inside the chamber headfirst, going right through Lilitu's astral body. The whole area sparkled with a sharp blue light, spewing electricity from wall to wall.

From upstairs, Josh heard Gilles' painful scream, but he also heard Lilitu's hair-raising wail.

◦◆◦◦◦◆◦◦◦◆◦◦◦

"I guess you were not expecting that one, did you, Lilitu?" asked Gilles in obvious pain. "You see," he continued speaking with difficulty as he stood, "During all the years I spent in solitude, I tried the same as you just did. But I only managed to hurt my astral self much more than the human I tried to dislodge." He clenched his mouth tighter, talking through his teeth. "Your pain must be ten times greater than mine. Finally, even if it is for the last time, I can cause you pain; and you are in pain, aren't you?" His triumphant, but forced smile told Lilitu he was about to destroy her body.

With lightning speed, Lilitu entered her body; something she had not done in centuries. The sudden realization that she might roam the Earth for the rest of eternity filled her with panic.

Gilles sensed her desperation, knowing he had finally won the battle. He looked at the red button on the front panel of the glass coffin; A row of five blue switches lay to the right of it, and a smaller green button at the end of the row. He followed his instincts, pushing the red one. A loud hum permeated the room, making the walls vibrate. A large antenna pushed upwards from the back of the glass, as the hum got louder. Then, suddenly, the noise stopped. Nevertheless, nothing happened. He could still sense Lilitu inside the glass container; her anger grew exponentially.

Nervously, he punched the next five switches, and heard another set of five strange sounds, one for each switch. Still nothing. That only left the final green button. He quickly pushed it, and the lid of the coffin opened with a loud 'swoosh', startling him backwards.

A sudden rush of air, condensed by the vacuum inside, entered the coffin. Lilitu's body slowly crumbled. Her mouth formed a frozen, but silent scream of terror as her fully formed body deteriorated. He still felt her presence, but it lasted until the Succubus known as Lilith, was nothing more than a pile of dust.

FORTY-FOUR

Gilles took a deep breath, attempting to regain his strength. His eyes drew to a slit when Josh called out for Lilitu from the top of the tower. That bitch made a crass mistake when she thought to challenge him with a child. He could take care of this pup with his hands tied behind his back.

The torch on the floor dissipated slowly. He picked it up, but only to throw it into the slush, at the bottom of the pit. As much as he hated darkness, this time it would be his ally. With no light from his side, the kid upstairs would never see him coming.

He stepped out of the chamber and looked up. The kid kept calling out for Lilitu. Quickly moving towards the first rung in the staircase, he called out to Josh.

"Please help me," he said, his voice sounded strained and hurt. It was not far from the truth, but he wanted to give Josh the impression of being worse off than he was.

"Where's Lilitu," asked Josh.

"She kept her part of the bargain. Why didn't you?" As he spoke, he slowly began his trek towards Josh. The strong echoes in the tower disguised his location, although he attempted to throw his voice downwards. Hugging the moss filled walls, every step brought him a little closer to his goal. At no time was his prey out of his sight. The torch on the second level gave him just enough light to see Josh, but the closer he came to it, the more vulnerable he became. He silently passed the third level, and was now directly underneath Josh. Across from him were the door on the second level, and the torch on the wall.

Another step up and Josh would surely see him, but he had to take the chance. If the kid was armed, he needed to find out.

"Why do we have to be enemies?" whispered Gilles. "Do you not trust me to let your mother go?" There was no distant echo this time; his proximity was obvious. The boy stirred nervously above him, but got no answer. "Are you not even going to tell me your name?" Still no answer. Looking around the steps, he saw a rod of rusted metal that had fallen out of the broken gate above. If anything, he could use it as a weapon.

After taking a bold step forward, the boy saw him. Josh took a potshot at him, but Gilles managed to step aside in time. Moving back under the steps, he took a deep breath.

"That was not very friendly!" Startled by the suddenness of the boy's attack, his abrupt movement underscored the pain of his broken wings. The pain was unbearable, but now he knew the exact position of the boy. If he hurled the piece of metal at him, perhaps he could knock the gun out of his hand, and if he was lucky, he could kill the son of a bitch.

Josh quickly answered back. "You wanna' see friendly, show me your face aga…"

That was all the distraction Gilles needed. As the boy spoke, he swiftly stepped out again and threw the metal rod straight at him. It flew like an arrow deep into Josh's right shoulder. The gun fell from Josh's hand into the pit below.

Gilles smiled wickedly. The shrapnel pinned Josh to the wall; there was no way he could get out of it without tearing off his shoulder blade. The wound on his other shoulder reopened, making any kind of movement extremely painful.

This was no standoff; it was his moment of triumph, yet he was about to hyperventilate with frustration. He cursed and growled like the caged beast that he was. After neutralizing Josh, the jump to the next level was too big; he might not make it with his disabled wings.

As Josh struggled, Gilles studied the situation. Suddenly, he saw a possibility. Three steps up, by the passage door to the Dining Room, he could almost reach the rusted Iron Gate. If the Gate held, and his legs provided enough momentum, he could do it. Taking each step with delight, he enjoyed seeing the boy thrash about, trying to free himself from the wall behind him. It was an unexpected bonus, to see the terror in Josh's eyes as he realized he was about to die.

Josh looked at the Gate knowing exactly what was on Gilles mind, but his efforts to free himself from the wall proved futile.

Gilles positioned himself in front of the door preparing to make the jump. Then just as he sprung, the passage door opened suddenly. The door hit him squarely in the hips; his interrupted flight pushed him further to the right than expected. Flying forward, with one hand, he desperately managed to grab the bottom of the Iron Gate. The excruciating pain kept him from getting a good hold.

Mircea staggered out from the passage, his body covered with spiders. Although maddened with pain from spider bites, his will for vengeance was unbending. He held a knife. He spotted Gilles vicariously hanging across from him. Snarling at the monster with his knife high in the air, he sprung towards him like a cat. The blade struck deep into Gilles' back. Mircea tried to hang on, but Gilles kicked him off, sending the gypsy straight to the bottom of the pit.

The knife remained embedded between Gilles' shoulder blades. With great effort, he pulled himself up a little, and found Josh's foot. If his body died, this little shithead was going down with him. Now that he knew the power of soul transference, it was just a matter of time before he got a new body. Lilitu had been his main concern, and now she was permanently out of the way. A new eternity awaited him now.

◆◇◆◇◆◇◆◇◆

Josh felt her before Gilles did. The sudden, overwhelming awareness of Lilitu's presence. For a split second, he looked towards Gilles. He felt her then, but was not prepared for her astral attack. She flew up from the pit with such fierceness, that Josh felt the blast of air against his face. The strong electrical shock, created by their collision, lit up the walls, filling the tower with ozone. As she penetrated Gilles' body, his hands opened, forcibly releasing Josh, and losing his hold on the Gate. During the long fall, Lilitu continued assailing his astral body until the final moment of impact.

Now, the slush completely covered Gilles; his lungs, about to implode for lack of oxygen. He thrashed, splashing congealed blood over the walls. It was useless; he could not breathe. His control over Laslo's shattered body was lost.

Desperately, Gilles tried to slip away, but Lilitu held him in place with stubborn determination. Her mouth opened wide over his face as she slowly began to swallow him. Sparks flew from within the bubbling bath of blood. Once Laslo's body expired, Gilles had no refuge. His astral self slowly dissipated into Lilitu and he was helpless to stop her.

In his final moments, he realized that Lilitu had sucked the life out of his soul.

●◆●●◆●●◆●

Josh, barely able to move his head, clearly saw Lilitu flying up from the bottom of the tower. She shone brightly, as he had never seen her.

"I... I don't understand," His voice was faint, slurred. "I thought you were dead."

"We'll talk about it later...."

"My mother..." whispered Josh, hardly managing to form the words with his lips.

"Stay put," she said. "I'll get Zgeza to help you." With that, she crossed through the passageway into the Dining Room.

FORTY-FIVE

Inside the Dining Room, many dead spiders surrounded Malcolm and Zgeza. With a torch on each hand, they had kept them under control. If any spiders survived, they were long gone. Malcolm was the first to see her.

"Lilitu," he said, startled by her physicality. Her brightness lit up the Dining Room.

Showing herself in her shapely human form, she said, "Zgeza, go see to Josh, quickly. He is wounded and needs attention."

"Where is he?" asked Zgeza.

"Go through the Kitchen. You will find him by the tower door."

Zgeza hurried out, while Malcolm stood hypnotized by Lilitu's naked beauty.

"You stay!" she said to Malcolm. He could, not only see her, but hear her as well. "I may require your assistance."

"Yes," he replied. "Yes, of course."

She smiled condescendingly. The look on men's faces when she displayed her human simulacra never failed to amuse her. Malcolm tried to keep from staring at her, but failed miserably.

Wasting no time, she approached the wall near the entrance to Gilles' lair. She scrutinized the wall, closely studying every moss-covered brick, searching for anything that might call her attention. It did not take her long to find it. A few light scratches on the wall pointed in the right direction.

Taking a position directly in front of the spot, she slowly buried her face inside the wall. Most of it was solid wall, except for one brick; a false cover for the locking mechanism behind it. Carefully, her right hand reached into the wall from underneath, trying to push out the brick, but her hand slipped right through it. Removing her head from the wall, she addressed Malcolm.

"Malcolm…"

His eyes were all over her.

"Can you stop staring at me for a moment?"

A muscle quivered at his jaw. "Sorry. This is quite unnerving. I..."

"Would you rather have me change to my real form?" She knew the answer before he said it. "Get over here."

Malcolm came closer.

"Do you see this finger?" She stuck it out from behind the brick, wiggling it in his face. "Pull this brick out."

He looked at the wall and saw her index finger moving from within. Reaching with his right hand, he pulled out the brick.

Now, two small levers inside the hole were in full view. Lilitu buried her face inside the wall again, following the lever closest to the door. That one opened the door, but had a hidden wire attached to the other lever. The trick was to move the second lever first to release the hidden wire.

Lilitu pulled herself out from the wall and told Malcolm what he needed to do. He looked at the mechanism, then after a slight hesitation, released the second lever; the wire retracted, making a loud noise as it disengaged the trap. They froze momentarily, hoping. The tension in the air was almost visible. After that, he pulled the first lever. The door opened easily.

"Come," said Lilitu, as she floated down to release Mary Ann. "There is still work to be done."

When Mary Ann heard the door open, her chest felt as if it would burst. Not knowing what to think, she hoped for the best, but braced herself for the worst. Her skin pulled taut when a tall, bright figure stepped in from the shadows. It was slender woman with red, fiery eyes that glowed. Her rich, thick hair framed a pink complexion. Everything about her was beautiful and sensuous.

"You're Lilitu?" asked Mary Ann.

"Yes," she said. "Yes, I am."

"I can see you." Her eyebrows raised inquiringly.

"I know, but the effect will not last long. I have enough energy to be visible for a while. Let's not waste time and get you out of here."

Malcolm walked in behind her. Mary Ann's eyes brightened at his presence. "Where is Josh?" she asked.

"He is hurt," said Lilitu, "but he has a much stronger constitution now. He will recover quickly."

Quickly, Malcolm knelt in front of Mary Ann. He studied the shackles. "How the hell do you open this?"

"How hurt is he?" asked Mary Ann ignoring Malcolm. Lilitu's reply regarding Josh had stabbed at her heart.

Lilitu came closer to Mary Ann. "You need to *know* that he is no longer the frail child you knew. His wounds will heal four times as fast as a normal human. In a couple of days, he should be fine."

Mary Ann sighed with relief while Malcolm continued turning her hands over, trying to figure out how to open the locks.

"The keys are by the bed," said Mary Ann, addressing Malcolm. "What about Gilles?" she asked, turning to Lilitu. "Is he dead?"

"He will no longer bother us."

Malcolm returned with the keys in hand. Their eyes met just before he placed the key in the first lock. For a frozen moment, they studied each other. It was a brief exchange.

"Malcolm," said Mary Ann in a low, calm voice. Her hands moved up to his face. "The locks?"

"Oh," he reacted as if pricked with a needle. "The locks, yes, yes."

While Malcolm released her shackles, Mary Ann noticed Lilitu plunging her face into the walls at various places in the room. At that moment, it made no sense to her.

"There," said Malcolm, finally releasing Mary Ann.

"Thanks," said Mary Ann as she stood and moved away from the wall as fast as she could. She pulled Malcolm away from the wall for fear something might trigger the trap.

"Got it!" said Lilitu triumphantly.

Her exclamation pulled Malcolm and Mary Ann's attention from each other.

"What is it?" asked Mary Ann.

"Here," said Lilitu pointing at the bed. "Move this back from the wall."

Malcolm grabbed the bed and moved it away from the wall.

"See this?" said Lilitu pointing at a spot on the wall. There was a slight indentation, barely visible. "Get your fingers in there and pull."

"Maybe we'd better not," blurted Mary Ann. "That might bring the walls down or something."

"Trust me," said Lilitu. "Pull it!"

Malcolm carefully slid his fingers into the indentation and pulled. It was a small door, and behind it were several boxes full of jewelry and coins. Most of the coins, as well as the jewelry, were centuries old.

"I guess you won't have to worry about money for a while," said Lilitu with a smile.

A few minutes later, they were all out by the courtyard. Josh sat on an improvised straw mat by the stable while Zgeza washed his wounds. With the help of an iron pincer, she had pulled the iron rod out of Josh's shoulder. Although his bleeding had stopped, he looked worse than he was.

Mary Ann's face relaxed a bit when Josh smiled at her and waved at them. She approached him, wanting to embrace him, but afraid she might hurt him.

"You can hug me, mom," he said, "just do it softly. It still hurts when I laugh!"

She giggled between her tears, and knelt next to him, giving him a warm, but soft embrace.

"You know," said Malcolm, "I think we should leave this place."

"I agree," replied Lilitu. "Zgeza, are there any clothes you can find for Josh?"

"Yes, of course. There should be something in the Great Hall he can use. I'll get some clean rags for bandages too." Zgeza had closed the Kitchen door. The dead gypsies were now out of sight. "I think we should all wash up before going back to town," she added as she stood.

"While you're at it," said Malcolm. "Let's try to find a chest. The bigger the better." Malcolm saw Josh and Zgeza's questioning look. "I'll explain later," he said moving with Zgeza towards the Great Hall.

An hour later, they were ready to leave. Malcolm stood inside the courtyard, looking towards the Four-Wheeler that was parked out by the ravine. He had second thoughts. Driving it all the way down in reverse was downright dangerous.

Mary Ann and Zgeza stood next to Josh. He was already dressed and bandaged, but still sat on the floor of the stable, leaning against the wall. The clothes Zgeza found for him were a bit ill fitting, but they did the job. It was better than walking into town totally naked.

"Well," said Malcolm, "now is as good a time as any to leave." He bowed at Mary Ann and Zgeza, pointing his arms towards the gate. "Shall we…?"

"Could you leave me alone with Lilitu for a minute?" Josh asked the group.

They exchanged glances, and finally agreed. They walked towards the portcullis, leaving Josh and Lilitu alone.

"Don't take long," said Malcolm. "I don't wanna' stay here another night." Josh nodded, and then turned to Lilitu, who stood nearby.

It was a bit awkward to see Lilitu in all her farcical human beauty. She looked desirable and having those feelings in front of Mary Ann made him feel strange. His fear of her was gone, and he was sure Lilitu sensed his human desire for her. She flaunted herself at him, and seemed to enjoy doing it.

"What happened to you down there?" he asked, ignoring her flirting. "I thought you were dead."

"Josh," she replied, making a short pause after saying his name. "I wanted to die too. I thought my plan would work, but I underestimated Gilles too many times."

"I saw him jump right through you," said Josh.

"He reacted fast, and unexpectedly. A warrior's trait, I guess."

"From where I stood," added Josh, "I had no idea what was going on. It was too dark to see that far down."

"Gilles jumped through me, catching me off guard. The collision took a lot out of both of us. I was still in shock when I saw him reach for the controls. I panicked." She knelt next to Josh, and continued. "I have been alive for too long. The thought of not being able to die made me rush into my body, feeling defeated and helpless. This man fooled me at every turn, and now, I was conceding to him his final victory." As she spoke, her brightness and physicality began to dissipate. Soon, she would be invisible and silent again.

"Once he knew I was dead," she continued, "he was going to kill you, and you would have been no match for him. I lay there, behind the glass, looking at him, while he salivated with satisfaction. When he began to push the buttons, I could not contain myself. Although I was too weak to attack him again, an uncontrollable anger festered inside me. Then I felt my physical body dissolving. His face, his expression, was more than I could take. He thought he had won when he could not sense my presence anymore. To him, I was finally dead. But at that moment, I glided into the solid mountain below me. I was still weak when the rock enveloped me. I lost all awareness and, to put it plainly, I fainted."

Josh lowered his eyes, avoiding hers. Unbelieving, he tried to take in what she had just said; what she had done for him. "Lilitu…"

If she knew his thoughts, she gave no sign of it; until, she paused and looked at him.

At this moment, Malcolm started up the Four-Wheeler. Mary Ann turned to Josh, indicating they were ready to leave.

Josh nodded at Mary Ann, and then turned toward Lilitu. "Please," he replied.

"Maybe some other time," she said, playfully dismissing him. "It is time to go."

"Come on, Lilitu. Don't do this to me. Finish now."

"You are not one to take no for an answer, are you? I like that in you." She moved closer to him, a bit seductively – or maybe it was Josh's imagination. "When I came to," she continued. Her voice now almost a whisper. "I was dizzy. The vertigo turned my sense of direction inside out, but I knew I had to *scramble* back up. It took me awhile to get my bearings, and by the time I did, Gilles was almost upon you."

"And all along, you knew how to destroy him?" asked Josh, trying to ignore her proximity, but failing miserably.

"No. I had no idea that would happen. I just went berserk. I did not know what I was doing. My only goal was to make him suffer. I braced myself to hold on to him no matter how painful it proved to be. Believe me, the pain *was* excruciating." When she said it, she made pain sound delicious. "Do you like pain, Josh? Well, I do not. I would rather feel pleasure. We should let them go on ahead. We can catch up with them later. Now that this is over, we can…"

Josh remembered reading that warriors, after winning a well-fought battle, usually felt a sexual high. Lilitu seemed to be riding on the crest of that wave. Her teasing tone excited him, despite his protestations. "Lilitu, my mother is standing there, watching us. Just finish telling me…"

"Do you think I care? She owes me, you know." She brought her lips close to his ear. "You know, in all this excitement, we have forgotten to take care of… business."

Josh impatiently turned his head away from her mouth.

She laughed heartily, throwing her head back. "Very well. Tonight, then. Now, where was I?" She moved away from Josh and smiled at Mary Ann. The woman did not smile back. "Oh, yes. It was simple, really. I held him down with rage – not thinking what I was doing - and bit into his astral neck. I have never done that before; I had no reason to. The shock of two astral bodies colliding is difficult to bear. I do not want to repeat it again. Yet, at that moment, a sweet warmth met my lips, almost making the pain bearable." Her eyes suddenly turned bright red as she looked closely into Josh' eyes, smiling. "Then I swallowed… hard." For emphasis, she allowed her tone to go down an octave when she said the last word, yet at the same time, made it sound sexual.

Josh tried to separate her from her playful mood. "You took his soul?"

"I would not call that thing a soul." She stood as her voice and body dissipated a bit faster. "Whatever he was, you are right. I consumed him. That is why you can see me now. His life force made me shine."

Josh stood and looked at her. He saw her clearly for what she really was. "What you did for me goes against everything you've said. You saved my life, and now your chances of dying are gone forever."

"I know…" her voice trailed, but a sense of completeness filled her; something she briefly felt only once before.

"I also thought you hated humans."

"I know." As she said this, her body disappeared completely. Only a faint touch of pink remained behind. If Lilitu was capable of blushing, she did it now. The last Josh heard, from her disembodied voice was: "Josh, I cannot hate *you*."

Josh stood there for a moment, thinking about Lilitu, and knowing he would definitely see her again tonight… in his dreams.

THE END

A Fiend Unveiled

Author: Edwin Oliver

Meet the Author!
Book signing & Chat

Blood & Mayhem

- Available Now!
- In this bookstore
- Or in the Internet

Mystery/Horror
ISBN# 0595090494
Trade Paperback

A fiend Unveiled is an exciting first effort by Edwin Oliver, which could possibly be best described by the vividness of many of its passages. Here's a tiny morsel for those mystery fans who enjoy a good murder mixed in with their gore:

> Scattered about the room were several human bones, some high-heeled shoes, and plenty of rats. In the opposite right-hand corner, there was a coffin-sized pit, half filled with an ugly, brownish-red, foul sludge. To the left of the pit lay a partly eaten female torso with a fully bloated abdomen, covered with live, hair-like, red worms.
> Now he knew why most of Michael's victims were never found. Either Michael had turned cannibal, or these rats had been weaned on human flesh. A horrifying thought. Sooner or later, Michael would return to finish his work on the policeman, and here he was, utterly defenseless. Then, he remembered the gun, it was lying on the floor where the police officer dropped it. There had to be a way out.
>
> -- From A Fiend Unveiled

The main character (Daniel Hull) has the task of uncovering the villain while juggling uneasy interpretations of the dreams invading Rebecca. Somehow, all the moves of the villain seem to revolve around Rebecca, and her dreams of premonition make her life a living nightmare. The book has enough red herrings to keep you guessing to the very end. A locked room mystery is only the beginning of the adventure. As the truth behind the murder is uncovered, the story becomes an unstoppable roller coaster ride.

Made in the USA
Columbia, SC
09 July 2020